The Living on the Dead WITHDRAWN

Aharon Megged

The Living on the Dead

TRANSLATED FROM THE HEBREW BY

Misha Louvish

The Toby Press

The Toby Press LLC

Second English Language edition, 2005

POB 8531, New Milford, CT 06776-8531, USA
& POB 2455, London WIA 5WY, England

www.tobypress.com

ISBN 1 59264 113 4, *paperback*

A CIP catalogue record for this title is
available from the British Library

Typeset in Garamond by Jerusalem Typesetting

Printed and bound in the United States
by Thomson-Shore Inc., Michigan

Contents

Chapter one, 1

Chapter two, 7

Chapter three, 17

Chapter four, 21

Chapter five, 31

Chapter six, 41

Chapter seven, 55

Chapter eight, 63

Chapter nine, 73

Chapter ten, 85

Chapter eleven, 97

Chapter twelve, 107

Chapter thirteen, 119

v

Chapter fourteen, 121

Chapter fifteen, 129

Chapter sixteen, 141

Chapter seventeen, 149

Chapter eighteen, 157

Chapter nineteen, 161

Chapter twenty, 171

Chapter twenty-one, 175

Chapter twenty-two, 185

Chapter twenty-three, 193

Chapter twenty-four, 199

Chapter twenty-five, 203

Chapter twenty-six, 205

Chapter twenty-seven, 215

Chapter twenty-eight, 221

Chapter twenty-nine, 231

Chapter thirty, 237

Chapter thirty-one, 241

Chapter thirty-two, 247

Chapter thirty-three, 249

Chapter thirty-four, 255

Chapter thirty-five, 261

Chapter thirty-six, 265

Chapter thirty-seven, 271

Chapter thirty-eight, 275

Chapter thirty-nine, 281

About the Author, *283*

Chapter one

The third session ended a few hours ago. Whenever my counsel ejaculated 'Freedom to write!' I had a powerful impulse to shout him down. 'No, not that! "Freedom *not* to write!" That's a freedom I absolutely refuse to barter for...You can't compel me, surely, for Heaven's sake, you can't...' But no. I'll never be able to say it there in the courtroom, for straight away the retort will shoot across from the prosecutors' desk, sharp as the pen he keeps pointing at me: 'But your signature! Your signature!' Yes, he's right, and the judge, it seems, thinks the same—the judge, who throws at me from time to time, from the shelter of his bat-wing robe, a sidelong look of dark sceptical suspicion that compels me to lower my eyes. So it appears do the few spectators, who gaze at me in wonderment that I should even try to fight a battle lost before it started. And, so I am sure, in his heart of hearts does my own counsel, that bespectacled baldpate, thick-headed and thick-fingered, wriggling and writhing in the web of his arguments, building up piles of bombastical speeches—at every embarrassing moment I blush to see him smoothing down his bald patch as if it were a lad's untidy mane—the man who is to blame for most of these judicial tortures, with his foolish tactics of asking for repeated postponements in the hope that their ammunition will run out. Yes, they're right, all of them. I confess. And if I now set down this account, it is not in the illusion that it might serve as a brief for my defence one day, but so that Truth may conquer Justice.

The next session is on July 15th; that means I have five weeks ahead of me. I must finish by then, for after that, if the court returns its verdict, I shall be stripped of what money I have left, my resources will dry up, my room will be barred and bolted in my face. For the present I have time on my hands, from morning till evening, from evening till midnight. I can write twelve, fourteen hours a day if I am not disturbed. I don't need to dig up the words, I only have to roll them out like peas from a pile, and arrange them in rows. I must go back about two years and describe—sincerely—how it all happened, day by day, from the time I undertook that ruinous task until this moment when I am on trial for breach of trust, fraudulent conversion, affront to the dead and affront to the living, double dealing and theft. Sincerely, I say. I know that sincerity, like a chaste virgin, has her own kind of coquetry, alluring the innocent and simple-hearted. But I shall let the events speak for themselves.

It was on May 5th, a little more than two years ago, that I went to the memorial ceremony at Davidov's grave. On June 7th in the same year my divorce from Ahuva was pronounced.

This is how it happened as far as I can remember. One evening between these two dates as I sat at my desk—Ahuva sitting behind me in her armchair in the corner of the room, calm, sure of her husband, busily cutting out paper letters for her kindergarten class—I said casually without turning my head: 'It's time we separated, isn't it?' Something snapped in my heart. A stupefied silence filled the room as the swish of the scissors ceased. There was no sound but the tick-tack of a moth beating itself against the bulb that hung from the ceiling. I dared not lift my eyes from the paper in front of me so I did not see whether she was startled or if there were tears in her eyes or if she was wounded to the quick. After some very long moments I could hear the sound of the scissors again and she said something quietly—I thought it was 'Bastard!' 'What did you say?' I asked with a feeling of relief, for now it appeared that we would have that 'serious talk' I could revel in, armed from top to toe with conclusive arguments. But she repeated her remark, saying very softly with her usual disarming quietness: '"It's hard!" I said.' (Submissive soul! If she had wept, or cursed, or thrown the scissors at me!) The page was lying before me without a single sentence on it. I had only been doodling, as so often, far too often: nothing but geometrical shapes, triangles and circles and pyramids riding on top of one another. And after another few moments she said, still quietly, without a pause in the motion of the scissors: 'When?'

This 'When?' dropped from her lips so soft, so feather-light, that I wanted to get up and kneel before her chair, take her by the hand and say: 'Oh, let's drop it. I was joking, just joking.' But instead I said in a voice brittle as glass: 'We'll fix a date.' And with that I knew the die had been cast, like a heavy stone into the silence, and there was no way back. I hardened my heart, clenched it like a fist. And then there was the rustling of the papers as they slipped from her knees and she rose, went to the bed, and started taking off her dress and preparing for the night. Only later, as I lay beside her in the darkness, did I notice that her cheeks were wet.

Tears do not melt my heart, they make my hackles rise; I get bitter, malicious. So I turned my mind away from her. I thought about Davidov. About the journeys awaiting me to the ends of the country; about the encounters I could expect with the days of the past, the men of the past, in that land I knew from dreams; about the great adventure on which I was embarking; about the unexpected incidents, the mysterious surprises in store. Yes, and about the glory too—how I would gallop off on that fallen rider's horse, with his flag borne in my hand! Davidov, as I saw him first, many years ago, running with a barrowful of salt in the glittering salt-field at noon—a tall gypsy with glowing eyes, his pitch-black hair dishevelled on his brow…or on a moonlit evening, lifting his voice in a song…

'Let's go tomorrow,' she said.

I shuddered all over. Her voice in the darkness, calm as rain-drenched sand, knocked me off my horse with one blow of a blunt wooden sword.

3

'Where?' I choked down my agitation.

'To the Rabbinate,' she said in a dead voice. 'That's where they do it, isn't it?'

Oh, 'That's where they do it!' Do what? What for? Like an operation, I thought, in hospital, where I feel faint at the smell. And what's the hurry? Perhaps I'll change my mind. If she doesn't talk about it. If we say nothing for weeks and months and the decision remains hanging—as ever—by a spider's thread from the ceiling...

'All right,' I replied.

And she said no more. Lay with open eyes, her hands clasped under her head, until one solitary bird started to warble with a bustling, lively chirrup on the tree by the window, and through the slits in the blind a pale light stole on to the winding-sheets in which we lay.

The chirruping probed at my heart. I couldn't do it, I thought, I couldn't repay her so: this silent dove who for two whole years had gathered grains and brought them to my lips; couldn't offer her up now as an oblation to the memory of Davidov.

To his memory? Now, after all that has happened—and all that hasn't happened—when I think of it...

A knock at the door interrupted my writing. Lately every shuffling step on the stairs has been making my blood run faster. Was it the clerk of the court? My lawyer's messenger? The postman with a registered letter? The tax collector? No, thank God, it was Mrs Silber. She came in—now of all times, at this hushed hour of the evening—to ask about the rent.

'I'm not disturbing you?' she asked at the door.

'Sit down,' I said.

She sat herself down with knees apart on the edge of the bed, resting her pink hands on her spreading skirt. A motherly woman, ageless with faded hair, she always appears to have come, not to claim but to get a grain of satisfaction. 'She likes artists,' as I was told before I moved into this garret, previously occupied by an elderly, solitary sculptor who breathed his last, penniless, here on this bed on which I toss and twist in the nights.

'I only wanted to ask…You know, it's June already.' And a blush bloomed in her cheeks, two round patches that spread in an instant to her temples.

I looked down at a spot between the two of us and said nothing. I was ready to be silent like this until she lost patience. This 'petty malice' in me—to adopt a phrase Ahuva coined and threw at my feet—incited me to punish her with silence for interrupting my writing. Let it spread, this feeling of discomfort in my presence, all over her, up to her neck, her ears.

'You know I have a case pending in court,' I said finally, with an air of importance.

'I only asked.' Her fingers fumbled with the edge of her striped skirt. 'Of course I know…'

And after she had blushed some more, 'I don't understand how a clever man like yourself…Surely you could just…Why give them an excuse?'

A smile came up on my lips. (What do the 'People' say? What do the 'People' say about this fall of mine?)

'Did you know Davidov?'

'Not personally, of course, but like everybody else I know his life was a great romance, and that was just why I thought…'

Then she smiled at me, half in rebuke and half in apology.

'Forgive me for interfering, but you drink too much. That's the trouble with you.'

And with that she rose and smoothed the lap of her skirt as if shaking off a pile of potato peelings.

'I'll pay, never fear,' I said, opening the door for her to the flat roof.

'I never doubted it for a moment, Mr Jonas,' she said, offended, and immediately hurried away, her sabots clattering down the stairs to the bottom.

An oppressive heat weighed on the roof. Beside the door, mounted on a pedestal, was the tall statue swaddled in rags that had hardened with age and clung to the hulk of clay. The unfinished work of Polishuk the sculptor: that mummy, wrapped in sacking, from which I had never tried to peel off the cerements to reveal its face.

5

Chapter two

It was on June 7th that I was divorced from Ahuva, and only
this morning I noticed that yesterday, when I started to write these
pages, was June 7th too—which suggests the silly idea that my life has
been proceeding in cycles of two years: two years since the divorce,
two years of marriage to Ahuva, two years of study at the university,
two years of army service, two years in the kibbutz…I could go on
skipping down the ladder, two rungs at a time, till the fourth year
of my life, in which my father died, or till my second year, when my
parents left the Galilean kibbutz of Kfar Giladi and carried me in a
wagon, lying in a bathtub, towards the south.

No, I feel no remorse for the divorce. Our married life was
doomed from the beginning, it was neither one thing nor another,
neither fish nor flesh. I believe Ahuva was not happy either, though
she was so quiet that evening, hearing that malicious, casual statement: 'It's time we separated, isn't it?' How did she still have the
spirit to go on cutting out paper letters? For there was no storm
to forebode that earth tremor. But perhaps I'm wrong. Perhaps she
guessed it was coming and expected it any day, any hour, even if it
was delayed. Perhaps she used to whisper to herself: 'Here it comes

now, here it comes now.' Until that "now" came, and she accepted it as her fate. I don't remember any quarrel between us. I remember that I would long for a quarrel: for instance, when I came home late at night from aimless roaming about the streets and looked forward, armed for battle, to her slamming the door in my face or breaking a jug over my head or at least stinging me with inquiries...But nothing of the kind ever happened. I would come in on tiptoe in the dark, and almost always—yes, always!—her quiet, innocent, unconcerned breathing would be hovering in the room like a feather in the nest. And next morning, when she served my breakfast before going out to the kindergarten, even then she would ask no questions about my comings and goings. No, I was not grateful to her for never suspecting me. My masculine pride was hurt. I hated her on such mornings as she went about her housewifely duties. I could hardly help breaking out: 'Why don't you suspect me, damn it all? And what do you know about where I was?' So with a look I would drive her away to her kindergarten, the right institution for the likes of her. And in the evenings...in the evenings I remember only the nervous tremor in my back from her eternal presence, there in the armchair behind me, as she cut out paper chains, or letters to put together into mottoes like MAN IS BORN TO LABOUR or WE SHALL BUILD OUR HOMELAND—those mottoes that made me hate her celebrations and her children and her handicrafts. Was she to blame for that innocent, silent presence? We had only one room, though it was large enough; it contained my writing-desk, the bookcase, the wardrobe and the bed. But that was just what I couldn't bear: that infuriating quiet of hers all the time! For hours on end I would sit at the desk, pen in hand, doing nothing but eating myself up, furious inside me, hating inside me, my back bristling and my fingers scorching. I wrote nothing. And the only chapter I did write—one of the causes of the trouble I am in now—I wrote when she was away on holiday with her elder sister in the kibbutz.

No, I feel no remorse for the divorce itself. But the way it was done—it shouldn't have been done like that. Not like that! If you slaughter a bird, do it with a sharp razor, not a blunt knife. And do it with one stroke, sharp and smooth and done with, not irresolutely, not with saw strokes, so that she flutters in your hands with half her soul in her wounded throat.

Next day, after her return from the kindergarten, as she was serving lunch she said, midway between the cooker and the table: 'Have you been there?' 'Where?' I asked. 'You know. Where you said.' 'I had no time this morning,' I said. When I looked at her I saw her face suffused with a fiery blush; it glowed with a kind of soft light, like someone in a fever, making her beautiful, desirable. A thought stole into my heart: perhaps I was falling in love with her at that very moment. In the afternoon she went out, which was not usual with her, and did not come back until ten or half-past in the evening. For the first time I felt a twinge of anxiety for her return, and as I sat at the table I listened keenly to the steps in the street. I was panic-stricken at the thought that she might not come back, or perhaps she had done something...When at last I heard the grating of her key in the door I was as relieved as if she—or I myself—had been saved from some danger. I did not get up when she came in, did not speak a word. I went on sitting, pretending to write. But my senses lay in wait, restlessly. And when I heard the rustle of her dress as she took it off...Yes, that was what I meant when I said: Not like this! It was like an adulterous act, the vilest of adulteries. Very stealthily, like a cat stalking its prey, I went up to her and gripped her in my arms. She gave herself to me, after a brief moment of astonishment, with as burning a passion as my own; it was like a stolen, forbidden love. But afterwards...that silence, as I lay flat on my back in the darkness, not knowing where to hide. That empty chasm which makes a mockery of any word unspoken. That sadness which is followed by nothing but...No, I'd better not go on with this. All I remember is the lively chirping of the bird as the dawn broke, that impudent chirp; the protest of innocence against the crime perpetrated behind the window.

Then came intervention by her family: her father, her sister Geula. Two or three days after that night, towards evening, there was a hesitant ring at the bell, and when I opened the door I was startled to see him, pale, with quivering lips, in his shabby trousers hanging from his twisted belt and his sweaty shirt, as if straight from his shop. (If only he doesn't get a stroke—not here, not in front of me! I said to myself.)

'Come in,' I said, as he remained standing on the threshold looking at me like a man in a state of shock.

He came in, looked around, as if he was trying to find the traces of a tragedy or coming back to a house from which a corpse had been removed, and sat down on the edge of the bed as if he had lost the power of speech. He was a little man and sold suitcases in a little shop. When he stood up in his shop his shoulders filled most of it, and when he sat down, tired out, it struck me that when he died he would no doubt fold up in one of his suitcases and no one would know he had ever existed. He had a sickly, careworn face, and his head was always shaking under its own weight. His feet shuffled along the pavement as he walked with an eager, rapid shuffle, as if he was afraid he might be late, so we usually had warning of his arrival. But this time I had missed the warning.

'Is it true? Tell me, is it true?' he mumbled, shaking his head.

His watery eyes, light blue like his daughter's, threatened to denounce me.

'Yes, it's true,' I replied at last. I began to feel resentful, not against him but against Ahuva, who had loosed him on me as an advocate to arouse my pity, a father to reprove me, a sick and broken-hearted man, a mirror to the results of my sin.

'I don't believe it,' he said, his eyebrows bristling.

Yes, it's true. It's true! And what of it? Haven't you ever heard…?

He began stammering feverishly that he couldn't understand it at all, that everything had been all right between me and his daughter, hadn't it?—not a single complaint, all those years, never a cross word, a model of harmony between man and wife, and when he and her mother had seen the two of us…And how, all of a sudden? 'Tell me; after all, I'm her father. I've a right to know, haven't I? What happened?'

I said nothing, tight-lipped. I decided to punish him for Ahuva's offence in getting him to interfere. It was between the two of us, and I wanted no judges.

He looked at me as if he were trying to make up his mind if it was really I, or someone he had never known before in his life. Again he asked what had happened: if I had found fault with her in any way, if she had done me any harm, if she had not cared enough for me. 'Tell me, can't you? Tell me, let me know too.'

I was silent as a stone. I saw his eyes turning from blue to green, beginning to glow with hostility.

'Yes, that's how you pay her back'—he nodded—'for the two whole years she's kept you, worked for you, so that you, a healthy young man, could sit at home at your desk and write. What have you written, after all, in those two years? One story...'

'One chapter of a story.' I broke my vow of silence.

'Let me tell you,' he looked at me searchingly, 'when I read that story...'

'Chapter,' I repeated.

'When I read your *Hero of Our Time*,' he reproached me, 'I said to myself: he has real integrity. He sees clearly, and castigates where it's needed. Real moral principles there. Today, when I think about it...Oh, Jonas, Jonas, it seems to me that you're that "hero", yes, that very same "hero"...'

And with that he left.

About an hour later, when Ahuva came in, I was about to start up the quarrel that had been pent up within me all the time, during all those days of silence, having now found an excuse for it. But again she cooled my wrath even before it flared up. She got her word in first.

'Father's been here. I know. I want you to know it wasn't I that sent him. I told him not to talk about it. It was only when he came back from here that I found out he had been to see you. I'm very sorry. I can only assure you it won't happen again.'

Oh, that innocence! Killing me with kindness.

Was it inadvertently or out of malice that made me keep putting her off? Today I can hardly tell. 'A borderline case,' as the lawyers say. Every day I postponed the start of the surgical operation to the next, as if I was saying to the fleeting moment: 'Stay now; how unbeautiful thou art!' In the mornings I spent my time drafting notes for the Davidov book; in the afternoons I tramped from the publisher's to the lawyer's to discuss the terms of the contract. And meanwhile Ahuva pined and peaked before my eyes. Doubt gnawed at her silence, for she did not dare to ask. I did nothing to relieve or confirm her doubts. I nourished them as you do a tapeworm; by day I tormented her with my silences, and in the evenings I invited her to go out with me, so that she should torture herself with guesses about my intentions. Had I changed my mind? Was I still holding to my decision? Was I putting it off to a time I thought more suitable? I was capricious: sometimes hostile, sometimes friendly, one evening leaving her alone, another evening walking by her side and putting my arm round her waist whenever we met acquaintances. Hesitant hopes no doubt flickered in her heart at night, as she lay by my side, until it was the morning.

Twice more her father tried to breach my defences but was repulsed. Once it was in the early morning, just after Ahuva had gone. I was warned in good time by the shuffle of his steps on the pavement. I settled down and waited. I heard him climbing the stairs, halting behind the door. One ring, a second, a third (what a stubborn old fellow!)…six rings I counted. Then, after I was sure he had gone away, I went to the window and looked down, to observe his retreat. I saw him stopping on the pavement in front of the house, craning his neck upward. I pressed myself against the wall. For a twinkling, nevertheless, our eyes met. A second time, in the evening, he stole up like a thief. Not a shuffle, not a rustle. But by this time I was wary; when the bell rang I crept up on tiptoe and peeped through the spy-hole in the door: sallow, seamed face, jutting ears, sparse, faded hair, anxious expectant look. I went back into the room and put out the light, lurking in the gloom. Four rings stabbed at the darkness. Then I saw him through the slits in the blind, walking up and down in front of the house, up and down, stopping now and then, looking up with his heavy stare, anxious and careworn. All at once he moved off, dragging his feet one by one with the same rapid shuffle, as if in a hurry to get about his business.

One day, about noon—like a scorching wind bearing the scent of Galilee woods—I had a visit from Ahuva's elder sister Geula. She slipped her raffia satchel off her shoulder and sat down on the bed, took out her handkerchief and wiped the sweat off her face, reddened by sun and travel, and said, 'I suppose you can imagine why I've come. Don't worry. I've no intention of interfering in the relations between you and Ahuva. I was very sorry when I heard about it, but what's the use? This kind of thing has happened, is happening and will go on happening. Give me a glass of water if you don't mind, it's terribly hot here in town.' She fanned herself with her handkerchief.

I went into the kitchen, filled a glass with cold water and told myself I could keep cool: this Geula had left her husband about a year before we were married, though she had two toddlers, and gone off with a lad from Youth Aliyah six years younger than she was. What could she have to say to me?

'Hotter than in Galilee,' she said, taking a gulp of water. 'It's the humidity from the sea, I suppose.'

And after putting down the glass, lifting her skirts a little and waving them over her knees, she said, 'Look, Jonas, I'm not worried about Ahuva. She'll manage. She'll manage. A young woman, good-looking, with a job—believe me, she'll not go a-begging! Of course it's hard, the first time it's always hard. You live with a man a couple of years, you have experiences in common, you leave a part of you behind, you get attached…it's not so simple. Well, it can't be helped.'

Her eye was caught by the ceramic vase on the table. She rose, picked it up, turned it over in her hand, admired the glazing, remarked that they made the same kind of thing in her kibbutz, then put it back and sat down again.

'Well, as I was saying,' she continued, 'that doesn't bother me. Not so terrible. You have a crisis, of course, but that's natural. It's got to be like that, otherwise we wouldn't be human, would we? But look, Jonas…I find it strange having to talk to you like this'—she smiled at me, a girlish, immature smile—'but I hope you'll understand me. Look'—more seriously—'you can't do this to father. He's *broken*! Shattered! Just a wreck! I don't know if you've seen him lately. Believe me, I didn't recognize him. A shadow!'

'You mean to say that because of…' I started to say.

'I know, I know,' she interrupted hastily. 'Of course not. That's obvious. Don't imagine I have such bourgeois ideas. I know that for the sake of parents and all that you don't set aside the feelings of your heart! But I want you to understand me. Let him get used to the idea. Not now. A little later. I'm worried sick about him… You understand, it was terribly sudden. Nobody was prepared for it. Not even I, and I've different ideas about these things, you know. I myself…but that doesn't really matter. Look, Jonas, why should I go on talking? You're an understanding man, a sensitive man. You're a writer! You know very well…'

Her eyes flashed at me from her plump, healthy face; anxiety had not dulled their brightness.

'By the way,' she said, 'we all enjoyed your story a lot in the kibbutz.'

'*Chapter* of a story,' I corrected her.

'Chapter? Yes that's right. Doron was the name of your hero, wasn't it? You see, I remember. And the engineer—a classic type! And I want to tell you, the scene with Doron and the kibbutz secretary in the room—that's exactly right! So exactly that some of the fellows said they knew a case just the same. How did you get to know that type? Why, four or five years ago, a young fellow came to our kibbutz…'

A warm voice she had, quivering like corn in a light summer wind. Her body was ripe, luscious; my eye was caught by the bushy cluster of black hair that peeped from her armpits through the beads of sweat. I asked myself who that young fellow was on whom she bestowed her favours. 'Will you have a bite to eat?' I asked.

'No.' She was in a hurry. She got up, slung her satchel over her shoulder, glanced round the room, looked at the two pictures hanging on the wall, then turned to me again.

'I hope you weren't offended, were you, Jonas? I simply couldn't help telling you. I got a letter from father and it was just like a cry from the heart. By the way, Ahuva doesn't know a thing about my coming here. And don't tell her.'

She looked me straight in the eye and laughed.

'Funny I should be talking to you about all this.'

'Why funny?'

'Funny…I don't know why. But the fact is I'm sorry. Really

sorry. I thought you two of all people…Who'd have thought it? You were so…But that's how it is, you never can tell what's happening inside.'

'Jonas'—she gripped my wrists—'You'll do what I asked you?'

'I'll try,' I said.

'Put it off. For a few weeks, at least. He's suffering terribly, poor man. But he'll get over it, he'll get over it in the end,' she consoled me.

She took a turn or two about the room, her satchel swinging freely, stopped by the bookcase, glanced briefly over the books, then came up to me.

'By the way, what really happened between you? The eternal triangle, eh?'

'Not this time,' I smiled.

'Ah, we know you, you artists!' she cried. 'But it's really none of my business.' She turned towards the door.

'Any good films on in town?' She turned on her heel.

'A good film?' I tried to remember.

'Never mind,' she said. 'I'd better get back home. You haven't seen my children for over a year, I think.'

'How are they?'

'Oh, quite big. I must tell you a clever thing Zuri said, gripping the button of my shirt. 'I was taking him to the children's quarters and we saw a falling star. "Mummy," he said to me, "what will happen if all the stars fall and there isn't a single star left in the sky? The moon will find it awfully dull." Sweet, isn't it? The kibbutz is crazy about him! Come and see us some time, after all…' She twinkled a smile at me.

And on the threshold she said: 'Put if off. Do it for me. O.K.? You'll see for yourself afterwards that I was right.'

She was so right that next morning I went to the Rabbinate and fixed a time for the divorce proceedings.

Chapter three

I thought I would write this story at one stretch, the tale unfolding like a carpet. But they won't let me. Every now and then the blood rises to my head and I feel myself choking when I remember that damned trial. I fling the pen down on the table and throw myself on the bed like a sack, lie there plotting how to get out of the trap. Is it my fault? Yes, it's my fault. So what? Must I pay for my mistake by remaining fettered to that ghostly shadow for seven years of my life? Fourteen? This morning I was summoned to my lawyer again, and again he repeated the same things I had heard from him over and over again: 'We shall do everything in our power, of course. We shall lose here, then we shall appeal to the District Court; we'll lose in the District, so we shall go to the Supreme Court; but these proceedings are liable to go on for years and in the meantime you will be swamped by expenses that you cannot afford. Perhaps after all we should propose a compromise. You can undertake that within a year, let us say...'

'I can't,' I told him for the hundredth time.

'Why not, after all?' His spectacles gleamed at me with the clever twinkle that always appears whenever some idea for getting round the law is born in his big head. 'Actually you are not binding yourself to quality, not even to accuracy! You contracted to supply fifty thousand words. Write fifty thousand words of drivel, even if they are not the slightest use to anyone—and you'll get off scot-free from the legal point of view!'

'I can't,' I said.

'All right, if that's how you want it,' he said, after staring at me for a long moment, as at an idiot who must, nevertheless, be treated with respect. 'After all, I am only your representative.'

(And the visit cost me another twenty-five pounds.)

In the evening, when I returned to my room and picked up the pen, my right hand forgot her cunning. Like a curse: If I forget thee, O Davidov…There was a used envelope lying there and I sat doodling: figures, figures, totals of debts, expenses, the balance of my dwindling savings, the savings I had accumulated—yes, by false pretences.

I went out on to the roof to get a breath of air. The sea murmured close by; the breeze gave some relief from the heat. A falling star scraped across the sky. On a distant radio the last strains of the national anthem melted away. I pondered how I had come to this. First my pen had stuck in the middle of a story I had started; then it had revolted against a story I had undertaken; now it had gone on strike writing a story about a story I hadn't written. I recalled that chapter from *A Hero of Our Time* which had been published in the paper in three instalments, which had won me such a reputation that they said: 'Look, a new star!'—and but for which I might not have been in this mess now. After the chapter had been printed (yes, chapter, not story—for some reason everybody got it wrong, though below the title, which I had borrowed, of course, from a well-known Russian work, it said expressly: 'From a Novel in Progress') I had tried to continue, but simply couldn't—like the evil eye. I blamed the beautiful eyes of Ahuva, always bent over her handwork. I fumed in my chair. I felt as if her scissors were shearing my locks and sapping my strength. As I made my way back after that memorial service in the graveyard, stepping down the hill between the striped shadows of the cypresses, blinded by the network of light that gleamed between them, Abraham Shai overtook me and begged me to undertake to write a book about Davidov. 'Me? Why me?' I was taken aback. 'I hardly knew him—only for two short periods with a space of about ten years between them.' 'Oh, the man who painted such a striking picture of Margolin in *A Hero of Our Time*', he said, his hand on my shoulder, 'could easily paint a striking picture of Davidov, I'm sure, particularly since Margolin was a fictitious character, while Davidov...' I would have no lack of material, he said; hundreds of people all over the country would be willing to help me. And after all it was a duty to the nation. The duty of the present to the past. The duty of the treetop to the root! (Yes, Abraham Shai was one of the top people.) And besides, there was a drop of Davidov's blood in my veins too, wasn't there? (Here of course he was referring to my father, one of the pioneers of Kfar Giladi in the north, and later a well-known Haganah fighter in Tel Aviv.)

(Here I have to note, with mixed feelings, that the legend of my father has pursued me for years, ever since my childhood. 'You're Saul Rabinowitch's son, aren't you?' the veterans used to say affectionately, sometimes stroking my hair, while I, as a boy, would hang my head in shame. Whenever I kicked over the traces in school the teacher's glance would rebuke me silently: 'Well, well, Saul Rabinowitch's son...' And even years later, when I was already a grown-up young fellow, I would be met from time to time with 'You're Saul Rabinowitch's son, aren't you?' But by then I had trained myself to reply with an arrogant nod: 'Yes! I'm Saul Rabinowitch's son.' As if to say: 'And what of it? Do I owe you anything?')

I refused. What had Margolin of *A Hero of Our Time* to do with Davidov? No resemblance at all. And what had my father to do with Davidov? And why did I have to carry the burden? And in general...But in the end (as if something old, torpid and dormant had stirred within me and disturbed my rest: wasn't it like the fulfilment of a suppressed desire?) I weakened and agreed. After I had agreed (and suddenly felt myself riding on the wings of that eagle!) I felt so exalted that I plucked up courage to tell Ahuva that quiet evening: 'It's time we separated, isn't it?'

Perhaps I ought to say a few words about that chapter from *A*

Hero of Our Time which won me so much praise, endless hand-shakes, claps on the shoulder; that chapter which a number of critics, eager to unveil new 'talents', swooped on like chickens scrambling for a grain of corn, crying: 'Look, a new star!'—and which I myself believe was never properly understood and was so fulsomely praised for that very reason. They thought (and that was how it was interpreted by some of the critics) that I had con-fronted Gabriel Doron and Margolin the engineer as examples of bad and good in our generation. Here on the one hand was a young snob, mendacious, corrupt, a sinner and a seducer; and on the other, the veteran engineer Margolin, a pioneer of the Third Aliya, refined, well-mannered, intelligent, broad-minded—a model of the integrity and nobility that is rapidly disappearing; while Doron was supposed to be a degenerate branch of the sturdy trunk whose sap was drying up. That was not what I meant. No doubt it was an ironic tale, but I wonder why they did not realize that the irony was not only directed against Doron, but also appeared between the lines in the description of Margolin and also of the kibbutz where they both stayed as guests.

The chapter was published in three instalments in the paper and won me much praise, because people found in it a 'real slice of life', as Geula said, or because it 'threw light on a characteristic clash between typical representatives of old and young in our country', as one of the critics wrote—Margolin being a model of all that was noble in the pioneering generation and Doron of the corruption of the new generation. I intended to continue with the story of Doron's adventures in the city, with his meteoric rise in the social scale (thanks first to Margolin's letter of recommendation and later to his own talents) until he had become a prominent public figure. But, as I have said, I remained stuck at the end of the first chapter and could not make another step forward.

No wonder, therefore, that from time to time I was asked by some reader:

'Who, after all, is your "Hero of Our Time": Gabriel Doron, or Margolin the engineer?'

Chapter four

Polishuk the sculptor. For two years I have been occupying this room on the roof where he lived. These walls absorbed his breathing, were chipped here and there by the blows of the chisel on the stone, echoed no doubt to his death-rattle. This couch with its groaning springs was his bed. This chair bore the burden of his loneliness. If he knew how wide open his room has been these two years; who has sat here, who has slept here, what things have been said, what sights seen! It is only now, when I have shut myself up, hardly going out and hardly letting anyone in, that I think of him sometimes. No, it isn't thinking, but—especially in the evenings, when only the breathing of the sea near by steals into the room—I sometimes shrink from the last manifestations of his lingering soul. A woodworm scrapes in the darkness—I shudder: Polishuk. The lintel creaks—that's him, I say. A cockroach scampers at my feet—his reincarnation. Or that statue which stands by the door like a corpse swathed in rags. I do not believe in ghosts, but its silence speaks to me. Sometimes at night, when I go out on to the roof for a breath of air, I feel suspicious. Perhaps it has a sword at its thigh. What do I know of him, of Polishuk, apart from what the landlady tells me casually when she comes in to collect the rent or make some remark about water or electricity? Whenever she mentioned him it was with a sigh, with a tear in her eye. 'He suffered, poor man, how he suffered! Sometimes, when I heard him at night walking up and down, up and down—for hours!—I used to wonder why those walls didn't cry out. You understand what it means when a man like that is forgotten all of a sudden? Suddenly it's as if he was no longer there! Thirty years ago, when he made that statue of the "Unknown Pioneer", the whole country said he was a genius! Ussishkin wrote about him, all the great men of that time—and then, no Polishuk! He worked and worked—no one knows that better than me—and it wasn't just working, but with all his heart and soul, he was burnt up, burnt up inside! I tell you, it was as if the suffering inside went right into the stone through his hand, and became...delicate, very delicate, so delicate that you couldn't tell that it was just like someone cutting pieces out of his own heart. And what happened? No one wanted to hear of him. Simply took no notice of him. Don't I know what went on between him and that kibbutz in Jezreel when he offered them his monument to the fallen! I saw the letters. I saw the sketch. They'd paid him already, he'd started the work, and there were recommendations—from everybody under the sun—and at the end...like throwing away a wornout shoe! And he was a genuine person, so genuine...You've heard of Marc Antokolski? No, your generation doesn't know him. He came from my town, Vilna. I remember as if it was today his "Dimitri Donski" and his "Ivan the Terrible" and his "Talmudists" and his...Believe me, Polishuk was our Antokolski. I'm not exaggerating. But what's the use? Today they like different things! A monument to our heroes—it's got to be like a kind of burn-out motor car, like some kind of accident or I don't know what—and that's what they call genius! That's art! And they stand and gaze at it in admiration, and of course remember our boys who died like heroes. That's how it is. The world keeps moving—but backwards...'

Once she showed me a photograph of him: porter's shoulders, with a stubborn and rebellious head riding on them.

I took this room about two weeks after his death. He died a lonely man, without an heir, and about a dozen people came to his funeral. Once I opened the door of the laundry, where the landlady had collected the remains of his belongings. Plaster dust hit me in the face. The sunlight fell on piles of junk. The big bathtub was heaped high with heads of clay, stone, bronze; like a pile of severed heads. One washtub was full of hardened clay, cracked like scorched earth. In a second tub there were a number of stands carrying miniature models of groups. A few crates held books, notebooks, big sheets of sketches. What pioneers were there, in the bath and the tubs! Brandishing hammers, grasping picks and hoes, carrying rifles; girl workers in head scarves, pregnant women, *hora* dancers, leaders' portraits. Alas, all covered with dust!

I must go on with the story of the book.

I affixed my signature. 'In evidence whereof I have affixed my signature'—that was the last line of the contract for the Davidov book, with its twenty-three clauses spreading over four pages; and at the bottom my name, as the party of the second part, inasmuch as the party of the first part was interested…Yes, I want to emphasize this important detail: that the party of the first part was the interested party, that it was not my initiative, that in point of fact I refused from the beginning and stuck to my refusal, and that if there was any mistake here—and it certainly was a mistake—it was not only mine: it said expressly in the contract, right at the beginning: 'Since the party of the first part is interested in the issue and publication of a book on the life and death of…'

I come back to that memorial service in the Jerusalem hills, on the fifth anniversary of his death. Memorial service, I said. Nonsense! When I picture the convoy of gleaming cars that rolled along the road and climbed with triumphal hoots up the road to the cemetery and shone in a pool of sunlight as they paraded on the parking ground; the sight of the exultant people, shaking hands with each other, bleating 'Hello! How are you!' and putting their arms round the shoulders of men and women they had known in the old days; when I remember how the entire congregation irrupted among the tombstones in groups like sheep feeding in the meadow, and how the flock was scattered and dispersed while that dried out fellow, meagre as a starved horse in his khaki shorts that hardly hung on his body, delivered his eulogy, which the wind scattered to the winds—that was a picnic, not a memorial service! I tried hard to catch a single sentence of the speech of that man from the kibbutz, with his eyes screwed up tight and a dry spittle collected at the corners of his mouth, but I could not hear a thing. I stood there chewing at a stalk of oatgrass with one foot on a cracked tombstone, trying to catch one or two flying words, when some girl with flaxen hair and cornflower-blue eyes came up to me and said: 'Listen, aren't you Yossi Gal?'—and when I shook my head she asked again: 'Weren't you in Professor Halkin's literature class?'—and when I shook my head again she smiled. 'Funny how serious you are.'

Later, as I was making my way down the avenue, Abraham Shai caught up with me and, biting at a big apple, taking good, healthy bites at the unripe fruit until his teeth were set on edge, spoke to me about the writing of the book.

'Got a car?' He threw the core of the apple away into a thorn-bush.

'Not yet,' I said.

'Come along, I'll give you a lift,'—laying his administrator's hand on my shoulder.

In the car his wife was waiting. She had been sitting there, apparently, all through the ceremony. Dark glasses shaded her eyes.

'You know Jonas the author, Eva?'—pulling the keys out of his pocket. A sunburnt arm emerged from the window of the car and a damp hand pressed mine.

'Haven't you read *A Hero of Our Time*? he said.

No, she was ashamed to admit, she hadn't read a Hebrew book for months and months. She had a disagreeable voice like the grating of broken glass, and her face seemed to have been gnawed by worms.

Shai made himself comfortable at the wheel, wiped the wind-screen, started the engine, manoeuvred, and when he reached the road continued with his extravagant praise of that chapter (which he called, of course, 'the story') to his wife, who looked back at me from time to time with her ravaged face as if to get my confirmation or to compliment me with a smile.

'By the way,' he said, 'that passage about Gabriel Doron putting the pistol on the table and telling Margolin: Shoot me, I'm a good-for-nothing, I'm a skunk—that's Dostoevski! And I'm not the one to throw compliments about, ask Eva.'

'He's very sparing with compliments,' Eve confirmed, a melancholy smile adorning her thin lips. Later, as we were coasting down at Shaar Hagai, he came back to the question of the Davidov book. He was sure I could do it, and I wouldn't be sorry. All I had to do was start and I would be gripped, for Davidov was not just an individual. An entire era, which must not be forgotten. All the beauty, the wonderment, the youth of this country, where the present was so rapidly wiping out the past. And I was the man—both because I had met Davidov and also because…'I have a feeling for people,' he said.

'Abraham has a very good feeling for people'—his wife turned her sunken cheek in my direction.

I thanked him for his confidence in me. I told him I was completely engrossed in writing the continuation to *A Hero of Our Time.*

'How much do you still have to write?'

'About half the book. More.'

(Eva asked if a writer couldn't work on two books at the same time. In case he suddenly had an idea, for instance. Oh no! not me, I replied.)

When we got out to fill up with petrol he continued with his entreaties, as if he had made up his mind to show himself that he could overcome any obstacle. He was not asking me to stop the work I was engaged on. In any case it would take half a year to collect the material. I would have to meet dozens of people all over the country and note down their stories. In the meantime I could go on with my own book, and no doubt I should be finished by then. Only after that should I sit down to work up the raw material into a novel, or something like a novel. (The spear-tipped pines on the slope of the hill cast long shadows, and the carpet of needles emitted a sharp, dry smell which reminded me of a hushed, rustling, twilight journey towards the posts of the Arab Legion in 1947.)

Later, as we drove on, he baited his hook with memories of 1952 in Beersheba, where he had met me when he had been manager of the P.W.D. and both of us together had met Davidov. Did I remember that evening in the café when we arrived in a jeep from Kurnub C and Davidov, who had had a drop too much to drink, banged on the table and cried: 'Troughs I want to see here, sheep-troughs, not houses!'?

Yes, I remembered it well. I also remembered that some argument had arisen between him and Davidov. I hadn't asked him. Since he had been working in the Ministry of Defence I had only met him a few times, by chance.

'And as for the money side...' he said.

He would see to it, he said. Karpinowitch—the man who had published the 'World's Great Men' series (and made a fortune out of it)—was a good friend of his. No doubt he'd be glad to publish a book like this which was certain of a good sale. He was an honest man too, and generous.

I refused. A week, two weeks. But Davidov! Davidov the galloping horseman! The knight of this wild land, now tamed and domesticated! The Samson who had severed the straps of its harness and set it free! Yes, the Davidov I remembered, whose name, image, background filled me with warmth, and now they were casting his cloak on my shoulders!

I refused. I wanted nothing to do with commissioned works. I had to go on with *A Hero of Our Time*. And another dozen stories were quickening within me. But I remember that evening, just an ordinary evening in the street—it was still light (a woman carrying an enormous basket of groceries passing by; religious souvenirs sparkling in the shop window; a gigantic Lollobrigida, bare-kneed in a tattered shift, dominating the town; flutter of starlings in the treetops) when the sentimental strains of 'Poppies', pouring from some radio, pursued me from one window, then from another, and then one more, bringing a lump to my throat, and I said to myself: Yes I'll do it! I'll do it!—and I went into the next chemist, dialled the five figures, and asked: 'Can I speak to Abraham Shai?'

Karpinowitch was a dry, pedantic man, sparing of speech. He owned an investment corporation and his publishing firm was a subsidiary branch of his ramified activities. When I climbed up to his office I had to wait for him for over half an hour, thumbing over half a dozen leaflets from which I learned all about the values of the bonds and shares of the Central Building Company and the details of its balance sheet.

'Mr Jonas?' He rose behind his table, tall, white-haired, with bags below his eyes. His fingers pressed my hand like pieces of wood. The office was spacious and air-conditioned, and a ficus plant in a pot in one corner gave it the freshness of an aquarium.

'I was glad to learn from Mr Shai', he said after we had sat down, 'that you are prepared to write the book about the late Davidov. We believe that it will have good prospects. Davidov was a figure well-known to the public, thousands knew him, and there is no reason why they should not purchase the book which will be written about him. Provided it is a good book, of course. Mr Shai has a very high opinion of you and I rely upon him in this matter. I understand that you will require a considerable time for preparation before you begin the writing itself. Four months? Six?'

'About that,' I said.

'About six?'

'Yes.'

'The writing itself would take…a year? A year and a half?'

'Approximately.'

'A year and a half?'

'Yes. About that.'

'What we want, of course, is a novel. A biographical novel based on the material. Are we in agreement on this point?'

'Yes, I think so.'

'I realize that you will also have to live during this time.' A weary smile glimmered in his eyes. His long, pendulous face looked as if it had been dusted with white talc. 'Have you thought about a monthly sum that you would like to propose?'

I shaded my forehead with my hand and considered. For two years Ahuva had been looking after all my financial affairs. I did not even know how much her expenses were. Two hundred and fifty was the highest figure that came into my mind.

'Five hundred a month, would that be fair?' he said, when he saw that I was in difficulties.

I stared, open-eyed. (But I stopped the stare in good time.)

'Five hundred and fifty?' he said.

'Five hundred would be fair,' I said. (But a warning bell of some kind of sin rang in my head.)

'Five hundred multiplied by eighteen makes nine thousand'—he noted the figure casually. 'So we shall regard that as an advance. Author's fees on the usual scale will be credited to you as the book sells. If they exceed the sum of the advance—as I hope—you will, of course, receive your due; if they do not reach the sum in question, you will not have to reimburse us in any way. Anything else?'

No 'anything else' came into my mind, except a fleeting thought that his fairness was binding me too firmly. His powdered face was waiting.

'So that's all,' he said. 'Yes, I should add that any outlay you may have in connection with the work, such as travelling, meals and accommodation away from home, will be at our expense. You will submit receipts and we shall pay.'

I thanked him.

Karpinowitch rose to indicate that the meeting was over, smiled his polite, niggardly smile and said, putting out his hand: 'You can expect to receive the draft contract from the secretary tomorrow, at about this time. Have you a lawyer, Mr Jonas?'

'I haven't,' I said.

'You really ought to have one,' he said. 'Mr Shai will no doubt be able to recommend one. Better that everything should be clear before you sign the contract, so that you should not feel you have been unfairly treated or that any clause has been smuggled in that might give you trouble. It happens sometimes. I believe that is all for the moment. It has been a pleasure to meet you, Mr Jonas.'

When I brought the two-page draft contract to Shiloh, my lawyer, he raced over it with his eyes, smiling to himself as if to say 'Ah, what swindlers!' and, muttering angrily every now and then 'absurd, absurd', turned over the contract again and scratched vigorous, angry strokes of the pen under every third or fourth line, then threw it away from him on the table and announced loudly: 'No, my friend!' From the way he spoke it appeared that they were deceiving me, leading me astray. Every single clause was riddled with gaping loopholes; worse still, vitally important parts of the structure were simply not there. What about translation rights, stage, film and radio rights? What about the transfer of rights to a third party? What about checking the accounts? Or possible delays due to *force majeure*? And above all, above all—Shiloh picked up one page of the contract as if he were holding a reptile by its tail, striking the page under it with the back of his hand—there was no clause whatever about compensation!

'What compensation?' I asked.

'What does it say here?' Shiloh vigorously turned over the first page and impatiently rustled the second. 'Here, clause twelve, the last one: The two parties waive the need for the sending of solicitors' letters, and any statement that may be sent by registered post...and so forth and so forth. But why is there no clause relating to breach of contract by one of the parties?'

'What kind of breach, of contract?' I blinked.

'Anything might happen, my friend,' he said, with a look threatening disaster, war, death. 'What will happen if the first party thinks better of it, changes his mind? Doesn't publish the book? What will happen if for one reason or another he doesn't like the manuscript? Or if this Karpinowitch goes bankrupt? That could happen too.'

'In all these cases', I replied, 'it says in the contract that I keep all the advance payments I get every month and I don't have to give them back.'

'Is that all you want?' His spectacles gleamed. 'Why, you might suffer damages worth much more than the wretched sum you got.'

'Nine thousand?' I said.

'And if they stop after the first month? Or the third? And if, let's say, Karpinowitch dies in the fourth month? We must take everything into account! That's what you make a contract for.'

'What losses can I incur?' I asked.

'What losses? Let us imagine, for instance, that you have been offered some other literary work, for a fee double what you're offered here, and you've refused it because you are bound by this contract. Let us assume that because of these obligations you are unable to accept some important post for a salary higher than what you get here. Or even that you have interrupted the writing of some important work of inestimable value. And all that is apart from moral damage, mental suffering, loss of reputation and so on. No, my friend, here we have to put in a special clause about the damages that the first party will have to pay to the second party—and, of course, the same the other way round: the second party to the first party—in case of any breach of contract.'

A week later I had in my hands a new draft of the contract, composed by my lawyer, Shiloh, containing four pages instead of two and twenty-three clauses instead of twelve, including a clause on damages that each party must pay the other in case of breach of contract, to the tune of five thousand Israeli pounds. When I submitted the draft to Mr Karpinowitch he examined it calmly and when he had finished reading, he said, 'You have a good lawyer. Many of the things here are super-fluous in my opinion, but I have no objection. We can sign, I think.'

On the first of June I signed the contract for the book on Davidov. On the seventh I divorced my wife Ahuva.

Chapter five

We stood on the pavement in the midday heat and did not know which way to go. Should we separate? Should we go on together? Which way? The light was dazzling, as if we had emerged from a dark cinema after a depressing film. There had been something of the taint of death there inside, all through the proceedings, half bureaucratic and half ritual, with the funereal clerics who conducted the ceremony. The dusty, noisy street did nothing to wipe out the impression of nightmare. Should I go to the left? Should I go with her? Finally Ahuva gave me a strained smile—as if it was I who needed pity—and said: 'Come, I'll make some lunch. After all, you've nowhere to go now.'

It was strange to hear her voice after the way she had stood there in the room like a cast-off slave-girl, when she was instructed to hold her two cupped palms to catch the parchment I had to throw into them with a contemptuous gesture.

'Let's celebrate the occasion.' I tried to make a joke of it.

We took the bus to Jaffa and walked idly up the street. Ahuva paused every now and then at the shop windows, as if we meant to get ourselves a wedding present. Beside a men's-wear shop she remarked that black shirts looked particularly well on me. If she had some money, I thought, she would buy me a parting gift. She looked cheerful, like someone who feels easier after weeping his fill. We went into a restaurant and sat down in the greenish shade, with the cruets of oil and vinegar between us.

'Our funeral banquet,' Ahuva smiled.

The food was so peppery that tears scalded my eyes. When we came to the coffee she encircled the china cup in both hands and rolled it back and forth for a long time.

'What are you writing now?' She looked up at me gently.

'We'll see…I'll try to go on with what I started.'

She lowered her eyes to the cup, and when she raised them again there was the flicker of a bitter smile.

'Why didn't you tell me…about the Davidov book?'

'It wasn't settled then.' I blushed.

Ahuva looked at me as at a naughty boy.

'How's mother?' I asked.

'All right,' she said.

And then, with a melancholy smile:

'Actually she's not sorry.'

I sipped my coffee morosely. Her mother was a large, dignified woman. I respected her. All these weeks she had kept away from us and in my imagination I used to visualize her at home, pronouncing the ban on me. If she had come to me to fight for her daughter…

'You know she was never very fond of you,' said Ahuva.

'Yes.' I swallowed my phlegm. Suddenly, it seemed, what she thought about me was important. 'Why?' I asked.

'What does it matter now?' A smile quivered on her lips.

A few flies above the table disturbed our silence. I searched for something to say about our two years, something fitting for the occasion, something solemn and sad and full of feeling—but couldn't think of anything. If I said something conciliatory, it would sound false. I did not want to apologize or anything like that. Anything I might say would grate on the ears.

'You shouldn't have agreed to do it.'

'Do what?'

'This job, the book.'

'Why not?' I said, beginning to take an interest in the conversation.

'It's just a feeling… Don't know.'

'Why?' I insisted.

'It's not the thing for you. Perhaps I'm wrong, but I feel you won't be able to understand him…Davidov.'

'Why not?'

'There's nothing in you that's like him.'

'Is that necessary?'

Her candid look scrutinized me, as if she was seeing me for the first time, or summing up to herself what she had been thinking about me in the last few days.

'Actually, you're not so honest,' she said with a faint smile, more in sorrow than in resentment. 'I always thought you were very honest. But I was wrong. You have a kind of…a kind of…petty malice.'

'What else?' I smiled to hide my irritation. I wanted her to pick my character full of holes, to pay me back tit for tat, and then we would be quits. I cast her off, she spits in my face, and the game ends in a draw: I owe her nothing.

'Do you enjoy it?' She laughed as if reading my mind.

'It's interesting to hear,' I said.

'Are you really interested in my opinion of you?'

There was a sad quiver in her smile.

I found it strange that she had an 'opinion' about me. I always thought she admired me.

'Yes,' I said.

'Actually I always knew…' she said thoughtfully, looking into my face, 'but I didn't want to know. I suppressed it. I remember how you used to torment your mother with your silences when she came to visit us. After she died you used to torment me. A kind of vexatious malice, cowardly, surreptitious. You thought I didn't notice—I ignored it—I don't know why I was so frightened of any disparaging thought about you and always found excuses for you. Perhaps because I thought…that it was because you weren't satisfied with yourself. I wanted you to write, that was all I wanted. I prayed for you to succeed.

I thought that would make you better and everything would be different, like at the beginning. But actually it isn't this…'

Suddenly she shook her hair with a toss of the head and said:
'Oh, I'm just chattering,' and putting the cup on the table she smiled
frankly at me.

This innocent little lamb! I had never dreamt that she was
turning me over in her mind as she sat there behind my back. Now
I was ready to listen.

'Go on,' I said.

She was silent for a moment. Then she rested her chin on her
hands and said: 'You know, I've gone through an awful lot during the
last two weeks. An awful lot. All kinds of terrible feelings. At night I
sometimes thought my hair was going white. If I could write, I would
write down some time all I went through. But I find it terribly strange
that now…I don't hate you at all. I haven't even any resentment. It's
hard to understand, I even…Oh, never mind.'

Strange, strange, I thought, that my heart was heavier now
than hers.

'I even wish you success with all my heart.' Again she smiled
at me bravely.

The proprietor came up and put down the bill. Before I could
take my wallet out of my pocket Ahuva opened her handbag and
paid him. I sat on. We needed to spend a little more time getting
acquainted.

'You never told me what you thought about that chapter I
wrote,' I said.

'You never asked,' she said.

'I'm asking.'

Ahuva paused, and finally came out with a kind of forced
answer:

'It's all right.'

I swallowed the insult, hoping she would continue.

'Shall we go?' She emerged from her thoughts.

When we came out into the street the houses looked yellow.
Again we stood on the pavement and did not know which way to
go.

'Let's go home,' she said. 'After all, you've nowhere to sleep tonight.'

We walked along the shore; when we reached home it was already evening. When Ahuva switched on the light she was startled at the sight of a big cockroach motionless on the floor. She let out an '*Oi!*', sank into the armchair, and covered her face with her hands. I pulled off my sandal and pursued the insect as it ran about in panic, hiding under the furniture, slipping in and out, slipping away and appearing again. I moved the bed, pushed things around, and all the time Ahuva was sobbing, her head in her. She had never been afraid of insects, and now she was weeping like this, without stopping. Even after I had run the creature down and hit him hard with my sandal she wept and wept.

So I made Ahuva drink the bitter waters like the adulterous woman in the Bible, and recited the formula: 'Behold thou art permitted to any man.' The second evening, when she left me to myself, I packed up some of my belongings in a suitcase and went off to Ephraim Averbuch, a boyhood friend who lived in the south of the city.

When I rang the bell at the door of his humble, low house he came out in pyjamas, startled to see me with the suitcase in my hand, and whispered: 'Come in.' I asked if I could stay the night with him and he said: 'Of course, of course.' He didn't have an extra bed, but he would give me his and he would sleep with his wife. He brought me into the little kitchen and asked what had happened. When I told him he did not believe me. 'Yes, that's how it is,' I lamented mournfully, like a man who had suffered a great misfortune. He tried to comfort me and did not know how. Then he said sadly: 'Only a few days ago we were talking about you, Zippora and I. I told her about a dream I'd had about you.' 'What did you dream?' I asked. 'You'll laugh, but I dreamt you were dead,' he said, smiling a melancholy smile. 'Dead?' I laughed sardonically. 'A terribly strange dream,' he said. 'I was riding in a Jeep in a big field of thorns and suddenly the Jeep stuck in a deep hollow. I got out to extricate it, and I saw an old Bedouin standing beside me. I asked him what was in the pit, and he replied in Arabic: Don't you know? This is the grave of Jonas. Is

Jonas dead? I said startled. Yes, he said, dead, and his wife Martha brings a few stones every day and puts them on the grave. Why on earth I should have dreamt that your wife's name was Martha, I don't know. That's dreams. What happened between you?' When I started telling him he stopped and said perhaps we had better go out, so as not to disturb the children's sleep. At the same time he told me that they had had a third child two months before. He put on his clothes and we went out.

'By the way,' he said as he closed the door behind him, 'I read your story, *A Hero of Our Time*. I enjoyed it very much. I was angry with you, but I enjoyed it.'

'Why were you angry?'

'Because you didn't send me the paper. I only came across it by chance. Suddenly I see "Jonas" in print! I thought perhaps there was another Jonas, and then they told me it was you, Jonas Rabinowitch. I was really glad. Remember what I said about you in school? Even then I knew you would write. Only I didn't like the name. Not the name of the story, that was perfectly all right, but the name of the hero. What kind of name is that, Gabriel Doron? A name ought to be a name! And that was, well, an invention. Margolin—that's a name! You just see the name—and you see the man. But that's really a minor detail. I wanted to send you a postcard. But where to? I didn't even know the address.'

The night air was warm and the yards gave out odours from my childhood days, of woodpiles, machines, dust soaked in oil and petrol. One yard surrounded by a plank fence stood exactly the same as many years ago: the same yard where Ephraim had given a good drubbing to a boy who had shouted after me: 'Jonas, Jonas, teacher's pet, fell in the water and didn't get wet.' Ephraim admired me then because of my talent and what his mother called my 'refinement', and appointed himself my bodyguard; I liked him because of his honesty and because he admired me, and accepted his protection. Then our roads parted. I went to high school and he to learn a trade at Max Pine; after the war—during which we met a few times—I went to the university and he started a little car repair place in the neighbourhood where we had both grown up. When I got into trouble I used to remember him and our boyhood friendship and drop in at his house, not so much to get things off my chest as to make sure that he still believed in me. Even now he remained an overgrown boy, clumsy in body and speech. We walked along by the railway line and I told him something of my life with Ahuva. All the time he was silent, his hands stuck in his trouser pockets and his head sunk between his shoulders. In the distance, black by now, loomed the shadowy mass of the Mikveh-Israel wood.

'And all that time you weren't working?' He stopped and frowned at me.

'I was writing,' I replied.

'Writing all day?'

I explained that a writer's work cannot be measured in hours. That sometimes a man can sit at his desk from morning till night without putting down a line. That it needs time, time for thought, time for idleness, time for dreams. That the work produces itself like resin dripping from the tree, drop by drop, little by little. And all the time the roots absorb, and the trunk assimilates in secret…

'Two years not working!' He threw up his big hands in wonderment. 'I'll tell you honestly,' he smiled, 'if I'd been in Ahuva's place, I'd have divorced *you*! That my wife should support me and I should sit at home!'

I had no patience for his Tolstoyan views. It was only because of the debt I owed him for his hospitality in the middle of the night and his faith in me that I went on talking. With a little sophistical logic it was easy to get the better of this simple soul. So I gave him mate in five moves:

'Do you value a man's work according to his earnings?' I started off with king's pawn.

'Of course not. But…'

'If a man came to you and told you he was working hard from morning till night without having a thing to show for it, would you despise him?' I advanced my queen's knight.

'Well, Jonas, you know that…'

'Let's say he's had two whole years of drought and lost all his crops, would you hold that against him?'—pushing the bishop out into the middle of the board.

37

'But it's not the same, the thing is...'

'Would you tell him to abandon his farm and start some other job that he doesn't know a thing about?'

'Look here, Jonas...'

'And if he didn't do what you said and stuck to his guns, would you call him an idler?'

'I didn't talk about idlers. I only said...'

And now, mate next move:

'Well, then, why do you think my work—though I admit it hasn't produced much result—is less important than any other kind?'

The good Crito blinked his little eyes, deepset in his sallow face, at Socrates. Willy-nilly he must say: Even so, Socrates. No, I have no reply to that, Socrates!

'Perhaps you're right,' he said. 'I only thought it must feel funny to sit at home with your wife going out to work every morning. But perhaps I don't understand these things.'

Victory was not so sweet. I had to make some kind of concession.

'Yes, if it's feelings you mean,' I said, 'you're right. Not pleasant at all.'

We turned back. Now he talked and I was silent. I thought of many things that lay in store for me in my new bachelordom: café meals...new faces...free as the wind. I listened with half an ear to the moralizings of this paragon of labour. The country was full of parasites. Everyone was getting rich without working. Making money out of the land that good lads had shed their blood for. Lining their pockets with German reparations, flourishing over the ashes of the martyrs. Rot setting in at the foundations. Living on the dead! The whole country! No wonder there was corruption everywhere, from top to bottom! 'You tell me, Jonas, where will it all end? How can we go on like this?' I tried to speak my piece for the defence, half-heartedly, but he would not give an inch.

As we were approaching his house, he asked:

'And now that you're alone, what will you live on?'

I told him about the Davidov book.

The simple soul said nothing. Walked on beside me with his head bowed, silent.

It was two o'clock when we entered his house. His wife turned in her bed; in the corner near mine a child's breathing, feather-light. In the morning when I awoke I was alone in the room. There was a white light in the window, the kind of empty light you have in a southern neighbourhood, shining on a street without a tree in it. I remembered my mother, who used to wake me at this hour to run to the shop for rolls. That room was just like this one, low and whitewashed, with the tumbled, poverty-stricken bedclothes. From the kitchen I could hear the gurgling of an infant sucking at the breast.

A few days later I saw in the paper a brief item about the death of Polishuk the sculptor, all alone in an attic; the funeral was to leave from his house. The morning after, I went to the house and rented this room where I now live.

Chapter six

What I like about Clive
Is that he is no longer alive.
There is a great deal to be said
For being dead.

E.C. Bentley, *Biography for Beginners*

I now come to the story of the book. I imagine that few authors in this country have had as much publicity for books they have written as I got for a book I did not write. Davidov was known to thousands of people, old and young, who had settled all over the country. They were all waiting expectantly, and those I met would give me questioning and encouraging looks, as people do to a pregnant woman: How is it going? Is the baby kicking? When is it due? And I used to answer with vague hints—as if to avert the evil eye: Yes, everything's more or less all right, it's all going naturally, and, please God—stimulating hope, but appealing for patience, patience. If only Davidov knew...

I had met him at two of the stations in his wanderings. The first time it was at the Atlit salt-pans in 1944. He suddenly appeared, suddenly vanished, leaving behind a dusty cloud of nostalgia, like a horseman

41

disappearing at a gallop over the horizon. One evening the rumour spread through the camp: Abrasha Davidov is here! and early in the morning, when the surface of the salt was all purple, like a snow field in the dim sunrise...

(I must explain: it was 1944 and I was eighteen, and I was a member of a kibbutz—having been sent out to work for wages—and though I was somewhat out of step, slightly mutinous, rubbing from time to time against the yoke, I was still capable of getting excited at things that I greet today with a frozen face; and the year was 1944, when songs of the scout patrols echoed on the dusty roads and we wandered like flocks of birds from copse to copse, from village to village, and the waves spewed out scraps of wreckage on to the beach, and one's blood boiled at every report of curfews, arrests, arms searches, a defender falling somewhere at his post... So I'll make no bones about it: Davidov's name, which was always uttered in tones of affection and respect—though also with some jocularity—warmed my blood with fervent curiosity.)

I remember, then, that morning when the salt-pans were shadowy purple; I saw him some way off, holding a wheelbarrow with his long, steely arms—tall, handsome, the quiff of black hair dishevelled over his face. He held the barrow like a toy and he shouted at the loader: 'Fill her up, fill her up! No mercy!' Then he ran with it along the plankway, climbed, light and swift, up the slippery way, and, reaching the bridge, overturned his load on to the truck below as if he were shaking out the crumbs from a tablecloth, announcing the number to the accompaniment of a Russian oath: 'Twelve!' and an oath; 'Thirteen!' and an oath—as if to say: Now for the next one. Sordin the manager was standing on the bank at the edge of the salt-pans in his broad-brimmed Australian hat, riding breeches and shining topboots, his hands behind his back, looking out over the sparkling field swarming with scurrying ants like an estate owner surveying a horde of serfs. At noon, the salt steaming with sulphur fumes and sweat pouring from men's bodies, Davidov halted at the top of the bridge, the handles of his barrow erect on both sides of his waist, and shouted in a powerful voice that rang out over all the pans: 'Sordin, get out of there, damn you! You're annoying the workers! An-noy-ing!' And the laughter rolled over the blinding plain like scraps of paper in the wind. 'Sordin's afraid of him,' the men laughed, directing inquiring looks at the manager, who gritted his teeth and did not stir. I was washed out like a disembowelled sack, aching all over with the effort, and during the break, in the scant shade of the straggly tamarisks, Davidov sat down by me and, opening his basket, looked at me with a smile. 'Pissing blood, eh? How many have you done?' I mentioned a number. 'Not bad!' He looked at me, then he said: 'But you won't hold out like that, my lad. You're pulling with your strength, and that's wrong, you've got to do it with the spirit!' He laughed. 'How d'you mean, with the spirit?' I asked. 'You've got to let the spirit move you, you understand? Let it drive you along. Let's see your loins. Here, look, like a hollow pumpkin. You're working with your guts, and you've got to work with your chest, here.' And with that he took the sweaty *kefiya* off his shiny shoulders, wound it twice round my waist and tied it tight. 'Now see how you'll fly, like a donkey with pepper up its behind!' Later, as we went on working he would cast a pleased glance in my direction from time to time, as if I were somebody he had created, and shout from the distance: 'Carry on, Stakhanov! Break the record! How many have you? Thirty-five? Forty?' And to his neighbours: 'I'll get him up to fifty. Every salt-herring wants to grow wings!' In the evening we heard his voice from afar ringing out in the moonlight, alone and proud, singing some wolfish Russian song from the edge of the little colony.

A few evenings later, as I lay in my tent reading in the light of the oil-lamp, he drew aside the flap, looked in and cried: 'Aren't you ashamed of yourself? On a night like this! And they say there's still such a thing as youth.' He pushed in through the opening, and, sitting on the stool, snatched the book out of my hand. '*Oblomov!*' he exclaimed. 'In English!' '*Oblomov*—and in English!' he cried passionately. He leafed through the book, backwards and forwards, his eyes shining as at the sight of an old beloved friend; shut it; opened it again after all, and, after reading a little, decided: 'No, you can't read Goncharov in English.' Then he recited to me the first sentence in Russian and translated it into Hebrew. 'Ilya Ilitch Oblomov lay in his bed one morning, in his flat in Gorochovaya Street...' Those

Russian openings! I remember his extravagant praise of those openings in Russian novels, each of them like a chess-master's gambit, the first moves guaranteeing the preordained victory. (Remember *Anna Karenina,* he said, with the broken family, betrayal, strife, on the very first page: or *Dead Souls,* where the carriage arrives at the inn and straight away you can see the character in front of your eyes—all simple, practical, straight to the point, the whole plot coiled up in the opening like an embryo that will develop and grow.) I remember how he interrogated me afterwards: Did Goncharov love his Oblomov or not? And at the same time he spoke mockingly about those who do not understand what satire means, who regard it as an expression of the author's contempt for his characters when it is actually his own struggle with the qualities that exist within himself; that there is no satire without love and Goncharov too loved Oblomov and loved Zakhar his servant, and that it was Stoltz, the so-called 'positive' character, whom he did not love, and that was why he came out so colourless...In the middle of his flow of talk he stopped and said: 'Come along, let's have a little stroll, it's a wonderful night outside.'

Outside, the light of the full moon lay spread over chalky stones, straggly bushes and whispering clumps of pines, and quivered in the channels between the pans below on the plain. We walked on, side by side, on the road to the village, Davidov's shadow snaking over the rocks as he took long steps, like a man measuring out a field. I remember how he halted suddenly, lifted up his face to the moon, and said something about a nation's history beginning in the heavens, but without a moon... God, he said, took Abraham outside and told him to count the stars, but there was no moon. And that was the beginning of our history, which already contained the future *in embryo*—very serious, shadowy, sublime, unromantic.

Later, he said, the Jews used to pronounce a blessing on the moon when it was new, a mere thread of silver, an exiguous, seques-tered beauty, ignoring it when it was at the full and leaving it to illuminate the fields and barns of the gentiles... They packed away beauty in little magic boxes: the *mezuzah* on the doorpost, the cell of the phylacteries, spice-boxes, letters of the alphabet. Only now were the magic boxes opening up and the beauty breaking forth into the open. The poet Tchernichovsky, he said, understood what beauty is, but he associated it with idolatry, because he did not sense the natural beauty of this land. What have we to do with idols? he asked. Here beauty is one God, wide and abstract....

The chalky street of the village was wrapped in dreams; the moonbeams spread their nets over the farmers' houses and yards. From below, where a street-lamp glimmered by the railway station, a single laugh reached us, like that of a girl evading her pursuer. 'What an old and weary village!' said Davidov. 'Not ten yet—and fast asleep. As if their fathers had been farmers for generations. Have you ever seen their chickens? Arab birds converted to Judaism. The funniest breed in the world!' Suddenly, without warning, with the impudence of an inveterate jester (crazy Davidov—a laugh doubled up inside me—they'll chase him out of the place!), he lifted his voice in a Russian song of the steppes, which reverberated like a copper barrel rolling down the street. A shutter opened in one of the slumbering houses and a woman's voice called angrily: 'Quiet there!' 'Why quiet, mother?' he retorted, spreading out his hands. 'Why quiet on a night like this, when your heart goes out to the open spaces?' 'You want me to call the police?' asked a toothless voice from the window, and the shutter was slammed shut. Davidov stood for a moment like a chidden youth. 'Come on, let's go back,' he said. 'They're catching mice in their dreams.'

A few lads were standing in the workers' dining-hall, arguing about the trade union delegation to the congress in London, the Jewish Commonwealth idea, the Biltmore Programme. Davidov stood for a while listening, and I remember how he broke in suddenly: 'What are you talking about? What's all this?'—brushing aside all their arguments and bombarding them with questions: Why didn't they break in and release the refugees from the Atlit Camp near by? What were they afraid of? The British army? Casualties? Why did they submit to the disgrace of the leaders arrested by the British, and the disgrace of the refugee ship *Mafkura* wrecked on the high seas, and the refugees exiled to Mauritius? Suddenly, as if even he did not take his own words seriously, he stopped and turned to one of the group, the storekeeper. 'That's it! Now bring a water-melon, comrade. We'll slaughter it, drink its blood and cool our boiling hearts!'

Everyone smiled: another one of Davidov's famous lunacies.

'Go on, bring it! What are you waiting for?' Davidov rebuked him. 'We're thirsty my lad, we want a water-melon, don't you understand?'

The other stood grinning, with his hands in his pockets.

'Not allowed,' he said. 'At night we don't open up.'

'Hand over the key, I'll open up!' And Davidov stretched out his hand.

'Sorry,' grinned the storeman, holding on to the authority in his pocket.

Davidov looked at him for a moment in silence, as if considering what to do with him.

'Hand over the key,' he said quietly. 'You can say that I, Abrasha Davidov, stole a water-melon.'

'Only for meals. That's the law,' said the other, enjoying his authority.

'The law!' cried Davidov. 'Hand over the key!' He gripped him by the neck of his shirt. 'The law, he tells me!'—pushing him away against the wall. 'What law compelled me to come here, eh? A man's dying for a water-melon at night and they tell him—law! Fuck the law!'

Everyone burst out laughing and Davidov smiled too. 'Never mind, you're OK,' He soothed the fellow he had pinned to the wall. 'Only the water here's a bit salty. A terrible taste. You drink and drink and get thirstier and thirstier until your insides burn up.' He looked at him affectionately, then turned and went outside.

A few days later he disappeared as he had come. As I went on reading *Oblomov*, his figure flickered before my eyes from time to time like an illusion of salt and moon. About nine years passed before I met him again.

I had a list of twenty-seven people, and my first visit—a few days after I moved into the room where I am now writing these pages—was to Abrasha's oldest brother in Zichron-Yaakov.

I got there in the early evening. Joshua Davidov was waiting for me at the farm gate; beside him was a girl of about eighteen, brownish-complexioned, rather plump, with melancholy dimples in her cheeks. He was a thickset man, with a magnificent silvery moustache and smiling Mongoloid eyes sunk in his ruddy cheeks. 'Mr Jonas?' He put out his hand. 'Hope you had no trouble finding the road. Joshua is my name, and this is my little daughter Maxima.' Maxima gazed at me with a shining respectful look. Chickens scratched in the dust of the yard among pines and hibiscus bushes in full red blossom. A many-tendrilled bougainvilia straggled over the rough wall of the house, its tendrils clasping the shingles of the roof. Cracked tiles led to the door.

'Well, well, so they're writing a book about Abrasha.' Joshua sat down at the big table with a bowl of fruit in the middle. A somewhat sceptical look peeped out of his smiling eyes. 'What will you drink? Coffee? Tea?…Bring some tea for the gentleman, Maxima.' Maxima's eyes and hair were like her uncle's. The foliage of the creeper shaded the window and filled the room with a violet dusk. Joshua asked who the publisher was and, when I told him, said: 'I'll tell you straight, if it had been a national project I wouldn't have told you a thing. I wouldn't have had anything to do with it. The Jewish people owed a lot to Abrasha and never paid him back, and you can't make up for that by some kind of monument or something. He'd have had nothing but contempt for all that. He'd have got up at night from his grave, like in the legends, and smashed the stone. You knew him, didn't you? He was capable of that, eh? But if you say a private publisher, that's another story. Yes'—his eyes shone—'there's a lot to write about Abrasha. That's a great subject, a very great subject. You know what that man was? An epoch!'

Maxima brought tea and biscuits and sat down at the table, ready to listen reverently.

'You understand'—Joshua sipped from his glass—'now everybody has remembered him all of a sudden. Once a man's dead he's a hero, as they say. But when he was alive…Listen, for over thirty years that man worked all over the country, did all the hardest jobs, risked his life over and over again, and didn't take a brass farthing, as they say, from the public funds. Pay? Who thought about pay in those days? Did what had to be done and that was that. But when the war was over and he wanted them to give him a house in Beersheba, an old *ruin,* that he meant to repair himself, Abandoned property, they called it, then they said: No, nothing left! All taken! You're too late, they told him! Understand? Abraham Davidov, who was always the first—he was too late! And since Abrasha Davidov couldn't fight for himself—he never could—he died as he lived: a pauper! Everybody grabbed houses, groves, thousands of *dunams* of good olive trees and almond and vines, and he was left with only the shirt on his back, as they say. So now I hear they mention him in speeches and write about him and make him into a national hero. Their hero! By what right? Where's the justice? You want to know something? He was never one of them. You ought to know that.'

He pulled a handkerchief out of his pocket, wiped his moustache, got up, switched on the light, and sat down again, his narrow eyes twinkling as if he wanted to put his momentary anger out of mind.

'But after all, you're not to blame, you didn't come to listen to me scolding. You came to hear me tell you about my brother, isn't that right? What shall I tell you first?'—glancing at his daughter, as if taking counsel with her.

'Tell him about the Tartar soldier.' Maxima drew out the words in a nostalgic tone.

'The Tartar soldier…' Davidov thought a moment, then said forcefully, stretching out a finger to the paper in front of me: 'First of all, write down that Abrasha wasn't a Zionist. He was never a Zionist!' And when he saw the astonishment on my face he laughed. 'Yes, of course he was a Zionist, but not what they *called* a Zionist. You understand, parties, clubs, meetings—all that had nothing to do with him. Nothing at all! He hated it! What have you written there?'—pointing to the paper in front of me. 'Abraham Davidov?

You should have used his Russian name, Abrasha—he was more of a *goy* than a Jew!' His moustache quivered with hearty laughter.

'He really was a *goy*, you know,' he said. 'Well, he wasn't a complete *goy*, because he knew quite a bit of Hebrew before he came, he read a lot, could recite Hebrew poetry by heart and all that. But he had the soul of a Russian, a Russian *goy*, a peasant. If you want to know why, I'll tell you. Our family, we had an estate in Crimea, a farming estate where we grew sugar-beet and other things. You know'—as if remembering a joke—'at the time of the Revolution they used to say Russia was ruled by three Jews: Wissotsky, Brotsky, and Trotsky. Wissotsky was the big tea man, Brotsky was the sugar king…But that's not the point. To cut a long story short, in the whole of our neighbourhood there were hardly any Jews. Germans, Russians, but Jews—very few. Heard of Jenkoy? That's a farm that belonged to a German, Kleberer, and later they made it into a training farm for pioneers. Not far from Jenkoy was our farm. When we were little we hardly saw any Jews. But father brought us a teacher from Simferopol, an educated lad, who taught us a bit of the religious stuff and a lot of Hebrew literature, what there was in those days. Tell you the truth, I wasn't much of a student, but Abrasha loved it. He read a lot and played too. Oh, he knew music! A lot! He had a violin…later on I'll tell you about the violin—a very interesting story—but the soul of a Russian peasant! Loved to ride a horse, swim in the river, fight—just like one of them. He wasn't robust but he was very brave, didn't know the meaning of fear!…Maxima, bring over the album, let him see his pictures of those days.'

In the heavy brass-bound album there were sepia photographs, inscribed in sinuous Russian script. Abrasha could be seen among his family around the table, mounted on a horse at the great farm gate, sitting on a chair with a book on his knees, standing upright in his tight student uniform buttoned up to the neck. He was a lean, dark youth, smooth-faced, with sad, brave eyes. His brother seemed to be shorter, broad-shouldered and apple-cheeked, resembling his high-busted and round-chinned mother, who looked in her lace blouse, with her broad sash and the big medallion hanging round her neck, like a baroness. Joshua Davidov read the pictures with his fingers: This is father, that is mother, that's my sister Masha who died of consumption, that's Uncle Liova who was killed by the Bolsheviks in 'thirty-two…Uncles, aunts and other relatives with very serious, sad-eyed, proud and princely faces. (And among the photographs of uncles, the picture of old Tolstoy, ploughing with a team of horses. 'You know him, I suppose,' laughed Joshua.)

'Yes, I wanted to tell you about the violin,' he said when we had closed the album. 'That's not a story, it's a symbol! In those days, in the summer of 'nineteen, General Denikin's Whites invaded Crimea. He had bands of *Chechens,* barbarians, murderers, pogromists. They drove out the Reds and terrorized the whole district, robbing, raping, arresting anybody they liked, they asked no questions—Jews and Bolsheviks were all the same to them. They had a regimental commander, Sharov, who used to hang people in the streets. Every night you could hear terrible screams from the villages all around. Abrasha was at home at the time because the high school at Simferopol was closed. One night, when he was playing his violin, we heard knocks at the door and in came two White soldiers—they belonged to Slashchov's punitive battalion. They said they had heard that we had Bolsheviks hidden away and demanded that we should bring them out. Abrasha was hotblooded, he used to flare up in no time; before we could say a word, he brandished his violin over the head of one of them and—bang, one strong blow! The violin was smashed, of course, but the two picked up their feet, as they say, and—off they went. Why they ran away I don't understand to this day: perhaps because they didn't expect anything like that, perhaps because there were more men in the room, me, father, two Russian labourers—big, strong lads—but we never saw them again. Why do I tell you that this story is a symbol? Because when Abrasha smashed his violin, the most precious thing he had, over the Russian's head, he smashed all his dreams about Russia. That night he decided he was going to Palestine, and a new chapter opened in his life, as they say.'

'It's a true story,' smiled Maxima's dimples smiled apologetically.

Joshua Davidov watched the impression he had made with his

shrewd eyes, and continued: 'I left six months before him. Not because I was a Zionist—I wasn't, but…After that night we were afraid to stay in the farm, we left everything and moved to Simferopol. There were thousands of refugees in the town, lying in the streets, hungry, sick, dying. We had a bit of money left and with the help of the English Consul in Sebastopol we left by boat for Constantinople, and from there we reached Palestine. Abrasha stayed for a while, because at that time the idea of self-defence got into his head. You know what the trouble was with him? He took everything seriously. Trumpeldor had come to Crimea at that time to set up pioneer settlements, and he said: "Learn to fight and prepare to shed your blood for the homeland"—and Abrasha took it up heart and soul. He decided to join the "military pioneers," as they called them. But what was the result? He was the one who didn't go off with the others, he was the one who was too late to embark on the *Russlan* at Odessa, and he arrived here—alone. That was very typical of him.'

'Tell him about the Tartar soldier,' Maxima reminded him.

'Yes, the Tartar soldier…' Joshua's eyes shone. 'He told us all about it later, when he got here. He missed the *Russlan,* as I told you. And why was that? Because he was accused of stealing. He was working at Simferopol railway station and they said he'd stolen a sack of flour. In Russia they say: "All the acorns fall on the peasant's head." Lots of people took flour for the refugees, but he was the one who had to be caught. He spent about a month, perhaps more, behind bars, and then, when he was let out thanks to the intervention of the Community Council, he decided to make his way to Palestine on foot, through the Caucasus; as Trumpeldor said at the time: "To cross the mountains of Ararat on foot and conquer the Land of Israel." Well, to cut it short, Abrasha and another two lads left Simferopol on their way to the east. The trains were full of soldiers, and civilians had no hope of travelling on them. They had a bit of money, so they hired a cart and kept going day and night till they reached Vladicaucaz; from there they expected to get to Batoum and cross to Turkey. Russia, you know, was in a terrible state of chaos: Whites here, Bolsheviks there, Mensheviks over there. The Soviets were in power in Azerbaidjan and the Mensheviks in Batoum, which was in the Georgian Republic. From Vladicaucaz to Batoum you had to sneak across the border on foot over very high mountains covered with snow all the year round. They gave money to a Tartar soldier, a smuggler, who promised to take them across the border. When they got to the mountains, hungry, thirsty, dead tired, they heard that the Bolsheviks had entered Georgia. The Tartar was terrified and didn't want to go on. In the middle of the road, in the snow, he said he was going back to his village and wouldn't go on. What do you think Abrasha did? He pounced on him, snatched his pistol and said that if he didn't go on he would shoot him on the spot. So the Tartar kept going! They told him to walk a few steps in front of them, with the pistol pointing at his back all the time as if he was their prisoner. But then, when they got to Georgia, the Tartar took ill and couldn't go any farther. Dropping on his feet. The two fellows with Abrasha wanted to leave him in the mountains, but Abrasha said: "No! Leave a man to die in the snow? Never!" So what did they do? They took him with them, practically carried him all the way. When they reached Batoum the Tartar didn't want to leave them. He had got so attached to Abrasha that he said: "You saved my life, take me to Palestine." So they found a collier that was going to Turkey and took him with them as far as Constantinople. The Tartar disappeared later, that's another matter. But the story shows you what kind of a man Abrasha was. He could make a murderous attack on a man, but when he was in trouble he was ready to give his life for him…. Well, then they came to Palestine and he started to work on the roads, but that's a new chapter, as they say. No doubt you'll hear about it from other people. I didn't see much of him in those days.'

It was late by this time, and Joshua Davidov suggested that I should stay the night with him. I said I would try to get a taxi, and Maxima went out with me to accompany me to the centre of the village. On the road she told me how when she was a little girl she had stayed a few days with her uncle in his solitary house in a eucalyptus grove on the outskirts of Kfar Sava. The boys and girls used to meet at night in the packing-house of the nearby orange grove and Abrasha would teach them the use of weapons. Once she had crept up and peeped inside through the slits in the blind. 'I remember he was so secretive and so brave that I stood and quivered. A kind of fear—no, not fear—everything was terribly mysterious.' The guard had caught her, and her uncle had come out, pulled her by the hand, and, as he was taking her home, had told her that if she revealed anything of what she had seen, the house and the grove would be set on fire. Ever since then, whenever she remembered him she would see fire in her mind's eye, a great conflagration. 'And what I still remember is the throbbing of the well, the well of the grove, and the darkness of the night, as we walked hand in hand and I was trembling terribly—it was something I can still remember as if it was yesterday.'

Chapter seven

About a week after my visit to Joshua Davidov I received a letter from his daughter which I keep with another few letters, the last remaining scraps of the debris of my work which a malignant wind scattered in all directions.

> Dear Mr Jonas,
>
> I suppose you are now going over your notes for the book about my uncle, so I am losing no time in sending you this letter with two requests:
>
> a) My father asks you to correct one detail in the story he told you about Abrasha's flight from Russia. The town where he and his two comrades met the Tartar soldier was not Vladicaucaz but Piatigorsk (he remembered after you had gone and was very worried about it).
>
> b) I beg you, please, please, not to say a single word in the book *about me* or *about what I told you* on the way to the taxi station. My uncle's memory is very precious to me and I would not want a book devoted to him to contain something that is really of no importance and that I am now ashamed of

blurting out. I know you will not understand this, but perhaps I can explain it to you some time if we meet.

I hope you will carry out these two requests and I wish you (in my father's name as well) success in your important work.

Yours respectfully,

MAXIMA (DAVIDOV)

P.S. I found in the library the papers where your story *A Hero of Our Time* appeared. We read it, my father and I, and we both admired it very much!

('Yours respectfully'. I present this document to the prosecution as another piece of evidence against me. Here is an example of how the accused defiled the innocence of a simple soul who believed in him, who waited with humble patience for the clusters to ripen in his vineyard. Yes, I confess: when my glance now falls on this innocent, virginal, round handwriting, my ears burn with shame. I shouldn't know where to look if I actually met her somehow by chance. What should I say to her?)

I did not meet her. When I got her letter I stuffed it in a drawer. Scored out Vladicaucaz and wrote Piatigorsk. A few days later I set out again to track down her uncle. I went to see Hava Havkin, a nurse in Kfar Ata. I reached the clinic at midday, the time agreed, and waited in the corridor for her to finish her work.

'Forgive me for receiving you here,' said Hava Havkin as she washed her hands in the basin after inviting me to come in. 'I live in town and I've got to be back at work at four. I thought we had better meet here.' And as she dried her hands she said: 'Have you met Issachka Golan yet? You ought to meet him. He'll be able to tell you a lot about that period, more than me.' Then she sat down opposite me at the clinic table and, stroking her silvery, silky hair, said: 'Actually, I don't know if I can give you much help.... It's over thirty years since then, and my memory is not so clear any longer. But I'll try.'

She had a pleasant voice, calm and smooth like her soft hair, which was neatly parted and gathered at the back of her neck; like the fine network of wrinkles at the corners of her mouth and around her limpid eyes.

'So you're taking notes too?' She smiled, seeing me put down the paper in front of me. 'I shall have to be careful about every word I say...but then, otherwise I suppose you won't remember...'

She leaned her elbows on the table, shaded her smooth forehead with her two hands, as if erecting a barrier between us, or between the present and the days gone by, and pondered. Her eyes narrowed somewhat and the wrinkles at the corners of her mouth aged slightly. The odour of ether and medicaments cooled the air of the silent room.

'Yes'—her clear, sky-blue eyes opened—'I will tell you about a few episodes. We were working at the time on the Tiberias-Samah road. I expect you know how it was: rows of tents all along the road, some of the people bringing the stones, some breaking them, some digging, and others in the quarries. We were not used to the work and our hands burned with the blisters. It was particularly bad when the blisters burst, so burning and painful! Like salt on an open wound. But everyone was absolutely determined; they would have been ashamed to give in to the pain. I remember Abrasha's first day on the road. I did not know him, because he came after us. He came alone. Generally, at that time, people came to Palestine in groups and were organized for the work in the same way according to the towns they came from: the Orhov group, the Mohilev-Podolsk group, the Marini-Gorky group. He was from Crimea, but he did not come with the Crimeans. I believe he did not know a single soul. I sat at my heap of stones, in the blazing sun of the Jordan valley, and chipped away. Opposite me at another heap was Davidov, the new fellow. He was a very handsome young man, lean, tall, dark; with his red kerchief tied round his head he looked like a gypsy. I saw that he was trying very hard, striking and striking with his little hammer, but the stones were not breaking. My pile of gravel grew higher and higher, but his was small, minute. I went over to show him how to break up the stone—I was already a "veteran" at the job—but he rejected my help. "No need," he said, "I'll learn by myself." Very taciturn he was. About midday I had a big pile and he had a little mound. I felt that he was thoroughly depressed. It was a disgrace for him, a big strong lad, and here…but he said nothing. He carried on all day, and the same next morning. When it was almost midday and it was just the same again—my tall heap on one side and his little heap on the other—he suddenly threw down his hammer on the stones and went up to the foreman. Either the quarry, he said, or nothing at all. No more stonebreaking for him! The work at the quarry, you know, was very hard at that time. They used to work with a *balamina*, a long, heavy rod they split the big stones with. Very hard. The foreman tried to explain to him that he wouldn't be able to stand it because he was still fresh, but he insisted: either the quarry, or off he would go. They gave in, and the very same day he started working with the *balamina* down in the wadi. In the evening—in the evening I saw another man before me! Radiant, proud…' A glow of recollection shone from Hava Havkin's eyes. 'He had a wonderful voice, you know. Steely, strong, with a kind of broad resonance. They said that in Russia he used to play an instrument too. Why did I remember his voice? The same evening, as we sat on the shore of Lake Kinneret and talked—in those days, you know, on the roads, there was hardly such a thing as private life. You did everything together. Even the letters we got we used to show each other. Today it's hard to understand. And we were not tired at all! All through the night, after the hard work, we would sit in the open or dance or sing. No, it's not a fairy tale, it really was like that. Well, that evening, suddenly we heard his voice, singing in Russian. He was pouring out his soul as if to himself, and we all listened in silence, we could almost see the song swelling out over the Kinneret, like moonlight, and our hearts were so full…'

Hava Havkin looked at me from the distant days of her youth. 'I don't know if this means anything to you, what I am telling you. Unimportant things really. But you know, life is made up of little details. Sometimes I try to remember someone I haven't seen for a long time, and I find it quite impossible to recall what he looked like—only some trivial movement of the hand, how he would stub out his cigarette in the ashtray, for instance.'

Then she continued: 'Let me tell you about one episode. You know, in those days we were very young, enthusiastic, with great dreams about the settlement of the land, about a commune of all the workers in the Land of Israel…a kind of revolution, but in a different style, all our own. But it was sad, too. Yes, many left, many went back abroad. It's not only today you have people leaving the country, we had them then too. And there were suicides as well. There was a time when we were working near Migdal when not a week passed without a suicide. It's hard to understand today. Perhaps it was because people took life so seriously: either to realize the ideal completely or…better not live at all. There was no middle way. That was the psychology. Well, in Migdal we had a beautiful girl, the beautiful Saritchka they called her. Extraordinary beauty. Big, black eyes and a delicate, almost transparent skin. One night she went and drowned herself in the Kinneret. It was a terrible shock. Next morning we didn't go out to work, we all went to the funeral, hundreds of people, from all the companies of the Labour Corps. Even from Kfar Giladi. All of us—except Abrasha. He stayed behind, alone, in the quarry, and went on breaking stones. When they asked him afterwards why he hadn't come to the funeral he said: "To commit suicide is a sin. And a sin calls for judgment, not mourning. All this respect only encourages more suicides," or words to that effect. And perhaps he was right. If people had known that suicides would be excommunicated—as the Jewish custom is—possibly they would have drawn back…'

Hava Havkin passed her fingers over her forehead as if brushing away a cloud, looked through me, and recalled: 'Yes. One day Abrasha disappeared and we didn't know where he was. They said he had been seen walking along the road to Tiberias, but he didn't come back in the evening, or next day. We knew that he hadn't left for good because his things were still in the tent. We began to be worried. People were sent to the town and riders set out all over the district to look for him, but he was not found. We were very apprehensive. And then, two days later, in the evening, he appears in the dining-hut, radiant, and says he went—to the Hauran, across the Jordan. All alone. We were thunderstruck! You know, in those days some of us were considering the idea of the Kazachistvo—to establish settlements of workers and fighters on the borders. And Abrasha's dream was the Hauran. It fascinated him. Many people were fascinated by it—but only Abrasha was capable of leaving his work suddenly, without saying a word, and making his way across the river by himself. That's the kind of person he was. A wild stallion. Always doing surprising things, on his own initiative. He had scorpions in his feet, as they used to say at that time.

'Listen.' She laid her arms on the table. 'It's easy to say that Abrasha was an unusual person, out of the ordinary, a special type. But perhaps we were all like that. A little out of the ordinary. Strange. There was a kind of contrast like that: we lived together, and yet each of us was like a world in himself.

'How can I explain it to you? On the one hand everything was in common, everything! Nobody in this country has ever lived such a communal life as we did then on the roads. And on the other hand—such individualism! Every single one was a terrible individualist! Perhaps that was our tragedy…You know, sometimes I look around me and say to myself: Once there were so few people in the country and so many characters, and now—a mass of people and so few characters! It's funny, of course, what I am saying, but…. I've a feeling like that, perhaps because I am no longer so young, or perhaps…'

Again she shaded her forehead as if trying very hard to remember, and sadness hovered over the fine wrinkles. 'After you have gone I shall no doubt remember more things, it's always like that with me.' She gave me a melancholy smile and fell silent. 'Actually,' she said, 'he wasn't with us up to the end. I suppose you know he left the Labour Corps even before it broke up. In 'twenty-two or 'twenty-three. He went down to Nuris with us, and when the great debate with the Left began he went away. They said at the time that he supported Elkind and was against the Corps starting settlement. But I don't think that was the reason. He was just the kind of person who could not sit still in one place. The soul of a gypsy. To be a farmer—that was really not in his character. But…he loved the land, loved it very, very much.

'Well, what else can I tell you?' Hava Havkin pondered. 'I think that's all. Yes, of course there were love affairs, girls who fell in love with him and broke their hearts on his account. But for history that doesn't matter, does it? You see, I haven't given you much. My memory is getting a little blurred. You really ought to meet Issachka Golan. He knows a lot and remembers a lot.

'Strange'—she looked at me sadly—'such a little country, and just imagine: for fifteen years, since Zalkinson's funeral, I haven't met Issachka. That's how it is, our folk meet mostly at funerals. It's a good thing that you are collecting these memories. No doubt you'll work them up, too, into one complete whole. Abrasha was such a fine, interesting character that it would be a real pity if no memory of him was left.'

Chapter eight

Yesterday, Tuesday, July 15th, was the fourth session: 'D. Karpinowitch Publishers Limited versus Mr Jonah Rabinowitch, known as Jonas.' The session opened with a statement by the attorney for the plaintiff—a surprise manœuvre which stunned me, embarrassed my lawyer and brought an enigmatic smile to Judge Benvenisti's lips. The publishers, Attorney Evrat announced, were prepared to abandon their claim, forgo reimbursement of the advances, and waive the compensation due to them, on condition that I, the defendant, handed over in their rough, unfinished state all the notes I had taken of my conversations with the people I had met.

The judge, his head bent over his desk, looked up sideways in expectation at my counsel. 'Quite a generous offer,' he murmured.

Yes, Attorney Shiloh was deeply embarrassed. He blinked his bespectacled eyes and pretended to be examining the documents in front of him. I gazed at him more in enjoyment of his discomfiture than in concern. This fool had been building a rampart of sand that a single cannon-shot had wiped out as if it had never existed. To gain time, apparently, he stroked his bald head and said, 'To which notes does my learned friend refer?'

'I refer, Mr Shiloh, to those notes taken by your client when he interviewed twenty-seven persons who told him, each in his or her turn, about the life of the late Davidov, notes which were intended to serve as the basis for the composition of the book. This at least, we hope, your client did in return for the nine thousand pounds he received from the publishers—or perhaps he did not even do that?'

(How handsome, how skilful, how young, brilliant and candid is this lawyer in comparison with mine—clumsy, bald, heavy-headed and thick-fingered!)

Attorney Shiloh picked up the four-page contract, turned over the first page with an energetic rustle, and said, 'Will my learned friend point out where anything is said in this agreement about any notes whatsoever which my client was allegedly obliged to take?'

Attorney Evrat picked up the copy of the contract from his desk, raised it to his eyes solemnly as if he was about to recite the Magna Carta to the nation, and read in a clear voice:

'Article Four, subsection a): "The second party undertakes to prepare the said book, within the said period, according to and on the basis of the existing written and oral material which will be collected, edited and adapted by him, on all matters connected with the life and death of the late Davidov." I repeat: "written *and oral*"! Farther on, in Article Eight, subsection c): "The sums that will be received by the second party in the instalments and on the dates stated above shall be regarded as payment for the work of preparation and composition that will be done by him, including the recording of recollections and all other factual material about the deceased from persons who knew him, as well as the assembling and editing of such material"—and so forth. I repeat: "the recording of recollections and all other factual material"! I believe these points are clearly and expressly stated.'

My attorney's glance fluttered in the net of the articles of the document before him. With a twist of the head he extricated himself.

'Despite the undoubted familiarity of my learned friend with the details of the agreement,' he said, 'I do not see where it is stated that my client undertook to prepare any systematic notes whatever of the factual material. What was meant in drafting the article referred to, when speaking of "the recording of recollections", was the accumulation of the material for the sole use of the author, and this could also have been done by means of chapter-headings, notes, jottings and the like, not constituting any continuous and readable text which might be of use to anyone else except the author himself. In any case, there is no such undertaking in the agreement before us.'

'Your Honour!' Attorney Evrat jumped up. 'The plaintiff is prepared to call twenty-seven witnesses, each of whom will testify that the defendant made full, continuous and systematic notes of what they told him. These notes should be in his possession and we want to receive them as a minimal return, out of all proportion to the enormous sums he has received from the publisher. Such a return is quite inadequate to meet the demands of law and justice, and if my client is prepared to accept it, he is only making a generous gesture to a young author to save him from disgrace in the eyes of the public and of all those who honour the memory of the late Abraham Davidov.'

The judge looked expectantly at my counsel. Mr Shiloh, who was as well aware as I of what had happened to those notes, blinked again and drops of perspiration started up on his forehead, like pearls on his bald crown.

'Your Honour,' he said deprecatingly, 'it is not stated anywhere in the agreement that the author must submit any notes whatsoever to the publisher. It seems to me that in this respect my client has not deviated a hair's breadth from the text.'

The judge showed signs of impatience. He laid down his pen, leaned his elbows on the desk and bent forward.

'The plaintiff is offering to forgo the strict letter of the law, to relax the agreement rather than rigidly enforce it. I do not understand why you cannot accept this offer and finally settle this case, which is not to the credit of either side.'

'Your Honour,' my counsel replied sourly, 'I do not see why my client should agree to hand over to the publisher material which was specifically meant for his own exclusive use and which is in the nature of…'

'You insist on continuing these proceedings in accordance with the plaintiff's claim and ignore his compromise offer?' Benvenisti interrupted.

'Yes, your Honour,' replied my counsel gloomily.

Attorney Evrat now rose and, hand on hip, began once again to present the indictment against me. With the dexterity of an experienced fencer he read out each article of the agreement, pointing out how each had been fully complied with by his client while I had done nothing at all to comply with a single one: I, the living, who had undertaken to write of the dead, had defiled the honour of the living and tarnished the name of the dead. 'In his unparalleled cynicism'—his voice rang out in the courtroom—'a cynicism incredible in a man who calls himself a writer, this man continued to draw his remuneration, month after month, five hundred Israeli pounds each month, for a year and a half, without raising a finger, and—I fear—without turning a hair! All his work in return for the nine thousand pounds cash he received consists of interviews with twenty-seven persons, work that could have been done in twenty-seven days—and, in the light of the defendant's extraordinary refusal to accept the generous compromise offered by my client, there is reason to doubt whether any jot or fragment of the results survives. Mark, you well gentlemen! Nine thousand pounds, for work that any tyro journalist, any unschooled typist, could have done in a few days with the same efficiency, if not more! We placed our trust in this man, twenty-seven persons who favoured him with their most precious memories placed their trust in him; hundreds of men who cherish the memory of the deceased placed their trust in him—and he has betrayed them all. Your Honour!' Evrat smoothed his forelock to one side of his vigorous, dignified face. 'I know of only one case which bears any resemblance to the case before us, and even that is only a parable with a moral: the case of the two tailors in the tale of the Emperor's New Clothes. They took their generous pay, they shut themselves up and pretended to be engrossed in their work, they enjoyed the trust of the emperor and his ministers—and they did nothing at all! If there is, after all, any difference between the case under consideration here and that tale, it lies in the 'minor' detail that those tailors pretended to be sewing a garment for a foolish king, while the tailor who stands before us pretended to be sewing a robe of honour for a personality whom we all admire and of whom the entire nation is proud.'

There was silence. It was only with difficulty that I restrained myself from rising, approaching the rostrum and pressing Attorney Evrat's hand, in front of the judge, the curious crowd, and my stupid lawyer, whose look of depression on his face gave me a sweet sensation of revenge. What an extraordinary demonstration of gladiatorial power! What a brilliant oration by this young Cicero, denouncing Gaius Verus before the senators of Rome! What clean, elegant gestures, in comparison with the clumsy shuffling of my counsel, like a donkey kicking out at random!

But it sometimes happens that even a donkey's hoof strikes out sparks. After two or three moments' silence, during which every one seemed to share in his apparent disgrace, Attorney Shiloh rose and delivered his discourse. He opened his speech by declaring that he would not react to the vituperative statements made by the counsel for the plaintiff against his client, for when justice was done it would be clear to all that it was a case of the pot calling the kettle black. Instead, he would like to draw the attention of the court to one sentence in the agreement which had gone unnoticed so far...

And here he struck out that spark which made even me blink at its coruscation. At the previous session my counsel had built the defence on the argument of the author's right to produce a perfect work of art without limitation of time, even if such limitations were specified in the contract. ('The spirit of the agreement is incompatible with the natural right of the artist to freedom of expression, and the agreement is therefore invalid.') Now he abandoned all those entrenchments which he had constructed with so much toil and perspiration, and founded his entire case squarely on two words in the second article: namely, in the language of lawyers, '*force majeure*'.

'What does it say here?'—reading from the copy of the agreement in his hand. 'It says: "The second party undertakes to complete the writing of the book and submit it to the first party ready for printing not later than eighteen months from the day of the signature on the agreement, *unless he is prevented by force majeure* from carrying out this undertaking by the specified date." Your Honour, the defence intends to prove, and I believe that we shall prove, that this caveat applies to the case before us.'

Derisive smiles hovered on the lips of Attorney Evrat and his assistant.

'Do you mean to say', said Judge Benvenisti, trying to probe the depth of my counsel's meaning, 'that Mr Jonas was *ill* during a certain period within the eighteen months and could not finish his work in time?'

'Let him submit a medical certificate!' cried Evrat's stocky assistant.

'We have heard of authors writing by divine inspiration, but we have never heard before that an author was prevented from writing by divine intervention,' cried Attorney Evrat with a broad smile on his face.

My counsel ignored these pleasantries.

'Your Honour,' he said, 'the case in question is rare in the annals of jurisprudence and I should like to ask you to pay particular attention to this point. In establishing this reservation of *force majeure* the legislature was providing for the impairment of a person's capacity by natural means, preventing him from carrying out his obligations in due time, such as sickness, incapacity, accident, war or death. It is easy to prove that in each case the question at issue is one of the impairment of that human limb or organ which serves the individual concerned in the trade or profession involved in the undertaking. This reservation absolves the carpenter or the metal-worker, for instance, from the obligation to complete his work in time if he has suffered an injury to his hands. The same applies to a footballer who has been injured in the foot or a violinist who has gone deaf. What would be the parallel provision in the case of an author? Your Honour, it seems to be perfectly clear that the instrument of the writer's craft is not the pen, or the hand that writes—for these, surely, are at the disposal of any man—but *the creative spirit,* what we call "the muse," "the divine afflatus". If it is proved that this creative spirit was affected or impaired, or vanished altogether for a certain time during the period specified in the agreement, it is only right that the reservation of *force majeure* should apply to the case before us. I shall try to demonstrate this; moreover, I shall also prove that in this case the defendant's evidence about himself is conclusive.'

I had to admit that this was a brilliant and convincing polemic. I generally regard the finer parts of the law as incompatible with common sense, but this time there was logic in the argument. Perhaps he is right, I thought—that is, perhaps I am right. But the plaintiff's counsel thought otherwise. Mr Evrat rose and argued that if there was an iota of justice in the plea of his learned friend, there would be no point in any contract with any author, for at any moment he might be abandoned by the 'divine afflatus'. Later, when his turn came round again, he said that the work I had undertaken to submit was not a matter of creative literature at all, but came under the category of craft, and all the talk about 'the creative spirit' and the like was totally irrelevant.

'Is that so?' My counsel leapt to his feet. 'Why, then, did it have to be a writer that the publisher made an agreement with?'

'A writer?' cried Evrat's assistant from his place. 'It is not at all clear yet whether your client has any right to claim that title.'

I will not weary the reader with all the details of the vociferous war of words that was waged between the two desks, making me feel like a chicken in the market when they are haggling over a price. At the end of the session my counsel requested permission to call the Honorary Secretary of the Authors' Association as an expert witness at the next session of the court. Permission was granted, despite the opposition of the plaintiff, and the court retired after the judge's statement that it was closing for the summer recess and that the next session would take place after the Jewish festivals.

In the corridor Attorney Evrat came up to me and said: 'If you were a man of conscience, Mr Jonas, you would get up and admit that the notes are no longer in your possession. These futile evasions don't do you any credit as a man and a writer.'

Yesterday evening, for the first time since I started writing these pages, I left my room (my pen, like a refractory mule, refused to go on working) and went to the Cellar—that underground den whose alcohol-sodden air I had breathed on innumerable nights. The whole gang was there, just as in days gone by, already enveloped in the vapours of the place. They welcomed me with a flourish of trumpets as if I had risen from the dead: 'Dreyfus!' 'Socrates!' 'The Hero of Our Time!' 'The Victim of the Ink Libel!' Eliraz rose swaying from the table, pushed his neighbours out of his way, as well as a few glasses that smashed on the floor, fell on my neck and wailed: 'What are they trying to make you do, Jonas, breathe life…into…dry bones? Why? Why and wherefore?' He dropped his head on my shoulder, emitted a malodorous belch and, when I tried to keep him on his feet, ran like a slaughtered fowl in the direction of the lavatory. When I sat down, everyone insisted on hearing what had happened in court, for they had only read the brief story in the evening paper. When I told them about my counsel's shrewd stratagem they cheered again and burst forth into song, beating time and whipping up their enthusiasm with their fists: '*Force majeure—n'avez pas peur*! *Force majeure*—will open the door! *Force majeure*—heals every sore!'—and similar rhymes. The waiter came up and tried to stop the noise, but he was only adding fuel to the flames. Even I, after I had downed a few glasses, began to feel like a hero, and ordered a bottle in honour of my approaching vindication. Glasses were raised and clinked, Nakdimon pronounced a curse on me and my book, and Osnat chanted a couplet by Francois Villon:

> 'So in six foot of rope one day
> Neck must learn what buttocks weigh.'

Meanwhile everything started shimmering before my eyes as in the old days and, as I drank and sang, Hagit's arm was already coiled round my neck and her cheek rested on my shoulder. I dimly remember that she went out with me—the hour, it seems, was very late—into the cold air, stopped a taxi and got in with me. I also remember some vociferous argument with the driver at the entry to the house, cries of 'Quiet there!' from one of the windows, my stumbling ascent of the stairs leaning with all my weight on her limp body, and the prolonged search, accompanied by much laughter, in my pocket to find the key.

Once we were inside she kept on asking questions: Why did I shut myself up, why had I abandoned the gang, did I still see Nili? I said I was going on with the writing of the novel I had started three years ago. '*A Hero of Our Time?*' she asked. Yes, *A Hero of Our Time.*

I did not wake until noon, with a splitting headache. When I went downstairs my landlady, Mrs Silber, met me with an admonitory air. 'You're killing yourself, Jonas, believe me. And besides…it's beneath your dignity. Excuse me for interfering.'

Chapter nine

Beneath my dignity? Perhaps. 'I've drowned my dignity in a beaker, and sold my good name for a song.' But I hate sanctimonious piety. I would not say that the memory of the Cellar recalled the fragrance of spring flowers, or that I sensed the inspiration of the divine afflatus between its walls, or that sparks of sanctity floated upwards from its tables, or that I discovered in its choruses 'the secret of spirit cleaving unto spirit'—to use a Hassidic term. I spent many nights there that are blurred and hazy in my memory: idle, empty nights under the beams of the neon lighting; or nights of debauchery, overflowing into the street with its glimmering lamps and traffic lights and then on to song-filled night-clubs, finishing usually in the white morning in my room, finding by my side on waking a nude body, relaxed and exhausted, knees flexed, a cloud of hair spread out over the pillow, black or brown or fair (Nurit? Hagit? Dinah?). I have no nostalgia for all that, and for all those 'twenty-two sins' that had 'a certain licence' there, in W.H. Auden's phrase; especially not after that complicated episode with Eviatar and Nili (which I shall describe in due course) from which I emerged broken in spirit. But I hate those pious people who preach at me: 'Blessed is the man who walketh not...'—or sitteth not, or lieth not—and who want to plant me by rivers of water so that I may give my fruit in its season. That bondage to conventional rules and precepts which I have cast off...At any rate, the Cellar carries no particular blame for all this.

I first came across the Cellar by chance, one evening about two years ago. I was coming back from a meeting with a man called Ettinger (number four or five in the list), an elderly Jerusalem official who told me about the time when he worked with Davidov at the Ratisbonne quarry (in 1923). As I walked home from the bus, Nakdimon passed by. As I looked back, he looked back too, and both of us halted for a moment. He came up to me. 'You're Jonas, aren't you? Can't remember where we met. In the army?' (He remembered very well, the liar. In the corridors of the university he also used to pass me by and pretend he didn't know me, though we met quite often at the English literature lectures. Later I only used to come across his name in the weekend supplements, above poems with shapes which I can still see in my mind's eye: right-angled triangles, one below the other, or something like long-barrelled pistols, which were indeed loaded with highly explosive ammunition.) 'Perhaps,' I said. He looked at me with his expressionless eyes as if wondering what to say, and then said in his apathetic, drawling voice: 'Tell me, why don't you finish that novel? The beginning was not at all bad.' I said I intended to continue at the proper time. 'And in the meantime?' In the meantime, I said, I was collecting material for a book on Davidov. 'Might be a particularly educational book,' he said (and there was not a shadow of a smile on his puffy face). 'What's wrong with an educational book?' I said, 'I didn't say it was wrong. I suppose it'll get you the Israel Prize,' he muttered. I laughed. 'I mean it,' he said, 'Davidov was a national hero, wasn't he?' With that, he asked where I was going and suggested I should come with him to the Cellar. On the way he said: 'Interesting type, that Davidov, eh?' I said I found the stories about him very enjoyable. He halted by a bookshop and looked into the lighted window. When we moved on, he said: 'Listen, who was Davidov actually? Just an ordinary man who knew how to work well, and from time to time killed a few Arabs. Anywhere else in the world a man like that is born, lives, dies and is buried. Once a year his wife visits the grave to put a wreath of flowers on the tombstone, accompanied by her second husband. Here they make a hero of him.' And after a few steps in silence: 'Not only of him. Every year on the eleventh of Adar according to the Jewish calendar they wring tears from the schoolchildren and sing with great feeling: "Once there was a wondrous hero, one arm alone he had." Who was this wondrous hero, after all? An ex-officer called Trumpeldor, not a bad soldier, who defended his home against robbers. So what? There are any number of them like that all over the world, but nobody remembers their names. Here for almost forty years we've been standing to attention in his memory, singing the anthem, waving the flag, sending the kids home at eleven and letting the teachers lie down to rest.' He spoke slowly, dragging out the syllables as if he were smearing dough on a board: 'Or Joshua Hankin. Another hero they call streets and villages after, and plant forests in his name, because he redeemed the soil of the homeland. A shrewd real-estate dealer, that's all. Or A.D. Gordon, "the philosopher of labour." A nice old man, I'm not saying he wasn't...What do we need heroes for in this country? We get all romantic about every ordinary act that people do because they have to, like cultivating the soil, keeping watch, defending their lives. The Eternal of Israel! The Chosen People! Want to convince you that a position of necessity is a position of choice. So that they should have a sense of choice, they stuff you with the Bible and national poetry, exhume the dead to make them into national heroes. Who needs it all? I live in this bloody hot, sweaty country because I was born here, that's all! I don't need Davidov for that. It's laughable! Laughable! They send wretched Moroccans to the Negev whether they like it or not, and hang up a sign at the gate of the village: "The wilderness and the solitary place shall be glad for them; and the desert shall rejoice." What's all this rejoicing and gladness? Who's happy? Who's glad? Apart from the speakers at the cornerstone-laying who go back home in their cars? Even the flowery phrases once had some truth in them, but today...? Why don't they sell the national anthem to the Arab refugees? They could sing it today in our stead, with tears in their eyes: "To return to the land of our fathers..." Might get a good bit of money for it.'

We went downstairs to the Cellar and approached a small group sitting round a table. Nakdimon gave an indifferent look at one of them who wore a black beard, and said: 'That poem of yours in this weekend's paper wasn't so bad. True, you pinched the last line from me, but never mind, you're not the first.' The other slowly extracted a fly that was floating on the soup in his plate, shook it on to the floor and laughed: 'How much should I pay you? Two lines of my own?' 'Of your own?' said Nakdimon. 'You've got nothing of your own. Perhaps a table.'

Here is the Cellar, then: four walls adorned with a few drawings of the nude and miniature oil paintings by Darius, the price of too much drinking in periods of insolvency; the handsome Polish waiter, who sees all and keeps his mouth shut; the plump Hungarian cook who despises the gang ('Artists you call them? Animals!' the fat cow used to fling at us); a one-room café bare to the neon-lights, three steps below the pavement. (When we sat opposite the doorway, we could see the lower halves of the people in the street passing before our eyes as on a conveyor belt. Sometimes, when we had nothing to do, we would compete with each other in guessing what the faces of the girls who passed in the street would look like from the appearance of their feet and thighs. 'The General' would dash out, come back and announce the results, and the loser would pay by ordering a bottle for the rest. It was an amusing pastime, which sharpened our skill in perceiving 'the recondite connection between the ethical and the aesthetic parts of the feminine body', as Gumpel used to say.)

Let me take the reader inside, as my guest for a while. Allow me to introduce: Nakdimon. (He does not reply to our greeting; poetic licence.) The one with the black beard and the soft, sensual monkish face is Eviatar. A poet. (He is always dressed like this, in tight jeans, with the same grey shirt and sandals. He nods to us with a delicate, inquisitive smile.) The girl sitting by his side is his wife Levia. (Nervous as quicksilver, restless, easily excited. At this very moment she is furious. 'He doesn't understand a thing, that man!' she cries, beating on the table with her little fist. 'How could anyone say that Nakdimon is a nihilist? A poem like "Cast-off Slave-girl"—is that nihilism? Can't they feel that every line is drenched in pain—true, deep, abysmal pain? Or else he doesn't know what nihilism is. Then why does he write at all?') The little fellow on her left, in spectacles, who accompanies his excited talk with vigorous gestures, is Shraga Gumpel, a young critic who is Nakdimon's disciple and claims a stake in him as the man who discovered him and made him famous. (Behind that mousy face lies a brilliant incendiary mind, subtle and casuistical.) The young fellow with black curls, whose arm shelters a girl with long eyelashes, is Darius the painter. The girl (she is not his wife) who nestles drowsily against his breast, like a pet animal that has found peace and quiet, is unfamiliar. The man sitting in the corner, contracted into his meagre limbs, melancholy, pensive, is Uri Grabowitzki, who is known as 'the General'. By his side, the one with a scarred face, slowly and listlessly sipping from the coffee-cup, is Yohanan Hochberg…

When I arrived—almost every evening, like a donkey running to his stall at the end of the day's work—I would already find at the table Yohanan Hochberg and Avner, the smoke of their cigarettes rising up like incense and the gloom of *Weltschmerz* on their faces. As I entered they would look up at me for a moment, as if awaiting tidings of salvation. Later, when Eviatar and Levia came in, the lethargic silence would be broken all at once. 'That was awful, that poem you printed!' Levia would launch a fiery attack on Avner. 'How can anyone write like that? It's nothing but plagiarism! Such obvious plagiarism…' Eviatar would grip her by the wrist and she would shake herself free. 'Why not tell him openly? You think just the same, don't you!' When they were seated Eviatar would try to tame the shrew by clasping her to his shoulder and pressing his lips to her cheek, but she would cast off the yoke of his arm from her neck from time to time, and all his attempts to soothe her were in vain. ('You're a hypocrite, Eviatar,' she would throw at him in our presence. 'And I don't care if I say it here. At home you told me yourself that I was right.')

Later on Osnat would come in like a high wind, dishevelled, bewildered, as if she had just awakened from sleep, always asking for someone who was not there, always expecting some great event to happen, always disappointed when it did not happen, and fleeing into the street as if seeking him whom her soul loveth. At about midnight,

as the theatre and film shows ended, the street would inject another
few excited couples, flushed and voluble, like football fans on their
way back from a match. Eliraz and his bulky wife, her face shining
like a great sunflower; Abraham Avivi, the successful author of light
comedies, and his Miri, like a slender creeper clasping his thick trunk.
Saul Nunn would run down the steps like a bullfighter entering the
ring, look around him, greet the company, gird up his loins for battle,
and sit down at the table, inspiring us all to fill our glasses, to drink,
to sing, to curse, and to pinch the cook's tender flesh. (Saul Nunn was
a living legend. He had published one solitary story five years before,
an excellent war story in the style of the medieval tales of chivalry,
and since then everyone had respected his silence.) When Nakdimon
arrived, wrapped in mystery, with stealthy, feline steps, we would fall
silent in respect and apprehension. He would inject his venom in
brief spurts like a snake, and any poor wretch who was bitten would
shrink in his place, paralysed for the rest of the night. Later, Hagit
also started to come to the Cellar—she was picked up one night by
chance and the same night flung herself around my neck.

It was the eve of the fast of Av, when the pious mourn the
destruction of the Temple. It was only on my way to the Cellar that
I remembered that the restaurants would be closed. When I arrived I
found Avner, Eliraz and Saul standing on the pavement in a mournful
mood. We were thinking of going back separately to our lodgings
when we saw Nakdimon approaching. 'The gates of mercy locked,
eh?' he apostrophized the impenetrable door of the Cellar. 'Mourning
for the Temple,' said Eliraz, shaking his head. Nakdimon proposed
that we should go back to his house. On the way we met Eviatar and
Levia, on their way, arm in arm, to the Cellar, so we turned them
round and took them with us. When we arrived at his home—a
comfortable, spacious flat which was entirely at his disposal, since
his parents were abroad—he brought out drinks, sliced meat and
cheeses and various snacks, and set them out in the drawing-room.
We sat on the couches and devoted ourselves to drinking and talking. Warmed with whisky, Nakdimon brought out a bundle of new
poems he had written and recited them. He read well—in contrast
to his way of speaking—emphasizing the rhythms sensitively, without

exaggeration. After each poem he stopped and looked at us, a faint smile hovering on his face. When he had finished he tossed a drink down his throat in one go, turned a glass upside down, rose and, to raise our spirits and break the respectful and deeply impressed silence, put a record on the gramophone, grasped Levia by the hand and started to dance with her on the carpet. He had a heavy body, but when he danced he limbered up and waggled his hips with great dexterity. He swung Levia round his finger and she followed him with difficulty, watching the acrobatic movements of his feet to keep in time. After a few moments, seeing that he had left us in the role of spectators, he stopped and declared that he would not allow us to sit there like mourners. Taking Saul Nunn with him, he announced that he was going out to bring some 'virgins girded in sackcloth for the midnight threnody'. We were quite tipsy by this time, and Eliraz—a freckle-faced clown, thin as a rake, who was excellent at singing choruses and playing the buffoon—looked for the Bible in the bookcase, opened it at *Lamentations* and began chanting to the synagogue melody, adding trills and rhymes to every verse. At his command we sat on the floor and chanted the responses, swaying from side to side: 'Comfort, O Lord our God, the mourners of Zion, and the mourners of Jerusalem, and the city that is in mourning and laid waste…' And we all accompanied him with weeping and wailing, with heartbroken sighs and moans, until the tears came into our eyes. Suddenly the walls were breached and the room was invaded with howls and shrieks of laughter by four girls led by Nakdimon and Saul. While we were still wondering who the new arrivals were, the music began to wail from the gramophone and three couples started twisting and wriggling and waggling their hips, drumming with their heels and snapping their fingers. Someone rolled up the carpet and moved aside the furniture, someone put out the lights, leaving only a single red watchful eye, and laughter broke out from time to time in the glimmering half-light.

At about midnight our ears caught some quarrel that had broken out between Eviatar and Levia. 'You can make eyes at anyone you like, I don't care. Just don't come home, that's all I ask!'—we heard her furious voice in the doorway. The door opened wide, Levia rushed out, Eviatar was seen sallying forth in pursuit, from the staircase came sounds of hasty whispers and a kind of rap or knock, then her voice: 'Don't imagine I'm blind! Don't deny it at least! Don't deny it!' and then rapid footsteps running downstairs.

Shall I describe what went on later in the three rooms of the house, the rustlings, the whispers, the giggles, the murmurings, the creakings, the moans? Or the unseen struggle that proceeded somewhere between Eliraz and Saul Nunn, both of whom had taken hold of the same woman, like the claimants with the garment in the Talmudic paradigm, one whispering: 'You're all mine', and the other: 'No, you're all mine'? Or how the pale dawn rose over the room—after all the fires had died down—and lit up the scene? No, I will not describe it. Nor would I say anything about Hagit—that slender, green-eyed girl, 'crazy about literature' ('light classical', as Nakdimon described her), who from that night onward started to frequent my room—had it not been for the unfortunate incident with Ahuva.

Strange how she had slipped out of my mind all those two months since our separation. I had no idea what she was doing, nor did I ask; I did not see her even once, or think about her, as if that separation, which the divorce ceremony had sanctified with the seal of God and man, was capable of wiping out with one stroke all that time had written on our daily calendar, page after page, for two whole years. There was something cruel here, unjust, a wrong done to that unfortunate soul whose only consolation—perhaps her only pitiful vengeance—was that some memory should remain of those uncountable moments of quiet affection, sadness, subdued suffering, daily cares and daily joys—a memory that would be engraved on the heart of the one who had left her. Only consolation, only vengeance—she got neither the one nor the other. When she appeared again, unexpectedly, it was really an ugly incident.

It was late morning. I was sleeping the sleep of satiation. Not alone. A knock at the door woke me, but I did not open my eyes. At the second knock I muttered: 'Just a minute!' lowered my feet to the floor, and lazily wiped the sleep from my eyes. 'Who's there?' I called. And then the reply came from the other side of the door, in a hesitant, expectant voice: 'It's me, Ahuva.' Perspiration broke out all over me. I looked down at the pillows—'from whence cometh my help?' What was I to do with that impudent body sprawling here on the bed? Where could I put it? Where could I hide it? 'A minute, I'll just get dressed,' I called, distraught, at my wits' end, in the direction of the door. 'What's wrong?' Hagit opened her eyes and stretched her arms, yawning, on the coverlet. 'Get out quick,' I whispered. 'Take your things and get out.' I snatched her clothes from the chair and her shoes from the floor, and swept her with them in the direction of the bathroom. I slipped into my clothes and threw the cover over the bed, like dust over blood. I darted another glance over the room and opened the door. 'I woke you,' said Ahuva standing there, her face sallow, with big eyes like a frightened child's. 'I thought at an hour like this…' 'I was working late last night,' I muttered. 'Come in, nice of you to pay me a visit.' She sat down on the bed, glanced round the room and said, as if with repressed pain: 'Lovely room.' I blushed; Hagit's nylon stockings were still hanging from the bar of the chair. 'I suppose you're wondering why I've come?' She forced a miserable smile on to her lips. 'Long time no see,' I said. There was some kind of mouse-like rustle on the other side of the wall. Ahuva was silent. Again, distractedly, she surveyed the room. Two puckers appeared at the corners of her mouth. She looked sick. 'What's that statue outside?' she asked gloomily. 'There was a sculptor living here before me. He's dead,' I said. Her body was limp as if it was melting away. 'I won't take up much of your time.' Her eyelashes quivered. Then she lowered her eyes to her fingers crossed on her knees, as if sunk in thought. She raised her head and, taking a deep breath, said: 'I'm pregnant.' My heart sank. At that moment there was a gurgling of water in the pipe which shook the wall. I bowed my head under all these disasters—let them all come together. (Why had she conceived? With whom? Why on earth? And what a fool I had been! I could have refused to answer when she knocked at the door. Or at least gone out and taken her somewhere.) 'I'm sorry to trouble you'—her voice quivered—'but…I had no choice.' (And all these apologies, too. And why did Hagit have to take a shower just now? The flow of the water in the pipe made my flesh creep.) 'Are you sure?' I said. A bitter smile flickered at the corners of her mouth. 'It's two months.' The flow finally stopped. Now the silence beat on my temples. Why had she come? Why did she have to tell me? I was busy, I was completely engrossed in the work I had started. I couldn't have my mind distracted now with all kinds of…. 'Have you been to a doctor?' I muttered. 'Yes,' she nodded. 'What did he say?' I asked. The tears that had filled her eyes ran over. She fumbled in her handbag, but before she could find her handkerchief the tears fell in large drops on her cheeks. A kind of impotent rage rose in my throat. Why me? After all, we had separated. Why again? 'What do you want me to do?' I asked, very quietly, to keep down my anger. Her shoulders quivered and she blew her nose. Figures flashed through my mind. A hundred, two hundred, three hundred—how much could it cost? How much had I got? Where could I get the rest? 'I can't tell my parents, you understand.' Her fingers twisted her crumpled handkerchief. The blood flowed to my head. It came into my mind that she might want to force me to go back to her. 'You're not thinking of having it?' I said, startled. She covered her face with her hands and dried her tears with her handkerchief. 'I'll bear the cost, of course,' I said. Something fell on the other side of the wall. 'It's not a question of cost.' She wiped her nose. My fury grew. I asked her to excuse me and got up. I went and tried the door of the bathroom. The fool had locked herself in, to crown it all! The scrape of the key chilled my blood. I went in and adjured Hagit not to move a finger in her hiding place—I didn't want to hear another sound. 'Bring me my stockings.' She smiled at me with her green eyes as she sat naked on the edge of the bath. I went back to the room and sat down. 'So what's the problem?' 'It's terrible when I think of it,' she said with a tremulous look. 'They all do it,' I said in practical tones. 'Yes.' She fixed her eyes on the window. 'It's easy to say.' 'Believe me, it's not easy for me. Not at all easy,' I said heavily. 'If I could divide the burden with you…But I don't know what I can do. I'll bear the cost, of course, as I said. It's my responsibility.' Ahuva gazed at me with a forced, pale, embarrassing smile. 'You haven't changed,' she said quietly. There was a silence. She fingered the handle of her bag. A long time passed. Finally she rose and, without a word, turned to the door and went out. Very quietly she closed the door behind her.

I sat there motionless. The room was nightmarish in the full noon light. The stockings hanging from the bar of the chair, the cover carelessly thrown on the bed, with the impression left by her sitting on it. The sheets of paper on the table from which Davidov peeped out. The walls that had ears, that had eyes. A hospital pallor hung in the air, like after a death. How had it all happened?

'You didn't expect that,' said Hagit, appearing in the doorway, with her delicate, understanding smile. She cast a wondering glance at me, sat down on the bed, and pulled a stocking over her outstretched leg. 'You look terribly despondent,' she went on, with a searching look. 'What's happened, after all?' And, as she put on her right shoe: 'Oh, Jonas, it's not so tragic! I understand her, of course. The first time it's always hard. Afterwards'—pushing the heel into place—'it's like pulling a tooth. Actually'—with a somewhat clouded smile—'I've had three'—squeezing her left foot with difficulty into the shoe. 'I can afford it,' she laughed. 'My brother's a gynaecologist.'

A week later I supported Ahuva by the arm as she went down the steps from the clinic of Dr Konitz, Hagit's brother. I took her home, settled the pillow under her head and covered her with a blanket, put the kettle on the stove and later brought her a cup of tea in bed. Some biscuits, perhaps? No, she did not want anything. There was a smell of ether on her breath. The room was just the same as before. The 'Burghers of Calais' on the wall, the slim vase on the table with the everlasting thistles. Rolls of coloured paper on the shelf of the bookcase. The scissors beside them. An atmosphere of distant hours. Letters from *A Hero of Our Time* seemed to leap to the eye from the desk at which I had written them. I closed the window, in case she felt cold at night. The whole thing cost me seventy-five Israeli pounds. Cheap.

Chapter ten

Two generations of our authors, wrote Shraga Gumpel in his article, 'Against Ideocracy', which was published about a year and a half ago, were parasites on ideas. The first battened on the ideals of emancipation and renascence, and the second on those of 'pioneering' and egalitarianism. In both of them there pullulated, in layers of putrefaction, 'a fungus-culture of *literati*'. An ideocratic society produces literary dwarfs because it shackles the free development of creative art, as a theocratic society shackles liberty of thought. In such a society, father-complexes or guilt-complexes arise towards ideas. Consciously or in most cases unconsciously, the author relates his work to the dominant ideas 'without legitimate artistic criteria'. The works are not measured by their significance, but according to this relationship. If there was any justification for this in the past—'in the context of the period' and for reasons external to literature—today, when the ideas themselves were suffering from anaemia and had in fact lost their spiritual significance in the chaotic situation in which we were living, any acceptance of their authority was tantamount to worship of the dead. 'The parasites have become necrophiles.'

'Necrophilia is not so bad,' said Nakdimon in the Cellar one evening when the conversation turned to this article, 'but take Jonas, for instance: he's a necrophage!'

I laughed with the rest. I was used by now to his barbs, which he would shoot in every direction, especially at Gumpel, his admirer, who mentioned him favourably in every article, and even in this one had cited him as an example of someone who 'has arrived at extraordinary aesthetic achievements by liberating himself completely from the chains of ideocracy'. Later on that evening, when the talk had turned to some reviews Gumpel had written denouncing certain bad books of poetry, Nakdimon addressed him:

'You're an ass, Gumpel—not a learned ass, though you have some learning, but a plain, ordinary donkey. And why are you an ass? Because you keep sniffing at droppings. Have you ever seen a donkey lowering his snout to a cowpat and lifting it high in the air, his nostrils quivering with tremendous enjoyment? That's you! Every couple of paces you find some worm-eaten poem, some stinking story; you sniff, enjoy, and then you let out a "hee-haw" that shakes the welkin. You're a copromaniac!'

Gumpel was a cadaverous young man with ears like bat's wings, whose limbs twitched as he spoke. His bespectacled face—like a morose, fanatical scholar's—darkened whenever Nakdimon needled him, and he would hunch himself into his corner with a sour smile of submission on his lips. 'And besides, you're a parasite as well,' continued Nakdimon, not letting go of his prey. 'Not a parasite on ideas, of course; you live on me! Suck my blood and swell! Why do I have to feed you, you leech? For every poem of mine you get paid for three articles that stretch over an area of five acres. The only thing I can't understand is how you can still stay so lean. I envy you, my lad!'

'"And give up verse, my boy, there's nothing in it!"' twittered Gumpel from his lair.

'Shakespeare?'

'Pound! Don't you remember "Mr Nixon's" advice: "Follow me and take a column!"?'

'Every word of yours is worth a pound, Gumpel, but your silence is worth two.'

At first I was a novice in this order of knights armed with

quills and venomous tongues, a stranger from afar who had joined
the gang somewhat late in nebulous circumstances and was regarded
with a certain amount of suspicion. I did not fail to observe, whenever I entered the Cellar, the censorious glance of Shraga Gumpel,
who wondered what this uninvited guest was doing in their circle
and whether he had come, perhaps, to spy; or the reserved look of
Nakdimon, who favoured me with special licence; or the jests of
Eliraz, hinting that I had been baptized in adolescence and, in secret,
apparently, still clung to the old faith. I used to sit down at the end
of the table, all my senses alert, noticing every flicker of movement:
the stealthy touch of a hand on an elbow above the table, the touch
of knee to knee under the table, surreptitious smiles of contempt, an
embarrassed blink, a grimace of disgust, a hasty whisper.

I was a novice; but little by little I learned the code language
of the band, which was easier to decipher than I had first thought:
when to smile superciliously at a reference to this name or that, and
when to maintain an oracular silence; what should be mentioned with
enthusiasm, and what with a curl of the lip; how to pay a compliment with a derogatory implication and how to use disparagement
tinctured with praise; when to put on a frozen face and say: Never
read it, never heard of it; how to flavour a tasteless literary stew by
peppering it with quotations; how to inflict tiny pin-pricks which
would be painful without drawing blood.... But those venomous
darts which used to fly in every direction were also like an intoxicating
drug injected into my veins each evening: the delicate, meaningful
hints; the polished witticisms that flashed between the contestants
with the dexterity of sword-strokes; the jests, in a secret code that
no stranger could understand; the erudite debates, the wild bursts of
laughter, or even the long silences, drawn out in expectation of some
tardy theophany...It was a world within a world, the Cellar.

I remember one night when the fraternity swelled like a flowing
tide, and the Cellar was filled with love like wine, emotional revela-
tions and 'confessions'. Avner's round face shone with satisfaction at
a story of the capture of Katamon in Jerusalem that Nakdimon had
told; a celestial smile rested on Osnat's face; Gumpel banged with
his fist on the table and cried: 'Sing! Sing!' And after a thunderous

performance, all of us swaying from side to side, waving our hands to the rhythm of the song, Hochberg put his arm round Eviatar's shoulders and howled from the depths of his heart: 'I love you, Franciscus! Your beard! Your poems! Your ascetic mug! All of you, I love all of you! What have we left but love? No God, no king—we're orphans! Lawless, miserable, degenerate, lousy orphans—but blessed are the orphans! And you too, Jonas!'—turning his glowing eyes on me—'Yes, I love you too! Although you've got a *hero* and perhaps a God too, perhaps even a king—and though you look at us like that, with a kind of irony, with a superior expression, with a sly mockery in your eyes and who knows what? D'you think you're any different? You're an orphan just like us! Yes, yes, though you imagine you're sitting on the moneybags. What's this legacy of yours? A couple of coppers! We've *no* legacy, Jonas, and neither have you. Empty hands! We've got to begin from scratch. Roll the rock up to the top of the hill. Sisyphus is happy, Jonas, because he's got no God, because the…the rock, yes, the rock, is the whole of his world!'

At the end of that kaleidoscopic night, which finished somewhere in the neighbourhood of Marian's Bar, in the pale dawn light I dragged myself along to Eviatar's house with him and his wife. We stumbled into the room and fell dead drunk, fully dressed, he and Levia on their bed and I on the floor. When I woke up, two or three hours later, Levia was already washed and combed and fresh. She suggested that I should have coffee with her before she went out to work (she was a secretary in some travel agency). I went into the kitchen with her, and over a cup of coffee she told me her tale of woe. She was worried about Eviatar: his excessive drinking was destroying him; he suffered from attacks of depression from which he did not recover for days. She could not induce him to give it up; she was at her wits' end. 'And besides, believe me, it's spoiling him as a poet. His poems have become so obscure, so confused…Death, death and again death…Not a ray of light.' When she got up to go she asked me to stay until he woke.

Eviatar was sleeping heavily, horribly. His face was pale and nightmarish. The soft hair of his beard quivered with every breath and groan that came from his lips. He looked like a martyr with rocks pressing on his breast. His mother's two pictures (she was a 'crazy' painter, divorced many years ago, who spent most of her time in France) above the bed were like great gaping, bleeding wounds. One of them was a red, fiery blotch, the other a broken red cross surrounded with a wreath of tiny blossoms like cornflowers. It was strange how few books there were on the shelves, only twenty or thirty: a few volumes of Hebrew poetry; Rimbaud, Villon, Baudelaire, Lorca and Eliot in the originals; the works of Saint-Exupéry, *The Brothers Karamazov,* some old volume of travels, a book about Giordano Bruno, albums of Breughel and Bosch, Élie Faure's history of art, Burckhardt. On the two bottom shelves there were a haphazard collection of large fossils and a rusty celestial globe. In one corner stood an asparagus plant, long since withered, in a pot. On the table, the dishes from yesterday's meal. I took a book from a shelf and sat down to look at it.

All at once, with a start, he woke up and dropped his feet to the floor. He rubbed his eyes and smiled at me. 'What's happened?' 'You tell me,' I smiled back. He rested his head on his hands, stared at the floor and, when he had returned to his senses, said: 'A frightening dream.' He had dreamt that he was lying on the operating table and had been given a drug. He had asked the doctor whether there was any hope, and the doctor had shaken his head in denial. He had asked if death was inevitable and the doctor had said: 'Yes, inevitable.' He had said to the doctor: 'If I recite a poem and don't stop, don't stop for a moment, death won't be able to take me.' He had started to recite a poem and had woken up.

He asked what had happened during the long night. I reminded him: Marian's Bar; the two hooligans who had threatened to put us out; the quarrel between Nakdimon and Gumpel; the seashore; the police car that had stopped beside us. He was astonished when I told him how he had fallen asleep on the edge of the pavement and how Levia and I had had to get him on to his feet and drag him along. 'Purgatory,' he said.

He went off to wash and when he came back sat down and asked how my book was getting on. I told him a few of the stories I had heard about Davidov. They amused him. He said that in his opinion I should not write a 'biographical novel', but a kind of garland of stories, like folk-tales. Many of the stories were no doubt untrue or exaggerated, but they were beautiful and that was the main thing. 'Let's drink something, eh?' he said, getting up excitedly. I refused. I told him about Levia's anxiety. 'What does she want? Am I supposed to drink milk? Suck from the breast? I was weaned long ago!' he cried like a naughty child, and quickly brought a bottle of cognac. As we sipped at our glasses, I told him the story of the 'sheep's milk', which my aunt, my late father's sister, used to tell me when I was a child.

When my parents left Kfar Giladi, when I was two years old, they hired a wagon at Metulla, loaded it with the few belongings they were allowed to take—two iron bedsteads, two stools, father's books and so forth—and put me in a bathtub lined with blankets. Three times I burst out crying on the way: once as we passed by Trumpeldor's tomb, a second time when we passed the cemetery at Migdal beside Lake Kinneret, and a third time when we reached Tiberias. At Tiberias my mother got off the wagon and brought me milk to stop my crying. I knocked over the milk angrily and went on crying. 'I understand why he cried by Trumpeldor's tomb and the graves of the Labour Legion at Migdal,' said my father, 'but why is he crying now?' 'Apparently,' said my mother, 'he is hankering for the sheep's milk of Kfar Giladi.' 'Ai-ai-ai!' said my father, I'm afraid he'll be hankering after it all his life, for we'll never find sheep's milk in Tel Aviv.'

'So that's your private myth,' laughed Eviatar. 'My family joke,' I said. 'When I was a lad I felt sad whenever I remembered that story. I saw my father as an exiled king, and myself in the wagon like a prince going into exile with him in the coach. When I grew up I used to remember with a smile the dreams of my shepherd's kingdom. Today…I'm quite accustomed to much better drinks than sheep's milk.' 'You should write about Davidov with a smile,' he laughed, 'without nostalgia.' Then he suddenly became serious. He fixed his eyes on the floor and fell silent, embarrassed. He looked up at me and said with a tormented smile: 'I envy you your memories of "sheep's milk".' 'I've no hankering for it now,' I laughed. 'I've been weaned. Long ago.' 'All the same,' he said, 'it's a good thing to have something to be weaned from. I've nothing. A kind of *Waste Land*…thorns and thistles.' He told me how he had grown up in his uncle's home like a foundling. His eccentric mother had come to visit him from time to time, but he had never managed to love her because she changed the colour of her hair between one visit and the next, and every time she looked different. 'There's no contact, you understand. Sometimes I even hate the words I write. Every word connects me with something I want to break away from. Not to break away, but…The words aren't mine, if you understand what I mean. The Bible, all our history…I'm like an impostor. A thief of property that doesn't actually belong to me. By what right…? And then, of course, there aren't any private words.' He spoke heavily, forcing out his sentences. Suddenly he jumped up, took the bottle, poured out for both of us, and when he had emptied the glass said: 'I mustn't drink. When I drink, the bands of my lips are loosed.' He stopped and grinned. 'You see, I said "the fetters of my lips I remember the "fetters of wickedness. Ha! The Bible again…."'

After drinking some more, he said with emotion: 'Come on, I'll read you a poem.' He jumped up, went over to the table, pulled out the drawer, searched and fumbled among the papers, finally took out a crumpled sheet, sat down again on the bed, lit a cigarette with a trembling hand and began to read. He recited two or three verses as if walking gingerly on sharp stones (in the poem he compared himself to a snail slowly crawling along a grass-stalk after the rain in a gloomy world, but the royal purple was produced from its blood) and fell silent in the middle of a sentence. The cigarette quivered like a glow-worm in his beard. Morosely he scanned the sheet, and when he reached the bottom gave the verdict: 'No good!' 'First class!' I cried. 'Nonsense,' he retorted, crumpling up the paper in his fist and throwing it out of the window. 'The snail goes back to the dust,' he laughed, gulping down another glassful.

From one glass to the next we got merrier and merrier, coruscating with witticisms, playing with words like jugglers' clubs. Eviatar prophesied 'a great day.' With a sudden access of strength he jumped up and said: 'Come along, let's go to Marian. No, first to Saul. We'll take Saul and go together to Marian's Bar. We'll drink all day and all night, and then another day and another night.'

'Levia,' I warned him.

'Levia?' he said, screwing up his eyes as if in an effort to remember. 'Oh, yes. We'll pay her a visit too, all of us. We'll buy a flight ticket to Athens from her, we'll all go to Athens.'

'Rome,' I said.

'No, Athens.'

'Rome.'

We compromised on Istanbul. Turkish baths. A paradise.

Off we went at top speed. The sun blazed in the sky. In no time at all we were in front of Saul Nunn's house. The shutters were closed. We called his name in two voices from the pavement; passersby stopped and looked up with us. Finally a gap opened in the shutter and Saul's sleepy face emerged from the frame, hair dishevelled, eyes bleary. 'Come on up,' he cried in a hoarse voice.

'Come on down. We're going to Marian,' called Eviatar.

'Come on up!'

'Bands of wickedness!' I cried.

'What?'

'Bands of wickedness!' cried Eviatar.

'We'll loose them,' laughed Saul.

We went up and burst into the room. His untidy dreams lay scattered all around. The blankets had dropped to the floor. Newspapers, books, a dirty glass. In a corner stood a big polished trumpet.

'Where's Gabriel?' cried Eviatar, taking hold of it. 'Going to blow the Last Trump yourself?'

'Self-defence against the neighbours,' laughed Saul. He was not left in peace to write, he told us. Radio from every window, at full blast. He had tried persuasion, entreaties, threats, but it was no use. So he had bought the trumpet. 'When they switch on the radio I begin to blow and they stop right away.'

Eviatar puffed up his cheeks to bursting-point but could not produce more than a few miserable squeaks. Saul took it from him and blew a long blast and a series of trills that echoed and re-echoed into the distance.

'Take the trumpet and let's be on our way to Marian. You march at the head and blow.' Saul pulled off his pyjamas and began to dress while Eviatar ran to and fro between the room and the kitchen looking for a bottle in the cupboards. Somewhere or other he found what he was looking for and brought it to the bed with three glasses. 'A prelude to the day!' he proclaimed.

After two glasses Saul began to awaken from his lethargy. As always, the liquor started him off on a story-telling spree. The stories led him on to an account of what had happened to Ignatius Loyola: how in his youth he led a riotous life and used to bring whores to his room; how he saved two women from drunken soldiers and raped them himself; how he once found a countess fainting in a field and took her home to her palace. 'And when do you think our Inigo got his 'revelation'? Not before he was badly wounded at the battle of Pamplona and apparently lost a good deal of his vigour. Founder of the Order of Jesuits! And later? After he had abandoned all the sins of the flesh? He had to hide away in a women's convent. And in Montserrat—Our Blessed Lady…in his pious visions it was always Madonnas he saw.'

'You Jesuit!' said Eviatar, pouring out for the three of us. 'So what are you writing about; him or the Madonnas?'

'Writing?' said Saul, mocking at himself. 'Who's writing? What writing? It's three years now I've been wallowing in this stuff…Yes, I've got the name of the book written, in big letters: *What Ignatius Loyola did on May 25th, 1523.*'

'What did he do?' said Eviatar, interested.

'He was in the home of Señora Pasqual in Barcelona,' Saul replied with a loud burst of laughter. And then he went on to tell how he would write about Ignatius's struggles against the wiles of the devil.

'Now tell us about Davidov,' he demanded, turning to me.

I refused, but he would not give up. 'Go on, tell us, the man interests me.'

After I had told two or three stories he broke in with a shout: 'Lies! Romantic nonsense! Don't write it.'

'Fact,' I defended myself.

'What fact?' he cried. 'There are no facts. The facts are as you see them.'

'Listen,' he went on, wiping his mouth with his wrist, 'listen to something interesting. Four years after the death of Francis of Assisi, Pope Gregory commissioned a biography of him from a certain Thomas Masilano. This man sat down and wrote an official biography of a saint, as was right and proper, reeking with holy oil, it was called *Vita Prima*. About fifteen years later one of the heads of the Franciscan Order commissioned a different biography from him, one more in keeping with the requirements. So this Thomas sat down and wrote a second book, *Vita Secunda*. Both were written according to the testimony of disciples, but there was no resemblance between them. The second one, which was closer to the truth, was banned or destroyed later. There's facts for you! Are you going to make a saint of Davidov? Did we really have saints? Who'll believe you?'

'A saint?' I laughed.

'Write about him contrariwise,' he cried tipsily. 'Or make it into a grotesque tale. Make him a Gargantua! Gar-gan-tu-a! Let him swallow six respectable citizens with his lettuce salad! Let him take down the flag from the headquarters of the National Institutions and use it to saddle his horse, as Gargantua brought down the bells of Notre Dame and hung them on the neck of his ass! Anything but that holy oil of the schoolbooks and the anthologies, with all the two hundred atmospheres of "national consciousness". At long last we've got to cock a snook at history.'

And with that he picked up the trumpet, put it to his mouth and blew a long, thick blast like a fart.

Eviatar held his sides with laughter.

'Enough!' Saul proclaimed. 'We go to Marian. No, first to Osnat. We'll take her with us and go to Marian.'

He tossed down one more glassful, wiped his lips, and said:

'Let's rape Osnat. She'll take it in the right spirit.'

The idea appealed to all of us.

When we came out, the sun was already sloping down to the west. The road heaved ahead of us, the streets were merry as on a holiday. In no time we reached Osnat's house, without knowing how we had got there. We climbed up to the third storey and Saul leaned on the bell-push without letting go. A loud and prolonged ringing reached our ears.

Osnat opened the door, surprised.

'Osnat, we've come to rape you,' announced Saul.

'Really? what on earth for?' she laughed.

'No reason at all. Just like that.'

'Not so easy,' smiled Osnat.

'Never mind, we'll manage,' said Saul, leaning again on the bell-push and producing another prolonged peal.

'What's happened to you today?' she said, her embarrassed, wondering smile surveying our faces.

We fell into the flat and collapsed into armchairs.

'Undress,' said Saul, 'we're in a hurry. We're going to Marian.'

'Now? At four in the afternoon?'

'Four!' Eviatar struck his forehead. 'How did we get to four?'

'Levia,' I reminded him.

'Four! Good God, the day's lost! Completely lost!'

'Get undressed,' ordered Saul from the depths of the arm-chair.

'If I do that it won't be rape,' laughed Osnat.

'Good, we'll decide later about the terminology.'

'"Terminology"—that's good,' cried Eviatar, breaking out into wild laughter.

'Well?'

'Well?'

'Well?'

'You haven't seen my new kitten yet,' said Osnat. With that she ran out and came back with a soft grey kitten in her arms. She stroked it, rubbed her cheek on its fur, tickled the back of its neck. 'Isn't it sweet?'

'All right, bring out a bottle then,' said Saul, changing tack.

Osnat tried to solve the riddle in our faces. Finally she set down the kitten on the ground, opened the sideboard and took out a bottle. 'What's the celebration today?'

'The festival of Mary the Egyptian. Haven't you heard about Mary the Egyptian? She's been declared a saint.'

At six we left her house and went to Marian. No, first to Hochberg, and from Hochberg to...

Chapter eleven

In 1923 Davidov worked at the quarries in Jerusalem. In 1924 he was taken on by Captain Walker at the railway workshops at Lydda. In 1926 he moved to Kfar Sava, where he married Zippora Horowitz, where he built his home—'the base from which he set forth on his wanderings', as Menahem Schweig put it; where two years later his wife bore his eldest son, that son who was killed in the fighting for Latrun in 1948. Until this day they remember in the village that night after the funeral when, from Davidov's isolated shack, they could hear his agonized cries: 'Nimrod, why have you left me? Why did they take you away from me? Why?'

'You know what that son meant for him?' said Menahem Schweig. 'What a love there was between them? Every free moment he devoted to him. It was really touching to see him walking hand-in-hand with little Nimrod in the village street, talking to him as to a man like himself. He cherished him, taught him, hoped he would be a great artist one day, dreamed of sending him to the Bezalel School of Art in Jerusalem. Used to bring him art books he bought with his last coppers. He really understood art! It was a pleasure to listen to him talking about a picture, a book...'

97

Menahem Schweig had invited me one day, in the late afternoon, to his office at Trade Union Headquarters. As I came in he was engaged in an excited telephone conversation. With his free hand he motioned me to sit down opposite him. I waited and listened to some angry talk about academics' salaries, grades, civil servants.

'Yes,' he said, putting back the phone, 'you want me to tell you about Davidov.' He had not yet recovered his equanimity. 'You have no idea,' he said wearily as he ploughed his greying hair with his fingers, 'you have no idea at all of the way their demands go rocketing sky-high. Beyond the wildest reach of the imagination. A man earning a thousand pounds—a thousand Israeli pounds a month—is ready to paralyse the whole machinery of the state, if only...'

Finally he wiped his anger from his face with his palm, and continued: 'It's a most important thing you're doing. Especially for the youth. Our generation knew many characters like that, but today.... Have you got a cigarette by any chance?' He patted the pockets of his trousers, pulled out two or three drawers from the sides of his desk, finally discovered a packet of Dubek in the depths of one of them, lit a cigarette and said: 'Right, let's begin.' He waited for me to get ready to take notes, then rose, paced to and fro across the room, and began to speak as if dictating letters.

'It was a time of crisis. The bourgeois mentality was dominant in the Jewish community. Speculation was rampant in Tel Aviv. The immigration of the middle class had brought over a horde of *Luft Menschen*, hucksters, petty traders in currency and real estate. The workers were doomed to hunger, degeneration and despair...'

He halted of his own accord, sat down at the table, picked up the phone and asked the exchange not to transmit any calls ('I'm not here...Don't exist...Yes, till seven!'). Then he went on to tell his story in a straightforward way.

At the time, Schweig was the Secretary of the Labour Council at Kfar Sava. In the winter of 1926 a group of young people who had left the Labour Legion arrived in the village; there were four men and two girls. Davidov was one of them. They were allotted a room in the hut of the Workers' Centre, where they stayed together. In the evenings, the sound of singing, the music of mandoline and mouth-organ and the steps of the Krakoviak on the wooden floor used to resound from the room. The labourers of the village, who numbered only a score or so, met there or crowded round the windows. At night the merry band sometimes marched through the only street, with the musicians in the van, and aroused the slumberers from their repose. Respectable girls would go out to the gates of the farmyards, watching the procession longingly as their mothers kept angry watch at the windows. Not a night passed without some prank or other. Once they smeared pitch on the front of Feuermann the planter's house; once they almost frightened to death the bookkeeper, a sickly man with a weak heart, when they appeared dressed in graveclothes at the door of his room. Things went so far that the farmers threatened that if the riotous crew was not expelled from the village, they would dismiss the Jewish labourers in their groves.

But in any case they had neither work nor bread. The four young men worked about two days a week for sixteen piastres a day, while the two girls prepared their meagre meals and did their washing. Zippora Horowitz was an energetic and capable girl. With her own hands she made stools and benches from cypress branches and carved dishes from dry, hollow pumpkins. Davidov worked at planting in the grove of Lampert, who employed only Jewish workers.

About three months after their arrival, Davidov applied to Schweig for a loan of thirty pounds. 'He came into my room,' Schweig told me, 'sat down on the chair, you hear, and did not utter a word. He was so pale, I thought something terrible had happened. "What's wrong, Abrasha?" I asked. "Well, what's happened is what had to happen, I suppose," he sighed. He sat there silent, like that, for a long moment, and then said, as if he was telling me of some shameful betrayal, "I'm leaving the group." He saw that I was looking at him with uncomprehending surprise, and then succeeded finally in bringing a smile to his lips. "Not alone," he said, "with Zippora." "*Mazal tov!*" I said "What are you so depressed about?" "I'm depressed", he said, "because all along I thought I was a very clever fellow and now I see that nature is cleverer than me. Just tricked me. My heart is joyful, Menahem," he said, "but my feet, my feet are suddenly heavy!" Later, when he asked me to arrange the loan for the building of a hut,

I asked him: "And where will you put it? You haven't got a plot, have you?" "Never mind," he replied. "There's plenty of waste ground in Kfar Sava, and I won't steal the poor man's lamb.'"

Davidov got a loan from the Auxiliary Plot Fund, and started to erect his hut in a clearing in the eucalyptus grove at the edge of the village. He brought a few camel-loads of gravel and sand from the Sidni Ali shore, bought a few sacks of cement, and some planks from the crates in which the immigrants used to bring their belongings. With Zippora he moulded a few score concrete 'bricks', and by the time the owner of the copse discovered that his territory had been invaded the four walls were already standing on their foundations. When Levitan, an irascible American Jew, came to the spot and saw what they had done to him, he almost had a stroke. He brandished his stick at them and threatened that if they did not destroy the structure the same day he would set the police at them. 'British police you'd set at Jews?' Davidov jested. 'But I haven't stolen a piece of land from you. I've built in a clearing, and it's all for your own good. Now, when I'm here, the Arabs will stop cutting wood in your copse.' Levitan, whose wrath was only fanned by this reply, went off in a rage to the village council to demand its intervention. But on the way, or perhaps as he lay awake at night, he calmed down, and what Davidov had said half-jokingly began to make an impression on him. Next morning he went back to the copse and agreed with the trespasser that he would let him stay if he would watch his trees, his grove and his cucumber patch without pay, and be personally responsible for any thefts. Davidov willingly accepted the condition. A few weeks later he was appointed village watch-man and received his pay from the council.

By night Davidov would ride round the village on a piebald Arab horse, with a hunting rifle and a cartridge belt slung over his shoulder, and by day his wife would grow radishes and lettuces in the small plot at the back of the hut. When they had saved a few pounds they bought a cow, which they kept in a shelter they built of eucalyptus wood. 'You know what made a particular impression on us in their farmyard?' Menahem Schweig recalled. 'The peacocks! Whoever bred peacocks in those days? Who breeds peacocks today?

But he—just to be different...How did he get such a crazy idea into his head? At Passover that year he and Zippora paid a visit to the Near East Fair in Tel Aviv. It was a very merry fair, very colourful, in a kind of old orange grove surrounded by a wall, where the central bus station is now, and people flocked from all over the country.... And there, in the yard of the Damascus Pavilion, strutted a few peacocks. Davidov admired them so much that he asked for a few eggs—and got them. He set a hen to brood on them, and in three weeks he had six peachicks. "What do you want peacocks for, Abrashka?" we asked him. "Why do people grow flowers?" he asked. "And what's the use of a garland round a horse's neck?" That's the kind of man he was. Loved beauty. And as a matter of fact,' said Schweig, 'it was a lovely thing to see the peacocks walking about among the eucalyptus trees. You suddenly saw something out of a legend, you know.'

Since Davidov was a watchman he was not shackled, as he feared, and did not shut himself up at home, as others feared he might. He had dealings with the Arabs in the neighbourhood, from the encampments of Abu-Kishk to Kalkiliya and Tira. In the mornings he could be seen holding his horse's bridle and walking alongside the old Arab tracker to find the trail of a thief; or galloping to Petach-Tikva to deliver a message to the district officials. And besides this he found time every day to pay a visit to the Workers' Centre and join in the arguments that went on among the unemployed about work, social assistance, the left-wing opposition, Yiddish versus Hebrew, and the like. 'When he slept I have no idea,' said Schweig. 'At night he was on the watch, by day he was to be seen in the village.... But who slept in those days?'

In the summer of 1927 came that amusing incident which is still remembered by many veterans of the Histadrut. 'They were holding the third convention,' Schweig said, 'the convention that was dominated by the mood of economic crisis and hunger. We went to Tel Aviv, about twenty of us, in two wagons, and found hundreds there who had come from all over the country. Arlozoroff delivered a great speech against "grandiose plans", against "hysterical Zionism", and in the course of this speech said jokingly that "when the worker in the land of Israel milks a cow he does not think about the milking but about Zionism." There was a tremendous argument about this, and every speaker who followed him spoke about the "cow". Davidov shouted from the body of the hall: "Why don't you ask what the cow thinks about when she's being milked?" There was a great burst of laughter, and cries were heard: "She thinks about how to run away!"—"how to kick!"—and so on. "She thinks about exactly the same as me," cried Davidov, "about food!" "About food?" cried the spokesman on the platform. "Do your milking well, and then you'll have food." "Yes, comrade," shouted Davidov, "but the trouble is that I'm being milked too!" And again there was a loud burst of laughter. Since then, whenever Davidov's name was mentioned, people would say: "Oh, yes, the one with the cow.'"

One morning in the winter of that year, Davidov appeared in the Workers' Centre and summoned every one there 'to march on Petach-Tikva.' Those were the days of harvest pickets in that village, when scores of jobless men besieged the groves and insisted on their right to work. About a dozen workers responded to Davidov's call and set off with him on foot to join the pickets. When they arrived they found themselves in the thick of a great commotion. Under the command of a British officer Arab policemen on horseback, egged on by the farmers, were charging the pickets with batons, whips and rifle butts. Davidov had a club in his hand and lifted it to strike one of the policemen, but, before he could bring it down, the baton crashed on his head, and he was dragged off bleeding to prison with another sixteen labourers.

When he came out of prison, with a big bandage round his head, he found an infant wailing in his hut. He called it Nimrod— 'We shall revolt'—in memory of the events at Petach-Tikva. It was a great occasion, but his jubilation was checked the very same day, when he was told of his dismissal. In the evening his cries were heard from the headquarters of the village council:

'One day you'll call for me! When your Arab labourers from Tira and Miska set fire to your groves! You'll come and beg me—but I'm damned if I'll help you to put them out. You can burn together with them!' For about two months he had no steady job, just crumbs here and there, tramping as far as Magdiel and Raanana, pushing barrowfuls of sand at the paving of Allenby Street in Tel Aviv, humping bricks at building sites. He went north to work at draining the Kishon swamps, had an attack of malaria and came back. On his return he was pestered by the police, after someone had accused him of being a communist. One night they came and made a search in his shack. They found a few pamphlets by Lenin, Plekhanov and Maiakovsky, and took him to Jaffa. He was about to be expelled from the country without a trial, as was done to many who were caught with 'subversive material', and it was only after Schweig's efforts and the intervention of several labour leaders that the order was cancelled. 'Have you ever seen a big, strong eucalyptus that has withered?' said Schweig. 'That's what he looked like at that time. You could hardly bear to meet him. A man so full of power and energy, and suddenly…. And do you know when it was hardest to look at him? When he sat in the evening at the Workers' Centre playing chess. Hour after hour he sat and played, one game after another, with a kind of nervous eagerness—without saying a word. Late at night he would leave and go off alone towards the copse. "He's sinking," people said at the time, "Abrasha's sinking…"'

But a wind of danger came and fanned the dying embers. On the eve of the 1929 troubles, the Haganahh—a self-defence unit—was organized in Kfar Sava. He was called to a meeting with two representatives of the National Committee and asked to assume the leadership. He laughed in their faces and refused. Never in the world would he take command, he said. They explained to him that his experience as a watchman and the fact that he was acceptable to the community qualified him for the post, that there was no one better. 'I am not capable of giving orders, or taking orders either,' he told them. 'My experience—certainly. My hut—by all means. My days and nights—willingly. But I won't take command.' So he rejected the title, but from that day onwards he assumed the burden. The well of the grove he guarded, Levitan's grove, became a hiding-place for arms. Its packing-shed became a training centre. At night the copse rustled with footsteps; passwords were whispered on the paths. Dry leaves crackled in the grove; the sound of clicking rifle-bolts and drill orders could be heard through the concrete walls. In Davidov's shack the oil lamp burned late into the night.

When the reports came of the Arab provocations at the Wailing Wall, and the scent of the encroaching conflagration could be sniffed in the air, Davidov came to the Haganah committee and asked to be released from his duties. He announced that he had decided 'to go up to Jerusalem'. A quarrel broke out between him and Schweig. "'What d'you mean: you announce?" I said to him. "You'll take orders from the Haganah command, like the rest of us." "There isn't any command," he said. If an Arab mob could break into the area in front of the Wall, run wild, burn books, beat old men, do their worst, without anyone stopping them, there was no command, he declared, and everyone must obey his own conscience. "You're talking like a Revisionist," I said to him. "You don't frighten me," he said. "If the Revisionists are right, I'll go along with them! With their black flags and their slogans of 'With blood and fire Judaea shall rise'?" He smiled, pulled out a parabellum pistol from his pocket, laid it on the table and said: "With this!" The blood rushed to my head. "Haganah arms you'd take to violate the orders of the Haganah?" I cried. "You're wrong," he said quietly. "My personal weapon. I brought it with me from back there." And next day he left everything and went to Jerusalem. When he came back we could hardly recognize him. The sight of the havoc at Ramat-Rahel, Talpiot, the Georgian Quarter, Motza, had made a terrible impression on him. "Shameful," he said to me, "humiliating. Like in Denikin's pogroms. I'm not talking about the massacre at Hebron, but the modern communities! That a few score Arabs from Lifta could run amok in a Jewish neighbourhood where hundreds of young people were living! You can't fight the British, officials like Luke, Chancellor, Keith-Roache and officers like Duff, with manifestoes of the Jewish National Council and deputations from the Chief Rabbinate. The Wall should have been defended by force, by armed patrols. What are we afraid of? Inquiry commissions?" Yes, he had the soul of an anarchist. Hated organization, discipline, orders. But he was always in the right place, always at the focus of trouble. He was a strong man. A man of conscience, inner conviction, iron will!'

Schweig picked up the phone and asked the exchange to get him a number.

'I only saw him crying once,' he remembered. 'You know, when the news of the riots came we moved the women and children to Ein-Hai, where there were arms and concrete buildings, while all we could display openly was the handles of our hoes. We brought most of them back after two or three days, but some of the families who lived on the outskirts of Kfar Sava remained there, in the homes of the Ein-Hai farmers. When Davidov returned from Jerusalem he went, of course, straight to his shack and found it empty. I was sitting at the time in the secretariat in the Workers' Centre, when suddenly he burst in, dishevelled, red-eyed, and gripped me by the shirt. "Tell me what's happened?" he shouted. "Where are Zippora and the child?" I told him where they were and went with him to Ein-Hai, to the family in whose house they were staying. When we got there he took the child in his arms, sat down with it on the bed, buried his head in its body and wept. Actually wept, with tears. I shall never forget it. A heart-rending sight…The only time.'

Schweig lit up a cigarette.

'By the way,' he said blowing out the smoke musingly, 'have you met Zippora?…She still lives in the same shack, in the same copse—they haven't changed since then. Only she herself is changed. Very much. She was very beautiful once. Lovely. Long black plaits, shining eyes…Actually, better not. No. Let her alone.'

A loud ring shook the telephone at his side.

Chapter twelve

In 1930 Davidov was arrested a second time when he was involved in a fracas with Revisionist workers by the gate of Edelman's grove. Two weeks later his daughter Reuma was born—the one who later, when she was grown-up, was seduced by an Australian engineer and left the country with him. In 1932 he moved to the north of the Dead Sea and began working as a locomotive driver at Novomeisky's Potash Works. In 1936...

The cardboard file was getting thicker and thicker. I used to come back from my journeys (once a week, twice a week), put my notes into the file, close it so that I should not see them, push it into a drawer and lock it hastily like someone closing the trap on a snake. The snake inside did not choke to death. It kept rustling and whispering. Sometimes, late at night, I would open the drawer very cautiously, take out the file, lay it on the table in front of me, open it and begin to read what I had written. A deep depression would take hold of me, a kind of stupor that filled the inside of my head and shrivelled my nerves. I would close my eyes and shade them with my hands. Strange sights, distant thoughts: an empty valley bathed in the dead moonlight, a kind of valley of ghosts; someone calls my name, I hide, some evil band enters hastily carrying a long table—it looks like the judge's table in court, no, it is a billiard table and two men start pushing the balls about with pointed cues...I open my eyes to the sight of the open file and the rows of little letters on the pages, shut it with a bang, tie it up and lock it away swiftly with a malevolent turn of the key.

Sometimes when I took a page out of the file I would feel as if it were scorching my fingers and would put it away hastily as if throwing a lighted spill back into the fire. Not now, tomorrow, tomorrow. I put it off from day to day, from one week to the next, until all the material should be accumulated. (It was a damning dossier that I was taking so much trouble to compile against myself. The file became fatter and fatter before my eyes, every week. Strange that I failed from the very beginning to perceive that I was rearing an enemy in my home, nourishing and strengthening him with my own hands.)

I had plenty of leisure, if a man can be said to have leisure when he is pursued by a shadow and feels a piercing gaze at his back. I would wake up late in the morning, usually with the fumes of drink hanging like a fog in my head and blurring my vision. I would lie with eyes wide open staring at the ceiling, which swayed sometimes like the roof of a ship's cabin, trying to get the events of the previous night into some kind of order. Where had I gone when I left the Cellar? What had happened? How had I got to some place where the tunes swam in the reddish light like goldfish in an aquarium? Who had been with me? Whom had I fondled? Who had responded so ardently? How had I got home? A complete blackout came down from a particular point onwards, and my memory groped blindly, unable to find a way out. I dived into the dark depths of oblivion to draw up remembrance of lost time but was plunged into despair, and I would close my eyes again, drift off into a pleasant doze, abandon myself to flimsy illusions which carried me away. Then I would open my eyes a little; and there, staring me in the face, was the keyhole of the drawer, like the eye of a snake which had been lurking in wait for me all the time. That was the start of the cruel game between the predatory eye and the eye of its prey, each staring at the other to see which would be the first to pounce and which the first to escape. All of a sudden I would jump up, absolutely determined to open the drawer, pull out the file, lay it open on the table, pick up my pen...but no. While the key was still in the keyhole I would collapse again on the bed, my hands dropping impotently on my knees. I would gaze at the window—it was already bright daylight: ten, eleven o'clock, the sun shining vigorously—and I would tell myself: tomorrow, next day—no, neither tomorrow nor the day after, but later, when the harvest was ripe...Slowly I would get up, dress, go down into the street.

Davidov's shadow followed me wherever I went. Suddenly, I imagine, he jumps at me from the pavement to grip me by the throat. I cross the road with a leap, barely escaping the wheels of a speeding car, and immediately on the other side come face to face with someone who asks: 'How are you getting on with the Davidov book?' When I escape from him and go on my way, suddenly, from behind, someone pats me on the shoulder: 'Well? Soon? In a little while?'...No escape! I walk along with sidelong glances like a thief evading the police. My back feels that I am being followed. While I am drinking my coffee in a restaurant, the morning paper lying in front of me, all at once I hear the rustle of the letters in the drawer in my room, like the rustle of thousands of ants rushing about, looking for an outlet, slipping through the cracks...Sometimes Hagit would sit opposite me, her chin resting on her hands, and examine my face with her green eyes as if trying to solve the riddle of my thoughts. 'What's troubling you? The book?' the little clairvoyant would say, and when I did not answer she would go on: 'Don't think about it. Wait till you feel like it. You've got about a year, haven't you?'

About a year. I had plenty of leisure. After a late breakfast I would sometimes go down to the sea, swim far out into the distance, abandon myself to sunshine and fantasy. (As I lay, cradled on the gentle, rippling waves, gazing up at the vertiginous skies, the effects of my drinking would melt away little by little, together with the oppressive burden of duty, and I would feel like a prince in the free kingdom of my dreams.) I would come out of the water, kick at the sand, do some exercises...Two or three hours would pass in this way. After a light meal at three I would return to my room, tired and sunburnt, fall on the bed, try to read and sink into a deep sleep, wake up in alarm—and there, already, was the twilight at the window. Again the keyhole staring at me.

Idle days—a little sleep, a little slumber, 'And time flies, flies never to return...' But none of the pleasures of idleness. Oblomov had a servant in his room as lazy as himself, but I had a master in my room who would not tolerate idleness! I had my drowsy morning reveries, my siestas; read books in the evening, made love in the small hours—but where was the pleasure in any of these when I was always haunted by a reproachful, menacing eye, and the day of judgment loomed on the horizon? Green-eyed Hagit, whose long, delicate feelers reached out to the hidden places of my heart, sensed it. 'Then give it up,' she used to advise me in her cold, unsentimental way. It was easy for someone who did not know Davidov to talk like that. How could you smash the image that lowered over you, the incarnation of incalculable forces of good or evil—especially as you were shackled to it by your own signature.

No inquiry came from the publisher as to the progress of my work. Every month, on the first, I would find in my letter-box an envelope containing a cheque for five hundred Israeli pounds, signed by D. Karpinowitch, which I deposited in my current account at the bank. Karpinowitch sent no one to dun me; but it seemed as if everyone else was dunning me. Who had spread the rumour? Was it the two or three newspaper reports that had caused me so much distress? ('Author Jonas, a few chapters from whose first book, *A Hero of Our Time,* made such an impression a few months ago,' read one of them, 'is now engaged in writing his second novel, which will be based on the life of one of the heroes of our time, A. Davidon—*sic!*) Or was it my own friends who had told the tale, derisively or in all innocence? Or perhaps those whose recollections I had recorded had told their friends, and their friends had told theirs, until the whole country was full of the news? Whatever the reason, not a week passed without my receiving a letter from someone, from some part of the city or some far-off village, expressing a desire to meet me, to 'contribute' to the best of the writer's ability, or to the utmost of his capacity, to my work, from his memories, information or opinions (and I must admit that I did not even trouble to answer these letters—I would tear them up rudely and throw them away, for the twenty-seven names I had were menacing enough); and not a day passed without someone stopping me to ask how the book was getting on, or to offer...

I remember Czeczik. I remember him with shame.

One evening as I was on my way to the Cellar I sensed rapid footsteps behind me, someone touched me on the shoulder, and when I turned my head I saw a short, balding, elderly man, with a melancholy smile peeping modestly out of his narrow eyes. 'You are Jonas the writer. Forgive me for troubling you. My name is Czeczik,' he said, holding out his stumpy hand. 'Czeczik...' I replied, trying to remember. 'Well, I suppose you don't know me...I used to act once. Ask people, and they'll tell you. I'd like to meet you. Not now, of course, I see you're in a hurry...' 'What about?' I said brusquely. (Another one of them—I gave him a hostile look—another willing, humble, apologetic, but unbearably irksome contribution!) 'I heard that you're writing a book about Davidov,' he went on, shrinking somewhat before my gaze. 'I should like to meet you. I shall not take up much of your time.' (Get rid of him, get rid of him at all costs! I steeled myself.) 'Listen, Mr Czeczik,' I said, restraining myself, 'if it's about material...' 'No, no, I know you've more than enough,' he hastened to reassure me, 'it's about another matter. I promise you I won't take up much time. And you'll not be sorry. Any time you like. Anywhere.' I fixed an appointment one evening in a cafe, just to get rid of him. That 'petty malice' of mine towards those who depend on me which Ahuva had known in her own person came to the fore: I did not keep the rendezvous, and it was not without pleasure that, as I lay in bed reading desultorily, I saw Czeczik in my mind's eye waiting for me half an hour, or an hour, at the café table, casting impatient glances at the door, going out to the pavement and looking out for me in both directions, wondering whether he had mistaken the time or the place...Next morning—at two A.M.!—I almost bumped into him as I came up from the Cellar, standing and waiting by the door. 'Ah, Mr Czeczik,' I said, almost stumbling on the step, 'you must forgive me...' 'Don't apologize, don't apologize,' he hastened to reassure me, 'you were busy. I know. No doubt you had to leave town and...' 'I couldn't let you know, I'm sorry.' 'Yes, I understood. So—when shall it be?' I took out my pocket diary and began riffling through the pages, as if trying to find a free moment. 'Perhaps I had better come to your house,' he said, looking at me expectantly. 'You live in Polishuk's flat, if I'm not mistaken.' 'No, that wouldn't be particularly convenient,' I said hurriedly, to put the idea out of his head. 'I understand. All right. Wherever you like.' I fixed another appointment. Again I did not go.

For some ten days he shadowed me, lay in wait for me, ambushed me at the most unexpected times and places. I am ashamed to repeat the lies with which I excused my failures to appear, making him out to be a fool, a liar or an idiot ('I was there, Mr Czeczik, but you weren't', 'We agreed on six o'clock, Mr Czeczik, not seven'), and which he accepted submissively, hastily exonerating me while the lie was still on my lips. But there was no escape from this obstinate pest. Finally I gave in and went to his house.

'I must tell you, Mr Jonas,' he said earnestly as he offered me a glass of tea and wafers in his little room, crowded with books, photographs and old theatre posters, 'I knew Davidov very well. I worked with him at the Ratisbonne, and in 1928 pushing barrowloads of sand in Shenkin Street. I met him many times, once when we founded Sede-Nahum, once at the Northern Fence...But I won't tell you about all that, although I've much to tell, a great deal. I only want to tell you one thing, from which you will understand why I was so anxious to talk to you, why I have been pursuing you for weeks—don't imagine I don't know that I have been a nuisance—and why this is so important to me. Well, I want you to know: The dream of my life is to play the part of Davidov!'

Czeczik sat at the end of a couch which was covered with a warm green plush bedspread, his two hands clinging to the edges as if he was holding on to keep from falling off. His watery, almost lashless eyes, which seemed to be filled with turbid tears, gazed at me.

'The dream of my life, Mr Jonas. Yes'—he nodded his head—'you are a young man and you don't know me, and perhaps you won't understand it. But when I heard that you were writing the book about Abrasha Davidov, this heart of mine started burning—here'—laying his hand on his heart. 'There is such a thing in life, Mr Jonas! A man's soul seems to be nothing but ashes, for many years just ashes, and suddenly—one spark lights up! The vital spark blazes up into a flame.'

I looked at him, at the tiny spark that glowed in his narrow eyes, and lowered my glance.

'Yes,' he said, 'you look at me and think: Who is this Czeczik? Who is he? Who knows him? A piece of junk! Who looks at the junk at the road side? Who cares about the dreams of a piece of junk? But…you are a writer, Mr Jonas. You, if I may use the expression, are concerned with matters of the soul! You understand what it means when the spark of a great hope suddenly awakens in a man's soul…'

Czeczik's eyes held on to me and would not let go. When he had delineated his truncated sentence in the air for a long moment, he got up from the sofa, seized me by the wrist, and made me get up from my chair.

'Look,' he said, pointing to the photographs on the wall, 'that is from the Shalom Aleichem evening, from *The Robbers of Casrielivka*, and that's me as the Third Robber, a small role but full of temperament. And here, what you see here, that's from *The Fishermen*, I'm Kapps, the book-keeper. The fishermen from the village come to kill Boss after the boat has sunk and I stop them all by myself. Here I'm the herald in Zweig's *Jeremiah*—"Arise, O People of Israel!"' He suddenly raised his voice, lifting up his hand as if brandishing a sword. '"Gird yourselves with strength, fear not, for Jerusalem shall stand for ever! To arms!"'

He shouted out the 'To arms!' in a tremendous voice and was silent for a moment to let the echo die down. Then he turned me round to the opposite wall; facing me was a photograph of a stage, with several large wooden cubes arranged on it and a kind of pyramid at the side.

'And here…' He pointed to the figure of a man enveloped in an ancient cloak standing on the apex of the pyramid. 'Here I am alone on the stage. Alone! The angel in *Jacob and Rachel*. As the curtain rises I stand on the stone at the foot of which Jacob lies asleep. I was standing in for the regular actor and after the show the late Sheinbaum came up to me and said—I remember it as if it were today—"Czeczik, you have lifted us all on a ladder to the heavens." In these words. And if I were asked to play the part this very night, I would go on to the stage and recite the whole of the text without any preparation. I have it all here, in my heart. "Who art thou? What dost thou here?" asks Jacob. And I reply: "To take thy soul I have come!" "Who sent thee hither?" "He that created the heavens and the earth!" "I shall not live, but die. Get thee up from here!" "Jacob, Jacob, the souls of all living things have been entrusted unto me!" That is the epilogue. And what you see here'—directing me to another photograph, showing a room as poor as Polishuk's—'this is a satirical show by the Teapot Company, and I play the part of the poet in a delightful sketch by Avigdor Hameiri. By the way, we put it on in Kfar Sava and Davidov saw me in it. But now,' he said in a ceremonious voice, as if he was coming to a surprise that he had kept to the end, 'you shall see something else.'

On the third wall, between two posters of the Palestinian Theatre, hung a photograph showing Czeczik sitting on a royal throne, his beard dishevelled, deep wrinkles carved in his brow, his arms lying limply on his knees and his entire aspect eloquent of grief. For a long moment he stood looking with me at the picture, his arms folded on his breast, and finally he asked:

'Who is that, in your opinion?'

'It's you, if I'm not mistaken.'

'Me! Of course it's me—but in what role?'

'King David?'

'Lear!' His eyes sparkled. 'King Lear!'

> 'Blow, winds, and crack your cheeks! rage! blow!
> You cataracts and hurricanoes, spout
> Till you have drench'd our steeples, drown'd the cocks!
> You sulphurous and thought-executing fires,
> Vaunt-couriers to oak-cleaving thunderbolts,
> Singe my white head! And thou, all-shaking thunder,
> Strike flat the thick rotundity o' the world!
> Crack nature's moulds, all germens spill at once

That make ingrateful man!'

Czeczik waved his hands and shook his head as he declaimed the
speech, and all the room was his stage. A scintilla of royal majesty
glowed in his shining face. He sat down on the sofa, puffing, and,
after he had recovered, said:

'We presented it at the Studio in Jerusalem. How the audience
received me I won't tell you. I will only say that at one of the perfor-
mances Sir Ronald Storrs, the Governor, was present—there was a
man who imbibed Shakespeare with his mother's milk—came behind
the scenes, and… I will never forget his handshake. I permit myself to
say, Mr Jonas, with all due humility, that I gave a new interpretation
of Lear, different from all the accepted views. Have you ever asked
yourself'—he bent over towards me—'why he went mad? Because
his daughters and friends betrayed him? No! Kings have always been
familiar with treachery—all kings, in all ages! They have been betrayed
by their wives, their sons and daughters, their ministers and servants.
There's nothing new in that. The subject of Shakespeare's tragedy is
different, something much more universal. The tragedy not only of
a king, but of all men who are relegated by old age to the margins of
life while they are still alive. The tragedy of a man who sees himself
deposed, mocked at, pushed aside, superseded—while he is still alive,
treated as useless and unwanted while he feels that he is still in command of all his powers. That is what drives a man mad! The madness
is a protest, you understand. A protest against destiny! That is how
Lear ought to be played. You must feel that this is you, you, the fate
which lies in store for you one day, which already lurks within you,
and that you can do nothing to avert it, nothing at all!

'My friend,' said Czeczik, clapping his hands on his knees
and leaning forward, 'anyone who has played Lear can also play
Davidov.'

His eyes were fixed on me, waiting for an answer.

'I'm only writing a biography, Mr Czeczik, and even that isn't
written yet.'

'I know, I know,' he said, as if he had been waiting for that reply,
'but…don't you feel the drama that lies at the heart of that man's life?

What a great subject for a play! Perhaps the first real Israeli play ever to be written! Just think for a moment what a character it is. What inner struggles! What contradictions! Romanticist—and practical man! Anarchist—and slave to duty! The dreamer who always longs for the things of the spirit—and the man who forcibly crushes it all within him...And his family life—the wife, the son who is killed, the daughter who goes to the bad. What dramatic material! In fact, if a man like Davidov did not exist, some writer would have to invent him as the hero of a play.

'I live him, Mr Jonas,' said Czeczik, laying his hand on his heart. 'I feel him, I know every movement he makes, every syllable he utters. And don't imagine that I come to you with empty hands. No, I've been thinking of it day and night, day and night. I have a complete plan ready. Every detail. You—all you have to do is just to sit down and write.'

And now he began to elaborate his plan, founded on six episodes from Davidov's life, all of them taking place between the four walls of a room which changes form according to the exigencies of time and place. First—in his home in Russia (a tragic farewell to a non-Jewish sweetheart on the eve of his departure for the Promised Land); second—in a hut near the Ein-Harod spring, as he leaves the Labour Legion; third—in his hut in Kfar Sava (with a bitter quarrel between himself and his wife when he tells her he is going out to the Dead Sea); fourth—at the Haganah command in Tel Aviv, when his offer to parachute in to Nazi-occupied Europe is rejected; fifth—at the post in the Jerusalem hills, where he is told of his son's death; sixth—in the hospital at Beersheba, an hour before his own death.

'A cross-section of an entire era,' cried Czeczik, slicing the air with his hand. 'A great and glorious period through the prism of the life of one man, who marched, as it were, by the side of the road, but marched as a pioneer from the beginning of the road to the end! That is my vision.... And if you ask me who will realize it, who will play the parts...'

He had already spoken to six actors, four veterans and two younger men, who had expressed their readiness to set up a company especially for this purpose. They were only waiting for me to write the play and give it to them.

'My friend,' he said, 'Davidov is the role of my life. I will not give him up. And I will not leave you alone! Never mind that I'm...somewhat short, going bald, with no external resemblance to that man. That's not what makes a part. The great Garrick was short too, even ugly, but when he played Hamlet, Lear, Macbeth—his head reached the stars! A role gives an actor wings! Does miracles! When I play Davidov I shall be him with all my heart and soul, with a sense of a sacred mission, in the profound conviction that I shall be bringing new tidings to a generation that has lost all its vision.'

To all my explanations—that I could not even think of it before I had finished collecting the material, before I had written the book itself, that I had obligations I must fulfil, that I had no experience in writing plays—Czeczik reacted with a deprecatory shake of the head: 'Only begin and you'll see how the wave will carry you on its back, you will not be able to stop, you won't think of anything else. You'll do it while you are writing the book, at one and the same time. We'll help you, we'll help each other.'

His ears were deaf to my refusals. Some of them he took as an affectation of modesty, some as the hesitations of a writer uncertain of his powers. As he continued to press and encourage me he pulled out a bunch of keys from his pocket, fumbled through it to find the right one, went up to the desk, opened a drawer, took out a bulky envelope, and, holding it out to me, said:

'Permit me, Mr Jonas, just an advance payment. A modest sum...five hundred...only so that you can make a start.'

I jumped up from my chair and put away his outstretched hand. 'I won't accept any money,' I declared. 'It's out of the question. If I ever do the work...'

'You insult me, Mr Jonas,' he said, looking up at me with a hurt, sidelong glance, his hand still stretched out towards me. 'Believe me, I am doing this...'

I walked past him and turned towards the door. 'I will accept nothing. And about the play, we'll talk later. We'll see.'

'You promise!' he called after me as I went down the stairs. 'Remember, I'm waiting for you...Remember...'

A few days later, I received his cheque for five hundred Israeli pounds. I did not cash it, but I did not send it back either. It has been lying in my drawer for over a year.

Chapter thirteen

The court sat today. The session lasted only ten minutes. My counsel announced that the Honorary Secretary of the Authors' Association was unable to appear because of illness. Attorney Evrat remarked, with a faint smile on his lips, that he hoped that the worthy writer would not be confined to his bed by *force majeure* for too long. My counsel protested against this gross discourtesy to an illustrious author and demanded that the remark be struck from the record. The remark was struck from the record. The next session will take place in two weeks time.

Chapter fourteen

I have to go on with the history of the book that has not been written, that will never be written now, but I feel I must describe an unfortunate incident that took place during this time: namely, a few weeks after my meeting with Meanahem Schweig, about two weeks before I met Rudi Ephrat. It concerned Uri Grabowitzki, 'the General'.

The General (a title that had been bestowed on him—a kind of gold medal on a pauper's rags—because he once told us that his father had been a senior officer in the Red Army, after he and his family had escaped from Poland to Russia) sheltered in the shadow of the group like a fern in the shade of the trees. He would sit at the side of the table, shrinking as if with cold in the compass of his meagre limbs; you could not tell whether he was dozing or listening to what was going on, and only when Nakdimon expressed some wish (or even before then, when he looked for something with his eyes, or wanted to call someone) would he bestir himself and hasten to do his will. He was always ready to serve him, to bring the salt-cellar to his table or a bottle to fill his glass, to support him when he staggered, to see him home when he was drunk, to quarrel with anyone who dared offend him. Nakdimon despised him more than any of his other admirers, with the patronizing contempt of a master for his favourite servant, and would take particular pleasure in calling loudly, often for no particular reason, 'General!' or he would scoff at his sordid job, behind the counter in a bookshop: 'General! You miserable salesman! Cast away your books and grasp the sword!' The General, as if enjoying his master's whip-lash, would smile humbly while everyone laughed.

His poems, which appeared at long intervals, like afterthoughts, on the back page of some weekly or monthly, were condemned to pass unnoticed. No one mentioned them in his presence, so as not to give him pain, or behind his back, because it was agreed that they were not worth it. They were written in the old style—candid, emotional, sometimes suffused with blood, sometimes like delicate pencil sketches from his childhood home in Poland—a small village with geese beside the brook, thatched roofs ('Tottering fence, a pool where the clouds lie prone;/My face like a candle flickering in the light of day;/My bare feet, bruised by every stone,/Flee from my shadow like the echo of a dream gone away.').

When he was thoroughly drunk he would sit and mope all alone in a corner, his head slumped forward on his sunken chest, his eyes tightly closed, his ravaged face concentrated around the furrows of his forehead as if he were straining to listen to some distant voice. One evening two street-singers, scarecrows dressed in rags, came into the Cellar and started to sing old-time Yiddish songs, one of them accompanying the other with a hoarse and screechy fiddle. After two or three songs which stirred the ghosts in the Cellar, Gumpel asked the waiter to throw them out: 'We're not in the humour for Polish funeral dirges!' Suddenly, as if stung by a scorpion, the General jumped up and cried, red with rage: 'Why put them out? Why?' Nakdimon looked at him severely and said, slowly and quietly: 'What's happened, General? Have we offended the honour of your motherland?' The General, stunned, started to say something, but immediately sat down and remained riveted to his place. 'Here, have a drink,' said Nakdimon, sending over a glass after the two had left. The General sat motionless, shrunk in his place. 'Drink, I said!' ordered Nakdimon.

'Here's a toast to Polish Jewry!'—raising his glass. The General peered at him for a moment from his lowered eyes and a bitter smile expired on his face. 'Don't imagine I'm so cynical,' said Nakdimon in a thin drawl. 'I just don't like an exhibition of deformities, that's all.' The General did not touch the proffered drink, but later he poured out for himself and drank slowly and copiously, glass after glass. After midnight, when nearly everyone had gone and the Cellar was getting empty, he remained in his place, hunched in his corner, eyes closed, as if holding his heart in his clenched hands. 'Come on, come on, it's late,' I said, trying to get him to his feet. He opened his eyes, looked at me hard and long, and, as if he had found a friend in need, said: 'Sit down, sit down.' Again he closed his eyes, shuddered, and after a long interval opened them again and said: 'What do they understand, Jonas? Nothing! They believe in…nothing! Nothing, nothing…they're absolute ciphers, ciphers…they aren't Jews at all!' He relapsed into his apathy. Then, when he had roused himself again, he stammered: 'Why do you think I…f-fawn on Nakdimon, eh? Because…because I'm…a lump of carrion. Because he was born here I…think he's cleverer than me…that he's got the whole country in his pocket…his private property.' He giggled, as if he was laughing at himself. Suddenly he screamed until the echoes rang in the empty Cellar: 'His country? If it's his country, it stinks! What does he know, anyway? What has he seen in his life? What makes him the boss here? He's corrupting the country with his cleverness. Do you have to be ashamed of believing in anything? Ashamed of being honest? Ashamed of being sad? If you've a sharper tongue, you're king! King!…Listen,' he said, forcibly gripping me by the shirt, his face distorted as if he was about to burst into tears, 'you call them poets? Writers? They don't believe! Have you ever seen tears in the eyes of any of them? N-nothing can stir them to tears…Nothing…When we escaped from our village, over there, on foot…two hundred kilometres…in the snow…I was seven years old…yes, seven…' He became tongue-tied. Could not find words. His lips moved soundlessly. 'Oh, what does it matter…' He collapsed against the wall and closed his eyes. Now his face was peaceful, unwrinkled like a dreaming child's. For a few moments he sat like that, as if asleep, and when he opened his eyes again he started to sing, in such a soft and melancholy voice, as if coming from a distance, that I felt a shudder run through me:

> *Gelozen die mamen alein in der heim,*
> *In heizel farlatet mit troier un leim...**

He sang to himself as if he was praying. The empty glasses glistened on the table and the waiter stood opposite against the wall, listening with moist eyes. Suddenly he stopped in the middle of a line, his head sank on his chest, and he shrank into himself as if gripped with cold.

When his book of poems, *Tracks in the Ashes,* appeared he stopped coming to the Cellar. One evening we noticed his absence and asked each other where the General was. It was Levia who said: 'Not nice. A man publishes a book, his first book, and we don't even drink a toast.... After all, it's a red-letter day.' 'We can drink,' said Gumpel, 'the only question is what to say.' 'We can say something, Gumpel,' said Levia blushing, 'with a little good will. After all, he has a few poems that are not so bad.' 'To tell you the truth,' confessed Osnat, 'I'm simply afraid to meet him. I got a copy from him with a dedication, he even took the trouble to bring it to my flat, and.... I just can't find a good word to say for it. It's not pleasant. Every time I see him in the street I slip over to the opposite side of the road.' 'You can always find a good word,' Levia asserted. 'More philanthropy!' said Gumpel, raising his hands. 'The book is bad! Derivative, anaemic, pitiful, stop. Anyone who rhymes "sky" with "sigh" today is a nincompoop, that's all there is to it. Get it into your head that we're not a charitable society, we must draw the line between personal sympathy and sincere artistic evaluation. Plato is my friend—but a greater friend is truth! Personally, I like him just as much as you. I'm prepared to put him up in my room, feed him, comfort him for all his sufferings. But what has that to do with literature? Why should we be guilty of the lie in the soul?' It was Nakdimon, of course, who

---

* Yiddish: I've left my mother alone at home,
  In a house patched up with sorrow and loam.'

pronounced judgment. 'Tomorrow evening', he proclaimed, 'we bring the General here and have a celebration in his honour. I'll speak first, Eviatar second, Hochberg third. Not Gumpel; he has enough lies in his soul.'

When we were all seated, the whole band with all its hang-ers-on, about twenty in number, Uri was not yet to be seen. Two of the group volunteered to bring him from his home in a taxi and came back in half an hour dragging him in by force. As soon as he appeared, Nakdimon declared: 'The General!' and we all rose as one man and sang with all our might the battle song of General Budioni's battalions. Uri was seated against his will at the head of the table (he tried to escape, struggled, and finally reconciled himself to his fate, forcing a smile on to his lips) and, after a few more battle songs, some Russian and some Israeli, Nakdimon, who had been drunk since the beginning of the evening, rose and delivered his address.

'Gentlemen,' he began. 'I have read this book by Uri Grabo… Grabo-whisky…'

A loud laugh rolled round the heated room. Nakdimon's face remained rigid. He waited till everyone was silent and continued:

'I have read *Tracks in the Ashes* from the first page to…yes, to the last…And I hereby declare that this is…the most powerful book of verse that I have read for…for…two years! I am moved, impressed, overwhelmed! It has truth! Integrity! Sincerity! It does not have a s-single line of f-f-falsehood! It is authentic, ladies and gentlemen! And when I say authentic…Wipe those *foolish grins off your literary faces!* he shouted furiously. 'What are you smiling there for like a titillated eunuch, you wretched rhymester?' he cried to Eliraz. 'If you'd scribbled a single line in your life like…the six lines…of "That Night in the Snow", I would anoint your head with holy oil, Eliraz!' There was an embarrassed silence. Nakdimon lowered his voice por-tentously: 'I want to read you…these six lines.' And he recited in a sepulchral voice:

'That night in the snow
Angels rode on my back.
My mother's voice froze in the river

125

And the end of me was black.

The angels fell as I went
I was bereft of my track.'

'That is a pearl, ladies and gentlemen,' he said quietly. 'A frozen
pearl, with treasures at its heart...Abysses of death! Yes! Abysses of
death! Is there one amongst us—a single one, I ask—who can extract
the hidden beauty from one moment of terror as...in these six lines?
Not in the lines, ladies and gentlemen! In the silences between them!
In the awesome silence at the end of them! If Eviatar, or Avner, or
Hochberg were capable of uttering such silences, they would have
been great poets, I say...Homage to the General!' he cried, raising
his voice. 'This is a book of verse which...for which poetry is too
weak a word! It is the blood of the soul. Tears that have congealed
into pearls! Dripping with truth! In the sea of cynicism in which we
are all...splashing about...'

Hagit, who was sitting beside me, took a paper napkin from
the table and scribbled: 'Don't you think this is sheer cruelty?' I
wrote: 'Perhaps he really believes it.' She replied in the same way:
'You don't know N. He's capable of believing himself even when he's
lying.' 'Perhaps,' I wrote, 'And the General feels it,' she scribbled. The
General sat with head bowed and his arms folded on his chest, and
did not lift his eyes from his navel for a moment.

'General!' cried Nakdimon, raising his glass, after he had
become entangled in complex variations on 'truth' and 'sincerity', 'I
lift my glass to the most tempestuous, overwhelming book of verse
that has appeared in...the last decade, to a book which is beyond
poetry, which is...life itself! To life!'

Eviatar refused to speak. Despite all pressure he would not utter
a word. A pained smile hovered in the depths of his black beard like
a wounded bird in a thicket. He resisted all the whispers, the hints,
the suppressed anger of Levia, who remonstrated with him under
her breath, even Nakdimon's vociferous rebuke: 'Do you think it was
easy for me? Speak! You can hold your tongue when you're writing.
Now—you must speak!'

Yohanan Hochberg rose of his own accord. He stood erect, rigid, his face a pale mask of restrained emotion, and waited for absolute silence.

'Friends,' he said, 'I will not utter praises. Praise is hard to say and hard to hear. I will only tell you about one evening some two weeks ago, when Uri brought me his book. He came up to my flat, knocked on the door and, when I opened it, stretched out his hand, thrust the book into my hand—I didn't know what it was—and fled. I called after him to come up and come in for a few minutes at least…No. He was already in the street. Then I shut myself up in my room, alone with the book, read the first page, the second page…'

Hochberg described how, as he read one poem after another, he had felt as if he was being enveloped in memories of days gone by, as when a man has a dream and when he awakens imagines that these things had happened to him before and the dream was only a repetition. He told us that he had arrived in Palestine at the age of two and remembered nothing of the land of his birth, and the poems were like a blood-transfusion of experiences that had vanished into oblivion. He went on to say that he had no criteria by which to test a poem, but he had an ear with which to listen to a melody. Here he had heard the melody of an individual, and 'wherever you have the melody of an individual and not the singing of a choir—that is poetry.' Then he spoke of simplicity in poetry, and of 'that quality which is so generally despised today—modesty'.

'Hear! Hear!' interrupted Nakdimon. 'Every g-girl who has nothing to b-boast about—what does she boast about? Her modesty!'

Everyone hushed him. Hochberg's pallor froze on his face. Again he waited for silence. He breathed deeply. 'I don't know of any great poetry', he continued, 'where the poet does not strip away ornamentation, put a certain restraint on his ability and talent, keep out of sight behind the words, so as to leave them on their own…'

'Sit down, Hochberg! Sit down!' cried Nakdimon, waving at him with both hands. 'You're talking rubbish! Lies…con-ventional lies of the illiterate! Show me a single great poet who was…m-modest!'

The constrained pallor on Hochberg's face was holding down

a hostility that might break out at any moment, but he controlled himself and continued. When he remarked on the melancholy in Uri Grabowitzki's poems Nakdimon interrupted him for the third time: 'Who's interested in melancholy?' he cried mockingly. 'Who wants to see your pus pouring out?'

Hochberg picked up the glass by his side and threw the drink in Nakdimon's face. 'Scum!' he muttered, his lips trembling. Nakdimon rose and swept all the glasses and bottles off the table with a clatter of broken glass as he leapt at his antagonist's throat. In the middle of the ensuing tumult, with the waiter, the cook and the owner rushing forward and threatening to call the police, the General went up to Nakdimon from behind, seized him vigorously by the arm and pulled him towards the door. As they left, we could still hear Nakdimon's drunken voice: 'Melancholy, he says.... So who cares?.... If someone's got a pain...'

After that evening the General disappeared. No one saw him, no one heard of him. Only a few months later Saul Nunn said he had seen him in Eilat, working as a building labourer. When Saul greeted him, he had not answered; he had turned his face away and gone on with his work. 'At last he's doing something worth while!' said Nakdimon when he heard about it. 'Building the homeland!'

Chapter fifteen

I come to the Nili affair, which became intertwined, as if by some freakish aberration of nature, with the story of Davidov. I shiver today when I remember that it was mere chance which led me on to this minefield; for it was by no means inevitable that I should meet Rudi Ephrat—né Freudenthal. There were two names in my list—his and Eli Rosenberg's—and either of them could have told me about Davidov's Dead Sea period. The choice was in my hands; I pressed the wrong button and picked Rudi. But that was not all, for even after the angel stood in my path and warned: Danger! Danger! I smote my ass, like Balaam, again and again, and ignored him. I set my teeth and insisted on finding this Rudi, although he seemed to be hiding from me, disguising himself. So it happens that some blind impulse forces a man who can choose between seven roads to step on to the one narrow path where Satan lies in wait.

'Rudi Freudenthal. Worked with D. at the Dead Sea from 1934 to 1936 (address unknown)'—that was what was written in my list. All Abraham Shai could tell me was that Rudi had been a member of the kibbutz of L. from 1939 onwards, but he was not sure if he was still there; I had received no reply to my two letters to the kibbutz.

(I remember how I sat in the evening at the table, with the list in front of me, considering: Perhaps Eli Rosenberg after all? No, Freudenthal; I must find him!) So off I went to the kibbutz. I would find out on the spot, I said. It was a few days after the incident with Uri Grabowitski and the atmosphere in the Cellar was stifling. A trip to Galilee would.... Yes, I definitely needed a little fresh air.

I arrived after sunset, the dust rising from the road and a broad veil of tranquillity spread out over the entire Huleh valley between the mountains on either side. As soon as I got off the bus I was told that the man had left the kibbutz ten years ago and no one knew where he was now. So I had to stay the night. I was not sorry. In the dining-hall there was the same festive tumult of supper after the day's work which I had known in far-off days, the same flurry of activity to find oil for the salad, vinegar, a spring onion, or the treasurer; the same jokes flying from seat to seat, from table to table; the same assiduous girls serving bowls of porridge and tureens of soup from the zinc-lined trolleys. Outside—a starry, sapphire night, alive with the croaking of frogs, and a warm wind carrying the fragrance of mint from the wadi and memories of boyhood hikes in the hills. As he showed me the room where I was to sleep, the secretary advised me to try my luck at Shavei Zion, where, so far as he knew, Rudi Freudenthal had lived for a year or two after leaving the kibbutz, when he was working at the experimental station near Acre. Tiny lights scintillated in the valley like fireflies on the surface of a dark lake, and glimmered from the wall of shadow opposite, as if floating on nothingness. I felt a heaviness in my chest, but did not know why. The secretary opened the door of the room and switched on the light. 'Your wife's name is Ahuva, isn't it?' he said, as he put down a pair of starched sheets on the bed.

I remember that vertiginous moment, when it was on the tip of my tongue to answer, 'Yes'—not because I wanted to evade the truth, but because I had suddenly become uncertain of the truth and I imagined that it was really so; I was confusing—perhaps because of the unfamiliar place—different episodes and periods; I did not know where I was in the chronological order of things, and what had happened to me, and in general...'You know her?' I said. 'I know your sister-in-law Geula,' he replied. 'Neighbours. We meet sometimes.' When he had gone there was a kind of cool silence in the strange room—isolated, as if it were all alone in the desolation of the night. At the head of the bed there was a bookshelf. I took out Maupassant's *Une Vie* and read a few pages until I fell asleep.

In the morning the Huleh valley was green, crystalline, washed in dew, and the mountains were close, clear and bare. Again I was gripped by a kind of vertigo of chronological confusion, a return to other days which perhaps I had really lived through—or perhaps they had never existed at all. Sitting in the bus, as it crossed the stony fields, approached and receded from the mountain wall, mounted to look down on the polished mirrors of the fish-pools and climbed heavily up the winding road, I asked myself why I was pursuing this Rudi Freudenthal. Who was he, what had I to do with him, what foolishness was this?

It was a long road from the kibbutz to Safad, from Safad to Acre, from Acre to Shavei Zion. It was already afternoon when I landed there, in a strange village. I asked several passers-by about Rudi Freudenthal, but they did not know him, had never heard of him. In the restaurant they said: Yes, there was a chap like that once, it was years since he had lived there, I could ask his ex-wife, Marga Amir, she probably knew. I plodded wearily to the end of the village. I was welcomed by the barking of a bulldog when I opened the gate. I knocked with the brass ring on the polished pine door. A lean, morose woman stood on the threshold. 'Yes?' she said suspiciously. I asked if she knew where I could find Rudi Freudenthal—I had to speak to him on an important matter. She measured me with a hostile glance. 'He's not here,' she said, and was about to shut the door in my face. Perhaps, nevertheless, she could tell me where he was living now. I had come specially, it was a most important matter…'I don't know, perhaps in the Weizmann Institute,' she said sullenly. The barking of the dog pursued me from the yard to the street. I was ready to cross the length of the land on foot to find this Rudi, of whom I knew nothing.

Next morning, I phoned the Weizmann Institute. 'Rudi Freudenthal?' answered a woman's voice. 'No one of that name here.' I said I was talking on behalf of Abraham Shai, of the Ministry of Defence, and the matter was most urgent. 'Wait a minute, please,' she said. The clattering of a typewriter and the twittering of female voices buzzed in the earpiece. I waited, and then the clear voice said: 'I suppose you mean Rudi Ephrat. Yes, he works here, in the Biology Department. Shall I give him a message?'

I wrote a postcard to Rudi Ephrat, and he replied that I could come to his house one evening; he would willingly tell me what he knew. I breathed freely. I did not know what was in store.

Treetops spread an atmosphere of prosperous evening tranquillity. Everything was tranquil, very tranquil—the little stone houses, the curved stone pavements, the island of greenery, the cars dozing by the gates like faithful domestic dogs, the silent lights filtering through the windows on to the interlaced branches....

'Come right in,' said Rudi, motioning in the direction of the living-room. And then—a radiance blinded my eyes. She did not rise when I entered, only raised her eyes from the book. She sat on the couch with her legs crossed, and the shadows from the red lampshade above her, like a royal baldaquin, set tiny fishes, shimmering as in an aquarium, floating over her face and her hair. My glance took in all her beauty in a single stolen glance: the proud, alabaster neck, the curtains of long, honey-coloured hair that covered her cheeks, the narrow, slanting eyes...When Rudi said: 'This is Jonas, I told you about...and this is Nili,' she only smiled with her full lips and nodded slightly. Later, when I had sat down in the armchair between him and the couch, beside the low table with its vase of tall red gladioli, she asked in her slow, deep voice: 'Will you have some coffee?'—though it was obvious that she had no intention of getting up. When Rudi started to talk she went on reading her book (it was Nevil Shute's *On the Beach,* in English) which rested on her open knees, and did not seem to be listening. But from time to time she touched her hair lightly, fluffing it out under her ears and glancing up cautiously for a moment.

I have to make a considerable effort today to assemble fragmentary memories and put them together to make up Rudi's story. There was Nili on my right, inflaming my face like a small bonfire;

on the left sat Rudi, bowed over the table, fiddling with the stem of his pipe or filling it, his dry, woody, tedious, monotonous voice mercilessly enumerating facts: 'Well, it was like this…' 'I don't know if this will interest you…'

I must eliminate Nili, and that roseate magical mist in which I was immersed, in order to see Davidov. Picture the valley of the Dead Sea, white-hot in the sun, with the gleams on the water and the wall of Moab opposite. The grey potash lorries climb up towards Jerusalem between the chalky hills and the bare mountains, and glittering cars race to Amman. A plain chequered with steaming pools, smoking chimneys, railway lines, canals, embankments saturated in petroleum. A great camp fenced with barbed wire, guarded like an army base, supine under the pressure of the heat and the strict supervision of watchful eyes. Davidov, his face sooty, drives a locomotive pulling trucks of carnallite from the evaporation pans to the factory. A Hero of Labour working two shifts a day. Abu-Hadid—the Man of Iron—the admiring Arabs call him. His Arab fireman invites him to his home in Jericho, brings him basketfuls of pomegranates. Novomeisky, the director of the company, comes down from Jerusalem and whenever he appears, he leaves his office to seek Davidov, his favourite. ('You know how it is with the Russians: whenever two of them meet and start talking Russian all barriers fall.') He talks to him as to an equal, consults him, invites him to meet the company engineers, Englishmen, Germans, in his office or on the veranda of the Kalia restaurant. Takes him along in his car to Amman, to meet Abdul-Rahman al-Taj, the manager. Davidov had a crazy idea that gold could be extracted from the water of the Dead Sea. Crazy, because the water contains less than eight-hundredths of a milligramme of gold per ton. But Novomeisky likes crazy ideas. Once, a strike breaks out over a fine imposed on a labourer after one of the rafts has been damaged; Davidov goes up to Jerusalem, meets the old man, and that's the end of the fine. Rudi, who arrived at this time with the first contingent of Youth Aliyah, works on the pontoons and shares a room with him. Rudi has books on biology, physics and chemistry, in German and English; Davidov swallows them in the evenings and delivers lectures on eugenics to Rudi. He has extraordinary powers of comprehension. He goes home only once a month and on the Sabbaths he takes Rudi along on hikes, to Ras-Fesh'ha, to Granadel, to Ein-Doch, to Wadi-Kelt. He has a weakness for monasteries; once they come to a Russian Orthodox monastery north of the mouth of the Jordan and he has a long talk with the abbot. On the way back he expounds to Rudi a logical and mathematical proof of the existence of God, according to a book by one John Scotus. ('He really was a strange man, you know. Sometimes one got the impression that he had no respect for all the work he was doing, that something was pulling him in a totally different direction.') Yes, in the warm, stifling, windless evenings he used to read. On Saturday evenings a dance-band played on the Kalia veranda, and the upper crust from both sides of the Jordan—Englishmen, Jews, Arabs—could be seen floating in dance rhythm by the light of the moon or of red lanterns.

As I took notes my face burned. My neck ached with the effort not to turn my head to the right; my skin tingled with her nearness; her upright posture, with her knees crossed, canopied by the lamp-shade, cast a spell on me. I wondered what she could see in him, in this Rudi, at least ten years older than her, with the hairline receding to his crown, with his arms hairy as an ape's, with his boring talk. What could she see in him and what was the meaning of her digni-fied, reserved posture, this manifestation of indifference? (Towards me? Towards him? Towards the subject of our conversation?) There was an English book lying on the table: *The Mechanism and Physiology of Sex Determination* by R. Goldsmith; and whenever Rudi paused in his story I fixed my gaze on it so that it should not be diverted towards Nili. Rudi spoke in a depressed voice, fiddling with his pipe, trying to light it but not succeeding, and again—again the glow of the burning Dead Sea valley, mountains of heat pressing on its scorched soil and the oily mirror of the water. One dry, hot day in May the workers assembled on the jetty facing the ship *Kalirohi*, which was laden with rafts, machinery and materials for the building of the sta-tion at Sodom. The waving of flags, speeches…anthems…Davidov wanted to go to Sodom, but Novomeisky kept him back and he continued to drive the locomotive. One day Davidov climbed up to the monastery on the summit of Mount Nebo. Davidov looked for traces of the Essenes…And what else? What else? Again the title of that book gleams before my eyes: *The Mechanism and Physiology of Sex Determination.*

After that I felt that Nili had suddenly begun to pay closer attention, that she had stopped turning the pages of *On the Beach* and from time to time was sending a cautious glance at her husband. It was when he started talking about the 'crisis' in Davidov's life.

'He had one difficult period, had Davidov,' said Ephrat, pressing down the tobacco in his pipe with his thumb without raising his head. 'He got involved. Not that it was all his fault. He was a handsome man, you know. And when a man is far from home…I told you he sometimes visited the restaurant at Kalia…'

Yes, there was a British engineer at the works called Henry Wood—they used to call him the Colonel. An expert geologist who had worked in India and Malaya. A dry man, who did a lot of drinking and little talking. His wife was a blonde, full of life and temperament, twenty years younger, who used to spend a great deal of time at the Kalia Hotel taking the rheumatism cure. The Colonel took frequent trips abroad. Katherine fell head over heels in love with Davidov. She used to break the rules by entering the factory area to see him, laughing up into the cabin of the locomotive. They were all witnesses of this crazy behaviour. The labourers used to make fun of her and tease Davidov, the officials smiled to themselves and waited to see what would happen. Davidov was embarrassed, like a virginal boy. He tried to keep away, to hide. In the end he was caught.

'He was not frivolous, you know. I think he really was in love with her for some time. But it depressed him. He became taciturn, dispirited. He would come back to the room at three, four in the morning, and by day he would be ashamed to look at me. He was a bit childish in this way. He would be careful never to appear in her company, and whenever the Colonel visited the works he would do all he could to be friendly with him. Talk to him with such humility that you could hardly believe it was he. People said that he was as miserable as if it was not he who had cuckolded the Colonel but the other way round. He really was wretched. He was a man of conscience, you understand. And that woman…a pretty dubious character. What saved him in the end was the disturbances…'

'The disturbances?'—a bell-like tone suddenly dropped into the tranquillity of the room like a pebble falling into a pond. Nili asked her question in a tone that seemed to imply that he had said something quite unreasonably foolish. Now, for a brief moment, I could see her again. The curtains of hair had shifted slightly and revealed smooth, sculpted cheeks sloping down to the rounded chin and the parted lips ripe as a strawberry. Her narrowed eyes rested on Rudi, waiting for a reply.

But Rudi went on playing with his pipe and did not look up at her.

'In 'thirty-six, when the disturbances broke out in Jaffa,' he said after the ripples of her voice had died away, 'he became himself again. He could not rest. Started talking about going back home. It seemed as if he felt himself caught in a trap. I don't know if you knew him. He had opinions that were unconventional at the time.'

Davidov was against the official Jewish policy of self-restraint and advocated attacking the marauders in their bases—that I knew. As far back as 1932, when Sheikh Aziz al-Kasam's Black Hand gang was running wild in the Jezreel valley. Now, too, at the Dead Sea he expressed similar ideas. When the news came of the attacks on Ramat Hakovesh, not far from his village—here Rudi concluded his tale—he packed his things and went back home to Kfar Sava.

Rudi clasped his hands behind his neck. A cloud of smoke rose from his pipe. He was looking straight in front of him, at a point somewhat above Nili's head. Her eyes were lowered to her open book, but she was not reading. I folded up my papers and very slowly put them into my little briefcase. The tense silence, Nili's restrained impatience, called upon me to get up and go, but I remained seated. The more I lingered the harder it became to rise. By staying on I made myself out to be an intolerable fool; I saw that they were asking me to get up and leave, that I was making myself odious…But, as if to torment them, or myself, I did not get up.

'Personal matters…will they come into the book too?' Nili's voice broke the silence.

Our glances clashed for a moment. Hers was sharp and wounding.

'I don't know yet…. Perhaps.'

'His wife is still alive, isn't she?'

'Yes…perhaps I'll skip a few details.'

Now I rose. So did Rudi. 'Going back to town?' he said. 'Of course,' I replied. 'I'll give you a lift. It's hard to get transport at an hour like this.' And putting his pouch into his jacket pocket: 'Come with us, Nili?' Nili put down the book and rose, slowly. We went out. As Rudi was locking the door he said: 'I hope Rami won't wake up.' 'Oh, he never wakes up, Rudi,' said Nili, with some impatience. I wondered what there was between them.

All the way Nili's hair was in front of my eyes. In the heavy silence I counted the shadows as they raced to the rear. When we got into town I asked Rudi to drive me to the Cellar. When we arrived I got out and thanked him. 'Perhaps you would like to come in for a cup of coffee,' I said with dutiful politeness. Rudi thanked me. 'It's late,' he said. 'We have left our little boy at home alone.' 'Let's go in for a moment, Rudi,' said Nili, opening the car door and stretching out a leg to the pavement.

From the Cellar we could hear Osnat's voice, reading something, reciting. Nili went in front, and as she appeared I could sense the men's suppressed whistles of admiration. She walked with a proud, erect gait, aware of her beauty, the beauty of the chiselled features, of the shining hair falling on her shoulders. We sat down at the table somewhat apart from the gang, Rudi on her left and I on her right. Osnat surveyed the company as if asking whether she might continue—and went on from the place where she had stopped:

Les jambes en l'air, comme une femme lubrique
Brulante et suant les poisons
Ouvrait d'une façon nonchalante et cynique
Son ventre plein d'exhalaisons.

'Baudelaire's "Une Charogne", of course,' said Gumpel. 'Too simple. Ask me something else.'

Osnat closed her eyes for a moment. Then she remembered, and recited:

> * *Ma femme aux seins de creuset du rubis*
> *Aux seins de spectre de la rose sous la rosée*
> *Ma femme au ventre de dépliement d'éventail de jours*
> *Au ventre de griffe géante...*

'André Breton,' said Gumpel. 'Next. Something harder.'

Nili listened, leaning forward, her chin supported by her hand. She was enchanted. When Osnat recited a few more verses she touched my arm lightly and asked in a whisper for the reader's name. I bent towards her; a warm wave flooded over me when I felt her hair on my cheek. Then she asked about each of those who were present. She knew almost all the names and mentioned their books. When I whispered Eviatar's name her glance rested on him and she remarked that she had liked his last book of poems. 'A beautiful book, isn't it?' she said, her head bending towards me. 'Not bad,' I whispered. 'Rather too explicit.' Osnat went on reciting fragments of French poetry and Gumpel never went wrong in identifying the authors. Again Nili touched my arm. 'What did you mean by too explicit?' she whispered. 'The symbols,' I said. 'Generally he's very reticent and restrained in his poems. But here...' She was silent, considering what I had said. 'Nevertheless,' she whispered, after a while, 'there's a kind of warmth...deep, dark...' I felt a twinge inside me.

Gumpel successfully met the test, and the duet splintered into desultory conversation. 'Shall we go?' said Rudi to Nili across my back. Nakdimon summoned the waiter to bring a bottle, banging with his hand on the table, and started the singing. All of them immediately joined in, and the chorus echoed, very clear and flowing, in the air of the Cellar. Nili raised her head, and her enthusiastic face absorbed the singing as if illuminated by a celestial light. I noticed how through her eyelashes she was casting from time to time a curious, stealthy look towards Eviatar, who sat, hunched and silent, with his hand on his beard. Rudi stretched his arm across my shoulder and touched hers. 'Let's go, eh?' he said. 'It's after one.' 'Yes, let's go,' she decided, as if awakening from a trance. She got up, as if making up her mind to break away from an enchantment before it should take hold. Outside by the car she shook my hand, a radiant smile of thanks on her face. I stood on the edge of the pavement and wistfully followed the car with my eyes as it sped away.

Chapter sixteen

The Honorary Secretary of the Authors' Association, who had recovered from his sickness, was brought in a taxi to this morning's session of the court. The usher led him to the stand, holding his skinny arm and hurrying after him to keep up with his rapid steps. The short, elderly writer's face was very pale and angry, and it was obvious that he was annoyed at having been obliged to come. The judge permitted him to sit while he was testifying, and his withered hand trembled nervously on the edge of the stand and his pointed little beard quivered. His replies were very peculiar. At first he did not seem to understand why he had been summoned and what was required of him, and then he gave irrelevant answers. This was particularly strange because my counsel, Mr Shiloh, had discussed his evidence with him about a month before the session. It appeared that he had forgotten the conversation. When Judge Benvenisti asked him whether he knew the defendant, Mr Jonas, he replied: 'Jonas? Who's he?…No, don't know him…Is that his name? A pseudonym?' Later, when the judge asked him if he had read any of my writings, he replied almost angrily: 'No, not a thing. I don't know. Haven't read anything the last few years except books connected with my work.'

When he was asked if I was a member of the Authors' Association he answered: 'Haven't heard of him. Haven't seen him at any of our conferences, at any meeting…Don't know. Is he one of the Young Guard?' And when he was told that I was indeed one of the Young Guard, he said: 'The Young Guard don't come to us. They have their cafés. I don't read what they write. You can't understand a thing. Their writing is confused, nonsensical. The first thing they ought to do is to learn Hebrew.' His voice was sometimes hoarse and sometimes shrill, and the judge did not seem to hear him properly, for from time to time he would turn towards him and put his hand to his ear.

My counsel enunciated his questions slowly and respectfully. 'I understand that your literary work stretches over a period…a period of some forty-five years, sir. Would you be kind enough to tell us how many books you have written during that time?'

'I don't know,' the writer replied impatiently. 'Fifteen, twenty. I haven't counted them. It's not of the slightest importance.'

'Now, if you will excuse me, sir, you have written a biography of…' Shiloh glanced at his notes and found it difficult to decipher them '…Rabbi Hasdai…'

'Ibn-Shaprut, Ibn-Shaprut,' the writer grumbled, as if resentful of the ignorance by which he was surrounded, now as always.

'I understand that you had to accumulate a great deal of material about…about the hero of this book of yours.'

'Yes, a great deal of material,' he replied contemptuously. 'No one can write a biographical novel without accumulating a great deal of material.'

'How long did you work on this book, sir?'

'Don't remember. Three years, four,' he replied impatiently. But when Mr Shiloh paused while selecting the next question he added of his own accord, though still as if resenting something: 'It was necessary to dig. Archaeological excavation. Collect the shards and glue them together. The information about Ibn-Shaprut is very scanty. Much of it is unreliable. To this day it is not known whether it was he who wrote the letter to the Khazars or another contemporary poet. Menahem Ibn-Saruk. Dunash Ben-Labrat. According to one view, the letter was not written in his time at all. All that had to be investigated. There are documents in Arabic, Spanish, French. I had to ask for copies of documents from the Arias Montana Library in Madrid. It took half a year before I got them. I could not write the chapter on Ibn-Shaprut's mission to Sancho, king of León and Navarre, without first examining the letters of Caliph Abdul-Rahman the Third. All that called for a great deal of work. The articles on the subject in such periodicals as *Tarbitz* and *Zion* are not of the slightest value. Mere conjectures by scholars who don't know what they are talking about.'

At this point Judge Benvenisti displayed considerable personal interest and asked the author if he had visited Cordova, where many documents from the time of Caliph Abdul-Rahman the Third were available.

'No, never. Haven't the money for it,' replied the author.

'When did this book appear?' the judge persisted.

'Six years ago. Seven.'

'Can it be purchased in the book shops?'

'I don't know. Never asked.'

My counsel resumed his questioning.

'Would you be kind enough to tell us, sir, from your experience as the author of several biographical novels, whether it has not happened sometimes that there is an interruption in the progress of the work...in the course of the writing of a novel of this kind?'

'Interruption?...I don't understand...What interruption?' the writer exclaimed, screwing up his eyes.

'I mean—does it not happen that the author may come up against...certain difficulties in the course of his work, and may be compelled, in consequence, to interrupt it for a while until he overcomes these difficulties?'

'I don't have any interruptions. No time for it. I work six hours a day. My time is short and I must get the work done.'

'What I meant was—by way of conjecture—if such an interruption is conceivable in the course...'

'Yes, yes, it is conceivable. And what of it?' the author interrupted him, irritated.

'From what causes, if I may be permitted...'

'What causes? Sickness, headaches, meetings, conventions. Or when a writer is summoned to testify in court—I don't know what for.'

'I deeply regret the necessity of troubling you and interrupting your creative work, sir,' said my counsel humbly. 'But your experience may help us to clarify several matters in dispute. When I asked about the causes I was wondering if there are *inner* causes...'

'I don't know. Perhaps,' he replied resentfully. But, after a momentary pause, he added irritably: 'A writer is not an artisan. If the holy spirit rests on him, he writes. If it vanishes—he had better stop. The spirit cannot be forced. Tied to the writing-desk. Too many authors have been springing up recently who will take on any job like building contractors.'

'This departure of the holy spirit, as you have so strikingly described it,' said my counsel, picking up heart, 'does not depend, then, on the *will* of the writer, but...we may say that it is due to the intervention of some *force majeure*...'

'I haven't studied the question. I don't think that a court is the right place for the discussion of the ancient philosophical problem of whether the will is free and under man's control or whether it is determined by a superior providence. Wiser men than us have failed to find a solution.'

'You are right, sir,' Judge Benvenisti intervened, 'but nevertheless, we should like to know your opinion on the subject.'

'I am not a philosopher. I am a writer,' he replied curtly. But a moment later he added: 'My personal opinion? My personal opinion is the same as Rabbi Akiva's—"All is predestined, but freedom of choice is given."'

'That is, there is freedom of choice after all,' the judge said, smiling.

'Yes, but all is predestined,' the writer asserted grimly.

'I understand from what you say,' said Attorney Shiloh, 'that it is *conceivable* that an author who has started a particular literary work may be compelled to stop in the middle for reasons that do not depend on his will.'

'I have already said that it is conceivable. I have heard of authors who have started writing a novel—biographical or not biographical—who have stopped and continued ten years later. Or they have not continued at all. There's nothing new in that. You can read about it in any book on the history of literature.'

'That is to say, such a thing is not unusual. It is in the nature of literary work.'

'Yes, in the nature, the nature,' said the writer, twisting in his chair.

Shiloh thanked him very humbly. 'That is all, for the moment, your Honour,' he said to the judge, collecting his papers. Then he sat down complacently with an expression of satisfaction radiating from his spectacles, took his handkerchief out of his pocket, wiped the sweat from his brow, and darted the glance of an exhausted victor towards the plaintiff's table. The usher came and set down a glass of water in front of the Honorary Secretary, but he pushed it aside impatiently. Attorney Evrat, his confident expression quite undimmed by my counsel's glance, rose, hand on hip, keyed up for the cross-examination. First he asked what qualities an author required in order to write the biography of a particular personality. To this the witness replied briefly and categorically: 'Love. That is all. You cannot write without love.' 'Love for the personality who is the subject of the book?' asked Evrat. 'Yes, love for the personality who is the subject of the book,' the elderly author agreed impatiently. And when he was asked to add other qualities—for surely, Evrat argued, love alone was not sufficient for the writing of a biographical novel—he enumerated diligence, persistence, powers of analysis and discrimination, narrative skill, and the capacity to express oneself accurately and clearly. When Evrat asked how an author chose the subject for a biographical work he replied: 'All according to one's personal inclinations, all according to one's personal inclinations.' Then he added: 'I was once asked to write the biography of Ussishkin, of the Jewish National Fund. I refused. Couldn't stand the man.'

'Did you ever contract with a publisher to write a book within a particular period, in return…'

'No contract. No period. Never in my life signed a contract. Never will,' he retorted, his little beard quivering.

'Are you not connected with a particular publisher?'

'Yes, I am. And what of it? I write and he publishes. I work and he eats. My book on Moses Hayim Luzzatto's letters has appeared in three editions and he didn't even tell me. An author gets no account of what happens to his work. They skin him alive and treat him as if he were dead.'

(A broad smile glowed on my counsel's round face at these words.)

'Do you receive advances from the publishers with whom you are connected?'

'I do.'

'Do these advances involve any specific obligations?'

'What obligations? They don't own me, I am not their slave. No writer with any self-respect would undertake any obligations whatsoever.'

Here Attorney Evrat raised his voice.

'Let me draw your attention, as Honorary Secretary of the Authors' Association, to the following facts. The defendant now in court, Mr Jonas, contracted with the publisher whom I represent in this case to write the biography of the late Abraham Davidov within a period of one and a half years, and in return for this undertaking received nine thousand Israeli pounds, in hard cash, five hundred pounds every month. He has not written a *single page* of this book! What is your opinion, as a writer, as an official of the Association, as a man with many years of literary work…'

My counsel leapt from his place and cried with a flushed face: 'This is demagogy! My learned friend is forcing his fantastic speculations on the facts, when he has no proof whatsoever that my client…'—but the judge silenced him with his gavel and ordered him to sit down.

'Mr Jonas has never undertaken to show you any unfinished work,' my counsel managed to fling at the plaintiff's table before he sat down.

'I shall prove that there is no "unfinished work" and never was any,' Evrat interjected briefly in reply. Then, turning to the witness again, he said: 'What is your view about a breach of faith of this kind?'

'My view? My view is that if he made his bed he should lie on it. He shouldn't have promised. If he did—let him pay for it!'

'Thank you very much, sir,' said Evrat, gathering in the spoils of victory. 'Let me repeat, to make it perfectly clear: It is your opinion that even if there was any impediment to the continuation of the work as a result of "the vanishing of the divine spirit," as the learned counsel for the defence argues, this does not absolve him from compliance with his obligations as laid down in the contract, and he must bear the loss.'

'Certainly. Certainly. That is only fair. Only right…' But after a moment, it seemed, the Honorary Secretary's pity was aroused by the distress of this apprentice craftsman of his guild, and he added, in a somewhat softer tone: 'Unless the publishers are prepared to give way. By all means. Let them give him time. Another six months, a year. Perhaps he may get over his difficulties…'

'Many thanks, sir,' smiled Attorney Evrat, turning suddenly to face me where I sat; in a high tenor, pointing his pencil straight at me, he cried: 'Mr Jonas, the publishers are prepared to grant you an extension of a whole year to enable you to carry out the work you have undertaken to do—are you prepared to sign such an undertaking or are you not?'

But as I sat, pale with surprise, my counsel leapt from his place as if to save me from stepping on a mine, and cried: 'The defendant is not obliged to reply! I request your Honour to censure this kind of surprise attack, the only purpose of which is to confuse and terrorize my client!'

The judge banged with his gavel and after explaining several points of procedure allowed the question and left it to me to decide whether to reply or not.

'Will you sign, Mr Jonas, or not?' Evrat repeated his question, head erect.

'No,' I answered.

'Two years, Mr Jonas,' he called out as at an auction sale. 'Will you sign?'

'No.'

'That was the reply I expected. Thank you. That is all, your Honour'—and Evrat sat down, pale with agitation.

The judge thanked the author, apologized for taking him away from his work, and announced the end of the session. The Honorary Secretary was led out by the usher, moving as fast as he could with his little steps and not turning his head to right or left. My counsel gazed at me from his place as if I was a hopeless case.

The next session was fixed for three weeks later.

Chapter seventeen

On the day Davidov came home from the Dead Sea a man by the name of Galutman was killed by Arabs on the road between Tulkarem and Kfar Sava. Next day two thousand trees were uprooted in a new grove on the edge of the fields of Arab Kalkilia, just opposite the village. The Arab labourers stopped coming to the Kfar Sava groves and Jewish workers were sent to replace them, accompanied by armed guards. A week later the packing-house in the grove bordering on the copse where Davidov's hut stood was set on fire. A truck on its way to bring back labourers in the evening after work hit a mine on a dirt track. At night, shots hummed from the direction of Miski, Tirah and the east. A company of British troops was billeted in the village, and soldiers accompanied the motor convoys on their way north through the Arab towns of Tulkarem and Jenin, along the dangerous road strewn with mines, nails and broken glass, running the gauntlet of stones and rifle bullets. One morning, after Davidov had left to dig trenches near Hamefaless, a platoon of British soldiers came to search his hut. His eight-year-old son stood outside beside his mother, who held her little daughter in her arms, and saw them through his scalding tears overturning the beds, pulling things out of the drawers, and taking up the floor tile by tile. When the soldiers climbed on to their truck and started to drive off he ran after them throwing stones until they reached the road. Towards evening, when Davidov came home and saw the havoc, Nimrod tried to comfort him. If he had had a gun, he said, he would have climbed the tall eucalyptus tree and wiped them out.

Listless and depressed, I travelled to Kfar Sava in the late morning to meet Shmuel Harari. I sat in the bus, my head buzzing, and said to myself: To hell with Davidov and to hell with this book. It was driving me to distraction. I plotted revenge on Eviatar, on Nili, on the whole world. The previous night, a little before twelve, they had come into the Cellar—all of a sudden, like a blaze of light in my eyes—Nili and Rudi. I was so startled that I behaved like a fool. I got up, shook hands with them, shifted chairs in every direction, mumbled all kinds of foolishness. Very soon I sobered down. Even as she greeted me Nili's glance floated over my shoulder as if she was looking for someone, and when we went to the table she manoeuvred so as to sit beside Eviatar. Rudi sat on her left, between us. So I lost her the same moment as I found her again. I was compelled to nod assent to the talk of her husband the biologist. They had come from the theatre and they had not liked the show. The play, actually, was interesting, but the acting...I hardly heard a word of what he said. My ears were strained towards the talk on his other side. (Such cordiality so soon! Such mutual comprehension so quickly!) Yes, Nili was talking very sensibly. The direction was not discreet. And why did the actors have to face the audience all the time? And ———'s acting had no charm, no grace, no nobility. And such pathos! And the scenery didn't fit the spirit of the play at all, too baroque, too ornamental, when what were really needed were straight, laconic lines, just a background and a frame...And Eviatar couldn't agree more. Nodded his head and from time to time, he added a quiet, apparently witty remark, greeted by laughter on her part (which made my blood seethe). Only Levia, who sat on his right, spoiled the harmony. Every now and then she broke in on Nili with her common voice and her sharp tongue: 'What d'you mean? Excuse me, but that's just what's so good about the production. Just that ornamental quality, as you say, because that's in the spirit of the period, because it's not a modern play, after all.' A servant-maid, a fishwife, against a princess! Nili did not even answer her. She went on talking to Eviatar, calmly, in a low voice, each slow sentence sinking into his heart. And all the time Rudi went on dripping his dreary sentences into my ears, his pipe in his mouth, while I nodded my head, anxiously listening to the conversation on my right so as not to lose a word of what was being said, my blood racing through my veins. At one moment, when Eviatar whispered something to Nili and the two of them laughed together as companionably as if they were old friends, I wanted to shout at Rudi: Take your pipe out of your mouth, man! Don't you see what's happening over there? Don't you feel the horns beginning to sprout from your forehead? And only when they rose to go did Nili smile at me again, and as she pressed my hand she said: 'Really delightful place. We'll be meeting again, no doubt.' I sat down and poured out a glass. 'Terribly arrogant type, isn't she?' said Levia later, turning to me. But I was already in my cups and deep in the dumps, and I went on drinking until the Cellar closed down.

Listless, depressed, cursing the evening when I brought Nili to the Cellar and the day I undertook to write about Davidov, I went to Kfar Sava. I got off in the main street and looked for Harari's transport office. ('Mulka Harari, former driver in the United Sharon Co-operative and an active member of the Haganah. Worked with D. in 1936–8'—that was what I had in my notes.) Two noisy lorries were standing in the square in front of the office; someone was shouting with broad gesticulations: 'Come on, get moving, and don't forget to bring the iron rods from Glickman'—and one of the lorries moved off with a deafening roar. Harari was a very fat man, with a tremendous head and a stained hat askew over his sweaty forehead. 'Come along, let's go inside,' he said, preceding me into the office: a narrow room which, in addition to the table, the two rickety chairs and a huge wall calendar with a picture of B.B. in the nude, was crammed with tyres, machine parts and parcels of all sizes. 'Sit down,' he said. 'Sorry I had to ask you to come at a time like this, but…' The telephone rang; Harari pushed the hat back on to his crown and roared into the mouthpiece. 'Not a chance, I said, not today. The Dodge has left already. You're wasting your breath. Send the boy. Yes!' Slamming the phone back into place, he paused for a moment after his outburst of temper, and concentrated on me. 'What have they told you about Davidov? That he was irresponsible? Write down that it's not true. That he was a man of whims? Write down that it's not true. An adventurer? Not true. Go on, write it down, don't be bashful. Write that Harari said so! Write this: Abrasha Davidov was a hero! You can say it in my name. I was with him at Kalmania, at Ramat-Hakovesh, under fire, night after night. People didn't know what kind of a man Davidov was.' Then he paused and went on in a softer voice: 'Talked to Zippora yet?' Then after a moment's reflection, he added: 'No, better not, leave her alone. Nothing'll come of it.'

Every now and then the door would open and somebody would ask something, or take something, in a great commotion; from time to time Harari would jump up, shout orders to the drivers outside, and come back.

On the day Davidov returned from the Dead Sea Galutman was killed on the road between Tulkarem and Kfar Sava. At night, searchlights were installed on the tops of the water-towers and great scythes of light stretched out into the distance, reaping the darkness over the pinnacles of the cypresses and the foliage of the groves, illuminating bare hilltops and secret ambushes. Signalling lamps pierced the darkness with dots and dashes, sending brief messages of warning, reassurance and encouragement. At the beginning of August, Davidov was put in charge of the defence of the area between Kfar Sava and Ramat-Hakovesh and established his headquarters at Kalmania, in the heart of the densely planted citrus area. At night he used to go out to inspect the posts facing the Arab villages, and by day he would make his round of the guards who accompanied the workers. For an hour or two he would go down to his house to visit his wife and children. He and Harari, armed with pistols and Mills bombs, would examine the dirt tracks and the deep sand between the groves before the passage of the trucks carrying the labourers. One day they came to a road-block of stones and noticed three figures with *kefiyas* on their heads, hiding among the trees. Shots were fired and Harari was wounded in the shoulder. Davidov threw a grenade at the attackers and chased them to the edge of the grove. When they reached the open road leading to Miski he hid behind the cactus hedge and waited for them. When they appeared again he threw another grenade and waited long enough to see one of them lying, shattered, in dust and blood. Then he went back to Harari and carried him on his back to the Kalmania farmyard, saving him from death.

'People don't know what Davidov was really like. An extraordinary man! I suppose you've been told he was a kind of crazy fellow, eh? Perhaps. But whenever it was dangerous he knew exactly what to do. Extraordinary!...Even before they organized the Assault Groups, even before the Palmach commandos, he led his men outside the area to attack the marauders. Got as far as Kakoon! You know what that meant in those days? Listen and I'll tell you what he told me once: In physics, he said, there is a law that any object can only be in one place at one time. With us, every man must be in more than one place at one and the same time. Why? Because we are building the land in violation of the laws of physics. And he did it! He did it himself! He was here, and he was there! In Kalmania and at the same time in the groves of Reiskin, Aharonowitch, Gan-Hasharon, and another dozen places. And at the same time he was so gentle'—Harari softened his voice. 'How he treated the men under his command! Everybody who worked with him. And what devotion! Listen to what I'm going to tell you: One day, his Zippora suddenly appeared at his headquarters in Kalmania and said the little girl was lying in bed with a high temperature and he must stay at home. What d'you think he did? Took the truck, drove her home, and in the evening—what a man that was!—he came back with Nimrod and the sick child, put them to bed in one of the rooms, and told the company nurse to look after them. Three days and three nights the children were with us, there in that building, together with the staff, and between his rounds he would look after them. Somebody will tell you, I'm sure, that the family meant nothing to him. Yes, you might think that, because in his yard the children always used to run about barefoot, dirty, like gypsy children; God knows what they used to eat and *when* they used to eat. Zippora was busy with the farm and the father was always away. But listen to what *I* tell you: He was a wonderful father and a wonderful husband! Yes, a wonderful husband too, don't believe anybody who tells you different. And what a heart! Listen, we had a disaster here with the truck that carried the workers from Meshek Ha'otzar to Kfar Sava. We left at half past two and after three hundred metres came up against road-blocks. We were fired at from Haj Abdullah's groves and our men had no arms—only the driver, Belkind, and he was hit right at the beginning. Two of them ran to get help and by the time the army came four men had been killed. You should have seen that man afterwards. He paced up and down like a madman. "It's my fault," he said to me. "Why didn't I have the road examined before they set out?" As if it was possible to examine it every hour. A terrible funeral that was! The whole village cried. He wasn't there. Shut himself up in his room and wouldn't talk to anybody. Such a heart he had…'

At the end of that year, when the disturbances died down, Davidov decided to acquire a seven-and-a-half-acre plot of untilled land with money he had saved from his work at the Dead Sea, and grow unirrigated peas. He bought the land and sowed it too, but when the time came for the picking he joined up with the Assault Groups. He went out for a month's course, and when he came back he was busy with patrols along the Eastern Line, from Tayibeh to Migdal-Zedek. His company intimidated the Arab villages and on one of his night patrols he blew up the hostelry at Miski, together with the marauders who were meeting there at the time.

'Got a bit of time?' said Harari, as he locked up his office for the midday break. 'Let's go over to Kalmania and from there you can see the whole front. To write about Davidov you've got to *see*. It isn't enough to hear about it.'

As we drove north in the truck Harari stopped from time to time and pointed out the dirt tracks branching off between the groves where mines and road-blocks had been laid. We went into the square farmyard of Kalmania and went up to the top of the water-tower in the centre. From there he showed me Kalkilia; the ruins of Arab Kfar Sava; the rocky spurs where the Assault Groups used to deploy; Tayibeh, blurred on the horizon like a heat mirage; the dusky blocks of citrus groves; the acacia avenues and the cactus hedges. He marked out boundary lines with his hand, and with his finger identified outposts, trenches, ambushes, here and there and over there. 'You ask where Miski is? No Miski. Wiped off the face of the earth. That house you see, the school, that's all that's left of that village of murderers, damn and blast it. But Tirah was left. Don't ask me why. Want to go over? Long time since I've been there.'

I remember that visit to Tirah now like a nightmare: the stone and clay houses, the filthy lanes, the minaret of the mosque, the dusty open spaces strewn with twigs, the pitted road crossed by trickles of turbid sewage…the gangs of children who ran after us shouting 'Shalom! Shalom!', the monotonous Egyptian songs echoing from the loudspeakers in the cafés, the adolescents lounging in front of the workshops, the obsequious Hebrew signboards, the bare clearing at the foot of the hill, swooning in the dusky heat. It all shimmered before my eyes like a mid-summer nightmare, hanging between the weary earth and the empty sky. It all seemed malevolent and hostile. Two filthy children ran out into the narrow road from the opening of a lane, and the truck almost knocked them down. A woman started to wail shrilly and some lads gathered round us shouting, until someone drove them off. Then a few toddlers followed in our tracks and ran after the truck until one of them fell down and burst out crying. A donkey-cart laden with bean plants, led by and old man, swerved to the edge of the road as we passed and was almost pushed to the wall. When we sat down on the veranda of the restaurant, and Harari started a conversation with an Arab he knew, I felt feverish and delirious. Through the heat haze I thought I could see Nili, Rudi, Eviatar, Davidov wounded and bleeding…'What's wrong with you?'—Harari's voice aroused me—'Feeling bad?' I had grown very pale, apparently.

Chapter eighteen

About a week later, I received a letter from Moshe Barnea, a teacher at the Kfar Sava Secondary School. Here it is, verbatim:

Dear Mr Jonas,

      I have heard from Mr Shmuel Harari that you are engaged in writing the biography of the late lamented Abraham Davidov. I was gratified by this news, but I regretted that I did not have the opportunity of meeting you face to face. First of all, permit me to wish you Godspeed in the great task which you are undertaking. For a long time I have felt that it is the nation's duty to one of its illustrious sons—though he was neither a leader nor a commander, but walked with God like one of the people—to erect a literary monument to Davidov, so that his image should march like a pillar of fire at the head of the camp, especially for the benefit of our youth, who knew not Abraham. Secondly, having been literature teacher and form-master of Nimrod, who sacrificed his life for our national independence, I should like to make my modest contribution herewith to the illumination of the one particular aspect of

Davidov's many-faceted personality which, I believe, has been concealed from the eyes of others.

During the four years in which I was Nimrod's form-master I had the privilege of meeting his father several times, though at considerable intervals. As you are aware, Davidov was generally far from home, and even when he was at home he was so engrossed with his duties that he did not find the time to pay a visit to our school. However, I was always impressed by the profound spiritual bond between father and son: "Saul and Jonathan, lovely and pleasant in their lives," and now—when they lie side by side in the hills of Jerusalem—we may say: "in their death they are not divided." Nimrod cherished a profound respect, which I, as his teacher, could sense, even though he never expressed it in words. And the father loved his son as himself. During my few meetings with Davidov I was always surprised at his extensive knowledge, the breadth of his horizons and the understanding he displayed for educational problems. However, it is not this that I wanted to tell you about, but only one meeting, some two years before Nimrod's tragic death.

Nimrod was not distinguished in scientific subjects, not because of incomprehension, but through slackness and perhaps indifference. I was seriously concerned, fearing that he might even fail in the final examination. As it was difficult in those times to expect Davidov to make the effort and come to the school, took that effort upon myself and one evening visited him in his hut in the copse.

It was quite late, and the two of us were alone in the room. Davidov, who was always hospitable, welcomed me with great cordiality and deference. He placed a bottle of vodka on the table, as well as olives and cucumbers pickled by his wife and pressed me to eat and drink. We chatted of this and that; I asked about his affairs and he replied, while he asked about the affairs of the school and I replied...I shall not on this occasion recall the details of the conversation, though any conversation with him was highly instructive. Then I expressed my concern about his son, and he made the following reply, which I now record as it is preserved in my memory:

'I will be frank with you'—so, more or less, he said. 'I am not particularly concerned about Nimrod's backwardness in mathematics and physics. Even if he fails in the examinations, I shall not regard that as a disaster. For me, the main thing is not the certificate, but the ideal: the ideal he follows in life. What should I like to see in him? A successful business?—No. A scholar?—No. A sociable man, well-versed in the ways of the world?—Not that either. What I want is that he should enjoy all those opportunities for the development of his personality which necessity and duty have withheld from me. Listen,' he said to me, 'I was not cut out from birth to be a labourer wielding the hoe or a fighter wielding the rifle. In my youth, all my dreams were devoted to music, literature, philosophy…And yet, since the day I set foot on these shores, I have not touched a musical instrument, and I can count the books I have read on the fingers of my two hands. I appear to be a free man, for I do everything of my own free will: no one compels me to do anything in particular; I am not subordinated to any framework. Nevertheless—I am not a free man. My will is inexorably determined. Necessity imposes on me things that are against my natural inclinations. True freedom is not the recognition of necessity, as the Marxists say, but something deeper: the free development of the spiritual capacities that are latent in the character of every man. But I have no complaints. I live in a generation, and in a country, in which men comply with the imperatives of necessity, not just willingly, but often with enthusiasm. This is an age of madness, but there is method in it. I have suppressed many of my desires, put them out of my mind, wiped them out. But I want Nimrod to grow up a different man: free as I understand the word; I want him to realize *himself,* to devote himself with all his might to those inclinations and talents with which nature has endowed him. And furthermore, I want him to be a man with an open heart and an open mind, free from prejudice, tolerant, respecting his fellow-men and independent in spirit. If this aspiration is realized, I shall know that all my work and the sacrifices I have made at my own expense will not have been in vain. I shall know that I have prepared the ground for him. If we regard life as one whole, continuing from generation to generation, if we think of my life as not ending at my death but continuing to exist in my son—a kind of immortality—then I have lost nothing and all this generation has lost nothing. And as for mathematics—a good mark or a bad mark—what does it really matter?'

That is what Davidov said to me that evening. I have not repeated it word for word, but that is the gist and the spirit of what he told me. And I believe that these words are sufficient to refute a view that is current among many of those who knew him: that he was a kind of outlaw, with no interest in the things of the spirit. He was a great humanist, was Davidov, a man of profound and sublime moral aspirations. And at the same time he was also a man who concealed a great pain in his heart, a pain which he never disclosed.

How sad it is to think that a life so rich in ideals, aesthetic values and practical achievements came to such an untimely end and that his dearest hope—to light a candle for the next generation—has been frustrated!

May his soul be preserved in the pages of the book to which you are devoting your labours, and may the book perpetuate the memory of the deceased, as an inspiration to us all and to our sons after us!

Yours very sincerely,

MOSHE BARNEA

That is the letter. I remember that it came on the first of the month, for the next envelope I drew from the letterbox contained a cheque for five hundred Israeli pounds, signed by D. Karpinowitch.

Chapter nineteen

I was the man who brought Nili to the Cellar; but Nili was never mine. Three victims fell at her feet, apart from the child: her husband Rudi, Levia, and I. In the end, Eviatar, like Sisera, also bowed at her feet and fell: where he bowed, there he fell. If I am to abandon the language of the Bible and express the situation in biological terms—to which I became accustomed perforce, when I was compelled, willy-nilly, to listen to Rudi's tiresome mutterings—I would say that Nili's penetration into the organism of our little group brought about a metaphase: the migration of the chromosomes to their poles in a redivision of the cell, after the balance of the previous entropy had been upset.

I used to watch her from the wings, as it were, out of the corner of my eye, after their visits had become very frequent: once a week, twice a week, after the show or the concert; but she gave me only an occasional glimmer of a smile or a scrap of a sentence, though she was very polite, very cordial, very grateful to me for bringing her to the Cellar that first night. Rudi did nothing to hold the fort, and had it not been for Levia, who was constantly on guard at her husband's other side, always on the alert, tense and ready to scratch and bite to save her dearest possession, the tinder would have flared up immediately. Nevertheless the fire glowed unseen, waiting only for the right moment.

Three victims there were, I said, besides the child; but the others also lusted for her, each after his fashion: Eliraz with flattery, Nakdimon with mordant wit, Avner with hostile silence...I will not enumerate them all. In any case they never had a chance. They devoured her with their eyes, leaving not a scrap untouched. Little foxes prowling around the vineyard.

Like a spectator in the wings, I saw how her face lit up at the sight of Eviatar the moment she entered, how she whispered to him as she sat by his side, how the unspoken covenant between them grew closer and closer, like a doom which no power, no will, could avert. I watched their self-control, the taut spring that joined them, gathering strength the more it was stretched, in preparation for the moment when it would be released. I sensed the desire that glowed in both of them—awaiting the longed-for opportunity when they would be left alone for a moment, one single moment, and then at last, with a sigh of relief from unbearable tension, they would fall into one another's arms. Or—in her absence—my senses would suddenly bristle at the sound of the telephone ringing in the Cellar, and the waiter would call: 'Eviatar, Eviatar, telephone!' and he would rise from the table (Levia darting at him a sharp glance of scorching suspicion), step like a cat to the counter, grip the telephone with his back to us, put his mouth close to the mouthpiece and speak into it, sweetly, glowingly, stroking the neck of the instrument as if it were hers—a very long moment of illicit love-making!—until he returned to the table with a guilty expression, trying to wipe out his sinful indulgence with a weak smile which still bore the traces of his enjoyment ('Who was it? Who was it?' asks Levia, and he fobs her off with an indifferent shrug, as if some persistent bore has been pestering him again over some old affair); or—late at night, in some bar somewhere in the undergrowth of the urban jungle—I would see the burning humiliation in her face, the humiliation of desire condemned to prolonged expectancy, no knowing how long—when with a suffering, dreamy smile she would watch Eviatar floating with Levia across the dance-floor, his feet keeping time with hers and his closed eyes dreaming a different dream. Suddenly, as if shaking herself free in an instant from her depression, she would rise, put out her hand: 'Shall we dance, Jonas?'—and then, as my arm embraced her and her perfumed hair caressed my cheek, I would wish I were dead: better be a servant gathering crumbs under her table, a dry twig under her heel, anything rather than a male nurse to soothe her sickness! But even these cruel mercies were rare; usually it was my fate to sit glass to glass with Rudi and listen with half an ear to his dreary lectures on the origin of life, courtesy forcing a question to my lips from time to time between the silences: 'In that case, what's the difference, Rudi, what's the difference between a living organism and a dead one, if the composition of the cells is the same in both cases?' 'Yes, that's a very good question. In point of fact I've never yet found a satisfactory answer'—Rudi continues his meticulous explanations, while all around us are sparkling melodies and tripping toes. 'Schroedinger has defined life as that condition of matter in which the uninterrupted increase of entropy is obstructed by the supply of energy. The result, then, is a continuous chain of physical processes which leads...' 'Yes, but is there no possibility of producing living matter from dead matter?' 'That, you understand, is what biologists have been trying to do for generations, and they have not yet succeeded in refuting the ancient rule which says *Omne vivum ex vivo,* although...'

Omne vivum ex vivo; but all Rudi's learning was not enough to prevent what was bound to happen by virtue of the iron physical laws of attraction and repulsion; or to hold up a biological process the end of which could be foreseen from the beginning. All it needed was the optimal temperature conditions to bring it to maturity, and these were provided on a night that was just right for the purpose—the enchanted night of the Purim festival, the night of masquerade, in Avivi's house.

All was predestined, but freedom of choice was given—on such a night as this, a night of enchantment and delirium, when bands of imps and demons danced in the light of lanterns of coloured paper, blinded and intoxicated by some demonic force; when every one was at liberty to embrace, to make love, to make a sudden escape to the dewy garden, to the near-by avenue, to one of the dark corridors; a night when Titania could fondle an ass's head and hold it to her breast. I wore a satyr's head—a *lovely* satyr, as Hagit told me in my room while she was fastening the goat's horns to my forehead and the goat's hooves to my feet. ('You shall have Nili tonight, poor boy, see if she doesn't fall into your arms as soon as you arrive,' she prophesied with an understanding smile as she stood in front of me and carefully painted my eyebrows. 'She won't catch Eviatar, he's too clever, too careful.') But by the time that we entered it was almost midnight, and the crowd of fairies, gypsies, aristocrats, courtiers and clowns were already dizzy with drink and dance. I knew that a Walpurgis Night was in store, to be followed by a bitter awakening. Hagit was torn from my grasp as we appeared on the threshold and drawn into the dancing whirl. I pushed my way forward alone to seek my beloved. My eyes circled the room, looking for her among a hundred laughing, drunken, mocking, threatening masks, but I could not find her. Nakdimon, in the guise of a corpulent, moustachioed, befezzed Effendi, offered me his hand, bellowing in an Arab accent: 'Mister Davidov, how are you? What is the meaning of these two horns on your forehead? Are they horns of plenty or the horns of a dilemma? Or have you come to provide us with a scapegoat?' He was immediately followed by Gumpel, who came up to me crowned with an owl's head, complete with owl's eyes, and breathed into my face: 'Mephistopheles! the Day of Judgment is here, the people are ready for it! Beware, the twilight of the gods approaches.' Osnat, her black hair dishevelled, her gypsy skirts flying, leapt at me and hung herself round my neck with a kiss, crying, 'Satyr of mine! How wonderful you are! How sad you are! Will you come to my kitchen tonight?'—but immediately released me and went off to seek other prey. Where was Nili? Where was Nili? I asked, my gaze flitting over the heads of the dancers; until suddenly—hallelujah!—I caught sight of Rudi on the other side of the hall, dressed as a French marquis, with a silvery peruke on his head and a monocle in his eye, advancing with measured steps, bowing to everyone he met, courteously kissing the hands of the ladies. 'Rudi!' I hurried towards him. 'What nobility! And where's Nili?' But Rudi inspected me with a glassy, monocled eye and said sadly: 'Ah, Nili!

Elle est au ciel! Le bon Dieu l'en a prise!' and immediately passed on to make his bow to others. I looked for Eviatar, but it was Levia I met, in a black nun's habit and a white quoif, making her way through the crowd of masks carrying a trayful of sandwiches. When she saw me she recognized me and said anxiously: 'Have you seen Eviatar by any chance? He's flown off! Since the beginning of the evening.' A paso doble flared up and the whirling throng of nymphs and satyrs stamped their feet and hooves. Nili was not there, nor was Eviatar to be seen. Beside the bar stood Eliraz, in a very short skirt and with two skinny plaits tied with red ribbons; on seeing me he crooned with a lecherous smile: 'So the devil is athirst, and he wants to know the worst: Who's embracing who?…Have a drink!' He put a glass in my hand…and then there appeared before my eyes—like a ghost at a witches' feast—the shape of Ahuva.

I stood beside Eliraz, holding my glass, watching the dancers swirling in the thickening fog, trying to peel with my eyes the masks from the faces of the tall girls, watching and wondering. Someone bumped into me as he hit the table in his caperings and pushed me against the wall. The drink was spilt and I was thrown off balance. And then, as I straightened up—there she was! How? Where from? Why? The blood drained from my face. 'Suits you very well, this costume,' she said, looking up at me with a pallid smile. 'You…' I muttered. She was sitting on a low stool wearing a white silk dress, a gilt Queen Esther's crown on her head, a white handbag on her knees. By her side stood a young sailor, his arm round her shoulders. 'How?…Here!…' 'You see; we meet,' she said with a smile that came from far-off, melancholy days. The sailor had big, black, sad eyes, which turned on me an indifferent gaze. 'Let me introduce you'—a slight blush mitigating her pallor—'this is Jonas, this is Abi.' Abi did not smile or nod; his big eyes compared me with what he knew, with what he thought. 'Sit down,' said Ahuva, pulling over a stool. 'What's new?' I said, sitting down. 'Nothing special. What about you?' 'Just as usual.' 'Still living in the same room?' 'Yes, on the roof.' 'Abi is a sailor,' she smiled. 'It's not a costume,' 'Oh,' I said, 'in the navy?' 'Merchant navy,' Ahuva replied. 'Which ship?' I bent forward to talk to her companion. '*Akko*,' he replied briefly. 'Oh, *Akko*,' I said. 'You're on the West African line, I believe.' 'Europe,' replied Abi. 'Europe!' I said. 'So you're in harbour, on leave!' I tried to put some life into the conversation, asked about this and that, about merchant shipping, oceans, ports, sailors' pay (Ahuva shared my sufferings, seemed to be sorry for me), but Abi did not respond. Remained alien and indifferent, in other waters. The silence reared up like a wall. Where was Nili? Where was Eviatar? I was shackled to my seat, the fire in Ahuva's face scorched mine. 'What about your book?' she asked. 'So-so, getting on. Like to dance?' I asked. Ahuva rose, the sailor's hand slipping from her shoulder. We turned towards the swarming dancers, her handbag still over her arm. 'Your handbag,' I said. 'Oh yes,' she blushed, going back and placing it on the sailor's knees. It was a honeyed tango they were playing. Her waist was soft, her feet inexpert. 'Friend of yours?' I asked. 'We meet,' she said. 'Very young,' I said. 'Not so very. Twenty-seven.' 'Terribly serious.' 'Taciturn.' Her body was unfamiliar and our steps did not fit. 'You've learned to dance,' she said. 'With difficulty.' 'I saw you once in the street,' she said. 'I passed you. You didn't see me, apparently.' 'Why didn't you stop and say hello?' 'You were in a hurry, I didn't want to hold you up. Black shirts suit you very well.' Once she dreamed of me, she said. She dreamed that I was carrying a sack full of stones along a street that was being torn up by pneumatic drills. A dog was chasing me and she ran to catch me up and warn me, but awoke with a cry. 'A strange dream,' I said. 'I dream a lot,' she said with a smile. 'Still in the same flat?' I asked. 'Yes,' she said. 'Same job?' 'Yes,' she said. There was a new headmistress in the kindergarten. At the spring vacation she would visit her sister in Galilee. In the evenings she was reading Agnon's *Yesteryear*. 'How's your father?' I asked. 'Sick,' she sighed. 'Sick?' I said anxiously. 'What's wrong with him?'

A long arm in a black glove waved at me out of the forest of dancers. At me? It waved at me again, with twitching fingers, as if trying to catch my glance. Yes, Nili! The blood flooded through my body, so powerfully that I felt it might spurt on to Ahuva's snow-white dress. In Eviatar's arms. A black, broad-brimmed hat on her head, with a crimson feather like a plume of fire waving over it. She moved farther off, was swallowed up, and later, when our circles crossed again, scorched my shoulder with her fingers, and cried joyfully: 'Jonas!' and continued to revolve in her orbit. 'Who is that?' asked Ahuva, and the music stopped.

I escorted Ahuva back to the sailor. A white bride to her safe haven. I meant to anchor there until the storm in my heart abated, but suddenly the firebird pounced on me, put her arm round my neck and cried, laughing: 'Jonas! A satyr! And that burning moustache!' My head reeled. 'Let me introduce you,' I said, 'Nili, Ahuva.' Nili made a deep curtsy, her black hand describing a broad arc in the air. Ahuva stood before her like a melancholy dove, a smile quivering on her lips. Then she sank down by the side of the silent sailor.

Shall I describe Nili's beauty? She was naked. No, she was dressed. The whole of her slender body—her long thighs, her hips, her waist, her breasts up to the bare shoulders—was encased in a sheath of black net, conforming to every contour, every curve, revealing secrets and covering more, and through it gleamed a green fig-leaf and another two. The black hat shaded her face and the black gloves accentuated the whiteness of her arms. The curtains of hair flowed, honey-coloured, over her white shoulders, and her eyes glowed and glittered. She was demonic. She was angelic. She was happy.

She was so happy that when the band started to blare out the samba she gripped me by the hand and pulled me into the riotous maelstrom, and I whirled round and round for I don't know how long. My arms lifted her into the air like a wheatsheaf at the harvest festival celebrations, guided her pirouettes, held her in the gallop. Through the vertiginous eddies I caught sight from time to time of Ahuva's white face, watching us as if through watery veils, the big sailor's eyes scrutinizing from a distance, Hagit chattering with Eliraz, her smile approving of my gyrations, Rudi pacing along by the walls making courteous bows, Levia, alarmed, flitting about, seeking; again Ahuva, the sailor, Hagit, Rudi kissing a lady's hand...And when the music flared up, driving the revellers on like leaves in the wind, and sparks flew through the air, Nili was as frenzied as a hell-cat. She twisted and twirled, waved her hands in front of my face in magical incantations. Her eyes sent snakes wriggling round my neck.

'Oh, I don't know what's come over me tonight; I don't know

what's come over me…' she breathed when the music stopped, falling on my neck, enflamed, panting, perspiring. Her head rested on my shoulder, her eyes closed. Suddenly she roused herself with a quick movement, shook back her hair, and turned away. Tall and slender, swaying like a somnambulist, she floated on through the tumultuous hall, farther and farther, until she disappeared into the cavern of the corridor. In another direction I saw Eviatar—in his everyday clothes, narrow trousers, grey shirt and sandals—perplexed, hesitant, lost in thought, then winding his way between the waves of the masquerade and following into the corridor, like the rope after the bucket.

And I saw her no more.

How much did I drink? Four glasses, eight? A score? With my glass of poison I wandered about—among couples and solitaries, among the exultant and the abandoned, flirting or melancholy—seeking her whom my heart desired. I wandered into the kitchen and looked for her among the revellers crowding round the fleshpots, but did not find her. I strayed through the rooms, seeking her among piles of clothes and retiring couples, but did not find her. I climbed the stairs like a bold mountaineer, searching amid the whispers and rustlings on darkened balconies. I butted with my head at the door of a room, entered and fumbled in the dark. Something glittered in the dusk on the bed. Nili? Oh, no, it was Levia, flat on her back in her black nun's habit. 'Who's that?' her voice croaked in the darkness. I came closer and put my hand on her cheek. 'Get out! Get out!' she screeched, and my hand was wet with her tears. 'Sorry, sorry…' I mumbled as I went out, closing the door on her. The lights of the city glimmered before my eyes like a revolving zodiac wheel. I crouched beside the banisters and closed my eyes. Did I fall asleep? How much time passed? A long time, apparently, for when I came down to the hall again it was like a battlefield after the fighting.

> The banquet is over and spirits go forth
> To clean up the empty hall.

Scraps of lingering melodies still echoed amid torn paper-chains. Splinters of smashed glasses lay scattered on the floor. Chairs and stools were heaped up topsy-turvy. A few isolated revellers wandered like ghosts seeking lost souls, and drunken figures embraced in the corners of the hall. Someone came up to me dripping spittle like a mad dog, and charged forward bellowing: 'Davidov!' I pushed him away, knocking him down. As he got up to seize me by the throat, I thrust my horn into his belly. We rolled over together on the dusty floor and someone—Avivi?—dragged me outside. I had a glimpse of the Marquis Rudi getting into his car alone, starting it up and moving off. 'Freudenthal!' I shouted. 'Rudi von Freudenthal!' But he hurtled off like a whirlwind into the darkness, far from my fading voice. The tones of 'I love you, I love you to eter-ni-ty' from a solitary singer accompanied me out of the empty hall.

When I awoke I found myself lying on the seashore. The day was cloudy and the sand damp. I felt cold and shivery. Through my glassy eyes I saw an old woman standing above me doing physical exercises. There was a network of blue sinews on her legs, her belly was distended, the empty bags of her breasts drooped when she bent down and flattened when she straightened up. Her flesh was withered, sandy yellow, and my head was heavy. I tried to remember how I had got there. Rudi had driven off alone. Where had Nili been? And Eviatar? I remembered that I had dragged myself along, solitary, in the night streets—car headlamps forcing me every now and then on to the pavement. The streets were long and silent; they grew paler as the dead houses were wrapped in the winding-sheets of the dawn. I remember how I went into some bar, abandoned by its band and its customers, sat down at the counter and demanded drink, and how some burly ruffian had taken hold of me and thrown me out. Why had he thrown me out? Had I tried to use force? Or had I perhaps drunk my liquor and not paid? I fumbled in my pockets, took out my purse, and found it empty. The old woman bent and straightened, stretched her wrinkled arms sideways and forward, her legs trembled. Then she went down to the sea, dipped her feet, rubbed her thighs, stood in the shallow water, and sprinkled water on her belly. The sea was at the ebb and the edges of the low waves licked the soles of my shoes. A crab passed at a clumsy run by my side. Where had Nili disappeared to? Night, night, pagan night!

Chapter twenty

W ho can recount all the exploits of Abraham Davidov? In 1938 he took part in the pioneering ascent to Hanita and in the same year he helped to erect the Tegart Wall along the northern border; in the summer of 1939 he was with the builders of the stockade and watchtower settlements, in the Beisan valley and on the white sands facing the palms and minarets of beautiful Acre; in 1941 he planned to break into the detention camp for immigrants at Atlit, and in 1942 and 1943 he roamed around the training camps of the Palmach commandos.

> *The winds of the desert knew him,*
> *His face was burnt by the summer sun,*

But I had no heart for Davidov in those days; I brooded in the Cellar, or in my garret room.

What had happened that night which so completely transformed Nili?

In the evenings she used to come to the Cellar—alone, no longer with Rudi; close to midnight she would rise hastily, say goodbye with a smile that concealed pain or humiliation, go out into the street, and wave her hand: 'Taxi! Taxi!'—alone; and between coming in and leaving again she would say little, drink less, and laugh seldom; only a word or two would pass now and then between her and Eviatar—like wounded birds stricken in mid-flight. She would sit silent, listening to the talk with her chin resting on her hand, sometimes lowering her eyes and sinking into a reverie—perhaps plotting something, at times raising her eyes, with smiling lips and bitterness in her look. She used to sit by me, no longer beside Eviatar, and when he spoke she would turn to me or to someone else, as if hiding or taking cover, and when Levia's flow of words flooded the table a spark of hatred would light up in her eyes; but hatred was becoming to her. Nili was beautiful when she hated.

Many things, pregnant with fate, intoxicating the blood, had happened that night, during those lost hours between midnight and the dawn when I lay prostrate in my drunken limbo: it was not only Nili who had changed, but Eviatar, and Levia as well. Eviatar had become more taciturn, more hesitant than ever; when he spoke he would hold back to the point of stammering; suddenly he would burst into a rage against someone or other for no apparent reason; suddenly—no one knew why—he would shower compliments on someone to whom he was not in the habit of paying them. And Levia had gone all cantankerous and prickly, had become more aggressive, more possessive than ever: what she had she would hold. She treated Nili as a woman of the streets, ostracized her with her look, with her silence, with the way she ignored her as if she did not exist.

I myself...

I grew a beard. That is to say, it grew by itself—first by neglect and then by design. It started as a matter of slovenliness, a kind of dejected indolence and incapacity to do anything, even to shave in the morning. I would lie for hours in the warm room, as in an oven, playing with torn and tattered fantasies, about Nili, about Eviatar, about things that had happened the previous night. Suddenly I would have a twinge of compunction about Davidov; the debt I had not paid would fill my mind like a thick cloud—the debt which accumulated day by day, which I would never get rid of. I would rouse myself all of a sudden, leave the bed unmade, go down to the beach, swim out as far as possible from the shore—if only I could sail out into the distance, as far as Tarshish!—then return to the shore, my hair wet, collapse on my bed, doze and dream, doze and dream…Little by little my cheeks, which had grown lean and hollow, were covered with a tender, light yellow down, an uneven growth like an untended field, close in one place and sparse in another. Then I saw that it was good and began to cultivate it—pruning the foliage, combing, straightening, refining, until it became handsome and dignified, smooth and round like a well-made haystack. Girls would look at me as they passed. Yes, a fine beard has certain advantages for a young man like myself—only at that time (between the Hanita chapter and the Atlit chapter by the chronology of Davidov) I had no mind for such things. The beard was more a sign of mourning than a work of art.

What a stratagem it was they wove—consciously against Levia and unconsciously against me; how well they marked it with silences, with modest lowered glances, with heart-breaking, self-controlled suffering! I found them out one afternoon. A circus had come to town and I went to watch with old and young. Here, as sometimes in the sea, I embarked on a long voyage to other worlds: to the heights of space with the breathtaking flights of the trapeze artists, to the Indian jungles with the great, heavy-eared and delicate-stepping elephants, to the countries of the north with the dancing of the ice-skaters, to Spain with the tempestuous melodies, the stamping feet and the swinging skirts, to Hungary, China, Morocco…Then three leopards leapt like fiery flames into the arena, and the trainer, an Amazon with a whip, a proud, long-haired tyrant, subdued their savage strength with the blink of an eyelash, a slight movement of the shoulder, quiet and masterful. With a crack of the whip on the floor, a lightning flash, the leopards, light and lissom, curvetted in their places, and at the second crack—at the second crack a laugh struck my ears like a whiplash, so clear, so exultant, brief and bell-like…Three steps below in front of me the two of them were sitting, his arm embracing her shoulder and her head close to his, her honey-coloured hair cascading over his arm. The leopards, the trainer, the rope-ladders, the clowns and conjurers and acrobats—everything dissolved in a mist. I could not take my eyes away from the backs of their necks, their heads; every movement they made was indelibly engraved on my heart. Now his arm slid to her neck and clasped it; now she whispered something in his ear and laughed again; now she straightened up for a moment and both of them tensed, watching the ring; now (the lions bounded into the arena and fiery rings were set up to face them) she gripped his hand as if in deadly fear; now she pressed herself against him and, as if no one saw or heeded or cared, pressed her lips to his bearded cheek...How Nili had ignored Eviatar night after night, how Eviatar had ignored Nili in the Cellar!

O that the reader may never know such jealous torments as I suffered in the days that followed, when at every street corner it seemed at any moment as if they would appear before my eyes clasped in each other's arms, and when my imagination sought out their hiding places; or in the evenings that followed, when I sat so close to Nili (as she suffered in silence), gratuitous guardian of their secret and consumed by it! I will pass over these jealousies and tell about that night when I swooped like a bird to the trap and enjoyed, as it were, an undeserved victory.

We were sitting in the Cellar, the whole gang, celebrating the appearance of the first issue of *Exclamation Mark!*...

Chapter twenty-one

I had to stop yesterday evening. First the sound of voices came from below—a cry, a blow, curses in Arabic. Then immediately afterwards Mrs Silber came running, startled, breathing heavily: 'Something terrible will happen there…Something's got to be done…Call the police…They'll murder her…' I ran downstairs after her, and when we reached the entrance two young men emerged from the door of Arditi the watchmaker's flat. Like sinister emissaries who had carried out their mission they hurried outside, climbed into a van that stood by the pavement, started up and drove off with a roar that sent the echoes flying from one end of the street to the other. Mr Arditi stood in the doorway like a half-drowned man pulled out of the water and mumbled with pale lips: 'To kidnap her?…By force?…' 'What's wrong?' cried Mrs Silber. 'That's your son, isn't it, that big fellow?' 'I have no son,' whispered Mr Arditi with misty eyes. 'If he comes again, I won't open the door. I'll call the police. May God forgive him, to do a thing like that to his sister! She nearly died.' He pointed to his daughter, who was lying on the couch with a damp cloth on her forehead. We went in, and from the mutterings and mumblings of the old woman who was sitting in the corner, wrapped in a black shawl, moaning and shaking her head without a stop, we understood what had happened: Yonina's brother, a labour-exchange clerk in Ramleh, had betrothed her after lengthy negotiations to one of his friends who owned a vegetable stall in his town. Yonina had changed her mind and did not want to complete the match. Now both of them had come to force her to carry out her promise. The brother, in a temper, had slapped her face, run amok, overturned chairs, smashed a flower-pot on the floor. As they left, they had threatened that they would come again and carry her off by force to her fiancé's house. 'They won't get her by force,' said Arditi. 'All the time I tried to persuade Yonina to marry him. No more. It's all over.' And the old woman, Yonina's grandmother, nodded assent: 'She's training to be a secretary and she'll find a husband. A better one.' 'I'm not worried,' added Arditi. The refinement of previous, better times still glowed from his sallow face, from his bald forehead whose nakedness was covered by a few strands of smooth, greying hair, from his long and delicate watchmaker's fingers.

Yonina limps, and her weak smile seems to be apologizing for her disability. I meet her once or twice a day. Her dress is sometimes dotted with blue stars and sometimes with red, but it is always shiningly clean. Her defect has not distorted her face as often happens, and apart from a little round blemish on her right cheek, the mark of an old scar, her face is smooth and open like a girl of ten's. Once she stumbled over the scraper at the entry to the yard, when she was carrying a basket of groceries with a big water-melon in it. The water-melon rolled to my feet and I put it back in the basket and helped her to carry it to her door. I asked her: 'Where do you come from?' and she replied: 'From Morocco,' and laughed lightly as if it was a joke. Since then she feels grateful to me and greets me every time with her warm eyes. That little coin-shaped blemish always attracts my eye, as if it were an ancient amulet inscribed with secret writing, and her limp seems to add to her charm. 'They won't do it by force,' I said to Arditi. 'We'll help you. All of us.' Yonina raised her head from the pillow and looked up at me sadly. Her left leg was withered.

Yes, we were celebrating the appearance of the first number of

Exclamation Mark! We passed it from hand to hand, admiring the
format, the cover, which bore a large exclamation mark culminating
in a shining drop of blood, the gleaming letters, the smell of fresh
printer's ink. Osnat put it close to her face, sniffed at it as at a baby
in its swaddling clothes, breathed in the smell—'Ah, lovely!'—and
respectfully turned over the first page. The title-page carried in large
letters a kind of manifesto called 'Thirteen Principles of a Non-credo!';
on the following pages there were poems by Eviatar and Avner, a
large essay by Gumpel on Nakdimon's poetry, a chapter of a story by
Saul Nunn, and so forth. On the two last pages there was an article
of mine—in small type—on 'Cycle of Nature in Gnessin's Stories,'
which I had written for my own benefit a few years before as a kind
of reader's notebook and had prepared for the press for this issue. The
magazine passed from hand to hand and when it reached Nili, who
was sitting by me, she kept it in her hand. Page four was crowned
by the title of Eviatar's poems: 'Three *Kerovot* for the Barber's Wife'.
'What are *Kerovot*?' Nili whispered. When I had explained to her
that these are a certain type of festival hymn, she looked down at the
page again, resting her chin on her hand, and immersed herself in
the poems as if she were alone in the room and wanted to decipher
their secret. When I tried to turn the page she put the magazine on
her knees, her face flushed. She touched my arm and put her finger
on the word 'roquelaure' in a line which read:

'Barber's blade at the midnight hour,
And he in his roquelaure.'

'What is "roquelaure"?' she whispered. I shrugged my shoulders. I
wanted to snatch the magazine out of her hand and to throw it away.
At that moment I heard Levia's voice, reeking with resentment and
hate: 'How long are you going to hang on to it? There are other people.'
Nili looked up at her, startled, as if aroused from a dream by a shock.
Then she held out the magazine to her across the table with both
hands and said with a malicious laugh: 'Take it. I didn't want to rob
you of it.' 'Thanks,' darted Levia venomously, taking the magazine.
Eviatar, as if trying to extinguish the conflagration before it flared up,

put his arm round Levia's shoulders and whispered something to her with a soothing smile. Nili lowered her eyes. Nakdimon, who was sitting near us and had not failed to observe the comedy, filled Levia's glass, then Eviatar's, Nili's and mine and started to declaim in praise of Avner's 'Two Poems of Despair'. 'I always wonder', he said in his oily voice, 'how a fellow like Avner can produce such wise songs. You look at him—a stupid face. You talk to him—he has nothing to say. Or when he does say something, you simply blush for him—such banalities. But the poems…'

Levia was engrossed in the magazine, which was lying on her knees. She seemed to be trying to decipher the riddle of the 'Three *Kerovot* for the Barber's Wife'. Now it was her face that was flushed. Nili swallowed down her drink and whispered to me: 'Ask her why she's keeping the magazine so long. There are other people…' 'A question worthy of consideration, the question of the birthrate,' said Nakdimon, pouring out another glass. 'Here we have four married couples amongst us who are not fruitful, neither do they multiply. Poetry has no obligations to society, as Gumpel has written. But the poet! This is flagrant irresponsibility, gentlemen. The state needs manpower! Healthy, exultant cadets, officers for the Defence Forces, shrewd and talented officials! Only think of the security situation…' Levia shut the magazine and threw it on the table. For a moment she sat looking in front of her, a stratagem visibly taking shape, then she said to Eviatar: 'Come, let's go.' 'Why, Levia?' said Eviatar putting his hand on her shoulder, 'it's not late yet.' 'You can stay. I'm going anyway,' she said, taking her handbag and rising. 'Let's stay a little longer,' said Eviatar, gripping her hand entreatingly, but she pulled it away and started pushing her way out. Eviatar got up and followed in her wake. 'Going to do your duty?' cried Nakdimon after them. Nili poured out another glass.

Midnight came—the hour for Cinderella's hasty departure—but Nili did not get up. She sat in her place, the mist of her thoughts setting up a barrier between her and the surrounding chatter, witticisms, talk and laughter. From time to time she poured out another drink and sipped a little, still dreaming perhaps, of a deadly fleece of gold. 'You're going too far,' I whispered to her when I saw her pouring out again. She shrugged her shoulders and went on drinking. Slowly, a kind of strange smile came to rest on her face, an angel's kiss from another world. How beautiful she was, like a somnambulist, her lips slightly parted! Everyone else got up and left—it was two o'clock already—but she remained seated, enveloped in cigarette smoke and the fumes of her liquor. 'Going?' I asked. She did not reply, but threw the lighted cigarette into the ashtray, and her head sank on her arms.' 'What's wrong with her?' asked the waiter who was clearing the tables. 'Tired out,' I said. 'Have you a handkerchief?' she asked without raising her head from the table. I took out mine from my pocket and gave it to her. After she had wiped her eyes she raised her wet face and stared in front of her. There was no one else in the Cellar, it was deserted like 'a hump-backed, weary night'. Suddenly she said: 'I hate her, Jonas. Oh, how I hate her! I pray that someone should help me to stop hating her.' Then, after putting my handkerchief in her bag: 'And him too. You don't know him, Jonas.' And then she spoke, spoke without restraint: Eviatar was fickle, cowardly, a weakling. He lived on lies, surrounded himself with lies, tied himself up in them. Once she had told him so, and he had replied that he left all the truth for his poems. But no, even in them he only expressed half-truths, for he had no courage, and a poet who was not courageous and relentless to himself would never go very deep. He was so afraid to take any risks! He was so afraid to be seen with her! Once when they were walking in the street they had seen me from a distance, and he had immediately pulled her into a comer. 'I took him by the hand and said to him: "What are you ashamed of? Jonas is my friend and yours; and what does he care? And what do you care?" No, he insisted...All these evasions, these stealthy meetings, this hide-and-seek, they're killing me, driving me crazy!' And why did he live with Levia when he did not love her? How was it possible to live a life of continual deceit? How could he bear this face-to-face contact, day and night, with such vulgarity, such complete mediocrity, and a face like that, like a sick hen's? How could he help feeling disgusted with himself? He was just surrendering to tyranny, giving in to compulsion, terrified for his skin. 'Surely poetry itself is an adventure—how can a real poet be afraid of adventure? Once I told him how indecisive he was, and then he quoted me some lines of Eliot, "There will be a time, there will be a time...to murder and create ...Time for you and time for me, And time yet for a hundred indecisions." Later, at home, I read the poem, and wanted to say to him, like the woman who puts her head on the pillow: "That is not it at all. That is not what I meant at all." But in any case he wouldn't have understood. A faithless type. Unfaithful to his wife, unfaithful to me, and unfaithful to himself with both of us.' The waiter came up to us and said apologetically that it was time to lock up. We went out into the street. I said to her: 'How will you get back now? Shall I get you a taxi?' She stood for a long moment facing the darkness, then she said: 'I'll stay with you tonight. If you don't mind. You can spread a blanket on the floor for me to sleep on. Anyway, it's all over.'

When we got into my room she fell on the bed and mumbled: 'My head's spinning round and round.' She covered her face with her hands to shut out the light and cried, as if in pain: 'Put it out! I can't bear it.' Later, in the dark, she said quietly: 'Come, come.'

That modest, monastic room of the lonely sculptor Polishuk! The sounds its listening walls had heard in the darkness! The sights they had been startled to see in the pale morning light! Disasters, historians say, repeat themselves, but never in exactly the same form. So it was in my room. Again it was late morning. Nili was sitting on the bed, leaning on the wall, smoking and dropping the ash into the ashtray she held in her hand. I was on the chair, facing her, afraid to know, afraid to understand what had happened, what was in store, who I had been for her, who I would yet be for her. Again, as last night, she talked and talked; the words poured out as if of their own accord. She would not go home again. Everything was destroyed, destroyed. She was only sorry about the boy, what could she do with him? She couldn't send him to her mother, a woman as selfish as herself who was living with some rich manufacturer. The fifth or sixth liaison since she had separated from Nili's father. When she was only eight her mother had betrayed her father with a certain engineer who had been his best friend even in his Russian days. She remembered it well. She had always wanted to be beautiful and proud like her mother, and here was another version of the same story. Heredity, she supposed. But that was just why her mother would not forgive her, she would send her away. And she had no illusions about Eviatar. He would never take a final decision. Perhaps he loved her and perhaps he didn't, but actually he loved himself more than anything else. But she could not go back. She would get work as a commercial artist, in the same office where she had been employed before by one of her poor father's friends who was now living in Haifa. She would rent a room and keep the child with her. It would not be easy, but she could no longer bear to live in that academic, bourgeois, boring suburb, with those stale conversations with the neighbours' wives, those petty intrigues over rank and position, those parties, sometimes in one house and then in another, made up of nothing but feminine chatter and flirtations by mutual consent to mitigate the boredom...'You don't know what it's like, Jonas, you can't imagine what a wretched life it is.'

There was the sound of steps coming up the stairs. Nili fell silent, crushed out her cigarette stub, and said calmly: 'It's Rudi.' I was panic-stricken, just like that other time with Ahuva. 'What'll we do?' I whispered. 'I thought he'd come,' she said. She raised her head and closed her eyes, as if prepared to accept judgment. A ray of sunlight gilded her long, soft hair. There was a knock on the door. 'Shall I open?' I whispered. 'Open it,' she replied, shrugging her shoulders. I got up and opened the door. Rudi was pale, dishevelled, unshaven. 'Forgive me for disturbing you,' he said on the threshold in a parched voice. 'Come in,' I said. He came in and sat on the chair. His suit was crumpled and his shirt-collar unfastened, as if he had got up in a hurry. He scrutinized Nili's face for a moment and said in a hard, dry voice: 'Look, Nili, I don't care what you do with yourself, you know that, but you can't leave me to look after the child. At nine I should have been in the laboratory. Now it's half past ten. It's not my job to dress him, give him his breakfast and take him to the kindergarten. I think you understand that.' Rudi stopped, waiting for an answer. Nili fumbled on the bed, found the cigarette packet, took out a cigarette, lit it and blew a long jet of smoke in the direction of the window. 'What do you want me to do?' she said quietly. The atmosphere was tense, quivering. The calm morning light filled the room, but it was saturated with the tremors of the previous night and Rudi's repressed tremors now. It was very sad, as if the end was near. 'I told you,' he said; 'I don't care where you spend your time and who you spend it with. You can sleep wherever you like. I want you to be home at seven. I don't have to listen to him crying "Mummy, Mummy" and tie up his laces. I haven't the time for it. I've got my work to do, you understand? And the same in the afternoon, and in the evening. You have certain duties.' Nili dropped ash on the ashtray in her palm and said nothing. Her silence lasted for what seemed to me a very long time. For some reason I found myself sharing Rudi's resentment. At last she raised her face and said: 'How did you know I was here?' Rudi's voice began to show his anger. 'It's been going on for over two months, this affair.' He flushed. 'I didn't ask you where you were going every day and what you were doing after midnight. So long as you looked after him at least. But now you've gone too far, Nili, and there's a limit even to my patience. If you want…if you want to finish it—all right. But this is not the way to finish. There are several things to be decided. You know how it's done. You can't live in the house and neglect everything at the same time. I make a fool of myself feeding him, looking after him. I'm losing time and money, it's getting on my nerves. I don't have to go into town in the morning to look for you in the cafes instead of being at my work…or to drive about in the streets…and pay fines on top of it all.' He pulled out a crumpled slip of paper from his jacket pocket and put it on the table. 'It can't go on like this, Nili.' There was a mocking little smile on Nili's lips as she looked at the slip of paper on the table. I stood by the door like a sentry, an unwilling spectator, an unwanted witness, a stranger in my own room, strange to myself. Rudi rose, fumbled with the keys in his pocket and said: 'I want you to be home at three to collect Rami from the kindergarten. If you want to come now, all right.' Nili went on smoking and did not stir. For a moment Rudi waited for a reply, then he turned to the door, saying as he passed me: 'Sorry to disturb you,' and went out. I went up to the table and straightened the crumpled slip that had been left on it. He would have to pay a fine according to Article Five, Parking in a Forbidden Place. Nili covered her face with her hands and said:

'I'm awful, Jonas, I'm absolutely awful.' I stuck the slip in my pocket.
'You've got to go,' I said. 'I'm a disgusting character, Jonas,' she went
on, with a sinful look on her face. 'And you know why? Because I
found the whole business funny, terribly funny. I could hardly help
bursting out laughing. Even now. As if it had nothing to do…as if
I was watching some play…so unreal…a kind of nightmarish joke.'
Then she looked straight at me and said: 'Actually, it's all your fault.
If you hadn't come then, that night…'

Chapter twenty-two

Today, the fourteenth of the Hebrew month of Kislev, is the fourth anniversary of my mother's death, and I dedicate the following lines to her memory. The reader can skip them; he will miss nothing of the story. I paid a visit to the cemetery and stood by her tombstone, but, however much I tried to concentrate my thoughts on her, I did not succeed. Various things distracted me. First my attention wandered to the inscription on the near-by stones; then an idea came into my mind for an amusing story about a rich man who bought a graveyard plot for himself and his wife, built a fine mausoleum, with a dome and an iron gate, and, after his wife died and was buried there, married again. His second wife made him swear that he would not sleep with the first one when he was dead, and when she died too he couldn't decide which of them he would sleep with. As I was turning this story over in my mind I remembered the Davidov book which I had not written, and the impending trial—my debt in money and my debt to the dead. Then some Sephardic funeral procession arrived in the row where I was standing and my attention was caught by a beautiful girl in a green silk headscarf, who was standing close to me, weeping bitterly into her handkerchief. She was dripping with cheap scent, which always stimulates in me some kind of desire. When she stopped weeping, I asked her who the deceased was. 'A fine man,' she replied, the tears sparkling in her eyes, 'a fine man.' 'What was his name?' I inquired. 'Moshe. Moshe Abulafia. Killed. Road accident. Terrible. So young. Only a month ago he bought a new taxi.' I stood and mourned for Abulafia and when the grave was closed I walked by her side to the cemetery gate. On my way home I was gnawed by compunction. There was no reverence in me. Thirty years of her life my mother, may she rest in peace, had devoted to me. No one had been closer to her than I. And yet, even when I stood by her grave once a year, even then I did not cherish her memory.

My mother Gita, née Yudelevitch, was a humble woman, acquainted with grief. Only a few years after she and my father had left Kfar Giladi she lost the glow of her beauty as a pioneer girl; she was absorbed in household cares and, after my father's death, in mourning. She no longer mentioned those far-off days. She had a little kiosk at the street corner containing two jars of syrup, one red and one green, some bagels, some sweets, and a host of wasps which buzzed about in the midday hours and eagerly sucked the syrupy taps. The urchins of the neighbourhood, who crowded noisily around the counter in school breaks, or in the early evening, used to get on her nerves. She used to shoo them away like flies from the jam, but they would stand their ground. They bought on credit; she never knew which of them had paid and which hadn't. Until eight or nine in the evening she remained at her post, and I remember how the sooty, smoky hurricane lamp which hung on a long iron hook above the counter would shed a reddish light on her careworn face. I was ashamed of her and her livelihood, before the children and myself, and I would keep away from the kiosk, to avoid being seen in its vicinity or in hers, as if to deny any connection between us. Every day I used to ask myself, bitterly, resentfully, why this kiosk had to stand so close to the school. In the evening, when she served me a modest meal—omelette and salad, salad and yoghurt—I would maintain a stubborn, mutinous silence, which none of her questions—What did the teacher say? How did you get on in the exam? Is your throat still sore?—could induce me to break. I never gratified her with good news, either when I got high marks or when I was praised for my compositions. When we studied Bialik's 'My Song' I saw my mother in that character of his who 'wasted her marrow and blood in the market'—but, unlike him, I felt no pity for her. On the other hand, I used to dream that one day I would be a great writer like his mother's son. Everything I was holding back from her—and storing up for myself—I would unload on paper in beautiful writing.

On Sabbath eves we sat together in silence at a table covered with a white cloth, in the same low, limewashed room, with melancholy shadows flickering on the walls. I can still feel the bitter taste of the honey spread on a slice of the soft Sabbath *halla* which I stuffed down my tear-choked throat. I used to yearn at such times for my dead father, whom I had known only from a few photographs and my mother's fragmentary tales. My father, Saul Rabinowitch, was a very tall man, with long legs, a bony head and very thick eyebrows. Although I was only four when he died, I still seem to remember his thick, warm voice, his moist cough, his deep laughter, to feel his big hands tickling my armpits and his half-bald head nuzzling my belly. My father died a peculiar death. He had a set of false teeth, which he used to leave in a glass every evening before he went to bed. Once he forgot to take his teeth out, swallowed them in his sleep, and choked to death. He bequeathed to us a wooden box containing a large wrench, a pair of pliers, two hammers and a rusty sign—'plumber: all kinds of repairs reliably executed'—which remained hanging at the yard gate for a few years after he was gone. In the rickety bookcase there were still a few Russian books which he had brought with him from the Ukraine, and whenever I recalled his memory I would open them and leaf through them: a large volume of Shakespeare printed on parchment paper, with fine etchings of Romeo and Juliet, Othello kneeling before Desdemona, the beautiful Ophelia floating on the water amid the willows; a large volume of Pushkin, with ink drawings of the delicate, sad-eyed Tatiana, of Onegin in the duel with Lensky, of Boris Godunov on horseback, girt with his sword, in front of some Tartar fortress; a volume of Faust, showing Mephistopheles with his spiky beard and twisted legs; a few Hebrew books, published by the well-known firm of Tushia.

I loved my dead father and boasted of him to my friends—that he had been a hero in Kamenetz-Podolsk, where he had killed two Cossacks; that he had been a member of Kfar Giladi and defended Tel Hai together with Trumpeldor; and here too, in town, he had been in command of a Haganah company…What had it been like in Kfar Giladi when my parents lived there? Very often I would weave fantasies about this kibbutz of Kfar Giladi, an eagle's nest on a pinnacle of rock, a precious little plot in my dreams, protected by watchmen dressed in Arab-style *abbayas*. What had my father done there? Why had he left and gone down to the city? Had he really been among the defenders of Tel Hai?…I remember how one evening two burly, heavy-moustached men, in old army coats and heavy boots, came to our house and talked to my mother for a very long time until I fell asleep, and in the morning she told me that these had been friends of my father's from Kfar Giladi. Later, people would sometimes say: Ah, Rabinowitch's son, from Kfar Giladi…Yes, my father was a hero in my imagination, and years later, in the immature stories I wrote, I tried to make him live again in some of my characters, but without success. His figure came out faulty and ridiculous; against my will he seemed to ridicule me; inadvertently I used to scoff at him.

Against my mother I felt an obscure resentment, and I was ashamed of her. When I was at high school she was summoned one day after I had been punished for some trick I had played on a wretched science teacher, and when I saw her in the distance I fled and hid in the lavatory in the yard for about an hour. Afterwards, when my friends told me: 'Your mother was looking for you,' I said: 'Impossible. What did she look like?' And when they described her I told them that she was not my mother but a relative who had come from Poland. To this day I do not know how she succeeded in keeping me at high school for four years with the coppers she earned by her wretched peddling. But the more she gave me, the more she showered her love on me, supplied all my wants and praised me to my face, as well as to the neighbours and my friends who came to see me—the more I denied her. I could not stand anything about her—her talk, her silences, her sad, soft voice, her infinite patience, her inaudible groans as she lay in bed on the other side of the partition, her thoughts which I could hear as she lay awake, her nightmares which I could see, her care for me, her care, her care…Had I no pangs of conscience? Yes, but these usually came when I was far away, when I no longer lived with her; and even then I would defer the payment of my debt to the distant future when I would be great and famous, and then I would build her a castle on a mountain peak, as far away from me as possible, where she would know neither want nor care and spend the rest of her days in tranquillity. When I joined the kibbutz I did so, not so much for its own sake, I believe, as to get away from her or to defy her, because she used to cherish the thought that I was going to study at the university. With fanatical fervour I rejected her entreaties. 'University?' I cried indignantly—'When the British are confiscating arms at Hulda! Besieging Ramat-Hakovesh! What would Dad have said about it?' The mention of my father was enough to make her lower her eyes in silence.

One Sabbath—a black Saturday it was—she came to visit me in the kibbutz. I had to sit by her side at the table in the dining-hall for four entire meals. To escort her into the kitchen because she had a notion to see it. To show her the poultry-run, the cowshed, the banana plantations, the clothing store! To linger with her beside friends I met on the paths, with whom she entered into conversation. The Sabbath morning was already lost, and for the afternoon, knowing that if she stayed all day I would also lose my Sabbath siesta (one of my consolations for the life of toil to which my natural laziness was never reconciled), I ran about all over the kibbutz to see if there was anyone driving to Tel Aviv. Yes, there was someone; and with the argument of economy I persuaded her to go with him. Thus I spoiled for her what she had dreamed of as a pleasant day, and I remember how she parted from me sadly, with a heavy heart, with moist eyes, her hand waving to me out of the window of the truck.

Later, in the army…was it because of the fear of death that my heart was softened towards her? I believe that those were the only happy days she knew with me, though she spent sleepless nights worrying about my fate. I used to come home for brief, hasty leaves from the outposts in the Negev, and I would talk to her as I had never done before, tell her about the fighting, encourage her, comfort her, kiss her on my arrival and my departure. 'Jonas,' she would mutter, holding on to my hand as if afraid that death would snatch me away. 'I know, mother, I know,' I would say, kissing her on the forehead. 'And write a lot, don't be mean.' I used to write a lot and not be mean.

But later, when I was studying at the university, it was the same all over again. In Jerusalem I had Rita, Shula, Naomi, and I had to put my mother out of my mind so that I should be able to sleep in peace. And yet she would appear in my dreams—always more beautiful than she really was, always splendidly dressed. Once I saw her at a ball in the Russian Czar's palace, bracelets at her wrists and a white silk dress trailing at her heels, leaning on the arm of a moustachioed officer. When she saw me she said, blushing: 'Allow me to introduce you, this is your father.' 'My father is dead,' I said with a shudder, 'my father is dead.' 'You are mistaken, my son,' said the officer with a foxy smile. 'I was in Kamenetz-Podolsk, in Kamenetz-Podolsk.' In another dream I saw her playing cards in a company of well-bred women, with a rose-coloured veil on her bare shoulders. She put a five of hearts on the table and then, a five of diamonds on top. I was standing behind her and whispered: 'The king, the king!' She looked up at me over her shoulder with a loving smile and said: 'You meant the joker, my son, the joker…'

After I met Ahuva, who was teaching in a Beersheba kindergarten while I was working in the Negev, I brought her to my mother's house one Sabbath eve. My mother was so excited that the flush in her cheeks made her look young and beautiful. She had prepared a festive meal, and all the time she never stopped singing my praises. Ahuva was a good listener and she gained the impression that evening that I was not only a brilliantly talented young man but also a model son, who would be a model husband. I took her home to her parents' house and when I came back found my mother awake, sitting by the table, reading the evening paper. She took off her spectacles, looked at me affectionately, and said: 'Will you pour me a glass of tea?' I felt moved to the point of tears: it was the one and only time in her life, so far as I can remember, that she had ever asked me to bring her a glass of tea to the table. Yes, she was very fond of Ahuva, who repaid her amply with affection and respect. No one was ever so kind to her as Ahuva was in those days. She showered her with presents—head-scarves, serviettes, household utensils which she hadn't got—she never came empty-handed. She used to wash up after the meal, clean up the house, decorate it. After we were married she used to drag me to my mother's house for a visit at least once a week, and then she made it a fixed habit to invite my mother to our house on Sabbath eves. It was too short a spring, in the evening of her days. Again I was gripped in her presence by the same spleen as in my childhood. I used to sit and hold my tongue, obstinately, maliciously, or find various excuses to leave the table—let the two women talk to each other. 'What a strange character you have, Jonas,' Ahuva once said to me; 'you're bad to those who love you.'

A few months after our marriage my mother fell sick and died. It was as if her heart—her simple heart, which did not foresee what was in store—assured her that she had left me in good hands, and that her life's role had been brought to a conclusion.

Chapter twenty-three

I reached Hanita in the afternoon, a few days after that night with Nili, and Rudi's visit next morning. The woods were all around, oak and terebinth, crab-apple and cane-apple, carob and Syrian maple, and the cool scent of pines filled the air. Far, far away, like a distant nightmare, were the alcoholic nights in the Cellar, the sick mornings in my room, the quivering expectations that brought up a cold sweat on my forehead. Very high were the heavens above Jebel-Lahlah and Jebel-Marda and Tel al-Hawa and Sahal-Bana, and from the mountain top the green valleys could be seen to the south and the west, as far as the blue sea licking at the Ladder of Tyre. We sat on a rustic bench in the garden of the kibbutz rest-house, the shadows lengthened, the twitterings of the birds filtered down from the murmuring treetops, and the pine-cones knocked against each other. Nahum Dolav was reluctant to tell his story. 'Look,' he said, 'you can't write about everything. There are some episodes...the time that's passed is too short; the people are still alive. It's not so simple....' I pressed him. He hesitated; combed his fair forelock with his fingers; let his glance rest on a wild mastic bush. He took out a packet of cigarettes from his pocket. 'Look,' he said, 'Davidov is Davidov. We all know.

A man who has become a legend. Or a symbol. You can't, well, so soon…. You understand, the time he spent here…it's left behind a kind of unpleasant residue. Of course, it was all very human, that sort of thing happens, and perhaps just because…. But in those days…. It was too open, and they didn't expect it of him, especially in those conditions. I understand that in a biography you've got to show the other side, the man's weaknesses and all that, but in this case…it's not so simple. Perhaps you can give the Hanita business a miss. Or just write that he stayed here two months from the day they put up the settlement till the middle of May, worked, stood guard, went on the march to Jerduya with Wingate…and that's it.' Only after I had given him my solemn word that I would show him the chapter before it was sent to press did he agree to tell me the story.

So this is the Hanita episode, which in any case would not have been included in the book, even if I had written it:

Davidov was in that convoy of four hundred men which reached the foot of the hill on the morning of March 23rd, 1938, when the kibbutz was built. With the other volunteers from all over the country he carried beams, tin sheets, rolls of barbed wire and tools up the hill, along the path that was staked out among the dense wild bushes. Many people remember him well on that day, for his voice rolled from the head of the line to the rear, singing, encouraging, spurring on the donkeys that carried the water containers. He is also remembered for the strength in his arms as he brandished the sledge-hammer to drive the fence posts into the rocky ground. That night, when it was nearly midnight, the great storm broke out that overturned tents, blew away tin sheets and did a great deal of damage. Then, immediately afterwards, the Arab attack started. Davidov was at the same post as Nahum, and when the alarm signal came from the western outpost they both ran there and found Brenner wallowing in his blood.

During the period that followed he went out on armed patrols, visiting the posts, scouting the surrounding heights, protecting the land surveyors and the men who built the stockades with iron sheets reinforced with rubble. Since he was expert in dynamiting rock he helped the road-makers, drilling the holes and inserting the explosives. It was in no small measure thanks to him that the work was completed—despite the bullets that whizzed by day from distant Arab positions on the heights—in only five days. When the motor pump was installed at the spring down below, he was there, advising and working with the mechanics, and every one vividly remembered how when the water reached the camp he exulted like a child, stripped off his clothes and stood, naked under the stream. On the first Sabbath he 'got lost'. He set out in the morning for Upper Hanita and did not come back. A search-party went out, but did not find him. When he returned in the evening he described how he had crossed the Lebanese border, reached the orchards of Alama and eaten of their fruit. No one believed him at first, but a *kefiyah* full of medlars testified to the truth of his story. The good land across the Jebel-Marda enchanted his eyes and his heart. He heard the call of Jebel al-Har, 'the Good Mountain', which one day in the future would be annexed to the heritage of Hanita. 'He was drunk, you understand…drunk with the landscape, the forest, the hills. You must remember that it was spring at the time, and spring here, with everything in flower, the sage, the orchids, the Judas tree, and the continual buzzing of the bees…especially in that atmosphere, with ninety men sleeping in tents or at their posts, eating under matting shelters, with Arab sheikhs and British policemen on horseback…He was drunk, just drunk. And perhaps you can't blame him—how should I know?'

Among the volunteers from Haifa was a girl called Erela, a nurse, the wife of Y.L., one of the managers at the Solel Boneh concern who was responsible for supplying building materials and machinery. She was beautiful, fiery, overflowing with laughter and passion. 'If it had been in secret, perhaps nobody would have cared,' said Nahum. 'It happens…and there are some things nobody has the right to judge. But here it was in the light of day, absolutely open and unconcealed. You could see them strolling together in the woods, sitting together at meals, going together to the posts. Sometimes he would take her with him to Bassa, to visit the police station or bring back supplies. And later in Upper Hanita…. And Y.L. was not just anybody. An exceptionally devoted man, popular with everybody. Almost every day he would come to the camp, make sure that the materials were supplied in time, ask if we were short of anything, help and advise. But for him we should never have erected the stockade and the huts in less than two weeks. And afterwards the generator and the dining-hut. It was all thanks to him. And you must remember what the conditions were like. Every journey to the camp and back was dangerous.... Of course he didn't know a thing. He would come for an hour or two and go back to town. He was pretty busy.... Look, I don't take it on myself to decide what's moral and what isn't, but there are some things, how should I say, that are like defying the order of nature, if I could put it like that.'

When Upper Hanita was taken, Davidov moved up to the top of the hill. From now on he used to set out from there to accompany the surveyors, the truck that maintained communications between the two points, the tractor that reaped the disputed fields. From time to time there was an exchange of fire with the Arab band that was stationed on the ridge to the north, or bickering with peasants who reaped patches of corn and charcoal burners who cut off branches in the forest.

Davidov asked for a nurse to be transferred to Upper Hanita, and Erela applied for the job. Both requests were refused. At a meeting of the kibbutz secretariat the hints developed into open indignation: this lawless love affair was spoiling the atmosphere; it was getting unbearable. When the road joining Lower with Upper Hanita was completed a large party was held in the new dining-hut. That night, after the singing and dancing, Erela was 'kidnapped' and went up with Davidov to Upper Hanita. After that, she spent her days down below and her nights up above. There was another consultation on the matter. Some people proposed that Davidov should be told to go home, or that Erela should be sent home, or both. But, out of respect for Davidov, out of respect for Y.L., and for fear the story might become known beyond the bounds of the kibbutz and a scandal break out, the proposals were withdrawn. Davidov built himself a booth in the crown of a broad-branched carob tree—a love-nest for himself and Erela. At sunset he used to go down to Lower Hanita and take his beloved back with him up to the top.

'The trouble was that it was too open,' Nahum repeated. 'They weren't ashamed, didn't hide. It was as if the two of them belonged to the same breed, gypsies, or Cossacks, or something—frank and passionate and freedom loving. They didn't care, they had no feelings of guilt at all. And perhaps that's how it ought to be, I don't know. Perhaps that's much more moral than doing it in secret…. But for us—you understand, it made us all accomplices without our wanting it, actually against our wills, accomplices in their liaison. Because when Y.L. came to the camp—and he used to come very often—no one, of course, would breathe a hint to him. Sometimes we would even help them, when we had to hide what was going on with all kinds of little lies. So, actually, we were the sinners, and they themselves…. And you've got to remember the spring, and the landscape, and all the romantic atmosphere: the patrols in the open country, the night journeys, the forest, the moonlight, Galilee and all that. Who knows, today when you look back on it all….' Nahum smiled as if he was somewhat ashamed, broke a dry branch between his fingers. 'Look, on the eve of Passover they both went home. On the day after the festival—the same day when four men were killed in a truck on the road to Nahariya—Davidov came back, bringing his son with him—he was ten or eleven at the time. He took him to Upper Hanita, to his booth. An interesting lad he was, serious, silent, mature for his years. Went everywhere with his father, and then…strange, after all…he wasn't a child. He saw, understood. He was here ten days. Yes, it's true, he built him a separate booth on another tree, and yet…but what do I know?'

One day, about two weeks after Nimrod was sent back home, Y.L. came to the lower camp at an unexpected time, at ten in the evening. He did not find Erela. They told him she was at the upper camp and offered to send a van to bring her. He declined and said he would go himself in his car. They signalled from the watchtower to Upper Hanita: 'Y.L. on way. Beware disaster.' The man at the signal post on top did not understand, or did not want to understand, and did not issue the necessary warning. When Y.L. arrived he did not find Erela. They shouted her name over and over again, but a long time passed before she appeared at the stone house, her hair dishevelled. What words passed between them no one knows. They were seen leaving the house, silent, and then driving down the hill in silence. Two days later Davidov took his pack and moved off to the fence-builders' camp.

Chapter twenty-four

It was at Ayelet Hashahar that I heard the story of the Northern Fence, which was built along the frontier to keep out marauding Arab bands. Mundik was heavy of speech and movement with years of hard work. He was a veteran commander who had gone back to his daily work in the vineyard, and now he was tired out with his memories and his day in the hot sun. In the evening, in his room, his face longed for rest and his hands were heavy on the arms of his chair. 'I haven't much to tell,' he said. 'He was with us from Malkiah until Bassa B, until the end. What can I tell you?' he mused.

When the fence reached Tarbiha, he said, the attacks grew more frequent. The neighbourhood was swarming with marauders in their hundreds and, together with the villagers from both sides of the frontier, they sabotaged the fence almost every night, breaking gaps and tearing up long stretches, mining the roads and stealing donkeys. Mundik, Davidov and another three supernumerary police in an armoured car patrolled the fence at night. One night the car came up against a barrier of stones, succeeded in getting through, came up against a second barrier, and overturned on the road. They came under a hail of fire and two of them were wounded at once. Davidov extricated himself from the overturned car and ran the gauntlet to the nearby police post. There he summoned help and came back with two other armoured cars. After a battle the marauders were repulsed, leaving six bodies behind them.

What else?

Yes, once there was a shortage of water for mixing the concrete. Near Sasa. They went down in two trucks to the village's rain-water pond to fill their containers. The Arab villagers crowded round and started to shout that the water was theirs. The men from the camp insisted that they had got permission from the authorities, and a fracas broke out. Davidov drove up in his armoured car. When the situation grew serious Mundik wanted to open fire, but Davidov dissuaded him. The water belonged to the villagers, he said, and their rights had priority over the official permit. He proposed drawing the water and paying for it. So they paid, and avoided bloodshed.

What else?

Yes, in Hurfeish. The fence, which was being completed, at a rapid pace of hundreds of metres a day, reached the Arab villagers' tobacco plantation, and the men were about to destroy the whole plantation to make way for the rolls of barbed wire. Davidov arrived when the workers were starting to cut down the plants, rushed forward furiously and snatched the hoes out of their hands. They didn't understand what farm labour meant, he cried. Labour was labour, no matter whose it was. They could shift the line of the fence north or south, but they must not destroy the fruits of anyone's labour. He submitted the question to the men in charge, and they decided to shift the fence. The episode was still remembered in Hurfeish.

What else? Mundik puffed slowly at his cigarette. The memories of a generation were buried in the wrinkles on his face, but he seemed to be too lazy to arouse them from their slumber. He was more accustomed to conceal than to reveal. Twenty years had passed. Now there was nothing but the vineyard, a world of dust and clods of earth and props and vine-shoots, into which I had intruded and was disturbing its routine. 'That's about it,' he said.

Perhaps something else?

No, that was all.

He went on smoking, as if he were alone. His trunk, which had seen sixty years of action, was dry, but he was still strong and hardy. And he was as good at holding his tongue, as ever. 'Have you met Dotan?' he asked through the smoke. 'You should meet him. He's got something to tell.'

Later he said: 'During the first month, when we were at Malkiya, I didn't even know he was there. There were about a thousand men in the camp, a great mob of labourers, guards, drivers and foremen. Most of them were new immigrants, who spoke Yiddish, German, Polish or Arabic. A complete tent town. There were very few veterans, men from the mobile fighting units or sent from the kibbutzim—hardly noticeable. Perhaps ten tents out of one hundred and fifty. It was only when we moved to Sasa that I discovered him. Just by accident.'

A faint ray of light, filtering through from those far-off days, rested on his face.

'It was quite ridiculous, actually. At midday the water truck used to pass along the fence. It would stop every hundred or two hundred metres and all the workers, markers, post-drivers, and wirers used to rush up with their mugs in their hands to drink. There were always shouts, quarrels, scrimmages, for there was not enough water. Grumbling against Moses, like in the Exodus. One day I was in the armoured car at the heels of the water truck, touring the guard posts that kept a look-out on the heights. The water truck was a little way in front of us and the workers were already crowding round. Suddenly I saw, on my right, inside the fence itself, a single man, stuck fast in a thicket of barbed wire. We stopped. I got off the armoured car and went up to see what had happened. How can I describe it? The man was completely trapped in the convolutions, enmeshed and entangled, his clothes held by the barbs. When I saw him he smiled sheepishly. "I've got all tangled up," he said. "Somebody will have to help me to get out." And then I recognized him. It seemed absurd to find a man like him in a situation like that. There was something queer about it. I find it hard to explain…'

Mundik's face grew more relaxed as he relieved himself of the burden of memories.

'During the last few weeks we were at Bassa B,' he said. 'There was a kind of sad feeling, you know, like before a parting. One day we were both standing by the fence, looking at it...Like a kind of river of sparkling silver, stretching away to the horizon. He said to me: "Do you really know why we built it? Not as a barrier, or a wall, or a border. The Arab bands can cross harder obstacles. In a few years, anyway, it'll rust, rot, and collapse. So what is it for, then? Perhaps as a monument to the stupidity of British colonial rule?" Have you passed it lately? That's really what it's like. The Wall, they called it then. Tegart's Wall...

'That's about it.'

And then he added:

'We were at Bassa for two weeks, and he never went up to Hanita, though it was only half-an-hour's walk away. Once when I was chaffing him about it he said: "Rubbish, every girl has only one springtime. Hanita has passed it already." He never went up there, though he knew the whole group. Strange, that man had a host of comrades, but actually—not a single friend.'

Chapter twenty-five

A mocking fate pursues me with a combination of malice and waggish humour. First it trips me up, and when I stumble it kicks me in the behind. A most diverting spectacle! Today, five days before the next session of the court, I get a letter from the Income Tax, official post, registered: the Treasury, Assessment Office, Chief Collector. Since I have not submitted a report on my income during the past two years, it is assessed at fifteen thousand Israeli pounds, and 'I hereby inform you that if within 5 days from the date of this notification, you do not pay the sum of IL3,350, I shall have no alternative, to my regret, but to act under Article 5 (4) of the Taxes Ordinance (Collection), which authorizes the impounding of assets, income, etc. etc.' Three thousand three hundred and fifty! How much have I left, anyway? I glance at my bank account: IL873.50—that is my total balance. For a year and a half I have been living on Davidov; all that time I have been consuming without working, paying my lawyer, paying court costs—and not earning a penny. That reservoir is steadily and rapidly draining dry, like the ones they dig in the sands of the Negev. Even if I convince them that I have not earned more than nine thousand, I should still have to pay more than I possess.

I ran at once to my lawyer and showed him the letter. He glanced at it, smiled and said: 'No need to get excited. We'll settle it.' 'Five days,' I cried, 'five days!' 'First of all', he said, 'we'll get a postponement. Then we'll see. They won't put you in jail for that.' Well, that's some comfort. If lawyers are good for nothing else, at least they do not abandon you to face the mighty machine that threatens to crush you all by yourself.

Chapter twenty-six

I go back to Nili, to the gang. Things had got more and more complicated since that morning with Rudi. Nili used my room as a humble sanctuary, an outlet for her suppressed desires, a place of refuge where she could turn to me for shelter, a hostelry, a harbour from the storm. Her time—no, her heart!—she would divide between Eviatar, me and her home. Things became very complicated, because she often spent the nights in my room (she had engaged a 'nanny' for her little son with money she extracted from her father), and on the following mornings, or at some time of day, she would meet Eviatar. To add to the complications, the three of us often met in the little restaurant near my flat, or for a visit to a museum, or to spend the afternoon at the cinema. It was a diverting sight, no doubt, and an excellent subject for gossip, when the three of us were seen walking in the street: blackbeard on the one side, yellowbeard on the other, and the golden lass in the middle. Something perverse, the reader may think, and so do I today; at that time my thinking was not particularly clear. I lived in a kind of stupor or delirium: sight somewhat confused, logical faculties deranged, every action seeming unnatural. Nor did I pay much heed to what people said or thought. An insubstantial state of mind, in which everything around assumed the colours and dimensions of unreality. Otherwise how can I explain my being with Nili when her heart belonged to Eviatar and she was still living with Rudi? And I loved Nili—yes, I have the right to spell out the word in black and white. She loved Eviatar—that was also written clear for all to see. And how can I explain the fact that, despite the jealousy that smouldered within me, I felt no hostility towards Eviatar?—in fact, a kind of undeclared friendship and concurrence reigned between us. How shall I explain why those hours which the three of us spent together in quiet conversation round a restaurant table (the tension of secret, undisclosed meetings and nights of desire in the darkness quivering deep below the surface, suppressed by the tranquil, tentative talk) were among the finest hours I remember from that time.

Yes, the conversations with Eviatar, by the cooling coffee cups. A sentence, then a silence; a sentence and an unfinished thought. Nili too put in her word hesitantly, looking up sometimes to him, sometimes to me. The three of us going down to underground passages, groping our way through. The chamber music of Braque paintings. The power of Romanesque frescoes. Why is the influence of Renaissance art weakening and the influence of medieval art on the upgrade? Why does pre-Bach music seem to have more to say to us today than Beethoven and Mozart? Take Monteverdi, for instance, or Purcell. Or the grotesques of Bosch. 'Moral' and 'anti-moral' art…Or what is the secret of the magic in a story: is it the way it resembles reality and the truths we know—or, on the contrary, the fact that it is so different from reality and truth?…I well remember this conversation, perhaps because of the circus metaphor that Eviatar suggested, and which aroused in me a poignant memory. A story has a magic power, he said, not because it expresses the truth we know, even with great skill, but because it is an illusion—but an illusion obeying laws of harmony, with an inner tempo which enchants us. Like the conjurer in the circus, he said. We all know that what we see is illusion, but we are all enchanted because we are captivated by a certain harmony which imposes its rhythm on us with a gentle hand. This is the truth within the lie. In contrast, there is the lie within the truth. A writer who tells a 'true' story embedded in reality, who describes what happened as it happened, is a liar because he is committing plagiarism. He is trying to imitate a rhythm which is not his, which already exists as a part of reality—the rhythm of the Deity, as it were, which He has imposed on Nature. Any such attempt is inevitably doomed to failure because it is less than the original, or a spurious substitute for the original. The best stories are illusion, imagination, fantasy, invention. And yet they are true, because they contain a projection of the author's inner rhythm, and if he is faithful to that he does not lie. Harmony, a new, personal harmony, hitherto unknown—that is the whole secret, in narrative and poetry, in music and painting, and then we no longer ask if the shadows or the colours, the objects or the figures, 'resemble' what we know or not. Then too we do not ask for ideas and purposes, any more than nature does. An illusion that has harmony, a 'lie' that has harmony. Isn't that so?

'Isn't that so?' Eviatar never made categorical statements, though the examples and comparisons and proofs he adduced indicated such erudition; he always presented a question for consideration. Yes and no. And still we have not exhausted the subject. And perhaps after all it isn't so at all, and the whole idea is unsound.

'But look, Eviatar,' says Nili, after the three of us have pondered in silence and considered all that has been said, each for himself, 'that's true, of course, what you said. But it seems to me…Look, you gave the example of the conjurer in the circus. The illusion that puts us under a spell. But in the same circus you can also see the tightrope walker…Now that's no "lie". That's "truth", "reality", and yet it casts a spell too. I'm trying to think: What exactly is the difference, that's to say, between the ability to introduce some kind of order into the reality we know and…It's not that I deny what you said, but there are other examples. Take Balzac, for instance: *Père Goriot* or *Eugénie Grandet.* Just because the material, the people, are so familiar…Don't you think so, Jonas?' She turns to me.

Jonas does not think. He sees the circus. His blood suddenly seethes when he remembers the two of them sitting three rows below, clinging to each other; when he tries to imagine where they meet without him, and what they do then…

'Yes, Balzac,' he forces himself to say. 'But Eviatar is right. That's to say, with Balzac the main thing is not the realistic material, but the "some kind of order" as you said, which is his inner rhythm…projected on reality, that is…'

Yes, I must admit that there was a great deal of pretence in this pious, scholarly, intellectual tranquillity—denying every evil inclination or unpleasant impulse—in which I cloaked myself. Jealousy? Bitterness? Resentment? No, perish the thought! I was saying, as it were, like Wagner to Faust: 'Hours of vain fantasy I, too, have had, but such an impulse never has attacked me.' When Nili and I were alone in the room together and I watched the clouds that flickered over her face after some meeting with Eviatar, trying to guess what hidden things had passed between them, I had to put on a variety of masks—that of the elder brother, of the father confessor, of the objective, uninvolved psychologist—so as not to fall in her eyes from my proud estate; speaking words of wisdom, measuring all things in the scale of justice, a faithful counsellor, a steward of the shattered household of her heart. I remember how one afternoon she came into the room, collapsed on the bed, and hid her head in the pillow without saying a word. Something had happened between her and Eviatar. What was it? My pride would not let me ask. So I sat and waited, silencing my heart as one smothers a troublesome clock to silence its ticking. I knew that in the end she would speak of her own accord. After a long time—enough to fray the nerves of an elephant—she sat up, took out a packet of cigarettes, lit one, blew out smoke, and announced quietly: 'We've finished.' (I hold my tongue. Damp down a tiny flame of premature joy. Put on, as I have trained myself to do, an expression of anxious surprise.) 'What's happened?' the elder brother asks at last, concerned for his sister's welfare. 'You have no idea, Jonas, how selfish he is, how selfish…' 'Selfish?' Eviatar's faithful friend asks in surprise. And then she goes on with the story of her own accord. They had met. (Where? where? that was always a mystery. She would always leave me to conduct my geographical explorations without map or compass, having to torture myself by combing the whole town, its cafés, parks and seashore.) They had had a long talk. 'A thorough discussion.' She had insisted that he should decide one way or the other, explained that she could not go on like that. He had pretended not to understand, hardened his heart, said there was nothing he could do. 'I told him we had better not meet again, and that's that.' Nili's vows! She kept this one for about forty hours. Of course, of course, they met again after two days, and it was a very thorough reconciliation apparently, for later, when she came to my room, she looked different, glowing with tenderness. 'Made it up?' asks the wise, farsighted psychologist. 'Oh, he's confused, Jonas, completely confused. And actually, he's a child, an overgrown child. What can I do, Jonas? I love him!' she declares, like a pampered little girl. The elder brother smiles, choking down his venom, smiles forgivingly at the pranks of his favourite sister. A moment later she sits down by his side, strokes his beard: 'What should I do without you?'—and with a kiss pays lip-service for his all-knowing, understanding, forgiving magnanimity. Two days later the three of us meet again. A long, quiet, meandering conversation over the coffee cups, about the arcane wisdom ensconced in the words of the Hebrew tongue.

Today, when I recall all this, I sometimes take my head in my hands and ask myself how I could have endured this trinity, how I could have borne the torments of her confessions, the oppressive weight of the masks, the alternation between the warmth of the nights and the chill mornings that followed, the guessing, the expectation...

One day, when I had waited for her in my room after she had promised to come at three o'clock, when five had passed, then six and still she had not come; when twilight had fallen and the shadows were lengthening, and I was heartsick with expectation, and even more with resentment, I found myself making my way to that house in the south of the city, Ephraim Averbuch's, whose dim light was always there, as it were, waiting for me whenever I should be in need of consolation.

Yes, there was a light in the windows of the little house. I stood in the shadows, an unseen watcher. The family sat round the table, Zippora stuffing the baby by her side with semolina pudding, which was smeared all over his face—one spoonful and then another, the pudding overflowing his little mouth. Ephraim was cutting bread for the two children. Zippora beckoned to him to bring something. Ephraim went out to the kitchen and came back with the bowl of sugar. The children quarrelled over the knife; Ephraim rebuked them. A moth circled around the light-bulb above. Zippora kept stuffing the child at such a rate that his mouth could not keep up. An overflowing flood of semolina…Should I go in?

The two of them welcomed me with cries of astonishment. The beard. They almost hadn't recognized me, they laughed. Like a sort of English actor, said Zippora, thrusting the spoon into the baby's mouth. The six-year-old and the eight-year-old opened their eyes wide in curiosity, as at a visitor from another country. I was to sit down, to eat, to make myself at home. They offered bread, butter, cheese, tomatoes. 'Make him an omelette, Ephraim, don't you see he's starving? What brings you…?' (What brings me is the fact that Nili is late and I haven't the heart to wait till nightfall.) The moth circled and circled. On the table the cottage cheese and the bottles of yoghurt gleamed. The yellow eye of the fried egg looked up moistly into mine. 'I think about you a lot,' says Ephraim, 'about that book.' The book? Yes, he says, that book. At first he doubted whether I was the right man to write it, but later he made up his mind that I was. No one else. The background, the foundation, the days gone by. What was I writing now? Strange things they wrote nowadays; he sometimes read them in the papers. The young writers too. 'I don't understand them at all. Explain it to me, what do they want? What do they want?' The conversations with Eviatar and Nili float in my head like a heavy cloud, the conversations in the Cellar like a yellow mist. Inner truth. The rhythm that contains a harmony. 'Perhaps I'm stupid,' says Ephraim, 'but I sometimes take a look at a poem. I'll be hanged if I can understand a word. One line doesn't hang on to the next. No connection at all. Words, words, you don't know where it all came from. Where did they grow up, these folk? They're making fools of us, I told Zippora.' Sacred simplicity! What do they understand? What do they understand of that world of enchantment, of fantasy, of the lie that is truth? Zippora's face is flushed with excitement as she speaks. She loves to read, but the more she reads the more angry she gets: no plot, no human beings, no time, no place, no life—don't they write for someone to read? Why was it that when she read Romain Rolland or Dostoevski or Steinbeck or *The Plague...*? I lower my eyes to the plate, fill my mouth with bread. '...Or you,' says Zippora. 'There's that story of yours, *A Hero of Our Time...*' The bread sticks in my throat, I must get out. Where can I go? Where is Nili now? In what dark and secret place? The inner truth is the main thing, I tell them, sipping my coffee. A writer cannot deny himself, I say, seeing Eviatar, and Nili in his arms. An author writes *out of* and not *for the sake of* I add after another sip. 'Of course, the inner truth,' says Zippora, 'but when I don't feel any...any connection with it...And what about Tolstoy—didn't he write his own inner truth? I wonder...' By this time the baby was sitting on her knees, sated, beaming with happiness, resting as in an armchair on her broad, full bosom, looking with an amused expression at my bearded face, his ruddy, rounded legs playing with each other by the edge of the table. I must go, I said, we'd never solve the problem. 'I'll see you on your way,' said Ephraim Averbuch, and comes out with me.

Outside the heavens are high. A smell of oil from barred and shuttered workshops. Here Rahamimov used to live, here Freedman, whose wife is paralysed, here Bloch the carpenter, whose daughter, they used to say, was put in the family way by an Arab from Jaffa and buried the baby in a grove at Abu-Kabir. On Saturday afternoons we used to go out to look for the grave in the grove, under the dry leaves that rustled like snakes. The foliage there was cool and shadowy, with the smell of stagnant water in the stone channels. And the Arab pond. Once there was a threatening voice from the dense foliage—apparently the father of the child. Yes, Bloch still lives here, said Ephraim, an old man, his carpenter's shop burnt down, his daughter in a madhouse. It was eight o'clock. Too early, too early to go back to an empty room. 'Let's go in,' I said, 'let's have a drink.'

We went into Baruch Daniel's Bulgarian restaurant, where I sometimes had a meal when my mother was too busy, or, years later, when I came home on short leave. Garage workers and carpenters' apprentices used to come in here at midday, and I used to weave stories around them which I meant to write down one day. Beside a table in the corner I used to sit with Ahuva in the early days, and she would pamper me with promises that she would earn enough to keep me so that I could devote myself entirely to writing. Baruch Daniel greeted Ephraim, but didn't recognize me. 'What will you have?' asked Ephraim when he sat down; 'shall we order a bottle of arak?' I girded myself for the fray. For my sake, he would drink with me for my sake. The innocence in his face would kill me one day, I thought. The little restaurant was empty. The walls were half green and half yellow; on the counter, as before, as always, gleamed the jars of green and black olives, and pink pickled turnips, and purple pickled eggplants; from the ceiling hung the rotating fan, a great, long-winged mosquito, dead and covered in dust. 'Tell me, aren't you Rabinowitch?' said Baruch Daniel, staring at me as he wiped the table with a rag. 'Yes,' I confessed. 'It's the beard, you see,' he smiled, illustrating with a hand to his face. 'Otherwise I'd have recognized you straight away. We never see you. Where are you these days?' 'Here, in Tel Aviv.' 'You never come here any more. Forgotten us, eh?' 'I live a good way off, in the north.' 'I can still remember you when you were that high'—lowering his hand to the level of the table. 'He used to come to me for a four-piastre lunch,' he said with an elderly smile at Ephraim. 'Four piastres, that was his top price. Four piastres was a lot of money in those days! And your girl, I remember her too. A lovely girl, so quiet. How is she? Bring her some time. They used to sit here'—he turned to Ephraim—'by the corner table, and talk and talk and talk. All the clients left but they sat on talking. How many children have you got?' 'None,' I said. 'No time to make children, eh? That's how it is with the younger generation.' And after he came back with the bottle of arak he said: 'I can even remember your father. Over thirty years ago. Ah, what a man he was! One in a million! A man with a heart, that was!'

Ephraim drank my health, half a glass. Wanted to know how I was getting on. The book, my stories, and all that. I said I wanted to leave Tel Aviv. To move to some other place: Jerusalem, Safad. Perhaps to Beersheba or Eilat. Here I could get no peace, no quiet, a man could not write. He thought it was a good idea: Beersheba, Eilat. Someone ought to write about the present, about the new country. The veteran community was only the office block of the new Israel, a parasite on its body, he said, a set of blood-sucking leeches. You can write about parasites too, I said. And also about leeches. Yes, of course, he replied, but only when you saw the whole body. He went on talking in the same vein. The more I drank the more I too began to like the idea of Beersheba, Eilat. I played with visions floating in the fumes of arak—I would go down to the tunnels of the Timna copper mines, or to the southernmost port, from which the ships set sail to Ophir. Furnaces of the sun, mountains of metal, lost sheep, rocks of Edom, dust-covered command cars, hot-blooded Moroccans, filthy desperadoes, Red Sea harlots. Yes, I said, I would stay two years in Eilat, I would work in the copper mines, in the nights I would write the greatest book ever written about this burning, wild land, the whole book glowing at a temperature of forty-five degrees Centigrade. Ephraim was with me with all his heart, his eyes already seeing me realizing all his dreams. It was not for nothing that he had believed in me all these years.

Oh, that belief and trust! That was what annoyed me, I think. I can no longer remember exactly how it happened. I believe it started when he asked me if I was seeing Ahuva and how she was. The arak was making me resent him. His broad face, with its innocence, was an indictment against me. No, I said, I was not seeing Ahuva. I was living with a beautiful woman, someone else's wife, with a child of her own. We were in love with each other. Happy. I saw his face darkening and the disappointment hardening it into immobility. He asked, half-heartedly, if she was going to get a divorce from her husband. No, I said, we were just living together like that. She divided her days and nights between him and me. 'And he knows?' he asked. 'Of course,' I replied, enjoying his pain. Pouring myself out another glass from the half-empty bottle, I told him about that morning when the agitated Rudi had invaded my room and found me with her. 'I don't believe you,' he said. I giggled. This morality of fools, like a mirror in front of my face, provoked me to shatter it. Yes, that's how it is, and that's the way I am, naked in front of you, and an end to illusions. He went on stammering something about honour, conscience. I believe he said—not about me, about her—that she was corrupt, or immoral. Later I found myself alone.

I do not remember how he happened to leave. Perhaps I insulted him when I protested against his censure. Perhaps he could not bear the disappointment. Perhaps he wanted to get away from defilement. I remained alone at the table. I sat and stared at the gleaming quarter-full bottle. Circles of light played on it, like the reflections of the sun on the wall of my mother's house in the morning when the window quivered slightly in the wind. A deep sadness descended on me from the gloomy green walls. Here my father sat—a man with a heart, one in a million!—many years ago, with his bony face, his long powerful hands; sat with his friends, discussing the defence of south Tel Aviv against the marauders from Jaffa. Or perhaps it was a legend. And Davidov was a legend, and it was all lies, except for the empty room waiting for me somewhere.

I got up and went over to pay.

'He's paid, it's all right,' said Baruch Daniel.

'*He's* not all right!' I cried.

'Why isn't he all right?' smiled Baruch Daniel, with his old deeply seamed face.

'He's not all right!' I repeated, with tears in my eyes. 'He's not all right! That's no way to leave a friend. I was his guest!'

'You're drunk, Mr Rabinowitch, that's not good for you.'

As I stood outside, I remember I was still uncertain which way to go. I had a confused and oppressive feeling that I ought to go back to Ephraim's house and beg his pardon. I cast off this foolish thought and set out northward, in the direction of the Cellar.

Chapter twenty-seven

It was like a tawdry operetta.

Three or four days after that melancholy evening with Ephraim Averbuch I asked Nili to come with me to Ein-Harod. I had to meet a man called Abraham Biederman who had been with Davidov at the establishment of a number of new settlements in 1939 and 1940. The idea that I should be with her—if only for a few hours of twilight and evening—far from my room, from Eviatar, from the Cellar, free to stroll on the slopes of Kumi hill, facing Mount Gilboa after sunset, in the rustling copse of the Harod Spring which I remembered from far-off days—the very thought enchanted me. Nili refused. She said she hated to visit a kibbutz—to sit in the dining-hall, the focus for hundreds of inquisitive, suspicious and censorious eyes, to sense the whispers from every side, to spend the night in a strange room on a strange bed—no, all that was not for her. And anyway, what would she do all the time I was listening to the fellow's recollections? She could listen together with me, I said. No, stories about heroes bored her to tears. Nothing was duller than tales of heroism, she said. And if I took her advice, I would give up the whole idea of the book. It was bound to be a book of adventure stories that might, at best, be of interest to schoolboys. I was hurt. I mumbled something about the debt we owed to the past, about the past that lived within me...Romantic nonsense, she said, outworn romanticism. 'Debt?' she laughed. 'We're all alive thanks to those who begot us. It's just our luck that the debt we owe them is always being carried forward and we never have to pay the arrears. If I had to think how much I owe my father...' I set out, with a bitter heart, without saying goodbye.

It was four o'clock by the time I reached Ein-Harod, and before Abraham Biederman finished his work and we had supper and went into his room it was seven. At seven o'clock, then, I began to take down his story.

In the summer of 1940, he said...

No. I will skip this chapter. In any case, I remember very little of it. I took it down without thinking what I was writing. It was a story about some convoy of lorries packed with people and building materials that set out at night from the Haifa suburbs and climbed up to the sands by the date-palm grove on the shore of Acre Bay. He described the building of a watchtower in the moonlight, with the sand like a snowfield and the waves whispering and moaning...He told his tale at great length. I was haunted by forebodings and wild fantasies. Something fateful was happening tonight in my absence. I saw Nili with Eviatar in some dusky room. Gleaming glasses, sweet confidences...her refusal to accompany me meant a cunning plan for a stolen night meeting ...I waited impatiently for him to finish his story, scribbling disorganized jottings.

At nine he finished. I folded up my papers and told him that I had to get home the same night. 'Tonight?' he protested in surprise. 'Why tonight?' He had already prepared a bed, and how could I leave at such an hour? I said that I simply could not stay, that I had to set out for the Negev at six in the morning, a special car was coming to collect me from home, I could not change the arrangements. Apparently he was convinced by the desperate urgency of my appeal for help. He said he would do his best to arrange some kind of transport at least as far as Afula. I waited for him by the dining-hall. I had made up my mind that if there was no vehicle available I would go on foot, to Afula, to Haifa—I would spend the night on the road, I had to get back, I simply had to, before morning. For about half an hour he ran about all over the kibbutz, looking for a driver or the treasurer or the secretary, coming back from time to time to tell me that there was still hope. Finally he found a volunteer with a Jeep who agreed to drive me to Afula.

I reached Afula at ten. It was actually a police car that took me to Haifa; there were no taxis, so I stood waiting on the road to Nazareth. The patrol car stopped and, after I had been cleared of suspicion, took me in. At eleven I was in Haifa. I tramped through the empty, dark, stupefied streets of the lower city till I got to the taxi service terminus. I had to wait an endless time for the taxi to fill up. I paid for an extra passenger to induce the driver to set out. Then came the long, long journey, the road streaking backward through an infinite avenue of shadows into the night pierced by the rays of the headlights. At half past two I reached the entry to my house. There was a light on in my room.

What a cheap joke!

As soon as I was inside the building's entrance I heard voices from above, and stopped. I recognized Levia's voice, completely unrestrained: 'But why did you tell me you were going out of town? Answer me! Why did you lie to me, why did you want…?'—and Mrs Silber's voice, interrupting: 'How dare you, at three o'clock in the morning, when everybody's asleep!'—and again Levia's voice rolling out at full strength: 'Tell it to your lodger, he's the one you let the room to, isn't he? He's…'—and Mrs Silber's rebuke: 'You ought to be ashamed of yourselves! In-tel-lec-tu-als!' I went up two or three steps, anxious, stunned, wondering what had happened in my absence, and then I heard Eviatar, trying to keep his voice under control: 'Yes, we'll discuss it all, everything—but not here! Not here!' My forehead was covered with perspiration. Who was still missing from the cast of the *commedia del'arte*, now that I had arrived? Was Rudi with them too? Neighbours had their doors open to listen, and the chemist's wife, who was standing in her doorway in a nightshirt, upbraided me: 'Shameful! Shameful!' Mrs Silber's sabots clattered on the stairway above my head, and when she saw me coming up towards her she cried: 'Good morning! Please come in! I didn't know that…' 'What's happened?' I stopped in front of her. 'I won't stand it any longer, Mr Jonas,' she cried, her face flushed. 'This is too much! I've been too patient! This isn't what I let you the room for, for you to turn it into a...' And as she continued downstairs, passing me without stopping, she spat out scornfully: 'Artists! Hebrew literature!'

'Don't imagine you'll get away with it!' Levia was saying, shaking her finger at Nili, who was sitting on my bed. And when she saw me on the threshold she turned, paused for a moment, and said, breathing heavily: 'How much do they pay you for it?' 'For what?' I mumbled slackly. 'For the use of the room,' she replied with a broad wave of the hand. 'Night and day...for three months now...' 'What do you want of him? Why blame him?' said Nili mockingly from her place on the bed, her face leaning on her hands and a malicious smile hovering over her lips, a smile of arrogant, queenly scorn at a serving-maid's ignoble outburst. Eviatar was burning with shame and embarrassment, and Levia stood there in an aggressive posture, ready to fire in all directions. 'Don't imagine you'll get off scot-free,' she cried at Nili, shaking her finger under the other's nose. 'You'll suffer for this, you'll see! If not me, then somebody else.' 'Take your finger away,' said Nili in a hard voice, with a glitter in her eyes. 'I don't want you to touch me.' 'I touch you!' screamed Levia, with a strange outburst of laughter. 'You're murdering me, and you're afraid I might damage that refined, noble, hypocritical face...' 'Levia,' I pleaded, trying to quieten her out of consideration for the neighbours, 'I beg of you...' 'You actually defend her!'—she turned her female tongue on me. 'After she plays with you, exploits you...' 'What's happened, Levia? What's happened, after all?' pleaded Eviatar. 'You know what's happened. You know you've been deceiving me, the two of you. That you came here only to...' 'I told you, I told you,' Eviatar interrupted, to prevent her finishing the dangerous sentence. 'We were in the Cellar till two, and Nili asked...' 'Lies!' cried Levia. 'You weren't in the Cellar. I asked! You were here! Here! You were here all evening, and I've known all the time, for the last three months, that...' She had a fit of coughing which grew more and more violent and, holding her hand over her mouth, she ran out on to the open roof. Eviatar got up and followed her, taking her by the arm. 'Shall I bring you some water?' 'Go away!

Get out! Don't touch…' She pulled herself away from him, putting her hand on her stomach, coughing harder than ever. I hastily filled a glass with water and took it out to her, but before I could put it to her lips she vomited. I stood with the glass in my hand, and the vomit poured from her mouth, one gush and then another, on to the tarred surface of the roof, which was dimly illuminated by the light from the room. I waited for her to recover a little and put the glass in her hand. She took it, drank, and moaned: 'My head's splitting, it's terrible.' Tears filled her eyes. 'Come on, lie down on the bed, rest a while, it'll pass,' I said, taking her arm. 'It won't pass, Jonas,' she mumbled, bending over the parapet. 'It won't pass, I know, I know…' Weakly, like a sick woman, she went on muttering, her forehead resting on her arm: 'He's been deceiving me all the time…I know…He's been meeting her…I know…I know all they've been doing.' Eviatar came up to her and said gently: 'Feeling better?' 'You can go,' she said quietly, without raising her head. For a moment he stood beside us, as if making up his mind, then he turned slowly towards the staircase and went out. I took hold of Levia's arm again. 'Come on, come inside, lie down and rest for a while.' She let me lead her. Nili was standing by the table, smoking. Through the smoke, with a superior air she watched Levia come in and throw herself on the bed. I knelt by her side and pulled off her soiled shoes. 'Give me a pill or something,' she whispered, her eyes closed. 'I've got a frightful headache.' Nili put her hand in her bag, searched and took out a tube of pills which she handed to me. I went out and brought a glass of water. Levia raised herself slightly on her arm, put the pill in her mouth and took a sip from the glass. Seeing Nili in front of her, she said quietly: 'You can go now. He's waiting for you,' and her head sank back on to the pillow. Nili went on smoking, blowing long, thin jets into the air. In her stillness, encircled by the dissolving smoke-rings, with the malicious look in her eyes, with her proud white neck, she was more beautiful than ever. Finally she stubbed out the cigarette in the ashtray, took her handbag and turned to go. She halted for a moment on the threshold, as if intending to say something, but did not speak and went out. I counted her steps as she went downstairs, slowly, deliberately, step by step, step by step, until they died away.

Levia fell asleep, crumpled up on the bed. I spread a blanket over her and sat down at the table. By now the light of dawn showed palely in the window, and a gentle morning breeze floated in like a sigh.

At sunrise she awoke with a start. After she had gone I took a pail and a rag and cleaned up the vomit on the roof.

Chapter twenty-eight

The battle over the notes raged for three hours yesterday in court. In the first stage, the shots were exchanged above my head between the two lawyers; in the second, I myself was in the centre of the crossfire. At first Advocate Evrat tried to get the court to subpoena my notes about Davidov. My counsel objected, for two reasons: first, these notes could not serve as evidence for the plaintiff, since they were merely rough jottings of no value to anyone but their author; secondly, the issue of such an order would be tantamount to a violation of professional secrets, which the court had no right to compel me to divulge; notes taken by a writer in the course of his work were materials to be cherished in his laboratory, his private domain—'the artist's sanctum'. 'Would it occur to the court to order *me*, or my learned friend the counsel for the plaintiff, to show anyone the notes we take for our own use in argument and interrogation?' cried Shiloh, picking up a sheaf of papers from his table and grasping it with a trembling hand. 'How much more when it is a question of creative work, which is done entirely out of sight when a man is alone with himself, and only its ripe fruits are destined to see the light. In such a case, we must say, like the Latin poet Horace: "We demand this liberty for ourselves and we grant it to others!"' (From time to time my counsel would astonish me with the breadth of his erudition; as his quotations showed, it was broadening with every session.) The judge accepted his view and the plaintiff's counsel gave way; but Evrat immediately asked permission to interrogate me, and permission was granted after the judge had instructed me about my rights as a defendant on the witness-stand. My counsel, who had foreseen some such development, had prepared me for it a few days before and warned me that if I made any statement, or gave any hint, that I had no intention of writing the book, I should be condemning myself out of my own mouth to refund all the advances I had received, to pay in full the penalty prescribed in the contract, and to cover all the costs of the trial. Against my will I had to adopt the line of defence he suggested, which was—in plain terms—to deny the truth at all costs. To keep up my spirits in preparation for this dangerous encounter, I had fortified myself with several examples from literary history, such as Dostoevski's involvement in his love affair with Paulina Suslova, which had prevented him meeting his literary obligations, or Balzac's failure to deliver his chapters in time to his publisher and debtor after he made the acquaintance of the Countess Hanska.

'You met twenty-seven persons in connection with the writing of the book,' said Evrat, examining the papers in front of him. 'The last meeting took place on the seventh of January last year with…'

'The deceased's wife,' I said, helpfully.

'Yes. Tell me, Mr Jonas'—looking me straight in the eye—'how did you record the statements of the people you met: word for word, or…?'

'No, certainly not word for word,' I said with a nervous giggle. 'How could I?'

'But you took coherent notes…'

'They were not coherent, in general, just jottings, chapter headings…'

'You relied on your memory, that is.'

'Yes. My memory has never failed me.'

'Excellent. On the fifteenth of August, about a year and a half ago'—glancing again at his notes—'you met Mr Menahem Schweig at Trade Union Headquarters; is that right?'

'That's right.'

'Did you take down his story coherently? The whole of it? Most of it?'

'Approximately.'

'Approximately what? Coherently, or just jottings?'

'Jottings.'

'Yes. And about eight months ago, you met Mr Ephrat of the Weizmann Institute in his home, and heard his account of the period when Davidov worked at the Dead Sea. Did you take down his story in full, or only brief notes?'

(Nili. Here. In court. The blood flooded my face.) 'I don't exactly remember. Perhaps...'

'Mr Jonas,'—Evrat's tenor rang out—'only a moment ago you told us that your memory never failed you! And if I tell you that Mr Ephrat can come and testify in this court that you took down his statement word for word in the course of two whole hours, what would you say to that?'

(Had Rudi betrayed me? In revenge? Had they had detectives watching me?)

'It's not true,' I said weakly.

'And if I tell you, my dear Mr Jonas, that Mr Schweig can also come here and testify that you took down an almost verbatim record of his story, since he had to stop his flow of words from time to time to enable you to catch up with him—what would you say to that?'

(A lost battle. My heart sank. They knew all.)

But there was no retreat. My counsel's gun was pointed at my back. 'That is not true. I did not show the notes to anyone; no one can testify what I took down and how.'

'Twenty-seven persons, Mr Jonas, twenty-seven persons can testify that you recorded their statements in full,' Evrat's voice rang out challengingly. 'And in fact these notes taken together constitute the story of Davidov's life, chapter by chapter; but you, Mr Jonas, refuse to hand them over, for reasons of which you have yet to give an account in this court.'

'Mr Evrat,' I summoned up the courage to say, 'even if I took down a complete verbatim report of the things I was told, even then, only someone who has no understanding whatever of literature could imagine that a verbatim report could ever be a work of literature. I am not a shorthand reporter; I am a writer.'

'Very well, Mr Jonas. Let us set aside the question of the notes for the time being. Let us try to examine the way you work as a writer. At what times—if I may be allowed to ask—are you in the habit of doing your *literary* work, Mr Jonas?'

My lawyer leapt to his feet. Objection, objection! His client was not a servant whose master could demand an account of his doings every hour of his life. But the judge perfunctorily rejected his plea.

'I have no fixed hours,' I said.

'As a general rule?'

'I can't answer that. Whenever the spirit moves me.'

'A spirit from the sea, perhaps?' smiled Evrat.

The judge turned an inquiring face on him: 'I did not hear that. What was your question?'

'I asked if it was a spirit from the sea that moved him,' said Evrat, 'because Mr Jonas, according to our information, is in the habit of spending several hours every day…'

Again my counsel leapt to his feet. 'Where is my learned friend leading with this line of examination? This is an insolent interference in my client's personal life, and I request the court not to permit it. It has no relevance whatsoever to the question of the times at which the writer does his work. It is not anybody's business.'

'Your Honour,' said Evrat, 'I shall prove that the defendant did no work at all for months, and that he betrayed my client's trust in the most cynical manner.'

'That's not true,' I said.

'We shall see,' cried Evrat.

The judge banged with his gavel and, after explaining several points in the laws of evidence, permitted the plaintiff's counsel to continue his examination.

'From the information in our possession, Mr Jonas'—Evrat returned to the attack—'it transpires that you were in the habit of spending the day on the seashore or in the company of friends, while you generally spent the night in a certain café called the Cellar, where you stayed until the early hours of the morning. Permit me to ask you, with all due humility and respect for your literary talents: When do you write?'

'Your Honour'—I turned for aid to a higher authority—'the counsel for the plaintiff is trying to present me as a liar, an idler and a debauchee. There are many people who know me in this city. They can be asked about me. I do not have to give an account of my doings to a man whose interests in the matter are purely juridical.'

Patiently the judge explained to me that I was entitled not to reply to certain questions, but in that case my silence might be interpreted as evidence against me, and he advised me, therefore, to reply to the best of my ability.

'When were you in the habit of writing, then?' Evrat repeated his question. I did not answer. It was obvious that my ill-wishers had been following me, spying on me, slandering me.

'No reply,' Evrat noted in conclusion. Then, after turning over his papers: 'Let us pass on to a second matter. When did you begin working up the material in your notes? After you had finished collecting all the testimony, or before?'

'Before.'

'A long time before?'

'A long time before.'

'Three months? Six?'

'Six,' I shot blindly in the air.

'How many pages did you manage to write?'

'About...about forty pages.'

'Forty pages. Forty pages are about...twelve thousand words?'

'Approximately.'

'That is to say, in the course of a year you wrote twelve thousand words, namely about thirty words a day if I am not mistaken.'

'I did not write them during a year,' I said, 'but in the course of about three months. Then I stopped.'

'In other words, in ninety days you wrote forty pages. That is, somewhat less than two pages a day.'

'Yes,' I said, taking heart. 'I am in the habit of writing every page six, seven or eight times. If I may be allowed to mention the example of a great writer—Tolstoy, for instance…'

'Never mind Tolstoy for the moment,' smiled Evrat. 'How far have you got with the life of Davidov?'

'Up to…up to about 1930.'

'Can you show us these pages?'

'No,' I said. 'I am not in the habit of showing incomplete work to anyone.'

'Do you mean to say that even the chapters already written are not yet complete?'

'No,' I said stubbornly. 'I may have to rewrite them.'

From my counsel's radiant expression I understood that I was giving the right answers. The teacher was pleased with his pupil.

'Yes,' said Evrat, with a suppressed smile to himself, examining his notes. Then he went on to the next chapter. 'From your counsel's statements at previous sessions,' he said, 'I understand that the cause of the interruption in your writing was…"a mental crisis" in your life. Is that right?'

'Yes,' I replied modestly.

'Can you tell us—of course you are entitled not to answer this question—was this "crisis" in the field of…your erotic life? Your intellectual life?'

'I decline to answer that,' I said.

'Decline?'

'That's right.'

'Permit me to ask you, Mr Jonas,' said Evrat, raising his voice, 'why you did not, the moment you experienced this "crisis" and stopped writing—why you did not come to the publisher and notify him accordingly, but continued to take his money month after month as if nothing had happened?'

I forced down a groan. Yes, I should have done that. Had I been afraid to admit failure? But how could I have done it, after all…?

'Because I hoped, and I still hope,' I said, 'that I'll be able to continue. There have been cases of that kind. It is known, for instance…'

'Don't you think it is a matter of elementary common decency for any man—especially a writer—in a position of this kind to come along at least and say this: I shall be unable to finish the work by the date specified in the contract, and I wish to request an extension. In that case the publisher who engaged you for this work would have had the alternatives to approve the extension as requested or not to approve it, to continue to pay you according to the agreement or not.'

My counsel rose in his place. 'May I be permitted to remind my learned friend,' he said, quietly but firmly, 'that under the contract the publisher was obliged to continue to pay my client his full salary until the end of the period specified in the contract, whether he completed the work or not.'

'This is new to me,' cried Evrat shrilly.

'That is what the law says,' said my counsel proudly.

'Which law?'

'One moment.' My lawyer raised the papers on his table to his eyes, pushed up his spectacles and said: 'I quote from the "Laws of Hiring Human Beings" in the Ottoman Code, Section 6, Article 581: "He that hires a wet-nurse for a specified time and undertakes to pay her hire—if her milk stops, or if the child rejects her breast, he is obliged to pay her hire as he fixed it in the beginning." For the purposes of our discussion, the case of the writer is similar to that of the wet-nurse.'

The laughter that filled the courtroom encompassed every one: the spectators, the plaintiff's lawyers, even his Honour the judge himself. Only my counsel stood looking round in astonishment, not understanding what it was all about.

'I am grateful to my learned friend for the light he has cast on the law,' said Evrat, wiping the tears of laughter from his eyes with his handkerchief. 'Only I intend to prove that this wet-nurse whose case we are now considering has not lost her milk, nor has the child rejected the breast.'

Another wave of laughter flooded the room. But this brief pause in the course of the battle, which gave me some respite for recovery, was a prelude to a renewed and crushing offensive, compared with which the previous exchanges of fire had been no more than a softening-up process. Every shell that whizzed in my direction from now onward was fired with 'And if I put it to you, Mr Jonas...' and burst with a smoke-cloud of 'What would you say to that?'

'And if I put it to you, Mr Jonas, that even these forty pages have never been written and you had no intention of writing them, what would you say to that?'

And straight away, when I protested—

'And if I tell you, Mr Jonas, that there never was any such "crisis" as you speak of, that it is merely an invention designed to justify a deliberate and culpable evasion of your express obligations, what would you say to that?'

And then, following hard on my confused stammers:

'And if I put it to you that you had no intention whatsoever of writing the book which you undertook to write and for which you received money, what would you say to that, Mr Jonas?'

'Why should I have undertaken the work in the beginning? What for?' I cried angrily.

'That is a question for you to answer, not for me,' retorted Evrat, his eyes flashing. 'But I have no need of your reply,' he continued quietly. 'Instead I shall read you a few sentences and ask you to identify the person who said them.'

Had I said something that could betray me? When? To whom? Where? I watched with terror as he leafed through the papers on his table, waiting for the crushing blow he was about to launch.

'Listen carefully,' he said, raising his eyes from the page, on which some poison pen had written words that were hidden from my sight. 'I quote: "Davidov...Who was Davidov, who was he? He was the greatest tyrant this country has known since it was rebuilt. He was a saint, yes, a great saint. But is there a more terrible tyranny in the world than the tyranny of the saints? The wicked may condemn you to suffering, torment, terror. But the righteous don't let you live! Against the wicked you can rebel; against a saint you can't even defend yourself. It's either he or we, my friends. The very fact of his existence—alive or dead—doesn't let us live in peace. His eye is always watching us. His name poisons our memories. His shadow pursues us. If we want to live, it is our sacred duty to wipe out his memory for ever and ever!

'Who said these things?' Evrat's voice chimed in the profound silence that had fallen in the courtroom.

I stood there stunned, overwhelmed. The silence screamed around me and I had not a word to say.

'Mr Jonas,' he cried with emotion, 'on the seventeenth of June, at night, at a party which took place at the home of the poet Nakdimon, in the presence of about a dozen young writers—it was you, it was you who uttered these words, and these words have sealed your doom.'

'It's a lie!' I heard myself declaring.

My head was going round and round. A tempestuous exchange of arguments between the two lawyers hummed past my ears without my understanding a word. I must have grown very pale, for the judge asked anxiously if I felt unwell. Then he banged with his gavel and announced the date of the next session.

Chapter twenty-nine

When I said it was a lie, I was telling the truth. But the truth is that it was not a lie. I recognized those words when Evrat read them out—and yet I did not recognize them. I felt as if he had read out some kind of unhealthy thoughts that swirled within me, sometimes in a whisper, sometimes with a scream—but was it possible that I had spoken them? Never would I have dared to express them in anyone's hearing! It was the wizardry of a cunning lawyer who was also a clairvoyant. Only later, after I had come home from the court, did I remember the details of that party in Nakdimon's house. A major poem of his called 'The Headless Ones' had been published in one of the weekend supplements, and we had come to celebrate the occasion with him. Fulsome praises flowed, and a great deal of drink. Osnat recited the poem, Gumpel elucidated it...I remember that later on, when we were in that state of intoxication in which the wit flows spontaneously and one *bon mot* follows another, Nakdimon delivered a statement that aroused much amusement: 'Our forefathers were hard-boiled pagans, and we are soft-hearted pigeons—except for Jonas of course, who writes paeans to the saints.' They all smiled, but his words rankled: was I really writing a paean to the saints? I, whose life was being made a misery by the book? I had drank a lot in the course of that evening, and I remember that Davidov's name had stung and stabbed at my mind all the time; I wanted to quarrel over him with someone, and later, after midnight, I think, in the heat of some argument I had started I made some kind of speech (which I completely forgot afterwards); and I now remember that while I was speaking Nakdimon said to Gumpel: 'Take down his statement so that it may be used in evidence against him one day' or words to that effect; and when I had finished Nakdimon went up to me, raised my hand high in the air and crowned me; and everyone cheered…All this was wrapped in mist; during the days immediately following that party various people referred to the speech and told me that I had said 'wonderful things', but refused to tell me exactly what they were. Had my confession been passed on from one to the other by word of mouth, until it reached the ears of the plaintiff's side? Or of someone who remembered Davidov? Had the plaintiff's representatives made inquiries and heard about it?

What I would not say in court I must say here in these pages, for I have promised myself to tell the truth here, the whole truth. Yes, I confess: I hated my master. I had hated him ever since I had become his slave. I do not remember exactly when it started, when this malignant growth germinated which spread afterwards like a cancer throughout my body. Was it when I met Nili? No, long before that. Perhaps it was as early as after the first two or three meetings with those who admired Davidov and cherished his memory. Little by little this hatred grew, spreading like a disease in my blood. For a long time I refused to admit its existence; I was afraid to face it, even to breathe its name. I tried to get rid of it, as if it were an infected flea. But I felt its bite. The more stories I heard, the more I took down, the stronger it became. And the file that contained my notes—the more it thickened and swelled, the more I came to look on it as a criminal file in which I, with my own hands, was assembling evidence against myself. Why had I started it all? I believe the first time I confessed this hatred to myself was on the night I met Menahem Schweig in the street, when his disgusted face confronted my drunken one—it was one of those nights when Nili's sudden disappearance left me like a mad dog howling at the car headlights passing in the darkness. I had just come up from the Cellar, dead drunk, Eliraz and Saul holding me by the arms, and I was shouting at a passing car: 'Freu-den-thal! Where are you going?' And again: 'Freu-den-thal!' Suddenly I saw Schweig in front of me, with another man dressed in a leather jacket, swimming before my eyes as in a yellow mist. I broke away from my supporters, charged at him, swaying on my feet, and thrust a finger into his chest. 'Schweig! Why are you silent, Schweig? Don't you see what's going on in this country? It's being desecrated, and you...' I could not finish, for at that moment the nauseating mixture of drinks I had swallowed came up in my throat. I ran to the nearest tree, leaned my forehead on it, and vomited. I heard this Schweig saying to his companion behind my back, with a kind of disgust: 'Shameful! And a man like that is commissioned to write the book about Davidov.' This spit in the eye was enough to sober me up in a moment. Beneath my arm resting on the tree I saw the two of them withdrawing, as if from something unclean. 'Idiot,' I mumbled to myself. Afterwards when Eliraz came up and asked who they were, I said as if still intoxicated: 'Oh, a couple of respectable labour leaders—they haven't seen a working man for twenty years,' and he burst out into loud laughter that echoed through the street. Later, on my way home, I kept on repeating to myself: 'I hate him, I hate Davidov, hate him, hate him.'

Yes, I did say those things that were thrown in my face in court, I recognize the tone of voice. No doubt I was exaggerating, and they smell of the fumes of drink. But I carried them within me like a call to revolt. For the more I heaped one period on top of another in my notes, the higher grew the load on my back—a mountainous load that threatened to crush me. All the hundreds of facts and minute details about Davidov in the Labour Legion, at Lydda, Jerusalem, Kfar Sava, the Dead Sea, Hanita, all over the country, interlaced and proliferated around me, every day a new shoot, like a climbing parasitic weed that stifles the trunk it embraces. I had meant to write about a dead man, and he was stifling the life out of me. I had sold my soul to a saint. I was no longer free; I could not cast off this shadow, the shadow of Davidov. It clung to my heels wherever I went; it grew longer and longer, and, although it had not the slightest resemblance to my own shape and figure, I was inseparably identified with it. I was regarded as its representative in the land of the living. 'Mr Davidov,' was Nakdimon's usual greeting. 'How is Davidov getting on?' people used to ask me in the street with the gleam of great expectations in their eyes, in the faith that very soon, there in the secret places of my scriptorial sanctum, the dry bones would be joined together, bone to bone, and I would give them breath and they would live. I had to defend him from detractors, praise him to admirers, conjure up his spirit for the benefit of those who cherished his memory—when I wanted to throttle him within me! The tyranny of righteousness! I thought resentfully when I sat down at my desk to try to arrange those notes and put them into some kind of shape. The letters I wrote on the paper were dead—compared with them, Ahuva's paper letters were full of vitality and movement. Why had he lived, why had he died, why was he haunting me, how had he succeeded in invading my life to lord it over me with his vigilant eye, with his surveillance of all my actions, day and night? Of my most intimate desires—which were my own private domain, in God's name, my private and personal domain! Didn't I have the right to do as I pleased—to lust, to hate, to get drunk, to make love—without his eyes watching me all the rest of my life? And that trial for a debt of a few thousands! They would be charging me with attempted murder by strangulation if they knew the truth.

The truth, I say. Is that the whole truth? I no longer know. I am beginning to doubt it. For after all, when I write that I 'hated' him, I feel the scraping of the pen grating terribly on my ear. Something stabs at me inside, urging me to score it out. Such a word cannot be written down like that in black and white, letter by letter. Perhaps it isn't right. Perhaps it isn't so. For when I call him to mind, the living man I knew, at that youthful meeting by the Atlit salt-pans or at our last meeting (of which I shall tell later) on the burning plain on the road to Sodom, something throbs within me, warm and yearning…. And surely there were many moments when, remembering him, I felt the touch of his hand on my shoulder. And there were moments when, listening to the tales they told of him, I would sense a kind of whisper like the whisper of the hot summer wind carrying the scent of chaff from the hills. Didn't I turn to him sometimes, in moments of distress, as to a father? Didn't I envy him his impetuous, insubordinate wanderings over the broad land, there in the Labour corps, at Lydda, Jerusalem, the Dead Sea, Hanita…? Perhaps, after all, I loved him.

No, score it out, score it out! I say to myself. That word can't be put down in black and white either without my hearing some demonic laughter from a distance.

So what? And why these feelings of guilt, as if half the country was insisting that I must settle some kind of debt that I had attested with my signature in my own blood?

Feelings of guilt, I say: how deep are they? I will not kill myself over them. Nor will I kneel like Raskolnikov in the heart of the public square to kiss the muddy ground. These are different days. None of us will say today with a heart tormented by suffering: 'Great is the riddle of life, greater than the riddle of death' or flee in terror from 'that blind, oppressive sadness which needs no consolation, even if it exists'. Did I love Nili? Did I not love her? Yes, I loved! But I have already forgotten.

This morning I went to see my counsel and said to him: 'Well, I understand I have lost.'

'Why?' he replied in surprise. 'Because of those silly things they claim you said? Even if they can prove that you really said them, what is the legal value of things that a man says when he is drunk, when he is not in his right mind? Nobody can use them as a stick to beat you with or present them as evidence against you. We can always argue that you were speaking in jest or in irony or that you were just being foolish—no one can prove the contrary. On the psychologist's couch there may be some significance in the things a man says when he is not in his right mind, but in a court of law…'

Apparently, then, the trial will continue.

Chapter thirty

I have written nothing for two days, but I do not regret it—not because of the doubtful favour I did to Arditi and his daughter, but because of an old, lost memory salvaged thanks to them.

A few evenings ago Arditi climbed up to the roof, knocked on my door, entered, begged a thousand pardons, and when I pressed him to speak out asked me, with a stammering humility that made it hard to refuse, to mediate between him and his daughter's betrothed. He wanted to make it up with the fellow. His daughter would never agree to marry him, but he admitted that the other had suffered shame and mental anguish, and he was prepared to compensate him: to pay him two or three hundred pounds—all his savings—just to settle the quarrel, which had caused a regrettable breach between himself and his son. He could see that I was a sensible and generous man and had a soft spot for Yonina, who was always singing my praises, and he begged me to go with him to Ramleh and help them to compose their differences. I agreed.

We arrived there the day before yesterday in the early evening. We went into an old Arab house, standing at the end of a muddy lane on the edge of a stony patch that stretched as far as a dusky olive grove. Elijah Khalfon sat with six or seven of his family round a big table with a bowl of dried melon-seeds in the middle. I was invited to sit down and crack a few seeds with the rest of them, but when Arditi said he would like to talk to Elijah alone we went out with him to the back yard. The electric bulb above the lintel outside lit up a broad-branched fig tree, a bench, a rickety wicker chair, a wretched little donkey-cart, and a sooty clothes-boiler resting on a circle of sooty stones.

I opened the negotiations by saying on behalf of Arditi that there had been an unfortunate occurrence, an unfortunate mistake, and that both sides should try to forget what had happened. Forget?—Khalfon's face flushed—how could he forget? All his family, all his friends looked down on him, laughed at him, his honour had been defiled…Yes, I said, Mr Arditi was well aware of that; he was deeply distressed and he wanted to do all in his power to prevent any slight on anyone's honour, but when the girl refused she could not be forced…. Forced? The girl?—Khalfon glared with bloodshot eyes. It was only his friendship for her brother and his own generous heart that had induced him to agree to the betrothal, for where would they get a fine, healthy man to take a cripple for his wife? So far as he was concerned, he would willingly have forgotten the whole business if only it hadn't become public talk and he had made preparations and laid out money…. If it's a matter of money—said Arditi humbly…

A bent woman in a red kerchief came out from the house with a copper tray and set cups of coffee before us. Arditi spoke about money and Khalfon about honour, while Yonina lay between them like a trussed lamb.

As I sipped the coffee my glance was caught by the big boiler on the sooty stones, with the twigs for the fire packed beneath it. Suddenly a lost memory broke through to the surface as from a distant dream. I was five at the time or less, and in the yard of our house, in the shade of the eucalyptus, stood just such a boiler, on stones like these, with a fire burning beneath it and steam rising from it, and my mother, with a red kerchief on her head, was stirring the washing with a stick. Then she lifted out the steaming garments and transferred them to a vat that stood on a stool. I sat on a stone, my thumb in my mouth, and stared at the fire crackling under the boiler, at the flying sparks and the rising steam. I asked—as I had no doubt asked many times before—when Daddy would come back. I knew what she would reply, and I knew it was not the truth. When she pulled out with the stick a long shirt, dripping with water, it seemed to me that she was pulling him up out of the boiling liquid, swathed in steam, only he had no body, for the body had been burnt away. When she stood beside the vat and scrubbed the shirt on the washboard I said to myself: She's washing him, she's washing him so hard…. It was hot in the yard in the noonday sun, withered eucalyptus leaves lay scattered in the dust, birds twittered in the topmost branches. Something bitter stuck in my throat, there was something salty in my eyes, as if from the smoke that spread from between the sooty stones. I had not known my father, but I felt him pressing on me as if it was his body that was being maltreated in the vat.

Arditi and Khalfon, under the fig tree, went on talking about honour, about money, about limping Yonina. On the way back I could not get that sight out of my mind. When I got back to my room, I jotted down the first lines of a story.

Chapter thirty-one

On the veranda of the Dan Hotel, looking out to sea, with two glasses of whisky on the rocks in front of us, I heard from Judah Dotan, a senior official in the Prime Minister's Office and a former member of the Haganah command, about Davidov's activities during the years of the war, the struggle against the British, and the illegal immigration. Everything glittered in the wind, the sun and the sea at that afternoon hour. Below, on the foam-licked sand, little balls flew between little round bats, figures in colourful bathing-suits lounged in the deck-chairs, brown bodies breasted the waves, sails fluttered in the distance. The whisky gleamed like crystal in the shining light from the sea. Dotan's silvery locks fluttered on his forehead and his blue eyes twinkled roguishly as he remembered the Davidov of those days. ('A visionary! What a fantastic visionary the man was! You can't imagine.') For a long, straggling hour he amused himself with his stories.

'For instance,' he said, 'for instance in 'forty-two, when Rommel was at the gates.... What a crazy idea!'

In 1942 Davidov proposed to the Haganah command that a kind of Jewish 'second front' should be opened in the heart of Europe.

They should contact the General Staff of the Red Army and suggest co-operation between the partisans in the occupied territories and Palmach units that would be parachuted into Poland, Rumania and Czechoslovakia to sabotage enemy installations. The Russians would supply the arms and the Haganah the men.

'And even before that, in the winter of 'forty-one...'

I shall not go into too much detail. The history of the period is familiar, more or less. In the winter of 1941, after the deportation to Mauritius of the illegal immigrants in the *Atlantic*, Davidov presented a detailed plan for breaking into the Atlit camp; in the summer of 1943 he joined the men who went down to the look-out posts in the Negev and spent a month at Beit-Eshel; in November 1943 he was summoned from home to help besieged Ramat-Hakovesh; in November 1945, on the morrow of the attacks on the coastal patrols he was arrested with the others and spent three months in detention at Rafah; in March 1947 he was on the shore at Nitzanim on the night when the *Shabtai Lozinsky* was beached, was caught and taken in the convoy to Haifa port, and, since he did not want to identify himself and mingled with the illegal immigrants, was put on the deportation ship. He spent six months in the Cyprus detention camps, organizing, teaching and training the deportees.

No, he was not in the Palmach commandos. In 1944, he wanted to join the Palmach as an instructor. He had actually been accepted, but his wife Zippora came along and intervened.

'In those days, you know, the command sometimes had to deal with family matters,' Dotan said. 'We used to know what was going on in every leading member's home. They used to consult us, not only on questions of work and livelihood and housing, but even on the most intimate problems. Sometimes we even acted as mediators in family quarrels. We knew, for instance, who had a love affair, who was on the way to a divorce, who had got entangled.... It wasn't that we kept on making inquiries about these things, but people used to come to us of their own accord to ask for advice, sometimes help. About Davidov we knew very little. There were rumours, of course, something at the Dead Sea, something at Hanita. But he himself never talked about his personal affairs. Except about his son. He often brought him to town. Took him to museums, bought him books on art. He had great hopes of him. I doubt if he ever mentioned Zippora. By the way, have you met her? No, actually there's no point in it. Well, one day she came to see me and said: "Listen, I've never interfered in Abrasha's work. He does what he wants and I don't stop him. I've got used to his leaving home for weeks and months on end. We have a seven-acre field and you can believe me that he's sowed it five times and never yet reaped the crop. Once it was beans, once vetch, once melons—we've never got a copper out of it. Only losses. Now I hear you're going to take him into the Palmach. That means he won't be home for at least two years. I want you to know what the position is…" And here she told me about their daughter, who was twelve or thirteen years old at the time. The girl had grown up wild, refused to go to school, roamed about the streets, had had to have psychiatric treatment. Finally she said: "I only want you to know that if you do this thing there will be trouble. That's all I wanted to tell you." She got up and went out. I was stunned. There was something in her piercing eyes, in her hard voice, that seemed to threaten disaster. We gave in; that is, he himself gave in. I believe that was the only time he gave way to her. There was something hard in him, that man. And at the same time—generous too, warm-hearted, full of contradictions.'

Dotan's name came over the hotel loudspeaker; he interrupted his story and rose. He had to meet some film producer from America. Before we parted he said, as if presenting me with an amulet for protection during a long, perilous journey:

'Remember one thing: Davidov was one of the few men who live and breathe history, who feel it in their bones. Perhaps that is the key to the understanding of his personality.'

Three or four days later a messenger boy arrived with an express letter. It contained an invitation to come to Dotan's house that evening for a reception for Mr Sheldon Zelnikoff, the American film producer.

The lady of the house, a tall, sharp-nosed woman, welcomed me in the salon of the villa with familial cordiality. 'You're Mr Jonas,' she said, taking my hand in both of hers, 'I'm so glad you could come.'

Then she whispered confidentially into my ear: 'Mr Zelnikoff is very, very interested in meeting you. Judah told him about you. You speak English, don't you? Of course!' Not-so-young, not-so-pretty women darted winsome glances at me from the couches—thanks, apparently, to my beard, which proclaimed me as the only representative of the artists' breed in the house. In the middle of the room, at a table adorned with drinks, stood a group of men in dark suits with glasses in their hands. 'Gentlemen,' announced my hostess in English, holding on to my hand with a warm and intimate grip, 'I want to introduce our writer, Mr Jonas.' The circle of men turned partly towards me, with hesitant bows or polite smiles which froze in the air halfway to me. 'Mr Zelnikoff, Mr Jonas. Mr…' Mrs Dotan introduced me to each of her guests like a superbly decorated cake, the pride of the chef. And to the two Israelis in the group, 'You know Mr Jonas, you've no doubt read his books.'

The company did not know what to do with their smiles and left them hanging in the air. The two Israelis who had read 'my books' nodded. 'Mr Zelnikoff,' my hostess declared with festive animation, 'this is the man my husband spoke to you about. You remember, I suppose.' Zelnikoff did not remember, but nodded his big, elephantine head, with its old, heavy eyelids. 'Yes, yes,' he said, giving me a searching look, holding the glass in front of him. At that moment Dotan himself arrived, gave me a hearty welcome, poured out a glass of champagne and offered it to me, said something to Zelnikoff about a talk they had had, then put his arm round my shoulder and took me aside. Zelnikoff, he said, with the air of imparting an important confidence, was looking for an original Israeli script, and he was prepared to invest half a million dollars in producing the film. While he was talking to him, as Dotan was suggesting various books and subjects, the idea suddenly came into his head that, actually, Davidov was *the* subject for a great Israeli film, a wonderful production that would embrace the whole of this land. The entire history of the new nation, the whole of that glorious and colourful pioneering era, were implicit in the life of one man who had realized in body and spirit the finest ideals of his generation. It was a miracle—an auspicious coincidence—that on the very same day, just before his meeting with

Zelnikoff, he had met me. As if there was a divine purpose behind it. When he had told Zelnikoff about Davidov's exploits—some of them, not all—the producer had been fired by the idea. He was most enthusiastic. 'Bring the man to me,' he had said, 'that's a great subject!' He had gone on to describe to Dotan how he envisaged the film and what advantages it would bring to the country as a whole, 'And to you, personally, of course,' he added meaningfully, 'from every point of view, and I needn't say more.' Zelnikoff was prepared to pay two thousand dollars plus royalties for the script if he liked it. He was ready to give a non-returnable advance of five hundred if he was assured that I was starting work. Government assistance was also certain. 'I don't want you to answer yes or no immediately. Think about it. Chew it over. I myself got the idea all of a sudden. But first of all talk things over with Zelnikoff. I want him to know you.'

Dotan put his arms on both our shoulders, mine to the right and Zelnikoff's to the left, and led us out to the garden beside the house. Zelnikoff remembered it clearly now. That pioneer from Russia, who fought the Arabs and the British. A story about the immigrant boat and the deportation to Cyprus. The son who fell in the War of Independence. 'A very exciting life-story.' The main question was the script. The script made the film. It would have to be of universal significance, speak to the heart of every man, Italian, Greek, Frenchman or American, even if he had no prior idea of the national or historical background. That was the secret of the success of all the great films: *The Bridge on the River Kwai, The Guns of Navarone, Gone with the Wind*. Davidov must be first of all a living man, a human being, with his own faults and virtues—not a symbol—that every spectator in the world could identify with, could say to himself 'That's me', or 'That could have been me'…Could I prepare a précis for him, about ten to fifteen pages, by next Tuesday? He was flying on Wednesday and would be back again in three months. He could take the script with him and look at it on the way. If he found it a good basis for a scenario we could sign a contract. Could I supply it by next Tuesday evening?

In the salon my hostess poured more champagne into my glass. 'My husband has great hopes for you,' she said, her face shining up into mine. On the couch beside me a woman with a pearl necklace round her shrunken neck was interested in my writing. Did I only write film scripts, or novels and plays too? Could an Israeli writer earn a living by writing? Was I married? At what hours of the day or night did I write? Was it a matter of inspiration? Had I perhaps read Herman Wouk's last book? 'Your English is marvellous,' she said, her pearls glittering at me.

Champagne works on me very fast. I become light, airy. Coloured ribbons sprout from my head. Laughter bubbles on my lips. I see bird's nests and radiant palaces, women with bright coronets on their heads, rivers of honey, mythical birds. After the fifth glass I kissed the hostess. After the sixth I paid my respects to the entire company and went outside. I saw the host of heaven like sheaves of fireworks, as on the night of a festival.

Chapter thirty-two

As letters continue to drop into a dead man's letter-box a long time after his death, so I still get letters about the book I am not writing. This morning I found one in my box from a man in Beersheba called Hayim Kafri, who used to belong to the Palmach and knew Davidov when he was working on the Sodom road in 1952. The letter was meant to correct one detail in his story which I noted down half a year ago and more. I present it here to avoid misleading anyone who may make some use of these notes:

Dear Comrade Jonas,

I suppose the book is now ready for the press, but I am sending you these few lines in the hope that you may still be able to make a few corrections in the Beersheba-Sodom chapter.

A few days ago some of the fellows came to see me, and we were telling tales about 'the good old days', as they say. One thing led to another and we started talking about Davidov, and I found out that I had misled you about several details in connection with the affair of the house. Perhaps you won't think it's very important, but seeing as I regard myself as responsible for what I said—and somebody might be offended—I shouldn't like to be the cause later of all kinds of charges and denials and goodness knows what. Well, the facts are as follows:

The house in Beersheba that Davidov was supposed to get (I believe I told you it was in a very bad state—an Arab ruin that was almost destroyed during the fighting) wasn't vacant at the time. True, it had been promised to Davidov, but since Davidov was working on the road and living at the Kurnub camp and told them that in any case he wouldn't be able to take possession for about another year, till after the work was finished, the house was temporarily entrusted by the Custodian of Abandoned Property to one of the managers of the Public Works Department, Solomon Davidson. In the meantime this Davidson renovated it, repaired the damage, built on another room and so forth, and altogether—so I was told—invested about five thousand pounds in the house. When Davidov came and claimed the fulfilment of the promise it was no longer possible to expel Davidson, not only because of his investment but also because he had a big family (a wife and four children), and Davidov, if he had moved in, would only have moved in with his wife, for his daughter, as you know, had emigrated to Australia some time before.

By the way, since nothing came of the business of the co-operative quarry at kilometre 18, I doubt if he would have moved to Beersheba at all even if he had got the house.

Naturally he was very angry about the business, especially because he was in a pretty bad state at the time, for reasons you know about, but, as I have now found out, it would be wrong to blame those who were responsible for the allocation of abandoned buildings in the town in those days.

I hope you will manage to make this correction and that I am not giving you too much trouble.

All the best,

HAYIM KAFRI

Chapter thirty-three

I pass over numerous interviews and numerous details about the years 1946, 1947 and 1948, and come to that terrible Tuesday, July 20th, 1948, when the father went out to meet his son and never saw him again.

In the evening of July 9th, at the end of the first truce in the War of Independence, Davidov was riding with the armoured column that took Wilhelma, Lydda airfield and Tira and reached Deir-Tarif. Next day he took part in the fierce fighting for Beit-Naballa. In the afternoon of that day the Arab Legion withdrew from the village and our forces entered. While the units of the Jephthah Brigade were mounting their pincer attack on Lydda and Ramleh, there were still artillery battles north and east of Beit-Naballa. On the Monday morning our positions were shelled by the Legion's artillery, who were repulsed to the hills only after four hours' fighting. During the next four days—after the whole of Lydda had surrendered, including the police fortress and the hundred Arab soldiers who were defending it—our posts in the village were still being severely shelled by guns and mortars and facing counter-attacks by tanks, armoured cars and infantry. Kula, about seven kilometres north of Beit-Naballa, changed hands several times, and at Hadita, to the south of it, the fighting continued. On the Saturday, after the second truce had been proclaimed, a fellow from the Emek Battalion brought a note to Davidov from his son which had been given to him by someone who had reached Barfilia through Hulda from Shaar Hagai, about halfway along the road to Jerusalem. The date on it was July 15ᵗʰ. The following is a copy of this note, which I have kept together with the few letters that have not been lost:

July 15th, 1948   *Deir el-Amar Post*

Dear Dad,

I am taking the opportunity of one of the lads going down to the plain to write you this hasty note, and I hope it will find you somewhere in the neighbourhood of Lydda-Ramleh. We are stuck here on an eagle's nest, about two thousand feet above sea level, and if I weren't short-sighted I might be able to discover you in the broad plain that stretches below as far as the horizon—tranquil, pastoral, veiled in a tenuous mist with puffs of bluish smoke here and there, as if there were no war. So far, everything has gone pretty smoothly. We reached this rocky peak after midnight at the end of a long, tiring night march, but almost without fighting. The night before we took Tzuba, using the old trick of Joshua's men at Ai which the enemy's soldiers didn't learn at school. We found the fortress empty and when day broke we could still see the last of them running away. Out of range, thank God (that 'weakness' of mine, the fear of standing face to face with the enemy, which you have tried to show me is not a weakness)! Well, we're advancing by leaps and bounds, and if the sun stands still on Gibeon for a few hours—unless they proclaim another truce (as the rumours say)—we'll meet halfway along the road, somewhere in the neighbourhood of Latrun. Then the newspapermen will have the chance to describe a 'dramatic' meeting between the two arms of the pincers, with father and son at the heads of the columns…If there's a truce after all (Bernadotte, they say, has decided to hand over Jerusalem to the Arabs, and if there's any idea in Tel Aviv of giving in to him then our chaps say: To arms! Civil war!) we'll go on sitting in the posts and I'll make a few more drawings of 'Soldiers at Rest'—quite amateurish (mostly of boot-soles). By the way, a few days ago we got hold of a week-old copy of *Davar,* and it had a report about a 'manifesto' of fifteen artists against the Artists' General Exhibition—something about the need to 'insist on maturity and eradicate all immaturity and dilettantism'…Of course dilettantism should be eradicated, but what's bad about 'immaturity'? Why should the ripe figs resent the green ones?

A military career is not for me, it seems; your son and heir will never be a 'war hero'. Every time we stop for a rest (and sometimes even on the march, when the webbing chafes your shoulders and the sun beats down on your head) I get a craving to draw, to draw in colour, to draw the landscape. War (perhaps this is a silly idea) changes the colour values of the landscape, seems to strip the materials naked. Everything becomes more intense. The rocks take on the colour of camels' skulls and bones. Arab ruins absorb enormous quantities of sunshine, like the marl of the Dead Sea plains. Something demented, like after an earthquake ('The mountains trembled and all the hills shook')—that 'fragmentation' or 'disintegration' which you once spoke about in connection with Goya, but more brutal here, perhaps because the sun is more brutal. Even at this moment, when I can hear very far away (from your direction, apparently) the muffled echo of gunfire, the sound affects the colours I see. If we talk about 'Israeli painting', it'll certainly be completely different from European, even Spanish painting, because of the powerful light which neutralizes colour contrasts. There is no red, no absolute blue, no absolute green like you see in El Greco or Velasquez. When we were in Abu-Ghosh and I looked again at that image of the Madonna on top of the church I was struck by the terrific contrast between that petrified marble and the disorderly movement all around. An *alien* image, without any connection either with the landscape or with the ancient past that pervades it. (Perhaps that was why there was such strong opposition to images being stationed here under the Greeks and the Romans?) 'The landscape is inside,' as you once said to me, but this 'inside' where I am concerned is strongly influenced by the 'outside'. It is changeable. It's quite different now, in these surroundings, from what it was at home before the fighting.

Apart from exhaustion (two successive nights without sleep, marches and so on), I'm in good health. All kinds of old anxieties have evaporated or dried up in the sun. Strange that it should be here and now, here in the post—when we are expecting a counter-attack that is certain to come in another hour or two—that I am not troubled by those worries about 'fear' and 'death'. Perhaps it's because I'm myopic, and time is 'refracted' for me into images…

I must finish. An infantry detachment arrived a few minutes ago from Jerusalem, to relieve us, it seems. I don't know yet where we shall go. Perhaps to another sector. In any case we'll surely meet soon. If you see Mum before me, assure her that she has nothing to worry about so far as I am concerned. 'We will pursue, we will overtake, we will divide the spoil.' The enemy flees before we can manage to catch him by the tail.

Love,

NIMROD

On Saturday and Sunday the fighting was still going on in the neighbourhood of Beit-Naballa. The enemy had concentrated at Budrus and was trying to recapture Hadita. He had made five attacks and been repulsed with casualties and damage to his armoured cars. Kula had been reoccupied by the Legion soldiers, and was taken again only at dawn on Sunday. Beit-Naballa itself was still being shelled. An armoured column that had approached the front line had compelled our forces to withdraw, and it was only after several hours' battle that the attack was repulsed and the whole village fell into our hands. On Monday a company of Haganah veterans arrived from Tel Aviv to relieve the fighting men and hold the place.

On Tuesday morning, July 20th, when the second truce was
already in force, Davidov got five days' leave. At about nine he reached
Lydda—a silent town, the debris of battle still scattered about the
streets: smashed armoured cars, dead horses, broken furniture, rolls
of barbed wire—and went to brigade headquarters, intending to
go home to Kfar Sava. A Jeep stopped in front of the entrance and
someone called his name. Davidov was delighted to meet Rozhansky
from Be'er-Tuvia, who had been with him in the shock troops in
1937 when they patrolled the 'Eastern line'. Rozhansky was on the
way to Jerusalem and Davidov decided on the spot to give up the
idea of going home and go up to the hills with him, hoping to find
Nimrod in one of the posts at Shaar-Hagai or Hartuv. 'All along the
road he was in great spirits,' Rozhansky told me. 'He was bubbling
with enthusiasm at the results of the ten days' campaign between the
truces, at the sight of the areas taken on both sides of the "Burma
Road". He showed a kind of open pride, which wasn't usual with
him. Laughed, told tales about the brave exploits of the lads who
had been with him in his post. About his son he said nothing. Didn't
mention him.' When they reached Shaar-Hagai they inquired about
the headquarters of the Jerusalem Battalion and were directed to the
lower pumping stations farther up the road. At the pumping house
Davidov inquired about his son's company and was told it had been
stationed there a couple of days before, but had gone up to Beit-Nuba,
above the road to Latrun. Here Davidov parted from Rozhansky,
went back on his tracks, and set out by himself to climb the path
to Beit-Nuba. When he reached the post at midday the officer in
charge of the company was shocked to find that Davidov did not
know about his son's death. He was sure that he had come in the
wake of the notification that had been sent to his home the previous
day. At first Davidov did not understand when the other mumbled
a few words of condolence. When they told him: 'He has fallen,' he
cried: 'Who?' The officer did not know what to say. 'I thought you
knew,' he stammered. 'I was asking about Nimrod, Nimrod Davidov,'
the father insisted, refusing to understand. Then he sank down on to
the sandbags and sat stunned, silent. The officer sat down beside him
and told him about the battle of the night of July 18th. At midnight

they had set out to attack the eastern outposts of Latrun. Two of the posts were taken under cover of darkness, but before dawn the Legion's armoured cars, with one tank, approached from the direction of Latrun. The company had no heavy arms. There was a panic, men ran away. The company was surrounded and threatened by the Arab posts above. At first light the order to withdraw was given. Nimrod was badly wounded during the retreat and remained lying in the open. When they got back to him he was dead. The bodies had been transferred to Kiryat-Ye'arim.

Davidov reached home in the evening. His wife had known of the tragedy the day before, but had refused to go to the funeral. At night the cries of the bereaved father could be heard from the hut in the copse: 'Why have you left me, why?'

Chapter thirty-four

In the summer of 1952 I came, together with another eight student volunteers, to a hutted camp at a spot known as Kurnub c, to help build the road to Sodom. There were about eight hundred men in this burning fiery furnace, through which the Tarmac serpent wound its painful way under white-hot skies, crossing a dreary waste scourged by sandstorms which rolled from one horizon to the other. Among the clouds of dust that spread from the chalk hills the air was filled with the deafening rattle of the pneumatic drills and the grating of the teeth of the bulldozers butting at piles of stones and casting them down into the abyss, or pounding with their chains the white, finely ground dust which fell down into the depths and rose in columns of smoke from the gorges. At midday the heat and thirst were unbearable if the water-truck was late, stuck fast somewhere in the heart of the desert, on the way from Be'er-Yeroham or Beersheba. Someone would go crazy, run amok, attack a foreman with a hammer or an iron bar, infecting with his madness an entire gang, whose cries would drown the noise of the machines that were gnawing at the mountain. On the glowing tin huts there was a big, glaring inscription in tar: 'all Ashkenazim thieves, all Sephardim good'; and the gunpowder that was compressed into the holes drilled in the rocks threatened a volcanic outburst that might bury the whole of the camp and its inmates. Fear of the police, who used to make a surprise raid on the road every few days, would drive all the dubious characters to the refuge of the rocks all around, where they would hide till the danger was over. A dynamite operator called Jackson, who had a robbery sentence hanging over him, used to change his appearance every day, framing his face in various headcloths, wearing a Mexican hat or growing sideburns, to escape from the arm of the law. An Algerian explosives expert nicknamed 'Indo-China', who used to risk his life by inserting T.N.T. in the upright walls of the wadi standing on the brink of the chasm, once hit a Druse quarrier on the head so hard that blood flowed from his mouth. Maurice, a pimp from Haifa, used to steal sacks of sugar from the camp kitchen and smuggle them by night to Beersheba. Budram Halfu from Tripoli, who was in charge of the meat supply, would put aside substantial cuts for himself and hide them in his tent. Mordecai Agabba, a sledge-hammer operator, used to keep three work-tickets in his pocket and triple his pay every week. The drinking-water was lukewarm and polluted; tiny worms floated in the cups. Four drivers were caught one night at an orgy in their hut with three girls brought from town. Matilda used to peel potatoes sitting on a stool by the store-room gate, with legs apart, and the lads used to walk backwards and forwards to peep at the private parts exposed to public view. Lime furnaces filled the air with choking fumes. A young fellow called Mendel, a survivor from Nazi Europe who had worked during the war in the Silesian mines at Katowice, was bruised all over his body when he was climbing down a rope-ladder to a rock-terrace and a fall of stones carried him to the bottom of the gorge. A Hungarian called Leibowitch, who worked on the embankment, used to talk incessantly about nerves, reflexes and *coitus reservatus*. Lads with red kerchiefs on their heads used to sing 'Josephine, Josephine' by the vats of boiling pitch. One day a new immigrant from India, Solomon Solomon, told his two companions on the shift that he was 'fed up with it all', went behind a rock and shot himself. The road clove its channel with grunts and groans between two arid mountainous slopes gnawed by scorpion-like bulldozers, and reached a wild rocky headland, from which it looked down on the broad plain of salt, a burning land of chasms, petrified in the throes of creation, like an ocean bottom laid bare after the deluge.

Davidov, in a Jeep, supervised the work; his name was a byword among the men. For some time I worked at stone-breaking and did not see him, but I heard he had fallen out with two men and expelled them from the camp. This is how it happened. Black-robed Beduin used to stand, solitary in the desert, at intervals on the edge of the Tarmac ribbon, with tethered sheep in their arms, to sell them for a trifle rather than see them die in the drought. The drivers of the trucks carrying stones, gravel, water and bread would halt for a moment, push a pound into their hands and get possession of the fresh meat, to roast or sell. Once a Jeep stopped beside one of them, and two fine home-bred fellows got out, snatched the sheep from its owner's arms and drove off at top speed towards Beersheba. The plundered Beduin walked for half a day through the wilderness until he reached the camp, and wandered helplessly from one hut to another, not knowing whom to ask for redress. It was Davidov who asked what he wanted and, when he had bewailed his loss, took him with him to the town. They found the two men in a restaurant. Davidov seized them and brought them with the Beduin to his encampment, where he forced them to empty their pockets in front of the elders. Then he drove them out of the camp in disgrace.

One day, when I was breaking stones for foundations in the noontime heat, a hand touched my shoulder. 'Give me the hammer for a moment, I'll show you how.' It was Davidov, from the Atlit salt-pans, years back. His temples had greyed, the glow in his eyes was dimmed. Only the arms swung as powerfully as then. 'Don't remember me?' I said when he returned the hammer. His glance rested on me and he said: 'At Atlit, I believe, wasn't it?' Without pausing he got into his Jeep and drove off at top speed over the stones on the downward road.

I thought he had forgotten. But two days later he stopped again. 'Hard, eh?' he said, and took me behind the embankment to work with the surveyors down below, on the slope, far from the clatter of the pneumatic hammers and the din of the breaking stones. 'Show him what to do,' he said to Sasson, 'and teach him to use the theodolite.' Sasson wore a brown pith helmet, a relic of his service as an officer in the Baghdad police. The theodolite was his talisman, the symbol of his honourable status in this mixed multitude of the wilderness. He sent me with a green flag to the lower part of the route to mark angles and distances for the lens of his eyepiece. All around was a wilderness of flinty expanses strewn with splintered stones like pieces of thousands of shattered pitchers; a hot wind rumbled among the fragments. I drove in pegs between the stones. When Davidov came back he rebuked Sasson from his seat in the Jeep for not entrusting me with the theodolite. 'I want him to learn,' he said, and drove off up the slope. 'A hard man,' said Sasson. 'What's he so angry about?' Then he added: 'But they're all like that here. It's this road. A man turns into a beast that eats stones, drinks tar, and shits asphalt.'

In the evening I met Davidov in the deserted dining-hall, in a waste of powdered dust and naked wooden tables and rickety benches, sickly in the yellowish light. He asked how I was, what I had been doing since Atlit, how I had arrived here. When I told him I was studying literature in Jerusalem he said it was a good thing that I had come. In this furnace a new land was being moulded. Eight hundred men from seventy countries, all of them being pounded and hammered into shape on this road that was going down to Sodom. At every kilometre they changed. By the time they reached the Dead Sea they would be unrecognizable. The burning desert had created the nation three thousand years ago, the burning desert was creating it again today. Anyone who did not pass through the furnace of the road would not know the nation. He spoke encouragingly, but his voice was not joyful; it was tired and lustreless. Then he pointed to an old man in an embroidered skull-cap who was sitting in a corner reading a book. 'Look at that fellow,' he said. 'A Tunisian. Shlomo Abusdrus is his name. Can you imagine what he's reading here, in this wilderness?' We went up to the old man, it was the *Book of the Zohar,* published by 'The Heavenly Lustre' in Jerba, Tunisia, with an Arabic commentary in Hebrew letters by Jacob Bashiri. Davidov, who apparently knew him well, induced him to give us one of his Cabbalistic sermons. Abusdrus said: 'There are three kinds of fire in Gehenna: fire that consumes and drinks, fire that drinks and does not consume, and fire that consumes fire. There are coals in it like mountains and there are coals like the Dead Sea and like large stones, and there are rivers of pitch and sulphur in it, flowing and seething. To what does all this refer? To the road to Sodom. For behold the day burneth like a furnace.' 'And what about you, Abusdrus?' said Davidov. 'You must be one of the wicked, for you're being roasted in the fire of Gehenna!' 'I'm middling wicked,' grinned the old man, revealing yellowing teeth. 'The middling wicked go down into Gehenna, are purified and rise again. The Almighty puts them into the fire and refines them like silver. He bringeth down into hell—and raiseth up!'

The Moroccans, Algerians and Tunisians were afraid of Davidov and did not like him. 'A hard man,' they used to say about him. 'Doesn't talk, doesn't laugh, isn't sociable.' The Rumanians, Poles and Hungarians knew nothing of his past. The few Israeli-born hesitated to approach him. He was locked up in his wounded silence, which wore an armour of severity.

During the days that followed, Davidov scouted among the hills in his Jeep to find a new route for the road, which was held up by a deep gorge. He wanted to circumvent the steep slope that descended to the plain, for the machines could not grip its protuberances. For two days I accompanied him in the Jeep, rattling and skipping over the stones, in the channels, across craters, on the sides of the rocky hills. From time to time we could glimpse, between sphinxes' shoulders or dinosaurian necks, a strip of the Dead Sea, polished in the sun, and, to the south of it, the Vale of Zoar with its green bullrushes, like a flourishing garden beyond the mountains of salt. From time to time we would reach the end of the terrace and halt before the valley. There were deep gorges separating us from Sodom. Once, as we sat on the stones facing it, Davidov said: 'Years ago I wanted to get to Sodom by sea and they did not let me. Now I'm trying to get there on land and again it can't be done, though I see it before me. I'm no righteous man. In the end, I suppose, I'll turn into a pillar of salt.' A faint smile lit his face like a flickering candle, and then the glow in his face was extinguished. His youth had deserted him, with his son, with his daughter.

He never reached Sodom. One night a shot was heard in the camp, and in the morning they said that Davidov had been severely wounded. One of the guards, a young student from Jerusalem, had heard footsteps beyond the fence, had asked who was there and, on receiving no reply, had pressed the trigger. He had not missed.

Later, a nurse at the Beersheba hospital said he had asked to be buried beside his son in the hills of Jerusalem.

Chapter thirty-five

The reader will ask what was the end of the Nili affair. In a novel an affair of this kind ends with an emotional scene, replete with tears, prolonged silences, agonized and inarticulate protestations; or else with a quarrel, the neighbours listening behind their doors and shaking their heads scornfully. Here I have to tell the bare and unvarnished truth, and the truth—so utterly unpoetical and undramatic—is that, after the unpleasant night in my room with Eviatar and Levia, Nili simply disappeared. Vanished. None of us saw her, either in the Cellar or in the street or in any of the bars we were in the habit of visiting from time to time. And in the Cellar everything was just as it had always been. The same old idle talk about some poem just published, occasional witticisms, occasional taunts. Eviatar would put his protective arm around Levia and she would rest her head on his shoulder. Everything was peaceful, tranquil—and deadly dull. No longer that electric tension in the air, no longer that gleam of expectation, desire, provocation in the young men's eyes. As for Nili herself…. A few weeks ago a friend told me that he had seen her in the academic staff quarters beside her house, her belly swollen, a basket of groceries in her hand, standing and talking with a neighbour who also had a basket of groceries in her hand. Her face had broadened and thickened, and it wore a look of lassitude, or perhaps satiation after sleep. Yes, she was still beautiful, her neck as slender and her hair as golden as before, but that radiance which had flowed from her...

I had interviewed another six or seven people since that night when I returned so hastily from Ein-Harod to my room: Dotan, Rozhansky in Be'er-Tuvia, Saul Avrahami in Jerusalem, Galili, Mendelson. Two days after my return from Beersheba where I had talked to Hayim Kafri, I fell sick. I had pains in my chest and a high temperature. No one came into my room and for almost two whole days I did not have a bite to eat. Weakened by hunger, I lay in bed, my mind wandering, staring at the square of sunlight on the wall as it moved little by little, with the slowness of the hand of a clock, from left to right, until it was extinguished. In my fantasies all the landscapes of the country were intermingled, shimmering in the heat: the Jordan valley, the mountains of Hanita, the Dead Sea plain...I would see myself in them, sometimes pursuing Nili, sometimes finding Davidov. My notes were complete. The cardboard file lay on the table, bulging to bursting-point. Twenty-seven chapters lay stifling within its covers, swelling—it seemed to me—like dough. It was only on the second day, towards evening, that Mrs Silber, who 'had a feeling that something was wrong', came in. She made a great fuss of me, got me up and aired the bedclothes, cleaned the room, put some water on to heat, went downstairs and brought me some food. All the time she never stopped preaching at me. 'That's what you get when you lead an abnormal life'—and so forth. She took my temperature, and when she saw that it was over a hundred she ran to call a doctor before I could protest. The doctor came at seven—a mannish woman with a heavy tread like a farmer's. In her deep voice she told me to sit up, to undress, to breathe, and examined my throat, my chest, my heart. Meanwhile she asked questions—about my work, my daily routine, whether I was not exerting myself too much. In the end she said she could find nothing. She left me a few pills and promised to come again next day. When she returned on the morrow my temperature was normal, but the pains in my chest had not stopped. 'What exactly do you feel?' she asked. I told her I found it hard to breathe. Stabbing pains whenever I took air into my lungs. General weakness. 'Nerves,' was Dr Gusta Buchholtz's verdict. 'All you need is rest. Complete rest. No working, eh? No sitting up till late at night. No writing. For two or three weeks no work at all. A trip to some quiet, beautiful place outside the city, and rest. And lots of sleep. And nothing to do with girls, eh?' She smiled through her spectacles as she fastened her bag. Then, as she stood on the thresh-hold, she said: 'You know what Goethe said: "*Wer immer strebend sich bemüht, den können wir erlösen.*"'

Yonina interrupted my writing. She came in towards evening, asked my pardon for interrupting me, and said she had only come to tell me the good news that the dispute between her father and her former fiance had been satisfactorily solved. Arditi had paid Mahlouf two hundred and fifty Israeli pounds, and they had parted friends. They had also made their peace with her brother. And it was all thanks to me. Thanks to me?—I laughed. What part had I played in this pacification? On the two occasions when I had gone with her father to see Mahlouf I had hardly intervened in the negotiations. No, she said, if it hadn't been for me they would never have settled it. It was out of respect for me that they hadn't quarrelled. Even my silence had created a calmer atmosphere and helped them to agree. I wished her good luck and said I hoped she would soon find a man after her own heart. Her eyes were wet. 'The one I want doesn't want me,' she said, a smile glowing from her cheeks like a ray at sunset. 'Oh, a nice-looking girl like you...' I tried to encourage her. She looked at the sheets of paper in front of me and asked what I was writing. 'I am writing a story about a book I haven't written,' I said. She laughed: 'You wanted to write and didn't?' 'Yes. I wanted the book but the book didn't want me.' 'Why didn't it want you?' she laughed. 'That's what I am writing about,' I said, laying my hand on the pages. 'Per-haps you've got a limp too?' she laughed. 'Perhaps,' I said. 'And what you're writing now—does it want you?' she continued playfully. 'I don't know yet,' I said. 'If I write the truth, no doubt it will want me.' 'Is it so hard to write the truth?' she smiled. 'Yes,' I said, 'with every step a writer makes he can commit a crime. There's a lie waiting for him in every word.' 'Why should he lie?' she laughed. 'So as to…Perhaps he thinks it will be nicer that way.' 'But it isn't nice to tell lies,' she said. 'Quite right,' I said. She looked at me more seriously: 'If I could write…I've got a lot to say.' I asked her what she would write about. About her family in Morocco, she said. They had a big family, and there were lots of stories about every one of them. And also how she had become lame. Perhaps she would tell me one day, and I would write it down. Finally she rose, took out something wrapped in paper from her handbag and said: 'Father asked me to give you this. A small thing. As a token of thanks.' I opened the parcel and found a table clock, round and gilded. I gave it back to her and said I would not take anything, that I was not entitled to anything, that I had done nothing. She put the clock on the table and said that if I refused to take it she and her father would never be able to look me in the face; they would regard it as a serious disgrace. With that she said goodbye and went out. I put my hand on the clock and listened to her halting steps on the stairs.

Chapter thirty-six

'Choose material proportionate to your powers,
you who write, and long consider what your
shoulders carry, what they cannot. Neither command of language nor perspicuous arrangement
will fail the author who has chosen his subject
wisely.'

Horace, *Epistle to the Pisos*

Now about the loss of the notes.

Deliberate, of course—in obedience to a repressed wish—
smiles the educated reader. Yes, I have read Freud too. Nevertheless
I must describe the course of events in their proper order:

I thought Dr Buchholtz's suggestion of 'a trip to some quiet,
beautiful place outside the city' was a good idea—not for the reason
she gave: so that I should have a complete rest, but in the hope of
changing my luck. Far from the city, I thought, cut off from my band
of companions, away from my room with all the memories in which
it was saturated, breathing a fresher air and living among men of the
Davidov breed, the afflatus would finally descend upon me and inspire
me to start the book. I wrote to my father's sister's daughter Judith,

who belonged to the kibbutz of N. in eastern Galilee, and asked if I could spend some time with her. Her reply came quickly: Of course, she would be delighted to have me, I should be no trouble—quite the contrary; and as for the payment I mentioned—not a bit of it, quite out of the question. Early in the morning—it was a Sunday, about six months ago—I packed a few clothes in a little suitcase, and put in a leather brief-case the file of notes, a packet of writing paper, two or three books and another few trifles. At nine o'clock I left town and at about half-past one I reached the kibbutz. Judith gave me a joyful welcome, laughed at my beard, which was a novelty for her, and led me to the room she had prepared for me—it belonged to a family who had gone away for the annual vacation and it was furnished with all the veteran's privileged luxuries. 'Here you can sit and write from morning to evening,' she said, 'and nobody will hinder you. You'll never find this kind of quiet in the city.' The window faced the mountains across the border, and the peak of Hermon, crowned with fleecy clouds, was just opposite. Towards evening she, her husband Freddy and their two little children Eitan and Aviva came and took me with them for a brief tour of the farm installations and then to the dining-hall. When the meal was over and the children had been put to sleep in their quarters they invited me to their room for a cup of coffee. For Freddy, a shrewd farmer and a scoffer, this was an excellent opportunity—which he had long awaited, apparently—to pour out his scorn on the 'Young Writers', who were isolated from life, from all the important developments and the country's real problems, and found pleasure in scraping their sores, 'while here, above our very heads, the Syrian guns are threatening us every day'. Judith defended me. 'But what do you want of *him,* Freddy? He's really writing about the things that ought to be written about today.' 'Yes, about Davidov—that's all right,' he said in a tone that conceded her point while implying some dubiety. 'I only hope you'll succeed.'

Next day—it was a clear, wonderfully fresh morning—I took out my file of notes, laid it on the table, and started to read the things I had taken down many months before. I read four or five pages.

I will not go into all the details. I stayed in the kibbutz from Sunday to Thursday. The place was quiet, very quiet, and the view was glorious. But this peaceful paradise got on my nerves. All my hopes of the inspiration that would come of its own accord, like a white angel swooping through the window to stand at my right hand, soon melted away. Something in me had been destroyed or blocked, it seemed, and 'The echo too had died away…and nought was left of the treasures of the past.' Like the palate of an invalid who could no longer sense the taste of the finest food, so my senses had ceased to perceive the savour of beauty. I used to abandon the written sheets and the white paper, which remained immaculate, leave the room, go outside the boundaries of the kibbutz and walk on along some path to the green plain, where there was a wonderful transparency in the air between the mountains veiled in a light mist, and there were pools polished in the sunshine with swords of light and water, and bee-eaters shot out from among the bushes as I passed by, and crickets broadcast brief signals to the silent expanse. But all this beauty only depressed me. Gloomy, absorbed in meditation, Onegin walked in the fields—'No longer did he rejoice/In copse and hill, field and meadow/They simply sent him to sleep.' Yes, this tranquillity simply sent me to sleep. And in the evenings…on the second evening the secretary of the cultural committee came to see me and asked if I would be good enough to lecture on the New Poetry ('Our members have a great deal to say on the subject, and this is an opportunity. And by all means—let's argue it out…'); on the third evening a girl came in with a notebook in her hand, blushing, hesitant, anxious, and stammeringly asked if I could have a look at her garland of verses and tell her what I thought of them ('I've been writing for an awfully long time, and I really don't know if it's worth anything…and actually, if there's any point in my going on…. and there's just nobody here to talk to about it…'); and after that the teacher of the top class in the school, and the counsellor of the youth group…and in the dining-hall, the looks, the whispers…and the dutiful visits to Judith's room every day for tea at five, to play with the children and listen to Freddy's boring talk about the situation in the country…No, I found no rest, the tranquillity of nature wearied me, the solitude did not change my luck. I read the notes over and over but the white sheets remained immaculate.

On Thursday, at seven in the morning...

Once again, for the thousandth time, I am trying to reconstruct in my memory the journey from the kibbutz to the city, and to understand how it all happened.

At seven I got into the bus that was waiting in the square in front of the dining-hall. I put the suitcase and the leather brief-case up on the luggage rack. Judith came running with a big bag of apples. I refused to take them, saying that I did not have enough hands to carry them. She said I should take down the suitcase and the brief-case and rely on her, she would find room for the apples. She opened the brief-case, took out the cardboard file, the packet of paper and the books, and emptied the bag of apples into it. Then she opened the suitcase and pushed into it what she had taken out of the brief-case. Again I put my luggage up on the rack and said goodbye to her. I sat down by the window and the bus set off.

At about half past eight we reached Tiberias. I got off, bought a newspaper and drank a cup of coffee. I got into the bus again. I sat down and read the paper. I did not touch my belongings until we reached Nazareth. After we had gone through Nazareth I took down the brief-case from the rack and took out a couple of apples. I looked for the book of Melville's stories that I had brought with me but did not find it. So I opened the suitcase, fumbled inside, found the book and took it out. I ate the apples and read the book until we arrived at Haifa.

At Haifa I had to change buses, so I put the book back into the suitcase and got off, carrying both pieces of baggage. I went into the station restaurant, sat down at a table, and ordered coffee and a cake. At about eleven I got into the bus for Tel Aviv.

Again I took out the book and put the suitcase up on the rack. Until we reached Tel Aviv I did not touch my luggage. At the Tel Aviv station I pushed the book into the brief-case and got off. At two I was back in my room.

It was only at five in the afternoon, when I got up after a sleep and began to unpack my baggage, that the situation came home to me. In the brief-case there were the apples, one book, my toilet things and a towel. In the suitcase: my clothes, the other two books and the packet of white paper.

The file of notes was not there.

The blood rushed blindingly to my head. I turned my belongings over and over, shook the brief-case and the suitcase, piled everything up in one heap and took the heap apart—but the cardboard file was not there. The blood rushed round and round through the maze of my veins. I sat down on the ruins and tried to put together the fragments of my frantic mind. What had happened? How was it possible? Where? When?

Perhaps Judith had not put the pile of notes into the suitcase but had left them on the seat. If so, how had I failed to notice it? Perhaps when I took the book out of the suitcase I had unconsciously taken out the file as well and left it on the luggage rack. Perhaps it had happened when I put the book back. Perhaps in the restaurant. Perhaps in Tiberias. Someone had opened it by mistake. Perhaps I hadn't taken it at all, and it had been left behind in the room at the kibbutz…But I *had* taken it! I remembered putting it into the brief-case, together with the packet of white paper. But perhaps, after all, I hadn't…

It was not by chance—says the shrewd educated reader. But if he had seen into my heart in those moments when I sat alone in my room in the twilight, bereft of all I possessed, the labour of months, the memories of twenty-seven people, the story of a man's life…. Panic-stricken, in a fever, I hurried back to the station. I inquired at the left luggage office, at the parcel counter, in the traffic manager's room. Not a trace. I asked for the number of the bus and the name of the driver, begged them to send a message to the intermediate stations. I went to the post office and sent a telegram to Judith: DAVIDOV FILE LOST PERHAPS LEFT IN ROOM REPLY IMMEDIATELY.

I went back to my room, empty, lost. At night I dreamt I was running down the slope from Rosh-Pina to the Sea of Galilee. Stumbling on the stones round dangerous curves. I came to a certain copse with a watchtower. Like a man with sunstroke seeking shade. Menahem Schweig, standing there with a stick, threatened me. I awoke.

Got up and searched again in the brief-case, in the suitcase, among the clothes, as if it had been a coin that had slipped into a crack.

At ten in the morning a wire came from Judith: not found.

I decided to go all the way back to the kibbutz of N. I set out at midday. Stopped at the Haifa station and inquired at the left luggage office, asked the dispatchers and the traffic manager, asked in the restaurant. From there to Tiberias. Inquired at the left luggage office, asked the dispatchers, and so on. At five I reached N. We went to the room where I had stayed, all of us: Judith, Freddy, and the children. We turned over every article, opened every drawer. 'But I'm sure I put the cardboard file into the suitcase,' said Judith, as stunned as I was. 'I put in two packages and several books.' We sat petrified, as at a deathbed. In the evening we went to see the driver of the bus. He consoled us: no doubt it would be found and handed in at one of the stations. After all, it was no use to anybody. Was my name written on the file? No, it was not.

The long night in the strange room.

Next morning—the long way back, the light dazzling my eyes, the light of white rocks and stony fields, then of the blue, tranquil, primeval lake, then of the road galloping between rows of dry thorns, the heat beating on my face…And perhaps the notes were scattered leaf by leaf all along the road, from Galilee to…That lassitude after all is lost.

Of course I could have inserted an advertisement in the newspapers, offering a reward to the honest finder. But what would all those who had entrusted me with their memories have said to that? What would Karpinowitch have said, if not that I should make the rounds again of these twenty-seven people and take it all down again from their lips? And afterwards…

Chapter thirty-seven

This morning I was awakened by the clatter of many footsteps on the stairs outside. More trouble. Messengers of the court? Representatives of the publisher? Income-tax officials? The door to the roof screeched on its rusty hinge and I heard Mrs Silber saying: 'Here you are, gentlemen, this way.' I stirred myself and slipped into my trousers. The steps halted just at my door; an abrasive voice said: 'And what's this? His?'—and Mrs Silber: 'It's always been like that, covered. He never unveiled it.' There was silence for a moment or two, then the steps passed on across the flat roof and I heard the door of the laundry grating as it opened. Not for me, thank heaven!

I went out on to the sun-drenched roof and approached that shedful of junk, now illuminated by a broad beam of light which shone through the wide open door and traced a shimmering halo of golden dust around the heads of three men who stood inside. The three of them were gazing silently at a clay statuette that stood on the palm of one of them. 'This is Mr Jonas, who occupies the room now,' said Mrs Silber, her face testifying to joy and anxiety at one and the same time. The three looked up at me for a moment with perfunctory nods and immediately concentrated again on the sculpture—the figure of a girl with a pitcher on her shoulder. Mrs Silber came up to me, took me aside and whispered excitedly: 'A delegation from the museum. They want to arrange a Polishuk exhibition.' 'Yes?' I wondered. 'What made them think of it all of a sudden?' 'I think it's some anniversary or other,' she said. 'Yesterday a special messenger came, and this morning…. I'm so glad. At last!' 'And will they take it all away?' 'That's what they've come for. To inspect. Perhaps they'll take it all. Perhaps only what they like. We'll see.'

I went up to the door again and saw the shortest of the men, with an aureole of white hair around his bald head, bending over the bath and pulling out the circle of *hora*-dancers, pioneer boys and girls with their left legs raised and their arms round each other's shoulders. He held the sculpture in both hands and looked questioningly at the two others. The taller, with the bushy eye-brows and the aquiline nose, said: 'Not bad…There's a certain rhythm, and a skilful organization of the space…Reminds you of the romanticism of the David's Tower School. What do you think, doctor?' The doctor, who looked morose and kept his hands in his jacket pockets, shrugged his shoulders disdainfully. 'And what's that? His too?'—turning his head to a marble bust of a woman, with a thick plait coiled round her head, on a shelf in the corner. The three directed their gaze at the bust. 'After Maillol, eh?' said the tall one after a pause. Baldhead bent over the bath again, extracted the figure of a tall, lean young man, his sinewy arms brandishing a hammer, and held it up for inspection.

'Imitation Rodin, of course,' smiled the tall one indulgently, 'but very plastic. There's the feeling for material. Note the stability of the leg. The heel…' 'Look here, gentlemen,' said the doctor, impatiently, 'the question is what we want to present to the public: memories or works of art? If it's memories—all right. Let us take out everything we can find here in the bath and we shall be able to fill an entire hall. But if you want to know my opinion, it will be a disaster! Look at this now,' taking the hammer-wielder in his hand and turning it from side to side. 'Even in Soviet Russia they don't sculpt like this any more! After all, you can't put the clock back to the 'twenties.' He put down the statue on the rickety table and brushed the dust from his hands. 'You're wrong, doctor, if you think

the public won't accept it,' smiled the tall one. 'With enthusiasm!
Old things are in fashion nowadays. Old songs, old memories…' 'If
that's what you think, then give them *kitsch*!' retorted the doctor,
quivering with anger. 'Give them *kitsch*! The question is whether we
have to lower ourselves to the public taste when it is our function
to guide it. I also have sentimental feelings about the Schatz period,
when art was in its infancy in this country, but I will not give my
name to a kind of…a kind of sentimentalism like this…to this kind
of provincial heroics. It's out of the question, gentlemen, with all due
respect to the deceased.'

Baldhead looked dejected. Mrs Silber, repressing her resentment, sent a rebellious glance in my direction from time to time. The
doctor had already turned to go, but the tall one pulled out of the
bath a lad in a stocking-cap with a sub-machine-gun under his arm.
'Look, doctor,' he said. 'Interesting, after all…The square lines of the
forehead…' The other turned to the clay statuette, and as he held it in
both his hands the boy's leg broke between his fingers. 'Disintegrat-
ing,' he muttered, with a kind of sense of guilt, and with a childish
movement tried to stick the leg to the knee. He gave it up and laid
the two parts of the body on the table. Mrs Silber boiled inwardly.

The three men came out, and as they reached the door of my
room halted again in front of the large statue wrapped in sack-cloth.
The doctor took hold of a dangling end of the material and tried to
peel it off, but it was stuck hard to the dry clay body and the fibres
disintegrated in his hand. 'Has he no heirs to look after this property
and prevent it being destroyed?'—he turned to Mrs Silber. Mrs Silber
did not reply.

After they had gone down the stairs I too tried to peel the rags
from the burly, tall body of the statue. It was like a bandage on a
bruise, and when a piece tore off it seemed as if the living flesh came
away with it. I shall never know now, it seems, whose image it is that
stands beside my door.

Chapter thirty-eight

I have still to tell about the last melancholy meeting with Zippora, Davidov's wife.

I reached the eucalyptus grove on the edge of Kfar Sava after sunset, when the golden twilight flickering through the trees was still strewn over the fallen leaves and the broken branches scattered on the ground. At the end of the path I saw a little woman scraping away with a besom of twigs at the few tiles in front of the hut. As I approached she interrupted her work, looked at me as if she had not seen a human face for a long time, and said: 'Yes?'

I told her who I was and what I wanted.

She looked at me askance as she leaned on the pole of the broom. Her unkempt hair was a tangle of black and silvery threads.

'A book? About Abrasha? Who needs a book about Abrasha?' She eyed me. She had a penetrating glance, much younger than her neglected appearance would have suggested.

I told her the book was being written at the request of many who remembered and esteemed him. I asked her if she could give me some time, not very long, and tell me...

'I've nothing to tell,' she said decisively. And after a pondering look at me: 'What do I know about him? I don't know a thing.' And she started sweeping the tiles again as if I had already gone away.

I stood, a little longer, hoping she would change her mind, then I begged her pardon and turned to retrace my steps.

When I had gone a few paces on the path, I heard her voice: 'Listen, now!'

She came up to me with rapid steps, the broom still in her hand, and said: 'Have they already told you about him?'

I told her I had taken notes from over twenty people.

She gave me a long, contemplative look, her lips resting on the end of the broomstick. Then she smiled strangely, with an impish expression dancing in her eyes, and said:

'What did they tell you?'

I said they had described his doings from his arrival in the country until his last days, and that everyone had been full of admiration for him.

'They told you he was a hero?' she said with a mocking smile.

'They told me things that happened,' I said.

'They did...' She fell silent, scrutinizing me.

'Well, all right, come in if you've come so far,' she said, and went in front of me.

Her boots were soiled with dried mud and her broad, grey skirt revealed the strong sinews of her legs above her heels. Beside the hut, which was covered in places with tarred paper, shone a fresh lettuce-patch surrounded by a wattle fence, and behind it was a cowshed. She set the broom down beside the doorway and went inside.

'Sit down,' she said with a wave of her hand as she went into the second room, which was apparently the kitchen.

A long table stood by the wall, with benches on both sides. On one wall a pair of dried pumpkins hung on a nail; on another, fixed with drawing pins, was an unframed charcoal sketch of working boots with gaping soles and dangling laces. In a corner stood a set of bookshelves made of cypress branches, containing, higgledy-piggledy, a lot of old books piled up in heaps, copy-books, and some square stained cloth satchels. Through the window I could see the tall cowshed made of coarse, cracked planks, twisted fence-posts, a few unpruned citrus trees, and luxuriant eucalyptus crests, with their hanging clusters of bells.

'That's Nimrod's,' she said as she came in again, pointing to the drawing fastened to the wall. 'There are more. Many of them'—pointing to the satchels on the shelves. 'I don't take them out. They're rotting away, I suppose. He could draw. Yes.'

She sat down opposite me, fixed me with her glowing eyes, and said: 'You know about Nimrod? They told you?'

I told her a little of what I knew about him. She listened distractedly and said in decisive tones: 'You know he was short-sighted? That he should never have fought? No, he shouldn't have died. He was sacrificed on the altar. You remember the story of the binding of Isaac: the father, Abraham, takes his son, his only son whom he loves, and offers him up on Mount Moriah. That's how it was. Exactly. But no angel. That is the truth that no one has told you.' She straightened her back and her little hand quivered on the edge of the table. She had a saturnine face and fine, full lips, cracked by the sun.

'Who sent you to me?' she asked after a silence.

I mentioned the names of Dotan, Harari, Schweig...

'Menahem Schweig?' she exclaimed with a hard laugh. 'He sent you to me? I find it hard to believe that he sent you to me. What did he tell you?'

I repeated a little of what Schweig had told me. In the middle of my story she clapped her hands to her cheeks and cried: 'That's what he told you? That Abrasha went to Jerusalem to help the Haganah because things were quiet here? But that's a *lie*! He went because he didn't want to stay at home. He never wanted to stay at home! All his life! The Dead Sea, the Negev, Cyprus—anywhere, but not at home. Even to prison, but not at home. Don't you know he didn't even want to be buried beside the house? Why do you think he asked to be buried in the Jerusalem hills? For Nimrod's sake? No! To be far from *me*! Yes, as far away as possible! Always! Even after his death!'

'About the melons, did Menahem tell you about that?' she asked with a suspicious smile.

'What melons?' I tried to remember.

'No, of course he didn't tell you. Why should he tell you how

I had a whole crop of melons impounded because of a debt of a hundred pounds to the shop, when Abrasha was at the Northern Fence? About the fence they told you, of course, but not about what happened here! Not that I had to look after the cows by myself—for years!—to go into the village every day with the milk cans, to look after the miserable plot we sowed and the debts he left behind him, to clean out the muck when the baby was screaming in the hut, or that I lay awake all night long during the troubles, when he was.... Don't imagine I don't know. I know. Everything. What was going on at Hanita and what was going on at the Dead Sea and what was going on in Cyprus. I know. Little birds tell tales, and I had plenty of birds, you can be sure. All round the hut. From morning to evening all I heard was the twittering. But why tell about all that? It isn't a nice thing to tell. Not nice to tell how Davidov's wife used to run about like a crazy woman all over the village to look for Reuma!' Here she bent towards me till her face was close to mine and her eyes glowed as she whispered: 'You know that at the age of fifteen Reuma was pregnant already and had to get an abortion?...You won't write about that, of course; you're not expected to!'

The sparks from her eyes seemed to dance in my face and the silence hummed in my ears.

'What else did they tell you?' she asked with the same strange smile on her face as she straightened her back.

I was silent. I had begun to feel afraid of her.

'Did you talk to his brother?'

I said I had been in his house and he had told me how Davidov came here.

'I suppose he told you about the fiddle, and the refugees, that he did a lot for them, and about the Tartar soldier...' she laughed. Then she said: 'All that's ridiculous. You really think he was capable of giving up his life to save some Tartar soldier? For his own daughter was he capable of sacrificing anything? *Anything?* Don't you know he abandoned her? And when he came home he used to beat her. He *destroyed* her! Why do you think she ran away to Australia? I have no daughter now!'

Her hands lay on the edge of the table, two little paw-like hands, the tips of their fingers roughened by dirt.

'You know what they say in Yiddish? There are three things worse than being dead: to be blind, to be a widow, to be childless. I was blind from the beginning, a widow all the time I was married, and childless—I have been for years. From Reuma I haven't had a single letter.'

She did not say this by way of complaint, but with the kind of hard composure that follows acceptance. She was beautiful, with the bold lines of her face, and the tempest raging in her black eyes.

'You're a writer, aren't you?' she said, gazing at me. 'Tell me, then, can a man love the whole Jewish people, the whole human race, and not love his own family?'

She stared at me, wrapped in thought. 'Yes, he loved Nimrod. That's right. But what did he do for him? You know that he was ready to abandon us all during the war and run away to Europe? He would have done it! If he didn't, it's only because I threatened him. I threatened to kill the two children! I'm a criminal, aren't I?' she said, with a brief laugh that made me shiver.

'You knew Abrasha?' she asked.

'Yes,' I said, and told her about my two short meetings with him.

She did not listen. Her face softened as if illuminated by a faint light.

'He was a handsome man, wasn't he?' she said smiling.

I nodded. Her smile lingered on my face, as if she was examining me to see if I was capable of understanding what she felt about him.

'Is the book written already?' she asked.

I told her I had not started the writing yet. I was accumulating recollections. That was why I had come to her.

'Look,' she said quietly, 'there are many legends about Abrasha. Many of them. I am the one who knows the truth. But why should I tell you? In any case you won't write it. What kind of book will it be if you write the truth I know? A black book. The Jewish people don't need a black book about Davidov. They need heroic legends! Well—let there be one more legend! Write about the roads, and the Haganah, and the immigrant ships…Write that he was brave, and devoted to the homeland, and a humanist, and…'

She lowered her head and pressed her fingers to her temples as if to smooth away a sudden headache. There was a deep silence. The wing-beats of a flock of birds that had flown off from one of the treetops passed like a wave outside the window.

'That's it.' She raised her head; her cheeks were burning. 'I've nothing to tell you.'

I asked if she could give me some letters or photographs…

'I haven't any,' she laughed. 'You see there isn't even a picture of him here.' She pointed to the walls. Again that melancholy spark glowed in her eyes. 'I burned them. All of them. Pictures, letters, everything. Heart of stone, eh? You're right, it's petrified. You see—I had a son I loved very much, I had a daughter—I loved her too, I had Abrasha…I had…that's all.'

She rose and accompanied me to the door. As we emerged, she said, 'Forget what I told you. It doesn't matter. Abrasha belongs to the people, as they say. For me he died long ago. Not six years ago. Sixteen. More. The people loved him and you ought to write nothing but good. In any case, I won't read what you write.' She laughed.

As I reached the end of the path I turned my head and saw her standing on the threshold, leaning on the doorpost with her hand on her cheek.

Chapter thirty-nine

I have come to the end of my story. I have no more to tell. There is a choking in my throat. Perhaps it is a feeling of being emptied, as if I had cut an artery in my wrist and all the blood had drained out. Perhaps it is the knowledge that a long time will pass, who knows how long, before I write again. The idle days will come back, haunted by apprehension of the next session of the court. I shall get up a little before noon, go to bed after midnight; in the evenings I shall sit in the Cellar, talking idly, yawning, musing on what I have lost, dreaming of stories I shall never write. A year and a half has been cut off like a hand from my body. The pain will not last, but the lack will remain.

The sadness of parting hovers over me. I thought it would take five weeks to write these pages. Five months have passed. I paused between one chapter and the next—on purpose, to stretch out the time. The naive illusion that 'confession' is much the same as atone-ment.... But I am unrepentant. In any case, I am a debtor on the run. In any case, my creditors still present their demands—inexorably, in speech or silence, with a questioning or an accusing glance—those who have entrusted me with what they had and those who expect me to supply them with what they have not. Give us our pound of flesh and blood! But no one can tear out of me what I do not possess. Whether I loved my master or hated him—

All I can do, therefore, is to address myself to the wind, which carried away the recollections I gathered: If you find the torn and crumpled pages of the Book of Davidov scattered about here and there over the face of the land—a page caught in a bush, a page fluttering from rock to rock, a page stuck to a stone dike, or drifting over the sands, or fluttering by the roadside—do not bring them back to me. Better that they should disappear into oblivion than that I should ever see them again. I do not want an ambush in my home, a nest of rustling memories under my bed, eyes observing my thoughts! I want to be my own master. I want rest.

Rest, I say…. This morning I paid a visit to my counsel. He told me that the proceedings in the civil case might last for years. Sometimes you can hardly see when it will end. He was trying to soothe me, to assure me that I had nothing to fear, that I could rely on the postponements. The fool does not understand that, so long as this trial hangs over my head, I cannot start anything new.

About the Author

Aharon Megged

Aharon Megged was born in Poland and came to Palestine at the age of six. He was a member of Kibbutz Sdot Yam between 1938–1950, and later, a literary editor and journalist. He has been a pivotal figure in Israeli letters since the 1950s. His many novels, short stories and plays reflect the complexities of Israeli society over the past fifty years.

The president of the Israel PEN Center from 1980–'87, and the cultural attaché at the Israel Embassy in London from 1968–'71, Aharon Megged is also a long-standing member of the Hebrew Academy. He has won many literary awards, among them the Bialik Award, the Brenner Award, the Agnon Award, the American Koret Award for the best Jewish book, 2003, and the much-coveted Israel Prize for Literature, 2003.

He has two sons, Eyal, also a writer, and Amos, who teaches history at the University of Haifa. He is married to the writer Eda Zoritte.

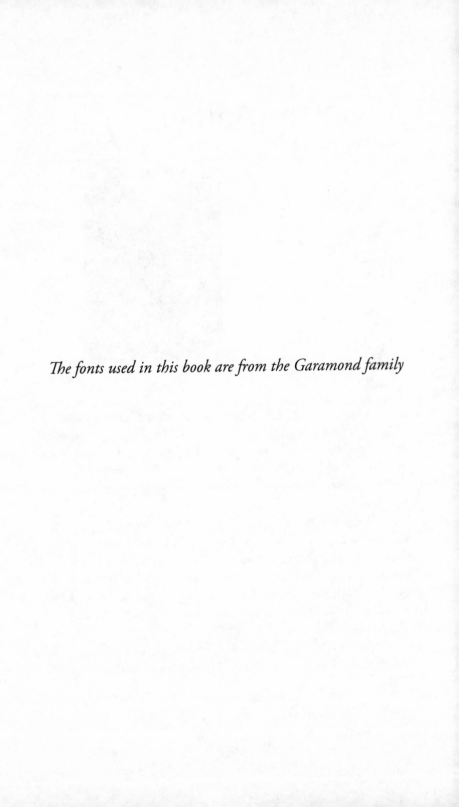

The fonts used in this book are from the Garamond family